THE FAR FACE OF THE MOON

By the same author

THE FAR ROAD

CLOSER TO THE SUN

The
Far Face
of the
Moon

BY GEORGE JOHNSTON

WILLIAM MORROW & COMPANY
New York, 1964

AUTHOR'S NOTE

THIS book is dedicated, with respect, to those many young men of the Air Transport Command, who once upon a time risked, and in many cases gave, their lives flying "The Hump" out of North Assam.

Veterans of the C.B.I. Theatre who were familiar with the strips at Chabua and Dibrugarh will, I hope, forgive the many licenses which a layman has taken. They will not need to be told that this is an entirely fictional story. "Zone Q-4" is an invention, as are Frisk's "command" and all the people in it. No character bears relationship to any real person, living or dead.

. . . like the martlet,
Builds in the weather on the outward wall,
Even in the force and road of casualty.
       —Shakespeare, *Merchant of Venice*

THE FAR FACE OF THE MOON

1

THERE was a fetish then about secrecy, a studied preoccupation with code names and ciphers which all seems rather childish now, in retrospect.

I think it was insisted on more than was really necessary simply as a prop to importance, since Frisk, the zone commandant, was quite consistent in labouring his point about logistics.

"We are not," he would constantly point out in that soft, lisping, deceptive voice of his, "a combat area."

There were even times when he would give little lectures on the subject, and when he did this one could never quite escape the feeling that one existed only as a point midway between a reality and a myth. Behind us was the very matter-of-fact reality of Frisk's problem of logistics; this immense assembly line of supplies and the movement of personnel. Far away from us, beyond the mists and tempests and rolling black storms and the peaks hidden in the whiplash of the monsoon, the murderous fighting had been going on for two years or more. But we would see nothing whatever of this, nothing of the dead nor of the wounded. No captives, sullen-faced and apprehensive, were made to walk beneath our speculative eyes. We were not—I can see Frisk now, looking up, trying to impose a steely skin across the bland blue innocence of his eyes as he reiterated his injunction—a combat area. We were a point in logistics. And this point, in signals, official correspondence, in Intelligence briefings, often even in the ordinary interchange of social chitchat, was known as Zone Q-4. There had been a time of less complicated secrecy when we were simply Zone Q, and I recall the day when Garnett Fleming, then the senior traffic and administrative officer, told me, with a definitely conspiratorial air, that we were to be redesignated as Zone Q-4. He gave me this information behind his hand, as if there was some immense importance attached to it.

In this world, as senior civilian liaison officer with the headquarters administration of Zone Q-4, I had found my particular sanctuary. I was both alien and civilian, yet I had my privileges. In exchange for the services of my specialized knowledge I had my place in the mess, the right to my monthly visit to Bergensen the paymaster, my ability to sign for an article in webbing or khaki drill at the damp, rice-smelling, DDT-stenched store of Quigley the quartermaster, my little luxuries from the commissariat, my tacit membership of the pilots' bar. I even believed then that I could hide there from myself, from what had brought me there, even from what had kept me there. Very foolish, as it transpired. . . .

The oddity of my being in Zone Q-4, attached to, if not totally involved in, a military organization which was almost entirely American, only infrequently occurred to me. At the time of the circumstances with which we are concerned I would have been about thirty-two. Tall and very lean; twenty pounds underweight for my height according to Robarts the MO, and none the worse for it. In the tropics the cadaver type wears better than the fleshy; perhaps the insects find less to tempt them in bone and gristle. I had spent ten years in these tropics and survived them pretty well. Brown hair, deep-set grey-green eyes, complexion over-sallowed by the climate, a long face too narrow below the cheekbones for the big brow. Not a very special sort of appearance, in any case. Nor a very particular background. An English vicarage boyhood—thin cucumber sandwiches, hollyhocks, tea kettles on a spirit burner, toast in the afternoons, the smell of leather and old books. St. Paul's School. Cambridge. A good degree. Some botanical writings, and at one time an entry an inch and a quarter deep in *Who's Who*, expunged long since because not kept up to date. A short and not specially distinguished period of service in the British Army, and an honourable discharge after being chancily wounded in a lugubrious retreat. After that, fortuitously, appointment as senior civilian liaison officer at Zone Q-4.

It would be difficult now precisely to define the terrestial boundaries of Zone Q-4, which, strictly speaking, was no more than an airfield complex hacked out of the jungles and tea plantations of northern Assam. We were indirectly concerned with a far wider area of geography—the hills and matted forests of Upper Burma, the plateau edge of Tibet, the mighty peaks of the eastern Himalayas and the Kaoli Kung, the distant uplands of Yunnan, in West China; with the turbulent, twisting courses of great rivers, the Brahmaputra, the Irrawaddy, the Salween, the Mekong. A wild, cruel territory this, a great deal of it mapped inaccurately or not at all, seldom explored, traditionally hostile to man. The reason for my appointment was a perfectly simple one. For almost ten years this had been the country of my adoption and concealment. There had been a time when I had loved it with intense passion, when with the indefatigable ardour of the young and the dedicated I had prowled a haunted, magic Eden. From the mosses and lichens above the timberline of the high places to the soggy soft growths of the river's flood-plain, through the temperate flowered hills and the tangle of the tropical rain forest, where iridescent butterflies and luminescent insects everlastingly surprised one with their mysterious presence on the satin-black gloomshine of the jungle floor, there was pretty well nothing of the plant life, this fecund vegetal world of poison and perfume and colour, and very little of the fauna, with which I was not familiar. My knowledge was expert in its field, wide in its general scope, and uniquely come by—after long years it became my credential for admission into the more complex world of Zone Q-4.

General Frisk, who appointed me in Calcutta, showed little interest in my botanical expertise, and, apart from some *Jungle Book* questions concerning leopard, rhinoceros, and python, was hardly more impressed by the zoological experience which I had acquired at some considerable personal jeopardy.

"We're hiring you, Strickland," he had said from the deep rattan armchair in the officer's club at Ballygunge, "because we figure to work our operations out of nowhere, across no man's land, and into limbo. We'll be just a point in logistics, Strickland, just a unit to move things on to some place else. For this operation, we'll probably be using tentative maps, untried equipment, raw kids. Those kids will be flying in conditions they've never experienced before. Most of them will never have seen a jungle . . . I guess most of them will never have seen a mountain above ten thousand feet. It's not going to be easy for them. It might be damned dangerous. And it won't have the glory of combat to boost their morale. So this is why we're using you in the outfit, Strickland. You know all the country in and around our zone of operations. You know the topography and the terrain, climate, the medical angles, you speak the dialects, you know the natives. So we're hiring you, Strickland, the way in the Old West they'd hire an Indian scout. We want you to be our Old Man of the Mountains, our Old Man of the Jungle. The guy *we* go to for local know-how."

Having lisped his little lecture, the general had grown immediately benevolent. The metallic film of earnestness dropped from his childlike eyes, he mixed me a martini *his* way, with an explanation of why the rind of a tangerine was better, and gave me the name of the tailor in Chowringhee who made his bush jackets. We toasted the success of "Operation Xanadu." His Old Man of the Mountains had had his thirtieth birthday the day before.

Within two years Zone Q-4 had come to occupy a fairly extensive triangular area at the northern apex of a sparsely populated plateau, much of which was humid jungle, bisected by the broad, turgid flow of the Brahmaputra. The river in these parts had become a slothful, repulsive thing which we tried to keep away from. The hot, steamy plain through which it muddily meandered was scarred everywhere by the marks of its earlier courses, like the shed skins of gigantic snakes. It carried little commerce, not even of the crude rafts of the apathetic natives, for both banks were fringed by many feverish, brackish lagoons and swamps where the anopheles mosquitoes bred by the millions. A place of malaria, blackwater fever, hookworm, typhus in its season, dysentery always, sometimes cholera. A place to steer away from. Not only that, the going was just too brutal on the treacherous flats, with deep soft sucking bogs hidden innocently beneath the thin, solid-seeming crusts of sun-baked mud. Dangerous. Occasionally fish taken from the river by the near-simian aborigines of the squalid riparian settlements a short distance to the south would be brought to the mess. They were big, dead-white, and flaccid and smelt always of rank mud. I never tasted the flesh.

[15]

Roughly five miles beyond the river the eastern hills began. Gently at first, in soft folding slopes, very green and
tranquil, quite like going beyond Hampshire towards the
West Country. Pleasant villages. Temples, tiny and tinselly.
Little farm plots carefully terraced, looking like the over-
coiffured wigs of Restoration fops. Agreeable people living
quietly amid water sounds and the tinkling of bells in trees,
slow-walking, arms linked affectionately, in the brief violet
ambience of dusk. There had been a time when Olga and I
would go there, at the right season of the year, to buy strawberries. Strawberries! In Zone Q-4 could strawberries be
imagined? It had become difficult enough to imagine Olga.
(She visited at times in nightmares, of course, but then that
is a very different thing from trying deliberately to will her
image back across the plains of pain.)

Like so much that is within the tropics, this attractive,
fertile hill country was very deceptive. Beyond the last of
the cultivated fields, the last trickling furrow of an irrigation
dike, one met the jungle again. An intimidating wall, dark,
matted, vine-entangled, alarming with secret life. And beyond this the hills became steeper and quite untamed, bare
and rocky slopes scoured and wind-blasted into the texture
of an elephant's hide. From the rugged tellurian pedestal
of these foothills sprang the buttressing spurs and shoulders
of the stone giants—those unearthly ridges and pinnacles
of the great alps, rising to far more than twenty thousand
feet. Aloof colossi these, dreaming in their clouds and the
streamer veils of driven snow. Wonderfully beautiful and
strange, and with a compelling challenge in their lonely
majesty. (Eight years earlier I had set out to climb to the
summit of what had seemed a reasonably accessible peak;
the upland tribes called it The Hammer: after twenty days
I had thankfully retreated.)

The alpine mass, and what lay beyond it, were the whole

raison d'être of Zone Q-4. What lay beyond was a desperate, brutal, and at this time a totally unpredictable war. Men were ferociously locked together on the plains of China, in the gorges of the Salween, in the green jungles of Burma. Our role was simply to move to within reach of these grappling millions all those supplies—human, material, even psychological—which would ensure that the killing should continue. *We were not a combat area.* This ferocious conflict with which we were bloodlessly involved always had some curious quality of unreality, a kind of *kriegspiel* where wooden blocks were moved around on maps marked off with coloured pins. The odd disconnection between our role and the reality was emphasized, I think, by the code names which, at that time, had such popular militaristic currency. I used to amuse myself at times trying to imagine the man back there, in Washington presumably, who had thought of them. Quiet, pleasant eyes, I would think, ready to smile, crinkling at the outer edges; blue, like Frisk's, and still young with the harboured visions of far places. White hair, silky, thinning above the brows. A neat brown face smelling sprucily of after shave lotion. A quiet voice, and hands at rest on his desk.

Our main target area in a hidden land we never visited was, like the airlift operation itself, known as Xanadu. Since none of us was able to refer directly to either Marco Polo or Coleridge, there were different opinions about pronunciation. Fleming, being a blunt, third-generation Irishman from Massachusetts, and a man of very fixed opinions, made four definite syllables of it, starting with an immutable "X," because, to him, that was the way it was spelt. I preferred the softer "Z" sound, without trying to impose it on anyone else. Frisk used the "K" sound, but the combination of his lisp and his soft intonation, often made it seem as if he was referring

[17]

to Canada, which made everything so much more remote than before.

The main point is that all our logistics depended on aviation. There was no way of getting anything into Xanadu, across that great wall of mountains and that desolation of jungle, except by flying it. Thus the centre of our own zone, the constant beat of its heart, was the two gigantic airfields around which our specialized little world was concentrated. One—it, too, had a code name, Kansas—fairly much resembled any other large foreign airfield. The usual geometry of runways, approach strips, fuelling bays, taxi lanes, emergency tarmacs, and flare paths. The trees felled along the approaches. That orthodox solid geometry, cubes, curves, and prisms, all rather shabby, of temporary-looking hangars, workshops, fuel pits, low buildings shuddering and rattling always under the hail of the slipstream dust. The coffee stand with its spread of bright chairs. The spindly control tower above the operations room which looked like something salvaged from the upperworks of an obsolete old dreadnought. The arched spiderweb of the primitive RDF looking like some image of a barbaric god. And at night a startling poetry of light lozenges, beacons, and smoky flares.

The second field, three miles away behind an obscuring belt of dahl trees, was coded as Rampart. It had been begun only a little while before the time with which I am concerned, and much of it was still being ruthlessly bulldozed out of a group of abandoned tea plantations. It was obviously planned to be considerably larger than Kansas, and all activities concerned with it were surrounded by a great deal of secrecy. Because of this there was a general assumption that it might have something to do with combat operations, although an alternative theory was that the longer runways were for a new type of larger, high-altitude freight carrier rather than for long-range bombers. All the Rampart

[18]

area was enclosed within a high fence of thick steel mesh and was guarded night and day by a battalion of special security troops, who wore white webbing belts and gaiters, and white low-cowled helmets bearing the letter "S" painted in black.

I had been through the high guarded gate and into Rampart on fewer than half a dozen occasions—and then only because of some urgent problem of interpreting or difficulty with the native labour which it was my responsibility to judge upon and settle. Each time I had been escorted by two of the armed men in white helmets, one on either side, pleasantly attentive, and never talking. Frisk had always accompanied me. Very taciturn on those days. Perhaps during those untalkative visits we made together he was working out in his mind a new series of little lectures to be used in the event that we did become a combat area after all. In any case, Rampart, like so many secret and ambitious projects of the war, was never finished. So there had really been nothing to worry about.

2

MY FIRST intimation of what was to happen—without any intimation of how deeply and violently I was to be affected by it—came, I remember, from Garnett Fleming.

I had gone with him at dusk to the village at the railhead which Frisk's lists showed to be "outside Direct Control Area," and which was classified as off limits to enlisted men except on Saturday nights from seven thirty until midnight, when a squad of pickets in the white "S" helmets would move about quietly through the muddy, musky streets and lanes. Their spruceness against the squalor of their surroundings never failed to fascinate me. And I am sure that their disciplined vigilance as they patrolled through the ramshackle bars and makeshift bordellos, tapping their batons nonchalantly in their cupped hands, decidedly discounted the psychological value, as a prophylaxis against boredom, of the men's weekly taste of exotic freedom. Certainly the enlisted men never seemed at home in the village. Their ribaldry was always uneasy, their drunkenness lacked conviviality, even their sexual nourishment had a kind of desperate edge to it, like a hint of rape. They were much more at home, much more like real people, back in

Frisk's "Direct Control Area," with their glandular titillation supplied two-dimensionally and with "Stateside" familiarity on the movie screen erected behind the Kansas hangars, and with their pin-ups beside their cots, and the unending circulation of the limp, ill-printed, evil-smelling novelettes of pornography which ceaselessly poured into the base from the distant booths of Chowringhee. With their beer and their bourbon they seemed to find a genial alcoholism much easier to attain than they ever did with the arrak and the fiery local brandies which the Hindu vendors sold to them at exorbitant prices. In Leromenos their laughter always sounded forced and grating, as if their nerves had locked midway between panic and brutality.

It must be admitted that the village was not exactly the sort of milieu that would inspire spontaneous gaiety. It was an entirely shabby village, sprung not from the fertility of the fields nor the run of water in the channels, as native settlements usually are. The true village is conceived by hunger, gestated by necessity, and born into some sort of harmony with its natural surroundings. Earthborn. Not this one. It had not even had a name until I gave it one. (Leromenos is the Greek word for "dirty," as distinct from "earthy": the sound of the word was not dissimilar from the native tongue; I had called it that out of amusement, feeling that I had a right to play at code names, too. I was pleased that it found its way into signals, then official stencils, and no doubt is filed away for posterity in old War Department files.)

Today the jungle and the monsoons have probably obliterated it, but then it housed a mixed native population of around two thousand. It was really nothing more than a swollen, shabby, parasitic growth fastened to the final half mile of the very primitive narrow-gauge railroad which came up from Bengal, in the south. The railroad terminated in

[21]

the very centre of the village in a series of crazy shunting loops and sidings leading to a kind of crude turntable worked by antlike gangs of skinny-armed natives in dirty *dhotis* who simply pushed and shoved at the locomotives until they turned round and pointed the opposite way. There was no station, only a fantastic, high, cane-roofed building which looked for all the world like one of the *tambaran* sorcery houses of the New Guinea headhunters, but which was dignified by an absurd painted sign identifying it as *Maintenance Running-Shed No. 7*. The jungle began again two hundred yards behind it.

The locomotives—there were only four in service at the time—were all small, black, squat, and as aggressive-looking as widows in bombazine. In front of each was an enormous iron cowcatcher, and above the boiler a strange, high smoke-stack, that went out and came in again in the form of a truncated cone. Childishly old-fashioned they looked—the stuff of science museums or the pictures on the cigarette cards one collected as a small boy. The engines burnt fire-wood, not coal, and everywhere along this very impermanent permanent way were distributed immense stacks of sawn billets of red, glossy wood. The locomotives hauled only flatcars, upon which passengers could clamber at will, getting on and jumping off more or less when they wished, since there were few stretches, and then only rockingly downhill, where speed was above a smart walking pace. Once embarked, the unofficial passengers would have to cling as best they could to the heterogeneous loads of freight —cement, sand, sawn timber, orange juice, chewing gum, ammunition, gelignite, gin, shaving cream, steel girders— coming up to Zone Q-4.

I had become very attached to the train and to its ram-shackle terminus. I liked the sudden gusts of steam misting up the surrounding jungle, wreathing the vines in woolly white. I enjoyed the bells and the snortings and the whistles, the clatter of couplings and the running drum rattle of the buffers. As the fruit bats swarmed over in the twilight and the smell of spices prickled at one's throat, and the sinuous robed figures dawdled past in the gloaming, laughing softly among themselves, there was something deliciously incongruous in those smoky hissings and clankings and the rattling rumble of metal wheels, and the sudden incandescent glow of an opened fire door, surprising one with momentary images of a world of Bosch punched out of Rousseau's landscapes.

Fleming loathed it all. It was too slow for him, too vulnerable, too inefficient. It represented at the nth degree a world and a way of life which he despised and detested. Fleming, of course, even then, was a man of the technocracy . . . a responsible officer of the technocracy. He visited Leromenos simply because Armand's brothel was there.

I used to think that this was merely another aspect of Fleming's efficiency. A girl, to him; moist, dark, naked, reekingly sweetly aromatical, writhing beneath the damp mosquito curtain, the smell of sweat and cinnamon, the panted breathing, the undulations of a silken shape, the clenching and unclenching of soft, strong fingers—they *did* give you your money's worth, those shy, strange girls of Armand's!— was not a girl so much as a necessary chemical prophylaxis against tedium and against foreignness, and a kind of symbol of *mens sana in corpore sano* translated into a few minutes of violent medicinal wrestling in a dimly lit room walled with cane. I think a whore was no more to him and no less than the bottle of B-complex vitamin pills on the mess table beside his coffee cup, or the yellow capsules he swallowed against the contingency of malaria, or the ten minutes of strenuous setting-up exercises he would force his strong thickset body into every morning. One thing—he never

[23]

talked about it. It had become a stable ritual with him. Mondays and Thursdays and always at eight o'clock. He would always look at his watch carefully to check the time before going in to do it. I would stay outside, at ease in one of the cane chairs on the verandah, talking or not talking to Armand and sipping at anisette or gin. The walls at Armand's place were very thin, soft-woven cane no thicker than a table mat, so that the sounds of copulation, the wilder breathing, the quick indrawn panting of the girl, a heavy grunt from Fleming, even the soft sliding sound of impacted flesh, were an inescapable obbligato to the murmurous relaxation which Armand and I shared on the wide dim verandah among the old copies of *The New Yorker, The Field* and the *Illustrated London News*. Yet this carnal background never intruded. It had cost so much in self-discipline to make sure that it could not intrude, but that was over now, and the very method and efficiency of the timetable ritual reduced it all to an accepted, unimportant undertone—like a fellow clubman in the far corner of the lounge clearing his throat behind his newspaper, or a waiter sorting silver over at the sideboard.

Armand kept twelve girls. They were not always the same twelve, of course, since they were said to be at their best only when they were young—around fifteen or sixteen— and although I am positive Fleming had been with all twelve of them, and quite a few times with some, he never knew any one of them by name. I often used to wonder about this extraordinary detachment of his, and from time to time I would find myself sitting on that shabby verandah, looking beyond the old blinking eyes and the nodding grey head of Armand, staring out into the darkness of that sordid street—a desert of dust at one season of the year and an almost impassable quagmire at the other—wondering what Fleming's reaction would be were I to discuss with him the true nightmare violence of the sexual act; were I to tell him about my wife Olga and what had led up to her death. Idle thoughts. Speculations. Drifting away like the smoke through the trees. Interesting enough, but merging into other reflections without ever forming into a decisive wish to tell. Not to Garnett Fleming, at any rate.

He had come out from the inside room looking as neat and clean as usual in his well-pressed suntans and shirt, spotless shoes, and gilt-buckled belt—a tall, well-set man with close-cropped pepper-and-salt hair, square shoulders and a rather heavy, rather humourless face that was, nonetheless, quite handsome in its way. No expression on the face to denote satisfaction or distaste. A man returning from the men's room. Or someone who had taken his vitamins. From behind the inner screens a soft rustling and subdued laughter were sounds of no more significance in relationship to Fleming than a mouse scratching at the wainscot or a squirrel teasing at the thatch.

Armand withdrew soundlessly to fetch the Scotch and soda, and the thermos jar of ice cubes which Fleming always had a boy bring across from the mess each Monday and Thursday afternoon. Fleming relaxed himself in the long cane lounger, lit his cigar, and carefully spread his legs.

"Jake," he said, after a time, and in a tone that seemed to reflect on something else, "what gives about this goddam monsoon?"

"When?" I glanced across at him idly. "Is that what you mean?"

He nodded, frowning away.

"I should say another week or ten days," I offered. "Why?"

Armand returned with the drinks and the ice on a chipped lacquer tray, soft slippers dustily shuffling on the woven mats; then withdrew again to his soft-spoken, soft-laughing

[25]

girls. Soft sounds always at Armand's. Fleming rattled the ice cubes around his glass—this sound an alien one, tinkling and hard.

"A week. God damn it to hell," he said, without venom.

I sipped at my gin and waited. The sulphur tints had seeped away behind the trees and the night was purple, with the fruit bats above flocking to the north like winged spirits. The shadows between the trees reminded me of thick, blobby liquorice sticks. Two of the girls came out and went to the far end of the verandah and squatted by the screen in their thin cotton loin wraps. Slender lemon-skinned girls with buds of small pale-nippled breasts and the huge timid eyes of animals.

"We're getting a bunch of people to handle," said Fleming. "Big shots. Special instructions. God damn it to hell," he repeated, still absently, as if he were too tired to put any heart into his cursing.

"You've had big shots before," I said.

"Sure. I don't care to have them sitting around, that's all. Getting in my hair," he elaborated. "Assing things up. And if the monsoon breaks they'll sit. Sure as hell."

I shrugged. I was not particularly interested—half my attention was on a train shunting up on the outside loop. But I said, "What sort of big shots?"

"Ask Old Frisky," he said sententiously, and cracked a grin that had malevolence in it. Fleming and the General had never got on very well with one another, and each went to some pains to make unnecessary difficulties for the other on questions of form and procedure. Frisk was a regular, and a West Pointer, and I always had the feeling that he could never quite forgive Fleming his bootstraps haul out of the broiling world of Boston-Irish politics into the uniform of a lieutenant colonel, nor the ribbons which his subordinate officer wore on his chest on the rare occasions when he dressed for company. Frisk had more ribbons, of course, but Fleming had been out in the Southwest Pacific and his were better ones. Some of them.

"He's been flapping about like a Westchester County hostess ever since the signal came," Fleming went on to say, and squinted at the half inch of ash on the end of his cigar. "So when he flaps we've all got to flap. It says so in Standing Orders." He brought the cigar closer and allowed the smoke to drift about his nostrils. I wondered if he would have the same expression on his face at his moments of culmination with the lemon-skinned girls in the room inside. I decided not. They were different pleasures. Indulged for different reasons.

"That goddam Jane Carson," he said, almost with a sigh. "And Vince Readaway. How d'you like that?" His eyes were closed against the cigar smoke.

I waited. He said nothing more. "Actors, aren't they?" I submitted guardedly, not being altogether sure, although it was the only connection that persisted from half-remembered fragments of *Time* and *Newsweek*. "I know the names," I added lamely.

He opened one eye and looked across at me whimsically. "Brother, have *you* been out of circulation!" he said. The eye closed. " 'Actors, aren't they?' " His mimicry of my accent was perfect. He could always take Frisk off, too. "Stars, my ignorant friend," he said wearily. "*The* stars. Ask Old Frisky. He can give you the whole works. I guess the guy buys up all those copies of *Movieland* and *Film Digest* at the PX. You ask him to tell you about Vince Readaway. He-man Vince, idol of the silver screen, daredevil of the comic strips. Hero of the mesa. The scourge of Tombstone. Christ!" He changed his tone and said casually, "You'd know about our Jane, though. Don't tell me."

"Well, I knew she acted," I said defensively. "I prefer ballet, anyway. I've never been one for the cinema."

"For pete's sake, you don't *have* to be. You read newspapers. You listen to the radio. She's always there. New husbands. New lovers. New scandals. I guess she's quite a dame."

"But . . . but how on earth does a person like that come into our setup?" I asked.

"Morale. For over there." His heavy handsome head tilted slightly. "It seems she and Vince are headliners with an entertainment outfit that's going to try to elevate the spirits of all those poor bastards on the other side. Take their minds off this other sordid business of getting killed. Next week *East Lynne*."

"But we're not a combat area."

"My friend, we are Pennsylvania Station and this is the Chattanooga Choo-Choo. They're not interested in *our* morale, bud. How we figure in this is just that we fly 'em over to Xanadu. We fix the connections. Well, we fix the connections and shift 'em over to Xanadu if the monsoon doesn't screw things up. That's all I was getting at." He turned in the lounger and yelled for Armand. "There's a senator coming too," he said. "The way this civilian traffic's building, maybe we'll be making out flight schedules for the Rockettes or the New York Giants!"

"I don't see why you should worry. You meet them. You billet them for a night or so. You move them on. It's routine."

"Sure, that's all. They send the packages, we consign 'em on. Anyway, Jake, it's not your department. You don't have to do a thing about it, except rub the mildew off your autograph book." He took the replenished glass from Armand, rattled the ice cubes again, and settled back. "The hell with it," he said contentedly. "I feel like a million dollars."

There were now five girls in the corner against the screen.

[28]

They stared across at us with big, blank eyes, like a group of curious children. Two of them looked down at intervals to play with a set of knucklebones. I had a sad, sneaking wish for a little of Fleming's uncomplicated virility. It was a thought of no particular fervour, the lightest brushstroke of longing, not even desire, yet for an instant the whole palisade of my protection seemed to tremble. Fleming clinked the ice cubes. Armand scratched at his backside and shuffled away. A train whistled somewhere down the line. The night smelt of saffron and nutmeg and dust. Zone Q-4. . . .

3

It was only a day or two after that that one could feel the imminence of the monsoon. Intensely hot and still, the leaves hanging like dead things, almost unbearably humid. At night, while the temperature dropped less than three degrees on the Fahrenheit thermometer, the dampness would increase, and as one lay sleepless inside the dank canopy of the mosquito netting the mosquitoes seemed to have the stridency of cicadas. The sky remained cloudless, but imperceptibly there had been a sickly paling off of colour, as if a wasting disease had drained from the atmosphere its capacity to sustain life—a space of steel that changed to bronze in the evening, when all the birds would become fretfully astir. The barrier of the alps had receded far away. Transparent washes on a pale watercolour, the spirit shapes of mountains.

It was only at sunrise that nervous little hot flurries of wind would start up, forming tiny dervishes of dust which would dance giddily across the compounds and suddenly collapse as if exhausted. The spasms of these dust imps left a nervousness inside one's head for the rest of the airless day. A trying, irritable time. Tempers on edge. Tensions jetting up, exploding, dying away listlessly. Minds working, I suppose, to the flurries of the wind: minds could be dervishes, too.

The general edginess was most pronounced among the pilots, especially the younger ones who had not yet experienced a monsoon.

I usually did my evening drinking in the pilots' mess. It had inevitably acquired something of the character of a tropical club, but it was a good deal less stuffy than the alternative refuges of Zone Q-4, and I liked the people there.

It was the one place where I really did feel to be Frisk's Old Man of the Mountains and the Jungle. Almost all the men were very much younger than I—when you are into your thirties how far away the early twenties seem—although a few of the senior men were around my own age. Bellini, Favell, and Hathaway, for instance, were old hands who had come back voluntarily to do a second tour of duty, and Major Peabody, who commanded the unit although still actively flying, was nearly through his third.

At that time a tour of duty called for the completion of one hundred and one flights each way between Zone Q-4 and Xanadu; after which the flier would go home on leave and, unless he revolunteered, would find some comfortable desk job in the command's administration or operations. It was not at all the sinecure it sounds, because although we were not a combat area, the casualty rate was considerable. Vile storms, unmapped peaks, icing, overloading, general accidents, the unpredictable violence of high-altitude winds, unsuitable aircraft, and the nature of the terrain over which these operations were conducted, were costing us at that time the loss of well over three hundred aircraft a year. It was an appalling country for accidents to happen in. Gradually we had built up a Search-and-Rescue group which, by contrast to the pioneering period, was comparatively efficient—we had more accurate maps, a few helicopters and some photo-reconnaissance planes; I had helped in the partial establishment of tribal depots and organized native search teams. But the percentage of recovery of personnel alive from lost aircraft did not amount to one in three.

Although the command was American, there were a few foreign volunteers—leftovers, as it were, from the pioneering period—who still flew on the operations. Favell came from Sweden, Hathaway was a New Zealander, Bellini had grown up outside Winnipeg. Favell and Bellini had both been commercial airline pilots—Peabody, also, had cut his teeth with T.W.A.—and Hathaway had been a Rhodes scholar reading Ancient History at Oxford when the war broke out. In the pilots' mess the five of us shared a special companionship, separated from the others not only as "the older group" but also, I think, because of our more unconventional backgrounds. Frisk had a guarded respect for his little coterie of experienced veterans, not entirely untinged by resentment: he felt that the operations of Zone Q-4 ideally should have been one hundred per cent all-American. In the case of Peabody, who was as American as hominy grits, his pique arose from the fact that the flying operations were directed from Washington and were not under his actual command. Let it be said for Frisk that he never allowed his resentments to interfere with the efficiency of the command to which he had been entrusted. The telephones on Frisk's orderly desk, the empanelled switches of his intercom system, the printed pads for his desk memoranda, were the paraphernalia which dictated the practical mechanics of his sprawling command, but they had no control over human destinies. Nor, I imagine, did Dalton Frisk believe that they should.

There were four of us at the bar drinking rye old-fashioneds—Peabody and Hathaway, myself, and a young second lieutenant who had been posted to Kansas six weeks before and who was learning the ropes on the not very pleasant job of flying gasoline tankers.

These were fat-fuselaged, rather slow, rather difficult freight planes fitted with quadruple belly-tanks into which the high-octane fuel was loaded in bulk. Hard to fly. Sluggish at high altitudes. And pretty tricky to handle at take-off and landing.

The system in operation had worked more or less since the establishment of the zone, and the pilot roster operated rather on a sliding scale of expendability. Recruit pilots had a preliminary shakedown period during which they flew copilot with one of the seasoned men. They graduated from this to the gasoline tankers—on the basis, I suppose, of "survive with them and you'll survive anything!"—rotated from there to general freight planes, then to "special freight," and after that to the transportation of military personnel. There was a final hierarchy of "special passenger personnel" —Fleming's impending "big shots" fitted into this category— but this was strictly reserved for the very senior men.

There was a basic and ironic paradox in the system, in that the brunt of the most dangerous flying had to be borne by the least experienced fliers. The reason for this was that while all passenger flights were forbidden during excessively bad weather, freight schedules had to be maintained night and day all through the year, good weather or bad, flying clear or flying blind. Frisk's pattern of logistics by this time called for the departure of a freight plane from Kansas every four minutes. When the alps were, as they would say, "socked in," passengers would have to just sit and wait for the weather to clear: there were times when they would be moping in our transient quarters for ten days at a stretch, although the normal flying time between Kansas and Xanadu was only about seven hours. The crossing, however, was never "socked in" for the freighters. It is hardly necessary to add that by far the greater percentage of losses occurred with these aircraft.

The young pilot who was drinking with us was a tall, good-looking, blond boy named Peter Strawlings. He had grown up on a farm in Indiana. I remember him for his broad mouth and his big capable hands, and the way his eyes would ingenuously examine you as if he had to seek the reassurance of some simpler values within the evidently complex framework of what he thought you were trying to tell him. There was something naïve, something almost of a pure innocence about him, that was difficult to analyze, but it gave one a sort of lingering sense of responsibility towards him.

He had touched down his empty freight plane only an hour before. He had changed into clean suntans which he wore tucked in to his heavy fur-lined flying boots. The boots must have been terribly uncomfortable in that heat—the sunset temperature had been eighty-eight degrees, and there was a quite hellish humidity in the mess!—but I remember the touch for its artless childishness. It seemed, somehow, to underline Strawlings' identity.

For some time he had been talking to Peabody, very respectfully and with a slow-spoken regard to technicalities, about his return flight from Xanadu. He had come over at low altitude, never above seventeen thousand feet, avoiding the high crests and weaving through the labyrinthine passages of the gorges and valleys between the peaks. He spoke of it as a man might speak of a meandering walk through the fields and woods on a fine spring day, with a throb of excitement beneath his account as if some inarticulate feeling for poetry was straining to burst through the uncomplicated simplicity of the man.

"But, gee, Major Peabody, you c'd see just every darned

thing, sir, just *everything*, like lookin' down into a clear glass!" he said. "Ridges. Rocks. Little things, too. An' we c'd pick up the big peaks, there, way up north, hundred miles away, I guess. Danny said, 'Take her down a smidge an' we c'n lick those glaciers like an ice cream cone!' "

Peabody smiled a little, and said, "What about turbulence?" Peabody, with all those flying hours behind him, had an essentially practical turn of mind.

Strawlings glanced at him quickly. "Well . . . sure." He nodded slowly, and frowned over the thought. "We got some turbulence, sure. Darned if we didn't. Funny, that was. Not a cloud in the sky big as your thumbnail even. No wind or drift to speak of. An' goddam it, sir, there we'd be tossin' up 'n' down like a kid's ball. Sure, we got turbulence. We bounced!"

"But, my dear chap, you *don't* bounce," Hathaway said in that mild, languid, rather affected way he had of speaking. "Not if you hit. That, of course, is the whole bloody point."

"Hit? We were way up, sir, an'—"

"Quite. This time you were way up. But just be a good boy now, and don't do hedgehopping over there, even on the nice sunny days. Never acquire bad habits, cock. Nasty rocks, those. And those clouds sometimes come down very quickly. Nasty clouds and just chockablock with nasty rocks. Unpleasant to a degree."

Peabody looked at Strawlings with his slow, easy, kindly smile. "Captain Hathaway's right, Strawlings," he said quietly. "Stay up. Stay up high, even on the clear days. Close your eyes, if you like. Take it on instruments. It took a lot of clever guys to work out those instruments."

"But there wasn't a cloud in the sky," Strawlings began to protest. "Gosh, you could see all the way to the river! You could—"

[35]

"Sure." Peabody nodded. "They take sightseeing parties to the top of the Empire State Building. Or the Pyramids. You can do yours when you get leave down to Calcutta. Listen, Lieutenant, that bouncing you did . . . you know what *that* was? That was just old Mister Monsoon lifting a warning finger. Just wagging his head a bit and saying, *tsk-tsk-tsk*. In a week's time, Strawlings, you can skip the sightseeing . . . you're not going to be able to see all the way to your own wingtips, not even to your own flaps. You're not going to see anything through that glass, bud, except a thick black soup shot through with fire. Blue fire. And what you've got to remember is just what Hathaway here has been telling you. That soup is full of rocks as well. Real rocks. Rocks you don't bounce off. So it's kind of wise to get into the habit of staying up high. Real high. When you've got to go on oxygen it's kind of inconvenient, but you do feel cozier somehow. It's always nice to feel cozy."

He put his hand for a moment on the boy's shoulder, then moved down the bar to the ice pail. After a time I joined him there. Strawlings and Hathaway had gone away, talking together, to one of the corner tables.

On the wall beside the refrigerator there was a big square frame of bamboo slats. Attached to it were the usual sentimental memorabilia with which pilots' messes the world over are decorated. Half a dozen snapshots of officers of a year before—one which I recognized was of a lieutenant now buried in the little cemetery across the railroad: another, on which had been scribbled the unintentional but ironic prophecy, *"Remember my silences!—Hank Goldman,"* was of a garrulous Texas major who had blown himself and his plane to pieces in the high timber of the Kaoli Kung. A festoon of corks from champagne bottles threaded on green silk ribbon. A little Pinocchio puppet. Somebody's mascot, but whose? A set of printed pulpboard beer coast-

[36]

ers bearing brand names and the location of bars in San Francisco and New York. The talismen of nostalgia. Most of the board was covered conventionally with pinned up pictures of girls. Mostly naked, a few in lingerie or G-strings. (Another bomb had not been exploded then; in the dark womb of language the word "bikini" had not even been conceived.) Two spectacular colour plates from glossy magazines of unclad voluptuaries were tacked up carefully below a hand-lettered sign reading *Park Your Pulchritude Here*. Next to this a more original wit had screwed on a stolen door sign in embossed enamel. LADIES ROOM. The rest of the space was filled entirely with monochrome clippings from magazines—in halftone, in offset, in rotogravure. But all women. Women without a doubt at all! Breasts for the most part, since this was then the fashionable territory of sexual desire, although there was a catholic interest betrayed in bottoms, in eyes, thighs, shining lips, hair falling loose. The votive offerings of the young. Totem of a carnal memory. The life-wish. . . .

A thought occurred to me. I looked more carefully at the board and said, "Is Jane Carson one of those?"

"I guess so," said Peabody. "Well, she'd have to *be* there." He examined the board curiously, as if he had never really looked at it before. He had a wife and three children in Omaha, so it is very possible that he never had. "Sure," he said after a thoughtful interval. "There. The one at the top, second from the right."

That was my first meeting with Jane Carson.

A page torn from a film magazine and trimmed up around the edges. A face and a body in grey halftones among all the other similar faces and bodies in grey halftones. Yet not quite the same as all the others when you looked at it more closely.

I suppose there is an unending fluctuating tide of change

[37]

in the fashions of feminine beauty, but I am sure there are always some women, a few of them, whose loveliness stands unimpaired and unchallenged outside the mores of any particular time. Jane Carson was such a woman. Sombody quite recently made the quip that "It used to be the *femme fatale,* but now it's the *femme foetal.*" Perhaps this goes too far, but certainly there is a kind of unformed almost foetal quality about the faces that stare out at one now from the magazine racks and the bookstands. Perhaps the secret self-assurance of the male has wilted a little under the pressures of this new sex revolution we read so much about, for adulation does seem to be reserved for adolescents with the qualities of the unformed, the childlike, the vulnerable, the nymphic not-quite-woman—as if these features offer a sicklier challenge to a shakier male ego. But in the intermediate time of which I am thinking, midway, let us say, between the *femme fatale* of Nazimova and Theda Bara, and the *femme foetal* of now, the cult figure was Woman. Real Woman. Neither the coy vamps of the twenties nor the weary Germanic sophisticates of the thirties. And certainly not the wayward delinquent schoolgirls of today. Jane Carson, even on that crowded bamboo board, had real rivals to contend with.

The picture showed a wide laughing mouth and white small teeth, eyes ever so slightly oblique in setting, soft pale-looking hair blowing away to one side. Smart photography, with a shallow depth of focus and a blurred background, bringing out the fine structure of her bones—a clever wind blowing something gauzy against a superb body. There was something about the picture though that did not quite accord with the cult image which, with as much attention to the technical aspects of allurement, everywhere surrounded her portrait. It did not quite fit into the cliché of provocation, into this hackneyed, mass-produced montage, swelling, curving, tempting, promising, which sym-

[38]

bolized the Woman Cult and gave it a shrine on a bamboo board.

Or was this a thought that occurred to me only later?

"She's coming here, you know," I said. "Passing through. Next week, they say."

"Sure. I heard about it," said Peabody.

"Fleming tells me she's quite a woman."

"You can say that again." Peabody laughed casually. "She sure is a tramp."

I studied the picture with idle interest. She didn't look like a tramp. Some of the others on the board did, but not Jane Carson.

"Well, I guess she's a tramp." Peabody added the qualification carefully. "She certainly acts that way."

"Don't they all?"

He shrugged. "She takes it further than most. It's publicity, I guess."

"Maybe you'll get to fly her."

"You scared me. I figured you were going to say something else." He grinned into his drink.

4

As it happened, the monsoon and Jane Carson arrived together. Or just about. The few hours' difference between these two events was not sufficient, at any rate, to mollify the fury of Garnett Fleming, especially as the difference was, from his point of view, in the wrong direction. The monsoon came first. By the time Jane Carson arrived the mountains to the eastward were "socked in" and all eastbound passenger flights suspended indefinitely. Fleming seemed to take this as a personal affront. "This sure has loused it up!" he grumbled bitterly, and I half expected him to launch into a tirade against cosmic inefficiency. In the end he blamed the meteorological reports.

The monsoon that year, in fact, hit us thirty hours before we had expected it. Up to a point, the seasonal coming of the monsoon is usually predictable. It strikes first hundreds of miles away to the south and moves north at a calculable speed, so that with reports from the southern weather stations one should theoretically be able to fix a reasonably accurate time for its onslaught upon one's own territory. The catch is that in that part of the world climatic phenomena have a knack of sometimes not working to the fixed rules. So it happened in this case. And it was, I think, the worst monsoon I ever experienced.

In its actual breaking it followed the usual pattern. That familiar breathless build-up when one's lungs seem to fight for air, and then the slow darkening of the sky to a heavy, almost apocalyptic blackness in which the most trivial sounds seem to scream with a penetrating shrillness. The squalls come first, frenzied rushes of wind at gale force howling in from every point of the compass, ripping the lighter branches from the trees, building a wall of coffee-coloured dust between Kansas and Rampart. Then a prescient hour of brooding stillness again before the thunder and the lightning. The Wagnerian moment, this. Drum-rolls of thunder that never cease, and mighty, ear-splitting claps of sound that seem to batter the shuddering earth with cudgels, and the sky blue-lit with an incessant flash and flicker of lightning—a world for three hours of deafening noise and that unearthly light which never failed to appal me. Finally, the rain.

The monsoon rain. Is it possible for anyone to describe adequately that first hammering tumult from the skies? That solid wall of water descending for hour after hour, with all life stunned and hushed and terrified beneath its roaring. To stand on the sagging, dripping verandah and to see, as in a flawed mirror, your own reflection on the falling wall of water. To watch rivers rolling where streets were, huts dissolving, trees sinking to the ground beneath the sheer weight of water. To see the earth restored to the cataclysmic violence of its primal birth. . . .

One of the corporals from Quigley's staff was caught on the way back from the airfield issue store, was beaten to the ground by the weight of the rain, and drowned before he could be rescued. In Leromenos, of course, it was much more disastrous. The death roll there was thirty-two, all natives, all drowned. Caught away from shelter or trapped in a collapsing hut—dying for want of air in a world turned to water.

The first deluge lasted nine hours, then slackened. Next morning the rain stopped altogether for three hours, and the world became an opalescent steam bath in which an unseen sun made a pale rubbing in our world of spectral mist. The sky blackened. The rain began again. Not quite so heavily, but heavy enough. And with a high wind now, tossing the trees violently. However, during that interval of three hours when all the world was pale they were able to land seven planes coming in from the west. One of them was the Fireball.

They had cocky, swashbuckling names for all the western services. Fireball was the direct service to and from the States—the *de luxe* service, one might say. The one to London, through Delhi, was Corsair. We also had Arrowspeed and Lightbeam. Confident names, with quite a swagger to them. But, in a way, confidence ended where we were, in Zone Q-4. If you continued on to the east the flights had only numbers. The continuity of assurance, of self-congratulation, of *belief* almost, existed, I feel, only behind us. There we could afford the arrogance of Fireball. It was the guarantee of our security. It comforted us in our delusions. But when we went on towards the jungles and the lofty silence of the peaks we were not quite so sure.

At the time I was not aware of the Fireball's arrival, of the coming of Jane Carson and Vince Readaway and the senator. I was in hip-length gumboots, floundering in mud, trying to organize rescue and salvage gangs in Leromenos. One of Armand's lemon-skinned girls was among the victims. Caked in mud and with her mouth and eyes open, stiff and naked, she had been trapped in the hut of a young railroad worker, also dead. She had had no business at all to be there. Armand was livid about it.

It was late in the afternoon before I got back to my quarters. The rain was pelting down again. I took the simplest solution and stripped off all my muddy clothes; threw them on the flooded ground and stood naked in the warm deluge of the rain until I was clean again. As I stood there I could hear the freight planes droning about in the overcast, fixed in their dismal flight patterns, waiting to make instrument landings. I decided to dress and go across to the pilots' bar and have a cocktail there. One was always conscious of a little chill of premonition and suspense in those first days of monsoon flying, and for some reason I found myself thinking, with a peculiar twinge of anxiety, about young Strawlings.

By the time I set out on the path across the compound it was quite dark. My gumboots sloshed thickly through mud and water. My head was bent against the sting of the wet wind, and the rain, cold now, drummed on the hood of my oilskin. So I did not see the small, vague figure in the darkness until I almost collided with it—an indeterminate shape in a pale raincoat and sou'wester sheltering uncertainly beneath a dripping tree at the rear of the billeting office.

Something in the unmasculine shape of the figure, something in its air of indecision, of being a *strange* thing in this wet, roaring night, prompted me to say, "You ought to have a flashlight. Almost knocked you over. You're getting wet there."

"I'm trying to find a bar," she said surprisingly. "There's got to be a bar some place. I need a drink."

"There are several bars," I said. "I'm heading for one now. I need a drink too."

"That's fine," she said. "I'll come along with you."

"If you like," I said.

That was how I really met Jane Carson. I could not see her face at all beneath the turned-down brim of the sou'-

wester, and her figure was shapeless under the raincoat, and I don't know why I had expected her to be six feet tall and Junoesque in the way of those showgirls who decorate the stairs and balconies of musical comedy sets—she was of average height and the crown of her sou'wester was exactly on a level with my shoulder—but I knew at once that this was Jane Carson.

Anyway, as she paddled with me along the compound path, she said, "I'm Jane Carson. Who are you?"

"Jacob Strickland," I said.

"You're not American."

"No. I'm English."

"I thought so. The way you talk. Are you in this setup then?"

"In a way," I said. "We're going to the pilots' bar."

"Are you a pilot?"

"No. I'm just a groundling, I fear."

"Are women allowed there? In this bar, I mean."

"I hadn't thought of that. I imagine so. They're not a stuffy bunch. Besides, they couldn't turn anyone away on a night like this."

"If they want to turn me away," she said firmly, "they've got to give me a drink first. I need a drink."

"Yes, you told me."

"That flight in . . . it was just terrible, all the way from Delhi. And I'm scared of flying at the best of times." She seemed to hesitate. "Do we have to go on from here, in this storm?"

"No," I said. "Only if it lets up—and it won't. I'm afraid you might be stuck with us for a day or two."

"That's wonderful," she said, with obvious relief. "That's the nicest thing I've heard since we left New York."

When I took her in I had a momentary twinge of embarrassment at finding the place so crowded, although I should

[44]

have realized that with the "sock-in" order in force there would necessarily be quite a few air crews with time on their hands. I was relieved to see that Strawlings was there, at the far end of the bar, with a bunch of youngsters.

The excitement and drama of the monsoon had given a heightened atmosphere to the place. The mood of the company verged on a kind of nervous hilarity as if everyone was trying a shade too hard. Jets of quick talk, over-loud voices, over-loud laughter. Two of the young men in Strawlings' group—they were all from the freight squadrons—were already fairly plastered. But every now and then there would be a tremor in the conversation, not a hush so much as a discontinuity like a cog slipping, and not everywhere in the big room but just here and there. In these fractional intervals one could hear the faint, pulsing drone of an aircraft moving above us in the black, wet night—a remote, sad sound, growing louder, wailing, fading, throbbing away, lost at last in the monotonous drumming of the rain on the thatch—and one sensed a flicker of inattention touching this group or that like an electric charge. This, of course, was something I noticed later. Not at first. Entering that company of men with Jane Carson gave me other things to think about.

She went in ahead of me through the swinging door and I followed with some polite platitude—something about hat and coat, you must be soaked—as she stood with an odd little attitude of expectancy on the rain-sodden, mud-smeared boards just inside the entrance. As I helped her remove the dripping raincoat she looked slowly around the room, her expression calm and unaffected. She took off her sou'wester and shook her hair. Every man in the long room was staring at her, all quite still, drinks arrested in fingers momentarily paralyzed. The smoke from cigarettes made vertical lines and then scribbled out into the drifting blue haze. There was not a sound save the slow drip-drip-drip of

[45]

water from my own oilskin, and from outside only the scampering shrill revels of the wind and the rain.

The sudden, unexpected intrusion of any woman into that all-male preserve would have been startling enough: the fact that it was Jane Carson accentuated and prolonged the shock. I remember thinking how absurd it was to have judged her by the monochrome magazine cutout on the bamboo board. Her hair, worn loose and shoulder length, was not blond, but of that tawny, pale, reddish-gold colour which we sometimes call "light Titian." Her eyes were beautiful in shape—even slightly more oblique than the photograph had indicated—and of the most remarkable colour: a vivid malachite green under dark lashes. Her nose, a shade too blunt perhaps, was an imperfection that added to her loveliness. Her skin was rather pale and creamy, her cheeks flushed a little by the wind and the rain, and there were drops of rain water still caught upon her face. Rather high cheekbones, and a pale lipstick to dissemble the firm, rich fullness of her mouth. No other evidence of make-up that I could see. No jewellery at all. And the famous body in a plain, sleeveless dress of some light, oatmeal-coloured material. She looked a little older than I would have thought from the photograph. I guessed her to be in her early thirties: she was, in fact, twenty-nine.

I saw Peabody's face among all the other silent, watchful faces, and since he was the senior officer I beckoned him across and mumbled something about taking a liberty, found her in the rain looking for somewhere to have a drink, hoped there was no objection. Peabody grinned and held out his hand to her and said, "Hullo. I'm Fred Peabody. What's the drink you have in mind, Miss Carson?" His invitation acted like the flicking of a switch, and there was a sudden buzz of conversation from all around, although no head was turned away.

[46]

I decided that the tactful thing to do was to leave her with Peabody, so I gave my oilskin and her raincoat and sou'wester to the sergeant, and moved along the bar to Strawlings. His greeting to me was rather absent. His attention was still on the woman in the doorway. I asked the barman to mix me a negroni, and turned again to Strawlings and said, "Were you flying in it today?"

He shook his head slowly. "No, sir, I'm scheduled for tomorrow morning," he said. "Four thirty. I guess maybe it'll ease off by then." He made the observation disinterestedly, and his glance drifted again to the far end of the room. Peabody had taken her to one of the tables, and quite a few of the men were crowding around, bowing politely, offering their hands. They were all smiling like dentifrice advertisements.

"It's quite possible," I said. "The first day is often the worst." I realized he was not listening. I also realized that Jane Carson had established herself as an honorary member of Zone Q-4 flying officers' mess.

She handled herself very well, I must say. I can't imagine what I had expected of a famous Hollywood film star, but I remember being rather surprised that she acted so naturally. There was about her, of course, that almost indefinable aura—authority? a sense of homage being taken for granted? —that always seems to surround the publicly famous, yet it was her charm and friendliness, more than her extraordinary beauty or this special and singular magnetism in her personality, that first impressed me. I was satisfied that I had committed no *gaffe* whatever by bringing her uninvited to the mess, and I was able with an easy conscience—indeed, with a glowing sense of having *contributed* something—to leave her to her admiring court. For half an hour I was left at the bar with no company but the corporal barman, who mixed my negronis in a very absent-minded way.

[47]

I was sipping my third when Major General Dalton J. Frisk arrived in a wet, shining yellow slicker several sizes too large for him and with the dedicated questing air of a man accompanied by bloodhounds. In a sense, I suppose he was—for behind him were two of the security guards in white helmets and black waterproof capes. Frisk's face was damp, pale, and petulant.

Let me try to reassemble the General in the vision of my mind. He was short and neat and tending towards stoutness, although he always tried to hold himself well, and he had rather puffy little hands that were always beautifully cared for. In some odd way his physical appearance exactly fitted his soft and slightly lisping voice. His eyes were blue, keen, and polished when he was alert, and wrapped in soft folded little pouches of flesh when he was relaxed or listening. His hair was his great pride. It was snow-white, thick and rather wavy, with a silky texture. He kept a tortoise-shell-backed hand mirror and a matching pair of hair brushes on the side table near his big desk. (Fleming's accusation that Frisk bleached his hair with a special chemical was almost certainly a fiction.) He was, on the whole, popular with the enlisted men but rather resented and mistrusted by most of his officers. The flying personnel detested him.

Since he was nobody's fool and aware enough of the pilots' animosity towards him, his visit to the mess on this particular and *very* inclement night had a quality of both rarity and urgency. That this involved Jane Carson was immediately clear, because when he saw her surrounded by her admirers he bit his lip with such obvious displeasure that a perceptible interval followed before he was able to summon an artificial smile.

Seeing that I had been responsible for bringing her there, I left my drink and began to walk down the room as Frisk, with a creditable attempt at surprised jocularity, moved

[48]

towards the woman with his hands outspread, saying, "Well, upon my soul, Miss Carson, so *this* is where we run you to earth! We've had half the base alerted, looking everywhere for you!"

She smiled quickly, and said, "I'm sorry, General. I didn't realize. I didn't expect there'd be any cause for anxiety."

"This weather, Miss Carson," said the General, with a solemn pursing of his mouth. He must have been very conscious of the faces of all those men steadily and expressionlessly watching him. "It can be dangerous, particularly when the terrain is unfamiliar. We've had casualties already, you know. It wouldn't do to have anything happen to you." His smile this time was under control. "And the others have been waiting, you see," he added mildly. "Mr. Readaway. Senator Vancourt. Readaway has been a pretty agitated guy."

The ghost of a smile seemed to touch her lips, but she said nothing.

"Well, she's been out of the weather here," said Peabody. "We've kept her dry and comfortable, and we have enjoyed her visit—for sure."

"I'm certain you have, Major Peabody," Frisk said, with only a trace of stiffness. "But the others have been waiting the best part of an hour. We're all going to my house for cocktails and dinner." The General was the only person at the base who had a real house. The rest of us shared hut quarters which, admittedly, were fairly comfortable. Preferable to Frisk's house, at any rate.

"Then all this is my fault," Jane Carson said quietly, "and I *am* sorry. I felt pretty shaky after that flight from Delhi, and I lay down for a bit, but then I wanted a drink so badly, and I didn't know who to ask, so I came out and I was brought here by . . ." Her head turned a little, her eyes searching.

"By me," I said, moving into the group.

[49]

"Yes." She gave me a quick smile. "By Mr. Strickland."

Frisk turned to me, the testiness assembling in his eyes. He was never at ease dealing with the pilots, and with Peabody especially, but *I* was a very different kettle of fish. One of his own staff. Not even a serviceman. Not even an *American!*

"It might have been more in keeping with procedure, Strickland," he said acidly, "for you to have kept me informed as to your social intentions. Half my staff has been—"

"It was nothing whatever to do with Mr. Strickland." Her voice, quiet in tone but very firm, cut him short. "I was outside. I was caught in the rain. I had no idea where to go. I met Mr. Strickland and I asked him to bring me here. He was kind enough to oblige. That's all, General Frisk. I'm sorry if there's been some misunderstanding. If there has, it's been my fault. Nobody else's."

"Well . . . let it pass." Frisk hesitated, clearly more discomfited by the directness of her attitude than by the awkwardness of the little scene he had precipitated. But after a moment or two he summoned a tolerant smile and said, "All right, let's skip it. The main thing, Miss Carson, is you've come to no harm, and now you will permit me to supply you with that drink you needed." His manner was genial enough but he kept fretfully tapping the fingers of one hand against the knuckles of the other as Peabody helped her on with her raincoat. Perhaps Peabody took too long doing it, because he turned to me sharply, and said, "Say, where were you at four, Strickland? I wanted you. I had runners looking everywhere."

"They could have found me, sir," I said. "I was at the railhead. I had some work there. Those casualties you were talking about."

"Report to me tomorrow," he said brusquely, very much

[50]

the commanding officer—for Miss Carson's benefit, I imagine. "O-nine-hundred. My office."

"O-nine-hundred, sir," I said, giving him his due.

I shook hands and said good night to her, and her smile was warm and sympathetic, and then I went back along the bar to my unfinished negroni. Peabody joined me a few minutes later, and said, "That stuffy little bastard!" then ordered an old-fashioned and sat with it for a long time, turning the heavy tumbler in his fingers and staring at the cutout picture of Jane Carson on the bamboo board.

"Do you still think she's a tramp?" I asked.

He just shrugged, and went on staring.

5

FRISK's office was big and airy, with drop rattan curtains on
three sides and a revolving electric roof fan over the desk.
The fan must have had a fault in the hub, because it
squeaked at every spin. (If Frisk stopped talking and you
closed your eyes, I thought, you could imagine that he was
a little pink mouse.) An arrangement of two miniature flags
in the corner set in polished brass 30-mm shell cases, one
with the Stars and Stripes, the other just with Frisk's stars.
On a rack below the flags a polished trumpet with a red
lanyard. Photographs in profusion—Frisk, baby-faced, in the
dress uniform of a West Point cadet; Frisk among all the
stiff, set faces in a big group of some graduating class; Frisk,
casual in a bush jacket, shaking hands with some orna-
mental native bigwig. A great many groups in uniform, all
including a Frisk growing older, growing more distinguished
looking, more beribboned—but, alas, stouter, too. And maps,
of course. One of them studded with coloured pins—the one
that Lieutenant Allison, the General's P.A., a studious, silent, bespectacled young man with cavalry badges, kept up
to date each afternoon. On the centre wall, immediately
behind the desk, a gilt and enamel facsimile of the eagle in

the Great Seal of the United States of America. *E Pluribus Unum.* At the edge of the big and remarkably tidy mahogany desk a varnished block of wood, triangular in shape, bearing in letters of gold leaf the modest legend, D. J. FRISK. Several silver-framed photographs on the desk, too, but all these of women and children and family groups. A Ghurka *kukri* in its black leather scabbard, and a miniature replica of the same knife lying on the virginal blotter. And, of course, the tortoiseshell toilet set arranged on the side table next to a prop-up silver frame containing a highly decorated version of Kipling's *If.*

There were just the two of us in the room. In the corner of the room Allison's smaller desk with the telephones, switchboard, and control consoles was not occupied.

"How reliable *are* these goddam met reports?" Frisk was saying. "That's what I want to know. Flannery, over at Weather, insists we'll have this sock-in a week, maybe ten days."

"It's possible. He really has no way of knowing, of course. Not for sure. At the best, met reports can be a guide only for the next twenty-four hours or so. Even then they can't be anywhere near infallible."

"Well, I guess you know as much about this climate as anyone does. What's your angle on it?"

"There's no way of predicting, General Frisk. We *could* have it bad for a ten-day stretch. It has happened before. But that couldn't be foreseen at this stage. In my experience, after the first day or two breaks can occur unexpectedly . . . in fact, there usually is a slight easing off in the early stages."

"Breaks of good weather, you mean?"

"Well . . . let us say, of *better* weather."

"Flying weather?"

"That's always for the control officer to say."

A shadow of irritation flicked across his eyes. "Would that apply on the Xanadu side too?" he asked.

I made a slight shrug. "I suppose it would apply," I said. "But you still wouldn't know whether it was clear *all* the way across until you actually *did* cross."

"We'd have met reports from both sides."

"Quite. Unfortunately, we have no meteorological stations in the mountains. And that's the really vital spot. The weather can build up there into something absolutely foul without our stations or the Xanadu stations knowing anything about it."

"The freighter pilots reporting in?"

"The freighter pilots, yes," I admitted. "You must still remember that a freighter might report it all clear over the main range, but if a passenger aircraft took off on the strength of that report—at this season, I mean—it could quite easily run into extreme monsoon conditions with a zero visibility by the time it got to the main alps three hours or so later."

Frisk considered this, squeezing his pink lip between thumb and forefinger. He must have been silent for quite two minutes, and then he surprised me very much by saying:

"Tell me, Strickland, how do we go about rounding up a bunch of native girls? A dozen or so, I guess. Good-looking ones."

"What?" I looked at him in astonishment.

"To stage those dances they do, the tribal dances." He fluttered his pudgy fingers. "In costume, naturally. We'd want to have that." He looked across at me brightly. "Sure, and musicians too," he added, with what was almost a tremor of excitement. "Let's show 'em the real thing."

"I'm sorry, sir, but I don't quite follow."

The eager expression altered to one of impatience.

[54]

"Listen, Strickland," he said, "my boys have been stuck in this neck of the woods a good long time, most of 'em, and they haven't had too much in the way of entertainment, have they? Some movies. That lousy dump by the railhead. A leave once in a while to Calcutta. Well, I figure to do something for *these* boys."

The enlisted men were always Frisk's "boys." He went to a lot of pains to cultivate his "fatherly" attitude towards them. I could only nod a polite agreement, since I still did not know what he was driving at.

"These things come down to a question of morale," Frisk went on. "Okay, we've got this stateside entertainment out-fit here. So it's for over there, on the other side. But my boys could do with a kick to *their* morale, too. Morale is a tougher problem behind the combat lines, Strickland, do you realize that? Tougher psychologically." He nodded profoundly and touched his fingertips together. "So we're going to put on a show, Strickland. A hell of a *good* show. We'll have half the program stateside entertainment, and half of it local traditional stuff. That'll please the visitors, and it'll please my boys. Yes, sir!" The idea seemed to please him also, because he nodded to himself several times, then beamed across at me.

"Here, you mean?" I asked. "At the base?"

"Why, sure. Lieutenant Allison's fixing the preliminary arrangements now. We'll have a proper stage set up. Lights. Curtains. Dressing rooms. All the trimmings."

"Do you mean Miss Carson and—"

"Sure, sure! They'll be tickled to take part. They told me so last night."

"Yes . . . well, that's a start, isn't it?" I said doubtfully. "But the trouble is you won't get village girls to come here. Not to dance. Not in costume. They're far too shy. You won't get musicians, either—not genuine ones." The thought occurred to me, fleetingly and ironically, that perhaps I could hire Armand's twelve little lemon-skinned girls—and then I remembered that now there were only eleven of them.

He frowned at this, then looked up with his bland smile. "But you'll try, Strickland, won't you?" he said smoothly.

"Well, I shall make inquiries, but—"

"I do want you to try, Strickland. To try very hard. You see—I always like to be candid with people, as I guess you know—there happens to be another angle on this. We have Senator Vancourt with us. Now, Senator Vancourt happens to be a pretty influential member of a Senate subcommittee which is interested in problems of command relationship and general morale. Obviously that is why he's travelling along with this entertainment group. I wouldn't like him to be disappointed in what Zone Q-4 has to show."

"Naturally." I nodded. I was beginning to see the light.

"So what we want you to do now, Strickland," he went on with the bland wisdom of an old adept instructing an acolyte, "is to help us all you can with the native angles. The exotic element. That's the sort of stuff these transients remember—this integration we've built up, harmoniously, without disruption of age-old customs and traditions. The simple native way of life. The sympathetic unity of a single cause . . . our little role, if you like, in the ultimate pageant of world brotherhood." His eyes for a moment dropped into their little pink pouches. His small neat hands rested on the unstained blotter. "You get it, Strickland, don't you?" he said quietly.

"Yes, I think so, sir," I said. I thought of the coolie gangs working at Rampart, of the festering, man-made excrescence at the railhead which I had christened Leromenos, of the guards in white helmets and the warning signs at the gates, of Armand's little girls. "However, I think I should point

[56]

out that—" I began, but he cut me short with a brusque wave of his hand. His eyes were bright blue again, and shining.

"What I want you to do now," he said, "is go talk with this guy Readaway. You'll find him a good Joe. He's eager. He's energetic. He's co-operative. Well, he's a trouper. He's agreed to kick this thing into shape. So what I want you to do is help him where you can or where he wants. Check?"

"Yes, but . . ." I began, and stopped. I thought of the collapsed houses in Leromenos, the running torrents and choked drains, the long row of wet corpses waiting for the rain to stop so they could be cremated. I thought of the ruined rice store in the village, the importunate thin hands holding out empty bowls, the epidemic possibilities in the increase of illnesses that always followed on the heels of the monsoon.

Frisk waited a moment to see if I intended to go on, then favoured me with an indulgent smile—the "fatherly" touch, even to me—consulted some notes on a scratch pad at his elbow, and said, "Readaway's in Number 62. Block J. Get over and see him now, Strickland. Let's get this thing rolling."

I went out into the rain, and splashed down through the lines of wooden huts to the transient officers' quarters in Block J, and Vince Readaway was there all right in Number 62.

He was sitting on the edge of his bed with his elbows on his thighs looking through a copy of *Life*. He was barefoot and wearing only a pair of olive-drab fatigue pants held up with a fancy white belt.

Even seated I could tell he was as tall as I, and about half as broad again. I remembered Fleming's words: "He-man Vince." He looked the part. His naked upper body—I had the immediate feeling he would strip to the waist when-

[57]

ever he could—gave one the impression that it had been moulded to a fresh perfection only that very morning. Shoulders, chest, pectoral muscles, biceps, forearms, even the inverted triangle of dark hair matting his chest and fading down to a point above his navel, all seemed almost too perfect. Like an advertisement on the back cover of a pulp magazine rather than a real person. The width of his shoulders made his head appear disproportionately small at first glance. He had soft, jet-black hair that was rather ruffled and seemed deliberately so, his eyes were brown, his features classically Latin with a touch of more Nordic strength in mouth and jaw line. He had that extreme, assured handsomeness which in another man almost invariably invokes an instinctive dislike. It certainly did with me.

He looked up at me without a smile, in fact, without much interest at all, and said, "Hi! What gives?"

"I'm Strickland," I said. "Headquarters liaison. The General sent me. I understand I have to discuss with you some plan about an entertainment show for the men."

"Oh that." He tossed the magazine down on the floor between his bare feet, and reached on the bed behind him for a pack of cigarettes and a flat gold lighter. He shook out a cigarette, flipped it into his mouth, lit it, and then threw the packet and the lighter back on to the bed behind him. He did not offer me a cigarette. Oddly, I had expected he wouldn't. But I did feel he could have motioned me to one of the two chairs in the room. Had he done so it would have been with a gesture, not by speech. I moved across to one of the chairs and sat down.

"So he's still on with that crap, is he?" Readaway said, and pulled a mouth. "That's all the sonofabitch could talk about last night." He blew some smoke and squinted at me through it and said, "So what do we do, chum?"

"Haven't the least idea," I said. "I'm supposed to help

[58]

you. If you want any help, that is." He looked blank. A stifled yawn tugged at the wings of his nostrils. "If there's nothing you want at the moment I could arrange to see you later," I suggested. "Actually, I have quite a number of other things I should be doing."

"Sure, let's talk about it later," he said without interest, and reached down for the magazine. "Maybe we can get together over a drink some place." He flipped through to the colour pages. "How come a limey's involved in this?" he said, without looking up.

"I beg your pardon?"

"Well, you *are* a limey, aren't you?"

"I am English, yes."

"Boy, is this the craziest setup! Say, does this goddam climate ever get over with? Or is it always this way?

"It's the monsoon."

"Sure, I didn't figure it was the southeast trades. Or the balmy breezes of Miami." He hunched forward on his elbows as if he had found something of particular interest in the magazine, then went even further forward with his left forearm lying along his thigh and the hand holding the magazine, while the right hand dropped down between his legs, rubbing at his bare toes. "Suppose we leave it at that," he said absently. "You look in here around seven this evening, we'll go find a drink somewhere and talk about it." He glanced up suddenly with a flashing white smile that was quick and insincere. "Be seeing you, Sinclair," he said.

"Strickland."

"That's right, Strickland," he agreed, waved me off, and went back to *Life* magazine and the rubbing of his toes.

6

MY ANGER, in fact, did not last to the guard gate of the compound. While one could resent his ill manners, at least the man's unpleasantness and disinterest postponed involvement with him. It relieved me of a chore which had become even less appealing since meeting Readaway than it had seemed when Frisk had proposed it. And it gave me some chance of attending to the far more pressing problems at the railhead village.

There had been no more casualties. On the other hand, physical loss and damage had increased a good deal since the day before. With the choking of runways and new floodings coming down out of the jungle, well over two hundred huts were now in ruin. The incessant downpour had bottled up an immense volume of water in the inadequate drains and channels, and the dammed-up pressures had found points of seepage everywhere through the crowded warrens of the village centre. Whole areas had subsided into muddy craters strewn with wreckage and litter. There were lots of dead birds lying bedraggled in the slime, with a special pathos in their bright ruffled plumage, and every now and then a dead ox or a swollen pig would go rolling down one of the channels that were still running.

The most serious disaster was that the roof of the communal rice store had caved in completely, and the rain kept pelting down on the sodden gunnies which represented the native food reserve until the next harvest. At one end of the big shed the swollen rice had burst through all the burlap sacks and precipitated a sticky, soggy, dirty-white, stinking avalanche that extended all the way to the mud outside. The unpleasant thought of beriberi occurred to me.

It was a relief to see that Quigley and a truckload of his GI's were there, making inventories and saving what they could. I waded across through the thick mud to see if he needed any help.

"No, no. Everything's under control," he assured me cheerfully. One of the very good ones, Captain Quigley, with his rosy moon face and his funny little waxy moustache and his irrepressible good humour. (I always saw him somehow in a high chef's hat, making wonderful dishes for gourmets at some expensive restaurant: that was the look he had.) "We'll have this cleared away in no time at all," he said, with admirable optimism considering that foul shambles.

I went down a half mile or so along the railway line to where a Negro engineers' platoon was busy on a section of the track where the ballast and the sleepers had been washed clean into the jungle. It was a chaos of muck, running cataracts, upended timber, and sagging, twisted rails. A massive, coal-black Negro from Memphis was in charge of the gang—one could just make out the sergeant's stripes underneath the mud and grease that smeared his coveralls—and he had them working in fine style in the sluicing downpour, and even singing as they worked. And all along the track at both sides, on the fringes of the jungle, the natives sat beneath the dripping trees, shivering, apathetic, scared. The sergeant gave a great bellow of laughter when I asked if he needed assistance.

"From them *there?*" he said, and roared again. "No, *suh!* We're havin' us a time! Jes' like workin' on the levees back home." He clapped me on the shoulder and bent to take up his crowbar again. As I trudged back along the trail to Leromenos I could hear them all singing:

> Longest train ah ever did see
> Was a hundred coaches long,
> Only man ah ever did love
> Was on that train an' gone
> An' gone,
> Was on that train an' gone . . .

Why didn't Senator Vancourt make a little tour of investigation along the railhead, I wondered? Why didn't Frisk show him that? Surely it was in circumstances like these that you saw the efficiency and morale of the men under his command? Show him the Memphis sergeant, and Quigley knee-deep in a squash of fermenting filth—and both smiling.

This train of thought persisted as I walked back from the village about four thirty. The rain had eased somewhat, but was still coming down steadily. I had quite forgotten the General's entertainment. In fact, I was trying to work out in my own mind what it was that constituted an American. No scope for any generalizations here, I decided; no point in looking for words like "average" or "typical." There was Frisk and there was Fleming. There were Peabody and Strawlings and Quigley and the Memphis sergeant and Jane Carson and Vince Readaway and little Benjamin, and perhaps there was Senator Vancourt himself, whom I had not met yet, although I had seen him from a distance on his way to the transient officers' mess—a slight, quick-stepping,

[62]

perky figure in the grey rain. A difficult race to understand, an impossible one to tabulate.

When I turned the corner by the depot workshops at the end of Kansas airfield—there were gangs of men working there, too, on bogged-down equipment—I saw Jane Carson ahead of me, alone, walking on the high clay bank to the right of the mud-rutted road. She was wearing the same raincoat and sou'wester. I found it strange that she was walking so slowly, at the pace one might choose for a warm, sunny day.

"You seem to like solitude," I said, when I caught up with her.

"I like walking in the rain," she replied, smiling at me from beneath that childish-looking, floppy brim of grey waterproof.

"*This* rain?"

"Any rain."

"You should stick around then. We get lots and lots."

"So I understand. It seems we *are* sticking around. Well, that's what General Frisk said at lunch."

"Do you mind?"

"Not specially. Vince does, though."

"Vince? Oh, Readaway—yes. What does *he* say?"

"He told the General that back home we don't stop airplanes because it begins to rain. He said we are supposed to have come a long way since that day at Kitty Hawk."

"Kitty Hawk?"

"The Wright brothers."

"Ah, yes. Sorry. General Frisk must have been delighted by your friend's observations."

She smiled. "He was the soul of tact," she said.

"Did he point out that back home you don't have *quite* this sort of weather? Nor do you have mountains in front of you that are quite so high. Mountains that aren't mapped at all, some of them. And no beacons. No RDF stations. No anything very much."

"It was Vince that said it, not I," she reminded me with that quick little twist of a smile, which at once changed into a funny soft muffled laugh, which she broke off suddenly by changing the subject.

"I hope you didn't get into trouble with the General about taking me there last night," she said.

"Not at all. He was the epitome of good fellowship and bland hypocrisy. He needs my assistance to organize this theatrical show for the men. He sent me to your colleague, Mr. Readaway."

"Yes," she said, without any special intonation.

"Miss Carson, *is* he as unpleasant as he seems?"

Her hesitation was momentary. "Yes," she said again, and I thought she would add something in confirmation, but instead she turned the subject once more.

"You don't have any rank in this setup, do you?" she asked, and there was a look of real interest in those incredible green eyes of hers. Once again she had raindrops spattered on her face.

"None whatever," I said. "A title, yes. Rank, no."

"Then what do you do?"

"Normally I don't organize theatrical shows, if that's what you're driving at. No, I'm the sort of indigenous Figaro, the civilian go-between. You see, I've lived in these parts for quite a few years. So I sort of fix things up. With the native peoples, mostly. And I do quite a bit of the organizational planning work for Search-and-Rescue."

"What's that?"

"Oh, it's one of the smaller units attached to the airfield. To try to find pilots and crews when their planes crash. And to get them back alive, of course, if it's possible."

"Do many planes crash?"

It was my turn to hesitate, but after a moment I said, "Quite a few, I'm afraid. Unfortunately. Well, it's not easy flying."

"And those men I was with last night, they're the ones who do it?"

"They are. They're the best bunch around here."

"They were sweet." Her voice had grown very soft and reflective. "They're so very young, most of them," she said. "Like . . . like boys just out of college. I guess I'd forgotten . . ."

"Forgotten what?"

"Oh, nothing," she said.

We splashed on in silence for a while, and then I said, "Listen, would you like to get out of the wet for a few minutes? There's the mess over there where you were last night. A brandy might be medicinal. Or you could even try one of my special negronis. A practical example of my role in all this. Because that was one of my more praiseworthy fixings, you see. *I* made them get Campari."

It was a duty hour and the bar was empty except for the sergeant sweeping away dried mud with a stiff bristle broom and the corporal leaning on the bar alongside the radio trying to sort something tonal out of the explosive crackling of the monsoon static. Our coming—or to be strictly accurate, Miss Carson's coming—snapped them both to attention more briskly, I think, than the arrival of any Four Star General would have done.

I deliberately took her to the far end of the bar—was childishly pleased that she agreed to try the negroni—and while the drinks were being mixed I pointed to the bamboo board and said, "There you are, that's you up there."

She smiled slightly and said, "My goodness, that's quite a party of girls! I'll give them a better one before I leave. That was taken years ago."

[65]

"I think it's a nice picture," I said, but she didn't answer. In fact, while she sipped her drink she had nothing to say, apart from a "Hmmm-*mm!*" and a nod of approval at the first taste. I knew the sergeant and corporal were in agonies wanting to talk to her, so I excused myself and left her to them, and went to the men's room. It was not until I was washing my hands that I examined the motive of my maneuver with a little more honesty. I knew that both the sergeant and the corporal were fond of me, and I hoped that courtesy would compel them to say nice things about me to her while I was away. I smoked a cigarette while I thought about this, so five minutes or more must have passed before I went back to her. At any rate, by then both NCO's were flushed with a dazed sort of rapture: so much so that the corporal insisted on buying the second round of negronis himself.

We had almost finished our drinks, when she said, "Are you married?"

"Not now."

"You said you'd been out in these parts a long time. How long?"

"About ten years."

"Isn't it . . . well, terribly lonely sometimes?"

"Of course."

"The solitude, I mean. Not having anybody."

I shrugged. "Oh, you can always walk in the rain," I said.

7

I WENT to Block J punctually at seven, and Readaway was there, sitting in front of a pigskin-backed travelling mirror, brushing his soft black hair. He was wearing a beautifully cut suit of white sharkskin, white shirt, paisley tie, buckskin shoes. For a moment it was as startling as seeing an apparition. I had totally forgotten what summer resort clothes looked like.

"Ah, our English buddy! Hi, Strickland!" he called jovially. At least he had remembered my name. "But say, I meant to send a note across"—his tone changed and he half turned in his chair and looked at me commiseratingly, still brushing at his hair with slow, reverent strokes—"to save you calling in. You see, there's no reason for you to be involved in this show business. I had a talk with our friend the little General. He's fixed it to give me this lieutenant in his office. Atkinson, is it?"

"Allison," I said.

"Allison, sure. That's right. I guess he's kind of overearnest, but the guy seems to be on the ball."

"He's very competent." I wondered if my relief was showing, and I didn't care if it was.

"I don't want you to get this wrong, Strickland," he said, turning back to the mirror. "I'm not anti this or anti that. But I figure that stateside ways need stateside folks. Your country makes doughnuts a different way from the way we make doughnuts. Get it?"

"I'm prepared to take your word for it. I'm not really any sort of authority on doughnuts."

"Sure, that's it. Didya ever know the English to make a good musical? They can't put it over, not that sort of show. Oh sure, they're fine on Shakespeare, or Peter Pan and Wendy . . . stuff like that. But they can't handle spectacle, vitality, the material with *oomph* in it, noise if you like. Can you imagine an English Judy Garland? Or a Merman?"

"Well, I must say I hadn't thought of it." I waited. He was pulling back his upper lip to examine his teeth. I mentioned Frisk's wish to have a troupe of native dancers, and Readaway gave a quick snort of laughter into the mirror. "Christ, he *told* me! We've canned all that. That sort of crap's for the birds!" Again I waited. Did he still want me to take him somewhere for a drink, I wondered? I hoped very much that he didn't. To my relief he said, "Well, nice seeing you again, Strickland," and frowned at his reflection.

I hesitated at the door, and turned back to him. "There's just one point," I said. "You're going to be in a hell of a mess if you go out in those clothes. Those shoes especially. The mud's about a foot deep between here and the General's quarters. And the rain's getting heavier."

"Oh, I guess he'll send a palanquin," he said, and dismissed me with an airy wave of his hand.

The way things turned out our earlier arrangement would not have lasted very long. Soon after seven thirty the weather deteriorated brutally. Within ten minutes a vile wind was screeching in broken squalls across the compounds, driving the rain in sweeping horizontal sheets that were almost opaque, shuddering against the walls of huts, tearing at the thatch. The thunder and the jagged stabs of forked lightning were hardly less spectacular than at the first breaking of the monsoon.

For the first time in months I could hear no aircraft droning about in the darkness overhead.

A little after eight, Pendlebury, the master sergeant from Flight Control, came for me in one of the airfield jeeps. We were old friends. Pendlebury had been with us since the establishment of the base. He was a man in his middle thirties, and of that special type that makes wonderful warrant officers—solid, trustworthy, intelligent, industrious. For over a year I had been giving him lessons in Urdu. He was a very good pupil.

Going across to the airfield in the jeep was more a voyage than a journey. We skidded, sideslipped, lurched into washaways, and for most of the time it was like surfacing and resurfacing over and over again in a submarine. By the time we could faintly make out the diffused glow of the control tower beacons in the raging wet swirl above us, we were drenched to the skin. Pendlebury, in between wrestling with the wheel, dodging cascades, and spitting out water, managed to convey to me the gist of the trouble . . . five freight planes were overdue beyond the safety margin of fuel range, one on the way to Xanadu and four returning.

"And that's not all," Pendlebury added grimly. "One of the gas tankers made emergency radio contact with a Xanadu station. They relayed the report in. Seems there was some sort of electrical explosion and the fuselage split. The pilot said they were hittin' the silk. Four in the crew."

"Did they get clear?" I asked.

"I guess so. The radio went dead. Well, there's nothing in parachuting—on a nice fine day. I wouldn't care for it

[69]

too much on a night like this . . . not at twenty-two thousand feet."

"Do they know where?"

"Roughly. Two of the Xanadu stations and one of our RDF outfits got cross-bearings on the call. Captain Rogers was working out an approximate grid position when I came across for you. Way off course, it seems."

"Do you know who the pilot was?" I asked, thinking of young Strawlings.

"Can't remember," said Pendlebury. "One of the new guys."

For more than one reason I remember that night very well. Partly because it was one of the worst I ever knew. Between sunset and daybreak sixty-seven freight flights were safely completed through that terrifying weather. But there were eleven freighters that failed to make the distance. Search-and-Rescue eventually located the survivors of two crews, and got some of them in alive. (Two men were seven weeks in the jungle before we got them out; one of them now is a successful automobile executive in Detroit, the other never got out of a madhouse.) We never located the men who had jumped from the gasoline tanker. They had had to bale out over the most savage of all our areas—a never-visited land of ice summits and glaciers, of rocky gorges and unscalable cliffs, up near the fringes of Tibet. We had no search groups within a hundred and fifty miles of the area; if we had had they would have been powerless to do anything. When we checked on the facts we found that the plane had broken up at an altitude of twenty-six thousand feet, so there was a merciful angle to it—when the four men jumped they either would have been frozen to death at once or died for lack of oxygen within a minute or so.

They showed me the plane's listing on the flight board, with a blank in the final column. It was not Strawlings. A

[70]

young Texan, they told me, making only his fifteenth flight. His name was quite unfamiliar to me and I have long since forgotten it.

It was a strange feeling, being back up there in that wind-shaken, rain-slashed control tower, with the curved windows all misted up and a solemn-faced tech sergeant endlessly circling with his long-handled squeegee, wiping them clear. Strange and intensely dramatic, and moving one at intervals to an emotional sickness that was almost physical. Quiet-voiced figures in the dim half darkness amid the coloured lights and the bulbs that flicked on and off and the eerie phosphorescent pointers on dials set within the sloping banks of black bakelite: and at startling intervals the sudden flaring of the primus stove in the corner, where Pendlebury was making cocoa. And in these sudden hissing explosions of light one would see the hard, strained, glinting stare of eyes all around the room—red-rimmed, exhausted eyes that would move back and forth, back and forth, between the chalked figures on the flight board and the winking instruments on the console panels.

There was not very much talk—usually curt words, mono-syllables. The facts of drama, of tragedy, of tension, scaled to silence. No comments. No discussion. Except on the fixed dimension of the factual, voices seemed subdued to a point below meaning. Sound was outside. The whole acoustic range was outside in the scream and roar of the wind, the rolling detonations of the thunder, the swish and slap of the rain. Sound, like experience, had become a thing external to us. We were no more than an enclosed bubble of perception, that was all, suspended within the rage of the elements. A complex sensory organ trained to listen, to expect, to watch for, to convey exterior messages and impulses to some interior nerve knot of collation and interpretation. An organ

[71]

to sift and classify impressions—impressions of the true experience.

And experience was far away from us, lost in the high tumultuous night. I remember that it was almost unbearably hot and humid in the tower, for no vent or window could be opened against the storm, and beads of perspiration were glistening on every face. I remember sitting there in my soaking clothes with the hot sweat filling up my crotch, and wondering about men freezing to death out there in the black chaos of experience, with their last choking breaths rimming their nostrils and their mouths.

Here, where we were, only the squeaking of the squeegee against the misted windows, the rasp, cough, and squeal of static, the stutter of Morse swelling and fading from some other station, the thin incomprehensible gibberish of a voice whispering in the headphones, the soft hissing of the primus in the corner. . . .

At intervals a plane would still come in, and they would switch to the microphone and the main speaker to fix the flight pattern and direct the touch-down. One would always see the landing lights quite suddenly as an unexpected blur in the distant pelt of rain, exploding into a dazzling wet halation rushing towards one, flicking a bright moment and passing from sight. And someone would call the time-reading from the chronometer and Pendlebury would take up his stick of chalk and mark it down in the final column of the flight board. Yet still nothing of sound from outside—nothing of that plaintive, throbbing, lost droning from overhead, nothing of the hiss and excruciating pain-screech of landing wheels touching the flooded runway, or the *swoooosh* of water flying.

Around midnight the storm must have eased off in the mountains, because after that we began to get an inbound freighter every ten minutes or so, and about this time the outbound flights, which Flight Control had suspended as a result of the earlier reports, were resumed again. But it was close to three in the morning before there was any noticeable improvement in the weather at Kansas. I realized that pencils were no longer rolling off the desks because of the shaking of the tower in the more violent squalls, but I continued to sit there. I had helped Rogers with the grid positions and given my reports on localities and there was nothing much more I could do until I sat down with Benjamin in the daylight. But I still stayed on. Sleepiness, strain, and the fug of the place had filled me with a deathly lassitude. I could only sit and stare, as if hypnotized, at that black flight board with those eleven hollow gaps among all the neatly chalked-in figures in the final column.

However, I eventually pulled myself together and said I was going.

"I'll run you over in the jeep," said Pendlebury. He tried to arrange his face into a smile, but fatigue had dragged at too many muscles. His eyes were blankly staring and bloodshot.

"You'll bloody well not!" I said firmly. "You're a damned sight more buggered than I am. It's a few hundred yards, that's all. I'll walk it."

"You'll drown yourself in a goddam ditch."

"I can swim."

"Well, you take this flashlight of mine. It's got a beam like a searchlight. If you fall in, it's your own business."

He went with me to the door, and said, "Captain Rogers is doing flight pattern. But he says thanks for the help."

"Don't mention it. I'm sorry we couldn't do more. It's been quite a night."

"Man!" said Pendlebury, and this time he smiled.

There was still a good deal of wind, flurrying and backing up, but the rain had slackened quite a lot, and there was no more thunder and lightning. It was not as dark as I had expected—a deep grey gloom with a kind of shine to it, rather than blackness—and I could see the glitter of water ahead of me, so I didn't use Pendlebury's flashlight. Not at first.

I only used it when I was walking up past the pilots' quarters—a long L-shaped block of single rooms which I had always regarded as the best billets in the area: comfortable, well-equipped, nicely furnished, private—and I only used it then because I could faintly make out two figures standing outside one of the rooms midway along the upper arm of the L.

One always had to be careful about stray natives prowling around the living quarters—after all, they were my responsibility, and there were some incorrigible thieves among them. So I walked on until I was closer, then flicked on Pendlebury's flashlight. He had not exaggerated the brilliance of its beam.

They were both standing there, just in under the overhanging eaves, close together and quite rigid, as if the ray of light had transfixed them. Jane Carson and young Strawlings.

I pressed the button and the light went out, and I turned away at an angle and went on past them without saying anything. I knew they would not have seen me at all against the dazzling brilliance of the light.

I don't believe I attached any significance to it at first. My brain was fogged and tired: time had lost its meaning, too, so that the fact of it being after four in the morning really meant nothing at all.

True, by the time I had turned round the corner of the L my mind began vaguely to nag at the problem—mostly to find an explanation and an excuse for her. After all, she seemed to be a solitary. She liked walking about in the rain. Perhaps she had been to the bar earlier. Perhaps she had lost her way. But why the pilots' quarters, a more cavilling area of my mind demanded? And why Strawlings?

But what business was it of mine, anyway? I was far too tired to grapple with problems. I splashed on home, sleepwalking through the rain and the puddles, soaked to the skin again and dimly glad of it, and overhead in the overcast the circling planes sobbed. The events of the night must have left me in shreds emotionally. Because I remember that word. When they were very high, or far out at the limits of their landing circles, the engines of the planes sounded exactly like somebody sobbing. Sobbing for whom? Not for me. Not for anybody at all. . . .

8

I WAS up, as usual, at seven, and took a quick mug of coffee and a sandwich at the airfield canteen to save wasting time over breakfast. I could have had a doughnut but it reminded me of Readaway, and that led me to wonder how the white suit and the buckskin shoes had survived the deluge. Then I went straight across to Search-and-Rescue.

The unit worked out of a small wooden shack lined completely with wall maps, and although I was there by seven thirty the place was crowded—two of the helicopter pilots, six or seven enlisted men, a second lieutenant from Frisk's general staff, and Captain Leonard Benjamin, the OC of the unit. (Benjamin is in Israel now, a brilliant academic figure at the Hebrew University in Jerusalem: but then he was much younger and the rare versatility of his mind was largely a potential.) He was very Jewish in appearance—dark, small, volatile, intelligent, subtle as a woman. Harvard Law School, and before this job in Zone Q-4 a rising young attorney in New York City. He should have gone, I suppose, to the Judge Advocate's branch, but even so he was one of those flukey army castings of the right peg into the right hole. The mind of a champion chess player, but quicker. I always had an immense respect for him.

His face was grave—all the other faces, too, for that matter—when I arrived, and I knew at once that the filling in from the night's reports could not have been encouraging.

The sombre gravity remained on his small, pinched face as he greeted me softly and said, "Thanks a lot for sitting in on it last night, Jacob. The preliminaries just came over from Rogers. They helped."

"What does it look like?" I asked.

"Lousy enough. There are three we can try, but it'll have to be native search parties. We can't get a helicopter any place near. The others . . ." He shrugged and made a little spitting sound through his pursed lips.

"There were three ships carrying gas," said Frisk's lieutenant. "Two had gelignite."

"No personnel?" I asked. "Other than crew, I mean?"

The lieutenant shook his head. "Socked in."

"Socked in's a laugh!" said Benjamin grimly. And then, with a sudden flash of anger: "Why don't these bastards fix a course and go through with it! They've got to damn well try to get above it, or try to sneak beneath it! There's no above it or beneath it in these storms, God damn it! They go up and have to carry a ton of extra ice, and that brings 'em down! They go down, and the rocks start from zero and go all the way up!"

"I guess they have to do it the way it comes," one of the helicopter lieutenants said mildly. "Maybe if they nose straight on the wings get torn off in the turbulence, or they get icing anyway and lose too much height and get right down there among those rocks you just mentioned. It's a piss-poor life for sure!"

"I know. I know. I just want to *do* something. Beef or shout or . . . or *something!* I just get so goddam mad at

[77]

sitting here and sticking pins in maps and not being able to *do* anything." He turned suddenly and went across the room and took a chair and turned it and sat astride with his arms across the back. "So let's get the horse in the shafts," he said. He half closed his small, shrewd, shoe-button eyes as he turned to me.

"Jacob," he said quietly, "pull up a chair and give me half an hour, will you? I want details on some villages and trails. I want food estimates—available, portable, and droppable. I want to know about some passes across mountains. Tribal attitudes. Hostility or otherwise. I want your guess on what weather conditions are likely to be right now." He paused and linked his fingers and seemed to study them with sudden interest. Benjamin still liked to use a good many of his little courtroom tricks and mannerisms. They were always simple, and always effective. "Jacob," he said at last, "how much do you know about Shingáli? Southern districts in particular."

"Shingáli?" I looked at him in surprise. "Shingáli" was another code name which we used then for a big section of the tribal country between Yunnan and the southeastern corner of Tibet. I said, "Why Shingáli?"

"I'll tell you why. We've been piecing together what happened. Now, what made the score so bad was drift. And, man, I mean drift! Above the main range there was a southerly blowing that must have been between a hundred and a hundred and twenty miles an hour. That's the estimate averaged from the reports of eight of the pilots who made it across. They were blown way off course, but they made it. And they all made it with empty planes, light, coming back. *Light* . . . and *coming back*," he repeated, spacing the words and tapping each one into emphasis with a forefinger jabbing at his thigh. "Now, of the eleven ships we lost last night," he continued, "we can check on three,

[78]

maybe four. One *could* be a duplication. The tanker that radioed Xanadu first seems to have gotten caught up in some loose lightning. The belly split. It was full of aviation gasoline. So the boys quit. It wasn't much of a choice, but the only one they had."

"That wasn't a choice," said the helicopter man.

"That's right," Benjamin agreed. "That wasn't a choice. Next point. Lieutenant Leason got back in here a bit after midnight. He had the shit of a crossing, but he broke through into a brief, strange little patch of clear above the long spur range"—he got up and went across to one of the wall maps and marked a spot with his finger which had already been ringed with red chalk—"and thought he saw something burning way down below. Well, you must have seen his report, anyway, Jacob?"

I nodded. "I didn't tie it up with that first one."

"Well, if it isn't duplication, that accounts for two. Personally, I'd settle for that *pro tem*. I'm damned sure high-octane couldn't burn that long. So let's say two. Well, now, after you'd gone last night radio reception got a hell of a lot better, and they got several other relayed reports they hadn't received earlier, or had received too garbled by interference to be comprehensible. These came in from the northern outpost stations. By this time they were eight or nine hours old. But interesting. They were relays of reports from two other ships. They both said the ships were out of fuel and the crews were jumping. Poor bastards!" He came back, turned the chair, and began to pivot it on one leg, first one way and then the other. "They got good cross-bearings on those signals," he said, staring at the chair. "Those planes went down *in* Shingáli," he said quietly. "One of them was three hundred and eighty miles off course."

He gave me a sidelong glance. I waited.

"So." He set the chair down on its four legs, lined the

[79]

front two up with the edge of a floorboard, and resumed. "The way I see it we lost all or nearly all of those planes within a period of around ninety-five minutes. Towards dusk. Of the eleven, eight were inbound. Empty. Light. We know that for a couple of hours leading up to and including that ninety-five minutes the wind up there was blowing a goddamned hurricane. Those empty crates just got blown away north to hell and gone. So our main search area has to be around Shingáli. Do you find this plausible?"

"Yes," I said.

"Winds of that sort of violence?"

"Yes."

His black eyes flicked across to Frisk's staff officer. "Brief the G side on what we're doing," he said. "I've got two dropping-planes standing by. We'll send six photo-recce planes off this morning to do a grid search of the area. They might spot smoke, flares, something. So." He moved across to his cluttered desk. "Corporal, go fix us all some coffee. Sergeant Garstein, get out your book. Let's go. And don't forget to spell out the native names for him, Jacob."

I was there another hour, and it was very arresting, but sadly anticlimactic to return to my own undistinguished little office, and to have the corporal hand me the mimeographed memorandum printed on one of General Frisk's distinctive pink forms.

Frisk had his own special set of forms and his own way of wording them. He always preferred forms to telephones. All the forms had his name, rank, and command position printed in small red type along the top.

MEMORANDUM:

A concert and theatrical performance, for all ranks, will be held Saturday. TIME: 1900 hours. LOCATION: Hangar A-2, Kansas Strip. All base and attached units will attend. Details will be posted with all units in due course. Officers will do their utmost to allow free time to enlisted men under their direct command, commensurate with the adequate staffing of all essential posts and duties. Attendance of civilians will be strictly confined to civilian officers attached to HQ Staff.

On my memo the word MEMORANDUM had been crossed out in red ink, and written across it, also in red, was: "Mr. Jacob Strickland, SCLO HQ Admin. *Special Attention.*" The last two words had been quite firmly underlined, which gave me a slight twinge of misgiving. Had Readaway misled me, I wondered, about my exclusion from the entrepreneur bloc? Certainly I had had nothing from the General's office to countermand his earlier direction. And Frisk, after all, did have all those cherished forms of his. I decided that it would be wise to find out exactly where I stood.

Frisk was in his office, and the staff sergeant at the desk in the outermost room—the General's administrative quarters were rather like a Chinese nest of puzzle boxes: there were three other anterooms between the sergeant's outpost and Frisk's gallery of photographs—said something into an intercom, and a thin voice squeaked a response. A few minutes later Lieutenant Allison came out and smiled at me in his usual polite, sad way.

"You can go on in," he said. "But only two minutes. He's got someone with him."

The someone proved to be Senator Vancourt, recognizable from my long-distance view of him in the rain, and also by something which seemed unmistakably *senatorial* about him. He was a small, neat figure in Frisk's big blue leather armchair, with hands neatly clasped across an almost imperceptible paunch, legs neatly crossed, and eyes neatly alert to my entrance. He gave the impression that he had

[81]

been neither talking nor listening, but merely waiting for my arrival. He was wearing GI khaki shirt and pants, the webbing belt, a thick-soled pair of combat boots which were rather muddy—the routine apparel, it seemed, for visiting American politicians. He had very blue eyes, close-cropped steel-coloured hair, a darkish skin more apricot than suntan, and a strongly modelled face in which all the features—the beaky nose, the craggy brow, the incised lines cutting down to the firm, rather heavy-lipped mouth, the square chin—seemed to belong to some much bigger person than this slight little fellow sitting with his legs crossed in the big blue chair. I remember thinking that his face exactly resembled one of those heavy, strikingly realistic Roman portrait busts. Of a senator, of course.

"Well, Strickland," said Frisk, giving his smile no time to settle. "What's on your mind?"

"This," I said, showing him the memorandum. "I wondered what was special about it, sir."

"Special? How, *special*? That's been circulated generally, throughout the command."

"Yes, sir, but this is marked, and underlined, 'special attention.'"

"Well, that's for you," he said with an edge of impatience. "That's for you, man. The native angle. Your department. *They've* got to be kept away, that's all. I don't want the whole darned base overrun by a bunch of goggle-eyed coons rubbernecking at everything. That's all, Strickland."

"I see. There's one other thing, sir. I am correct in understanding that Lieutenant Allison is now co-operating with Mr. Readaway?"

"Certainly. I told Readaway to tell you. Didn't he?"

"Yes, he did, in fact. But does that leave me out of it now? Or do you still want me to try about the dancing girls and the drum and flute players?"

[82]

I had put the question deliberately, and I was pleased to see that his chubby face grew pinker. His clipped laugh was uneasy with a twinge of embarrassment as he said, "Hell, no! We can skip all that folksy stuff. It was an idea, that was all." He put his fists together and gave his attention to the Senator. "I'd thought of letting some of the natives share in this show we're putting on," he explained. "Useful for this integration we have with the local people. But Readaway and Allison have located so much talent, so much *real* talent, among these boys of mine that there just won't be room on the bill. No, sir! I think we've got a real show coming up. A real show!" He turned back to me. "What do you say, Strickland, eh?"

"I hope so, sir," I said, folding the memorandum.

"Any other problems then?" he asked, genial now.

"No, sir."

"Beat it, then," he said with great good nature, and gave me a real smile—the indulgent smile.

Going back through the anterooms, it occurred to me to wonder why I had not been introduced to Senator Vancourt. There had been no absolute necessity for it, of course, yet I had the feeling that it was all very much a part of Frisk's deeply rooted all-Americanism. This was the true patriot. Firm. Unassailable in his beliefs. The certainties proven, the taproots forever sound. Fireball Frisk. To have revealed to the Senator that he had an Englishman on his administrative staff, and in a fairly responsible position, would have been as unthinkable to Frisk as for him to have pointed out to the Senator the fact that the second lower button of his fly was undone. Which it had been, winking its neat brown eye just below those soft, neatly folded hands.

9

THE incident left me with a better humour than I had known since the breaking of the monsoon. The exposed fly button had filled me with an almost childish pleasure. I was happy that I had momentarily discomfited the General. There was the relief of being relieved from any further association with Readaway and the tedious problems of the concert. And the rain had slackened to no more than a drizzle.

To the east the sky was still sombre and threatening so that even the foothills of the alps were invisible, and although our sky was also overcast the ceiling was high enough for the planes to be seen, coming and going, circling, waiting to fall into their patterns, shaking the air and the huts as they roared overhead on landings or take-offs. Even so, we lost another plane. For no evident reason at all it flew straight into a rock peak and blew up. No survivors.

I was active enough throughout the day, for there were any number of things to do in Leromenos or around the base, and it was getting late in the afternoon by the time I called in on Search-and-Rescue again. Captain Benjamin looked tired and dispirited. All the photo-reconnaissance planes had returned with negative reports. Visibility every-where in the search area had been zero.

"We'll try it again tomorrow," he said despondently. "But the met people say this letup is only temporary. We could even be in for another night of it."

While I was taking my shower I realized that it was Thursday. Fleming's night at Armand's. I had the feeling that he would still want to go in spite of the chaos in the village. Fleming was a firm disciplinarian about the private formalities of his own life. After I had changed I called in at his office—we were in the habit of meeting there—but his sergeant told me he had gone to his quarters about an hour before. I had never really quite worked out exactly why Fleming always insisted on taking me with him. He did not speak a word of the native tongue, so in the beginning I had assumed that I was taken along to act as his inter-preter if it was necessary. But he almost never talked to Armand—who spoke a pretty shapeless English anyway—and never at all to the girls. I imagine it was company he wanted—talk over the drinks after the necessity of the act . . . return to the haven. For my part, my escorting of the man preserved the discipline and gave me, I suppose, the prophylaxis I needed. Time and repetition had robbed it long since of its bitterness. It was no more than just another part of the protective structure.

For a while I chatted to the sergeant about this and that, expecting Fleming to put in an appearance, but when he had not come after about fifteen minutes, I decided to walk across to his room.

There did not seem to be any light burning, but I knocked on his door, and there was a stir of movement from inside. It was an appreciable interval before Fleming appeared at the door. He seemed vaguely discomposed, I thought, and he was not even dressed. He had wrapped around his loins

[85]

a narrow white towel, not very much bigger than the short-time towels one used to be given as souvenirs in the Chinese knocking shops in Singapore.

"Why, Jake," he said, and with obvious self-consciousness, "what gives?" His two hands were firmly gripped on the edge of the door and on the doorframe itself, and the door was hardly open at all. There was no light in the room behind.

"Well, it's Thursday," I said. "Are you going in tonight? I was waiting for you over at the office and—"

"Hell, I figured I'd skip it just this once," he said. "I don't feel up to it tonight. I've had the bastard of a day."

He smiled and nodded, closed the door, and that was that. I knew that there was somebody else there in the room with him—I had heard the faint rustling from behind his big figure blocking the doorway—but again I didn't connect anything.

My feeling, anyway, was entirely one of relief. I had had a bellyful of Leromenos for one day. And I was rather anxious to go to the pilots' bar to hear what had happened the night before.

Under the lighter drizzle the mud had turned into a glue-pot. From the darkness all around one could hear the bang and clatter of the chains on the wheels of jeeps and trucks.

It was still fairly early, and there were only five or six customers at the bar. Peabody was at a table in the middle of the room, writing a V-mail, but he closed it when I came in and called me over.

"Where's everybody?" I asked.

"Rostered, most of them. They've been doubling up all day to make up for last night. The schedule was shot to hell."

"It was a bloody terrible night."

"Sure was!"

[86]

"Were you out in it?"

"I did one schedule. And a shuttle relief."

"Bad?"

"Bad enough."

"What about Hathaway? I've not seen him about."

"He's okay. He and Favell have been flying specials. Two days now. There's some special Ranger regiment that has to be ferried in but fast."

"I thought it was a sock-in."

"Not for the Marines, bud. They're wanted in a hurry. Special directive from the Top Brass."

"Possibly they also think it's the same as running civil airlines in the States," I could not help saying. "Mustn't stop flying on a rainy day. They wouldn't realize the danger."

"I guess they wouldn't care," said Peabody, in that careful way he had of taking a subject and seeming to arrange it in special little piles for detailed examination. "Wars are supposed to be dangerous," he said. "For most of the guys who are involved. I guess it's still a case of get there fustest with the mostest if you want to have any darned say in the business. Why do we fly these freight planes out and back? A payload of aviation gas or a payload of Marines—what's the difference? It's all strategical material. The Marines get a better break, that's all. They get Favell and Hathaway to fly them. Those two bastards could fly a ship through thick clam chowder!" He paused and a slow smile came over his lean, swarthy, hawkish face. "I saw the big Swede this morning for a few minutes in the briefing room. He told me he'd made one milk-run, and for the whole trip, once he'd gotten altitude, the eighty-six was covered all over in Saint Elmo's fire, wingtip to wingtip, nose to tail—just one streaming sheet of electric-blue fire. Jesus! Can't you see it? He had sixty Marines sitting there in the bucket seats, parachutes on, jungle kits strapped around their bellies, looking out at that hell-fire through the plexiglass! Favell said that behind the oxygen masks there wasn't a single face among 'em that wasn't pure green! Even the Marines, you see!" He chuckled. "Come on, let's go fix ourselves some drinks," he said.

It must have been around half past eight when Jane Carson arrived. But this time she had company. Senator Vancourt, Readaway, and Lieutenant Allison. By now there were a good many more pilots in the bar, but it was still not all that crowded. Allison, frowning earnestly over his little tasks, took charge of coats and hats then returned, blinking doubtfully around the room. In this domain he was even less at home than his master; he seemed almost overwhelmed by the temerity of his being there. While he hesitated, Jane Carson took over. She murmured something to the Senator, then led the party directly up to where Peabody and I were standing. She smiled at us warmly and made the introductions.

"Major Peabody and Mr. Strickland were my first friends here," she explained. "I got caught in the rain, and they were both so sweet to me."

"Strickland I know," said Readaway heartily. "Happy to make your acquaintance, Major," he said, and shoved his hand at Peabody.

"Glad to know you, Major Peabody." Senator Vancourt had a pleasant bass voice, deep but muted, without much accent. "I think we have met, Mr. Strickland, have we not?" he said to me.

"Well, not met, exactly," I said. "I saw you in the Commandant's office this morning."

"That's right. I was asking General Frisk about you after you had gone. He told me you were his principal civilian liaison man. He speaks very warmly of you, Mr. Strickland. Very warmly indeed."

Had I misjudged poor Old Frisky, I wondered?

"Well, so he should," Peabody put in loyally. "Jacob here is a very useful guy to have around. There's none of us could do very much without him."

"What he means, Senator Vancourt, is that I'm the sort of unofficial *maître d'hôtel* here; I advise on the more exotic forms of hard liquor." I had intended to turn it with a light jest, but Readaway took it for his cue.

"Say, you fellers have certainly got it set up here," he said admiringly. He was not wearing his sharkskin suit, but his shirt and slacks of tan shantung were incongruously smart enough. "*Look* at those bottles there! Dimple Haig! Dubonnet! Black Label! Gordon's! Bols! Campari! Schenley's! Canadian Club! Say, Major, what would happen if I just settled for champagne and caviar?"

"You'd get them," said Peabody quietly. "Why, I guess we could even find an ice pail."

"This sure is a rugged war!"

"Rugged enough," said Peabody. "For some." I could tell from the way he spoke that he shared with me that immediate and instinctive abhorrence of Readaway which I had had in Block J. He turned away from the actor and said, "What will you drink, Miss Carson? Senator?"

Lieutenant Allison, emerging pink-faced and dutiful from his normal nervous melancholy, announced that he had fixed a table in the corner of the room. "Ummm . . . wouldn't—er—wouldn't we all be more comfortable sitting down?" he suggested diffidently.

The placing of the chairs put Miss Carson next to Peabody. My immediate neighbour was Senator Vancourt. Readaway elected to stay at the bar, drinking with three or four of the younger pilots, very much at ease, very big and strong looking and handsome; a friendly, talkative man who knew himself to be the centre of attraction. The one sentence of his which I overheard before getting involved in our own conversation at the table was:

"Brother! I just can't wait for this weather to lift, so I can get over there where *real* things are happening!"

How to win friends and influence people, I thought, looking at the faces of the young pilots.

"Last night was most distressing, Mr. Strickland," the Senator said in his quiet, deep voice. "I was very unhappy to hear about it."

"It was pretty bad," I said. It was odd in a way for us to be discussing it in this setting. The pilots themselves almost never did; there was a sort of unwritten rule that said, "No post-mortems in the mess."

"It is very tragic to think of those young boys flying out like that, dying like that. Well, one can say *c'ést la guerre*, I guess, but when one realizes that this is not even a combat area it makes it kind of . . . well, more melancholy, in a way." He coughed, as if to clear the emotion away. "I understand there is very little chance of saving any of them," he said.

"It doesn't look too promising," I admitted.

"Too bad." He shook his head slowly. "Tell me, Mr. Strickland, is there no way of lessening the . . . well, the operational hazard, if you like to call it that?"

"Oh yes. Ground all aircraft when the weather deteriorates beyond a certain point of flying practicability. Allow a much longer indoctrination period for the raw pilots. Spend God knows how many millions of dollars on new RDF and meteorological stations."

He studied me carefully with his sharp blue eyes. "Yes, Mr. Strickland," he said. "And then?"

[90]

"And then you wouldn't get your supplies or your troops through to where they're wanted," I said.

"But you'd cut the human losses?"

"In this command, yes. Almost certainly at the cost of much higher casualties up forward. In any case, you would only *reduce* losses here. You wouldn't eliminate them."

"You mean that the logical way to look at it is to write off these casualties as reasonable expenditure—well, say as reasonable as you can expect—for what has to be done?"

"I should put it this way, Senator. There must be some exact military equation—Clausewitz no doubt has gone into it—where the ratio of expendability makes final sense . . . where total accomplishment justifies the human sacrifice involved. Heavens, don't think that I like to see any of these kids crashing into a mountain . . . but perhaps in the circumstances it does add up to a sort of balanced logic."

He thought about this for a few moments, and then said, "Are you a flying man yourself, Mr. Strickland?"

"No. I am a complete layman in these matters."

"General Frisk, however, indicated that you had had service experience."

"A little. With the British Army. I was wounded in the first retreat from Burma. Discharged later as unfit. Not a very glorious military career, I'm afraid."

He smiled slightly, and cleared his throat again. "From my point of view," he said, "all this gives an added value to your opinions. You see, Mr. Strickland, I want to know how *you* feel—you as a layman, as a civilian, and particularly as a non-American—how you feel about the general morale here. I am referring, for the moment, to the active flying group."

I looked at him carefully. So even I was to be pumped for the Senate subcommittee!

"I think it's splendid," I said. "My admiration is without any reservation whatever."

"Hmmm. That's mighty comforting to hear, Mr. Strickland. You'd say the fibre was pretty tough, eh?"

"Yes, indeed."

"Yet I have been informed that three pilots from two of the freight squadrons were relieved of flying duties today on psychiatric grounds," he said deliberately.

I could feel a swell of anger rising, but I managed to control it. "Does that surprise you?" I asked quietly. "If it was me they'd have me in a strait jacket! After last night, the extraordinary thing is that there were only three."

"It's my duty to examine all these angles," he said mildly.

"One of those pilots under medical observation is only nineteen," I pointed out. "There was a Texas kid who was lost last night who was also only nineteen, and he'd only flown that range fifteen times. And don't you see, Senator Vancourt, that these kids don't have the thrill, the exhilaration of actual combat. Yes, I know that sounds ugly and brutal, but in the sense of an enemy opposition, in the killing magic, if you like, there's a dark, spiritual buoyancy that arises, whether you like it or not, out of human conflict." My vehemence had got the better of me, my voice was rising. "But these men, except in this bar at night, don't even get that mass comradeship and mass effort that fuses a company, or a battalion, or a regiment into a single unified entity. When they are involved with peril—and by God they are, you know!—they are involved *alone*. Every single pilot out there in the night storms and the empty weather is a solitary man in a monk's cell pitting himself against a black abstract. His enemy isn't tangible, hated . . . it's not even understood, really. Just a pure abstract of peril. The unknown. The uncharted. The unexpectable. The inexplicable, if you

[92]

like. Yet a man like Major Peabody here comes back for the third time, of his own choice, to do the job again."

I broke off quite suddenly, embarrassedly aware that there was no other conversation at the table, that Jane Carson and Peabody and Allison were all intently looking at me, listening; that my voice had even carried to some of the men at the bar; that Readaway, hands in the tan side slits of his shantung pants, had moved across and was looking down at me over Allison's shoulder.

"Well—that was *quite* a speech," I said awkwardly.

"I'm mighty grateful to you for it, Mr. Strickland," the Senator said quietly.

"Brother, what a press agent!" said Readaway, and whistled.

"Don't be greedy, Vince," Miss Carson retorted sweetly. "You *have* a press agent."

"Who's talking, honey?" he said with a loose smile, and drifted back to the bar.

I was grateful to her for having seen my embarrassment and covered it. Conversation moved to the collective and the impersonal. The bar grew more crowded. I saw Strawlings come in with three or four other men. It was some little time later that I realized he was drinking by himself at the far end of the bar. His face was set and sombre—hungry, in a way—and he never took his eyes off Jane Carson. The intensity of his gaze gave me a momentary feeling of uneasiness until I realized that almost all the pilots were very attentive to our group—attentive, and vaguely resentful, I thought, that the presence of the Senator and the General's aide put our table inside some invisible cordon of protocol into which they dared not intrude. The cordon was broken in a quite unexpected way.

I am not even sure that I heard the actual explosion, but certainly the blast itself was real enough because it banged the door and shook the thin walls and rattled the glasses in the wash tray.

Senator Vancourt looked up sharply from his drink. Miss Carson said, "What was that? Thunder?"

"Sure, thunder," said Peabody, but I saw the stillness of his hands on the table and I saw his eyes, and I knew that he, too, had heard the distant whining of the sirens and the thin wail of the crash truck.

It seemed a long time—although it could not have been more than ten minutes, really—before the orderly officer came and beckoned Peabody away, but it was well over half an hour before he returned. He came in through the door without saying anything to anybody and went straight to the wash room. I excused myself.

He was standing in one of the cubicles, relieving himself, staring fixedly at the water-filmed porcelain. I went across to one of the basins and turned the faucet and began to wash my hands. The place had a clean smell. Chlorine, DDT, carbolic soap. There were two spare rolls of Scott Tissue toilet paper on the shelf. Vince Readaway would have been struck by that, too. A rugged war, this . . .

"What happened, Fred?" I asked.

"One of the eighty-sixes went in," he said quietly.

"Who?"

"Favell," he said, and did up his zipper and came over to the adjoining wash basin.

I looked at him out of the corner of my eye. There was no need to formulate the question. He nodded.

"Burnt out," he said. "Couldn't get within fifty yards of it." He kept rubbing his hands together, staring down at the foam of soap on his knuckles. "How's that for a laugh?" he said, talking almost mechanically—anyway not talking to me at all, I think. "That Swede sonofabitch had a million miles behind him . . . all those goddam *hours* . . . and

[94]

this is the way the jerk has to do it! Light ship. Eight thousand feet of clear. Four motors singing sweet lullabies to him. An approach run as sweet as a widow's kiss . . ." Scrub, scrub, scrub at his foaming knuckles. "So the bastard has to drag his left wing along the dahl trees. Sure, he hit the runway all right! One wing down and rolling over! The rest of it's for Ringling Brothers! Jake, haul me one of those towels, will you?"

I tore it out of the container and handed it across.

"Do you feel like a drink?" I said.

"Why not?"

I stood back and watched him drying his hands. He took a long time over it. I knew how much Favell had meant to him, and I could only think of Favell's big, hoarse laugh and the uncontrollable thickening of his accent as he had described the green faces of the Marines behind their oxygen masks.

I had never known the Swede quite as well as I had come to know Peabody and Hathaway. He had always spread himself too widely. He was a boisterous, gregarious, good-natured fellow, coarse in his humour, and with an insatiable appetite for the company of his fellow men. But over the many months I had spent with these people I had come to understand the deep ties of attachment that held them together in this curiously lonely peril that they shared. It was always there, buried away behind the superficial dramatics, the practical jokes, the mocked-at heroics, lying like a strong steel band between Favell's exuberance, the easygoing unruffled taciturnity of Peabody, the brittle affectations of Peter Hathaway . . . yet to be developed out of the unseasoned searchings of young Strawlings.

"Remember those crazy songs the bastard would sing when he got really plastered?" Peabody said, talking down at his hands. "The 'Svenska Jazzenska!' You know, we flew together a couple of years with T.W.A.," he said musingly. "That squarehead could fly an airplane!"

"Suppose we go and get that drink," I said.

"Jesus, I could get high as a kite!"

"What's to stop you?"

"The halls of Montezuma and the shores of Tripoli." His smile twisted on him. "There are still Marines who've got to go over. And I've briefed myself for stand-by relief at o-three-hundred. Ah, the hell with it—we can have one for Sven, anyway."

Odd—I had never known his name was Sven.

We went back to the bar together, not talking.

The cordon had broken during our absence. Senator Vancourt had gone, and Lieutenant Allison with him. Jane Carson was hardly to be seen for the crowd of men around her, Strawlings among them. Readaway was still propped against the bar, holding forth. His black hair was attractively ruffled. He wore a fixed, loose smile that told me he was drunk. I could tell that, anyway, by the set, controlled faces of the two young pilots to whom he was talking.

"You just listen to me, fellers," he was saying to them, his finger jabbing out his points. "Say I take a ticket outa Dallas or Salt Lake City or Chicago. Well for Chrissakes I expect to *go*, don't I? I don't figure to sit aroun' an airport on my fat ass waitin' for the goddam showers to clear! There's a *war* on, for pete's sake! Do you think the Nips crawl in outa the wet because a cloud comes over, or sit round a nice warm fire 'cause they've got no rubbers to wear?"

I was glad that Peabody didn't overhear him, but Peabody wasn't listening to anything. He had his hands cupped around his drink, but he was not drinking, just staring down at the thick tumbler and the twist of lemon rind.

Neither of us realized that Jane Carson had left her party and come across to join us until I caught a whiff of her

[96]

perfume. I turned slowly, to find her standing between and behind the two of us, with a faint smile at her mouth which was partly amused and partly questioning. A tendril of tawny hair had fallen attractively across her forehead. When I looked at her she tilted her head a fraction, and made a little moue of reproof.

"What a fine pair of men you two are," she said. "First you both walk out on me. And then when you do come back you forget all about me and make for this bar like it's home base."

Peabody's gentle, engaging smile eased the strain and fatigue from his face. "Sorry about that, Miss Carson," he said. "I got the feeling you were fixed for the night with the Senator and the lieutenant. I'll go fetch you a stool."

As he moved away she put her hand on my wrist in a quick, urgent way, and said, "What happened?"

"What do you mean, what happened?" I countered.

"I saw his face. That wasn't thunder at all, was it?"

"No, that wasn't thunder. A plane piled up. On the air-field. Coming in to land. A friend of the Major's was flying it . . . a personal friend."

"And . . ."

I nodded. "He was killed. They were all killed."

"Your stool, Miss Carson," said Peabody. "Ah, that's just dandy. That makes you just as tall as both of us. And now . . ." He put his fingertips together very carefully. "This is a special drink," he said. "This is a drink to a guy called Sven. We were co-pilots once with T.W.A. He had a stomach of steel and a head of iron and he always drank *aquavit* when he could get it. I'm personally kind of loyal to the special Peabody rye old-fashioned. Jacob here has a fancy concoction called negroni. So there it is, Miss Carson—*aquavit*, old-fashioned, negroni, or the lady's choice. You to say."

[97]

"I guess I'll settle for the special Peabody rye old-fashioned."

"Deeply flattered, ma'am," said Peabody, and beckoned to the corporal.

That was the only reference Peabody made to Favell. Strawlings joined us a few minutes later. Still with that nervous, knotted-up, oddly hungry look. Biting on his lip. Acutely ill at ease.

"Hi there, young Strawlings," said Peabody. "What'll you take for it?"

"Thank you, sir, I don't care for a drink," he said, flushing. "I don't feel like drinking. I . . . I only came over to tell Miss Carson that . . . that I'll be sitting over there. I mean, when she's ready to go . . . well, I . . . I'll be happy to . . . to walk her across to her quarters." The poor devil's face was now scarlet, and his clenched fists were white-knuckled knobs at the end of ramrod-stiff arms. He gulped slightly, and said, "The rain's started up kind of heavy again, sir."

"That's awfully sweet of you, Peter," she said, and smiled at him with genuine affection, and her fingers fell for a moment lightly on his hand. "But there isn't any need, honestly there isn't."

"Gee, I don't mind," he said. "I figured on sitting around a while anyway, and so—"

"Yes, but you mustn't sit around just for me," she said with gentle firmness. "Because Major Peabody is taking me home, you see."

10

Both Fleming and the General had referred to an entertainment "unit," and the next morning the Fireball brought in the rest of it. They were very different from Fleming's "headliners"—what he defined as "a couple of real, honest-to-God, buck-and-wing pros." Fleming, of course, immediately invented stories about them. Both, he insisted, had been born in vaudeville wardrobe trunks—the boy backstage in a burlesque theatre in Little Rock, Arkansas; his partner in a railway waiting room at Gary, Indiana, with her hair already set in Shirley Temple curls.

The boy's name was Jack Consadine. In fact, he must have been about thirty but he had the look of one of those ageless theatricals one used to see on the London music halls who remain eternally "the boy."

The woman was his wife. Legally, Fleming told me in considerable surprise. He had seen their passports.

She was a small, glassy blonde battling against plumpness, with a prettiness that was just beginning to fade. Already she had passed the stage when habitually she would be referred to as "the girl." Her name was Pearl, but professionally she was Judy, for the alliteration. Jack and Judy.

Jack Consadine wore blue jeans and a black tasselled shirt and a real cowboy hat, and he played the guitar. He had an extensive repertoire of folk songs and cowboy ballads. When he played and sang *The Streets of Laredo* he always cried, quite genuinely. And he never liked any other person to touch his Stetson hat: it always had to be put down on a table, or the floor, in a very special way, and picked up, gently and carefully, by fingers accurately placed in the dents of the crown. The only time I ever saw Jack Consadine get angry was when a GI picked the hat up by the brim.

They had an astonishing amount of baggage, including Jack's guitar case, all of it plastered with hotel stickers and steamship and airline labels. Mostly American. A few brighter and carefully placed additions from a wider cosmopolitan field. All the stickers, both new and old, were clear-varnished for preservation, but this was a matter of professional prestige rather than the normal tourist snobbery.

The two of them were there when I called in at Fleming's office to arrange the weekly medical parade for the native dormitory servants. The Fireball passengers had just come in from the airfield—a bunch of replacement infantry officers going on to Xanadu, and some Pentagon people from the Adjutant General's branch—and among all the khaki and military insignia the Consadines looked a very odd pair. Jack had withdrawn to the farthest corner of the room, a tall thin figure with sagging shoulders and loose arms and legs. He had about as much military bearing as a stork caught in the rain, yet he stared around him with a kind of fixed rapture.

His wife, fantastically incongruous in a blue raincape with a pixie hood, stood plumply planted beside the baggage, her baby-blue, mascara-palisaded eyes fixed in a stare that was resolute and intimidating. One knew at once that if Jack was the artist, Judy was the organizer.

I had to wait while Fleming got his transients organized into billets, so I went to the desk phone and called Captain Benjamin. No photo-recce planes had taken off, he informed me unhappily, and his dropping-planes had been withdrawn from stand-by. The wreckage of one aircraft had been sighted on the Xanadu side, burnt out on a cliff side between the Salween and the Mekong. No evidence of survivors. "Well, *nil desperandum*," he said lugubriously, and hung up.

By this time Fleming had cleared everyone from the office except the two theatricals. He called me over and made the introductions.

"I've allotted their quarters," he said, "but they're supposed to contact Lieutenant Allison. You seen him about?"

"No."

He pulled an irritable face and went across to his sergeant.

Jack Consadine looked at me with a diffident smile. "Ah guess you're one of the flyin' men here, sir?" he asked. He had a polite soft voice, with a studied slow drawl which was rather attractive. ("The true *patois* of the Wild West," Fleming explained to me later, "and not too damn bad for a kid out of Jersey City!" Fleming *had* seen their passports.)

"No, I don't fly," I said, returning his smile.

"Mmmmm." He seemed a little disappointed. "Ah eavesdropped on yer on the phone. You were talkin' 'bout airplanes," he said.

"That's right. In this place everybody is always talking about airplanes. Either airplanes or the weather." I smiled again. I liked the look of him. His face was long and thin and deeply suntanned, and he had mournful, brown, doggy eyes.

"Ah'm plumb crazy 'bout flyin' machines an' flyin'," he explained carefully. "Sure am. It's been, well . . ."—he

[101]

rubbed shyly at his long chin—"ah guess it's been mah recreation, kind of, pretty near all mah life, sir. Flyin' machines an' flyin'."

"You've come to the right place then."

"Boy, that's fer sure." He pursed his lips and ejected a single strange shrill whistling note. "All the time Ah'm doin' drawin's 'bout . . . oh, hell, 'bout most everythin' . . ."

"Oh, Jack!" his wife said impatiently, but his hand had slid casually to the back pocket of his jeans, and then he was offering to me a small, spiral-bound sketchbook.

"Jack, who wants to see *that* stuff!" she said sharply.

He just smiled. He had a way of smiling that made me think that these old thorns which pricked his wife had never given him a moment's pain.

The sketchbook was filled with little drawings, all done with pen and India ink. He had a quite remarkable talent. His drawing and his sense of composition were highly professional, his line sweet and effortless. But it was the subject matter that astonished me, for every drawing and every page were concerned with aviation. Drawings of airliners, of pursuit planes, of bombers, of pilots in cockpits, of early balloons, dirigibles, kite-like contraptions with danglylegged little men harnessed to the frail wings, primitive gliders, the skeleton shapes of pioneer biplanes, even a marvellous little evocation of a 1917 dogfight between Sopwiths and Fokkers.

"But these are simply marvellous!" I exclaimed. His eyes shone. His wife gave a little smirk of pleasure. "Fleming!" I called. "Come here and look at these drawings." I turned back to Consadine. "You certainly know your subject," I said.

He looked at me gratefully, then lowered his eyes, and began to rub his hands against the seat of his jeans. "Yeah. Sure. Well . . . it's what Ah dream 'bout all the time. Guess

[102]

they've all kinda grown t'be buddies o' mine, like Ah'd bin to school with 'em or sumpin'. Montgolfier. Lilienthal. Bleriot. Hawker. Orville an' Pres'. Oh sure, Ah know 'em all." He looked at me from beneath the carefully rolled brim of his white hat. "Wow!" he said ecstatically. "Am Ah goin' to have myself a time 'round here."

"Well, we're certainly not going to *be* around here, Jack. We got our job to do, haven't we? We're going on." There was some quality of implacability in her undistinguished little voice that explained to me the fixed determination of her stare, that resolute stance beside the baggage. Her goal was elsewhere . . . her ambition to offer her mite, to do what she had been sent out to do. Another all-American patriot, I thought to myself. But quite different from Frisk.

Consadine tipped his Stetson back on his lankly drooping hair, and grinned down at her. "Well, there's planes there, honey," he said blissfully. "Planes an' flyin'."

Lieutenant Allison bustled in at this point. Very much the man of affairs. Two GI's in attendance with clip boards under their arms. Certainly the temporary backstage role seemed to be agreeing with Allison. (What was it?—entrepreneur? casting director? talent scout? lights? . . . or just errand boy for Vince Readaway?) And he was even smiling from time to time. Not his sad, everyday smile, either.

He offered a brisk apology to the Consadines for the delay, assured them he would keep them no more than a few minutes, then beckoned me to follow him into the adjoining office.

"I've been looking for you," he said, then came directly to the point. "Jacob, can I have two native work parties, forty men in each, with overseers. I'd like them trucked out to the airfield within an hour."

"If you can supply the trucks," I said.

[103]

"They're standing by. Say—can I have *three* parties?"

"Yes."

"Swell!" He beamed through his glasses. "We've got to get that stage knocked together in Hangar A-2. Readaway wants some acts run through this afternoon. And maybe a re-hearsal tonight."

"Allison, they're not really going to try to cram two thousand odd men into that bloody hangar, are they?"

"Sure, why not?"

"God help them!"

"Well, where else?"

"I don't know where else. I only know that it will be like a bloody oven. And the program set for the exact hour when the mosquitoes begin to swarm! Have you ever *seen* the moquitoes in those enclosed hangars?"

"Yes, but where else?" he repeated, spreading his hands helplessly. Suddenly he looked quite crestfallen. "It can't be outside, can it? You can bet it'll be raining. So where else, man?"

"I said I don't know where else. But you ought to warn people not to expect Radio City Music Hall."

"Jake, they don't expect anything like *that!* They will want to see Jane Carson. That's all. The rest is trimmings. Just Jane Carson in the flesh . . . that's all they'll be interested in. Besides," he added impatiently, "the General has ordered Hangar A-2, so there's nothing to be done about it."

"Well then, you put him right down in the front row and let *him* sweat it out." I smiled and patted him on the shoulder. "All right. If you get your trucks on the way round to the labour compound, I'll arrange those work gangs for you."

I went back into Fleming's office to use his telephone. Jack Consadine was drawing in his sketchbook, and his wife was standing by the baggage.

[104]

In the middle of the afternoon the rain stopped altogether. For about twenty minutes or so we even saw the sun. It was very watery looking, and it cast no shadow, but it was enough to begin the steam bath again. Thicker this time, like raw wool, and clinging close to the ground. All over the base any moving figure was just a disembodied head and shoulders sliding along quite uncannily above this opaque band of fog. Rather eerie to watch, and very strange to walk in, seeing everything so clearly and yet having to feel along with your feet. To be blind, I realized, would be distinctly unpleasant, but the aspects of blindness in reverse, as it were, also made a very uncomfortable sensation.

The ground fog was not the only queer phenomenon of that day. For some reason—and I could not recall ever having seen anything like it before—we had a plague of vultures during the afternoon. Possibly they were attracted by the village corpses, but there were even a few of the loathsome creatures perching on the roofs around the base. In Leromenos it was an infestation. They had come down low to roost in vigilant groups on the lower branches of the trees. The weight of the birds bent some of the branches almost to the ground. Here and there throughout the village they were even perched along the verandah rails of huts, ghastly to see with their scabby throats and viciously curved beaks and those unblinking quartz eyes. Hunched and squatting like ugly harpies.

The unit of coloured engineers whose men had been working on the railroad washaway—reinforced now, and under the command of a young Negro lieutenant—was putting a new roof on the rice store and getting some of the collapsed houses upright again. There was no sign of Quigley, but I saw that he had five or six dumps of reserve rice already established under neat tarpaulin shelters, each one watched by an armed sentry. There was no singing among the coloured men. They seemed very dispirited, and kept rolling their eyes at the vultures.

I went across to Armand's brothel and borrowed his old twelve-bore and bought a carton of cartridges, and banged away into the trees across the line. Not really trying to hit. No point in having dead carrion birds stinking up the place: it stank quite enough as it was. It was dishearteningly ineffective. One vulture hopped off a verandah and flew across to the unoccupied branch of a tree, and a few others shuffled about on their own branches. I gave Armand back the shotgun and the half-dozen cartridges I hadn't used. The Negroes seemed more subdued than ever.

A locomotive drawing empty flatcars came up the track with its headlight burning, so I supposed the steam bath was even thicker back where the jungle came closer.

Just before five there was an immense clap of thunder, and the vultures took off one by one, and soon the rain was sluicing down again. It was dark by six—another foul, beastly night for flying—but I could tell by the sound of the planes overhead that Flight Control was maintaining its tight freight schedule.

It was nine before I got over to the bar. I had native ration-and-remuneration accounts to check over with Bergensen the paymaster, and by the time this boring chore was done I had half a mind to skip the bar and turn in early. I would have made a call on Benjamin except that I knew we would only succeed in depressing each other still more. I was low-spirited enough. My visit to Leromenos, the vultures, the sad rolling eyes of the Negro troops, the trudge back through the pelting rain—God! how heartily sick of the monsoon I was!—the thought of Vince Readaway bigshotting his way through his bloody rehearsal . . . all these things had put my nerves on edge. I was in a filthy mood, but I soon found there was no sedative in solitude. I simply could not stand the thought of sitting by myself in my quarters with nothing to do but to thumb through a stale book and listen to the monotonous drumbeat of that infernal rain.

I found Hathaway in the bar, sitting at a table with Bellini, the Canadian. Hathaway was breaking match sticks. Neither of them was drinking. I went across and said, "Good evening, strangers. Where have you two been?"

"Specials," Hathaway said indolently, and gestured me to a seat, and went on breaking matches.

"How were they?" I asked.

"The Marines have landed"—Hathaway waved a limp hand—"and the situation is now in hand. Where, may I ask, is the venerable Peabody?"

"Haven't a clue. I thought he was on specials, too. After—" I broke off, hesitated, then said quietly, "You know about Favell?"

Hathaway nodded, and frowned down at a match stick. "Quite bloody!" he said. "Shit-hot pilot, too. And pranged it like a kid out of a Link trainer, according to the groundlings. Ah well, just goes to show, eh?" He made a quick smile and shrugged it away. The subject, I knew, was closed. That was his epitaph for Sven Favell. He would not expect a more florid valediction for himself. "Tell me, old cock," he said, "at what time do you produce your Jane Carson?"

"What? How the devil should *I* know?"

"*Comment?*"

"I don't know what time she comes. Nor even *if* she comes. My dear chap, she's not *my* Jane Carson."

"Come off it! The boys insist that you are her sponsor, cock. You brought her here in the first place, didn't you?"

"So what?"

He looked at me carefully. "In fact," he said, "I frankly cannot really see you, Jacob, in the sinister Svengali role.

[107]

Yet this is what I hear. However, the extent of your proprietorship is immaterial. You are sufficiently her sponsor to see that I *do* meet her. That's all I'm concerned about. After all, is it my fault that I am the only poor bastard who has missed out on the Theda Bara of Zone Q-4? Here am I, slogging on, keeping Old Glory flying, and—"

"So when have I met this dame?" growled Bellini.

"*You?*" Hathaway looked at Bellini along the thin ridge of his nose. "My dear chap, nobody counts *you*. It is axiomatic that all Americans find Canadians a people dreary beyond imagination. And rightly so. What earthly point is there in *your* meeting her? Do be sensible, Bellini." He turned to me seriously. "I, however, absolutely insist on an introduction to this woman. None of this trying to keep the whole loaf to yourself, now." He wagged an admonitory finger.

"I promise to do what I can," I said lightly. "*If* she comes, that is. I rather think they're rehearsing a show tonight in the big hangar."

"Really?" Hathaway brightened. "Well, dash it all, let's load up with some grog and pop over," he suggested.

"You can, if you like. Not for me, though. I used up the last of my energy in getting this far. Besides, if you go there you also have to contend with a certain gentleman called Vince Readaway."

"Ah, yes. Heard of him. Big line-shooter, they tell me. Contented with himself, it seems. The universal know-all. No, no—on second thoughts let's stick around here. In fact, let's have some grog. To tell the truth, I had tentatively planned on a *real* piss-up tonight, but now I think a more modest approach is called for. Pending the arrival of your Miss Carson." As he moved across to the bar he looked back and said, "Is this character Readaway one of the scheduled bedfellows?"

"What do you mean?" I asked, joining him.

"Well, does *he* tuck in with Miss Carson too? . . . I mean, reg'lar loik an' wiv 'is boots orf." The Cockney parody came glibly off his tongue.

"What the hell are you talking about?"

"My dear Jacob, you know how I hate using those four-letter words. But isn't this true that she's a bit of a nympho? Or is this only the usual bullshit of the boys?"

"What is all this?" He was beginning to irritate me. It did not occur to me to ask myself why.

"Sure, that's what they say, Jake." Bellini nodded and grinned at me. "It's all round the station." Steve Bellini had the sort of face that looked as if it had been assembled out of an automobile accident. The separate features seemed to belong to other people. Nothing quite matched. It was an ugly, craggy face with broken teeth and old pits of smallpox scars on his cheeks and chin. His black hair came down in the sharp cleft of a widow's peak on his broad and rather shallow forehead, and he had that blunt sort of nose one usually associates with pugilists. He was stocky and wide in the shoulders, and he looked Italian. Now, with that lascivious glint in his honey-brown eyes, he looked merely ludicrous.

"What *is* this bloody nonsense?" I protested, with a touch of asperity. "The woman has only been here a few days and you—"

"Exactly." Hathaway smiled briefly. "That's the whole ruddy point, man. Because already we have the dismal spectacle of poor Strawlings moping about all over the place with his nackers dragging, and Priapus only knows *who* isn't supposed to have had a bit!"

"She shacked up with that slob Fleming, over at administration, all right," Bellini put in quickly. "The orderly cor-

[109]

poral saw them go in, and he saw them come out. Last night it was Fred Peabody. She dragged *him* off."

"There is even talk," said Hathaway primly, and closed his eyes fastidiously against the thought, "of General Frisk!"

"And me, no doubt?" I said pointedly.

"Oddly enough, no. Not you." Hathaway shook his head firmly. "It appears that she is keeping it within the colours, so to speak. Only compatriots up to date. Which is why I'm rather anxious to try my luck on behalf of the colonies, dominions, and protectorates."

"If you want my honest opinion," I said, "I think you're both monsoon-happy. A little overwrought. You've been flying too hard."

"Hardly an original diagnosis, old cock. We're *always* flying too hard. That's why we crave a little—er—sexual stimulation. Might take our minds off it."

"Then I can only repeat that the woman is not *my* Miss Carson. What she does with her spare time is no business of mine. I happen to find her a perfectly nice, charming, normal, attractive woman. Well, an exceptionally attractive woman, if you like. I don't see anything unnatural in a kid like young Strawlings being bowled over by her. Nor anyone else, if it comes to that. But, for God's sake, why does she have to be classified as a nymphomaniac just because some man escorts her home through the rain?"

"Admirably chivalrous, Jacob. However, I should still like to meet her. Form my own opinion, if you see what I mean."

"Then I'd suggest you leave it until some other night. She isn't likely to be coming here now, not at this hour. So your opinion will have to keep."

"Green light for the piss-up then, eh?" said Hathaway cheerfully.

I stayed with them until about ten, and then left them

[110]

to it. They were both resolutely on the way. Jane Carson did not visit the bar that night. Nor did Peabody.

As I splashed back to my quarters through the rain I had a good deal to think about. Not at all a logical pattern of thought in which a equalled b and x was proved and the answer came out right all the time, for my reflections were rooted in a soil of doubt and some queer personal uneasiness that I would not, dare not, try to examine. The gossip of Hathaway and Bellini could not altogether be dismissed as the inevitable product of the situation. True, their basic interest in Jane Carson was understandable. They were young, vigorous men who for a long time had been denied any real companionship with women—and in a sexual sense this particular woman was a very formidable creature. They were slaves, too, to the contemporary idolatry: they had their own little votive shrine on the bamboo board. The carnal life-wish. But always *the wish*. Human desire is open always to an immense range of interpretation, but not for them by the Pythagorean balancing of mathematical symbols. Nor for me, if it came to that. Pythagoras could use it for life and the soul and essence and for a sort of God, too, but I wondered had he been able to use it for the simple element of passion. Simple? Words were only symbols, too, necessary to define delusion. . . .

Perhaps it would have been easier to think it all out if those other images had not been creeping around in the blurred, unfocussable background of my thoughts . . . she and Strawlings, rigid beneath the dripping eaves of the pilots' quarters, fixed in the bleak radiance of a flashlight beam . . . that soft, sly rustling behind the obtruded obstacle of Fleming's big, near-naked body . . . those cool words forming on her full, soft lips, *Because Major Peabody is taking me home, you see.* . . .

Disturbing reflections in the monsoon rain. How long

[111]

since I had thought in direct terms of any physical relationship between man and woman that went deeper than Armand's shy little girls? How long since I had thought like this about Olga? Careful, I warned myself. You will be whistling up the jackals. You will have only yourself to blame.

After I had undressed I lay for a long time stretched out naked on my cot staring through the diffused pallor of the mosquito netting at the soft blur of lamplight, and the raindrops gathering at the bottom edge of the window frame, and moving along, and dropping down the glass one by one like beads on an abacus, and the quick yellow gekkos darting after insects on the wall. Preferable, at any rate, to vultures.

11

AT THE beginning of the monsoon the weather often clears completely for a time, usually for no more than a few hours, but sometimes for as long as a day or two. It is always a phenomenon—for it has, in its sharp contrasts of light, brilliance, and dryness, the qualities of phenomena—which one must be very cautious about, for it is no more than a pause, a taking of breath, as it were, a resummoning of energy. The weather, after this brief respite, invariably turns bad again—never with the pyrotechnic drama of the initial stages, but with a longer span of endurance and a more sustained savagery. If one were to look up the statistical records of Zone Q-4—they must be somewhere in Washington, gathering dust in a cupboard—I am sure you would find that the peak loss and casualty rate for Operation Xanadu had always occurred in the second, third, and fourth weeks of the monsoon. I remember occasions, in fact, when our casualties over a given period of days considerably exceeded the casualties in the combat areas, although one must remember, of course, that monsoon conditions possibly would have brought most military operations to a standstill.

The ironical situation in this particular year was that the

weather began to clear around sunrise on the Saturday morning, by which time the arrangements for General Frisk's entertainment had been carried to an advanced point, and bulletins and general orders issued in such profusion to every unit in the base that any question of cancellation was unthinkable.

The General was said to have received an assurance from Flannery, the met officer, that the weather would remain clear for at least forty-eight hours—this, at any rate, was the substance of his later defence—so Frisk felt that he could have his concert and still get his VIP's off to Xanadu in clear weather.

As the day developed his confidence in Flannery's rather rash prognostication appeared justified. Not a drop of rain fell anywhere in Zone Q-4. The crossing to Xanadu was clear all the way, with the distant alps peaked and shining against a deep blue sky. Around the base it was intensely hot and humid, but with the stage already built in Hangar A-2 and the seating taken there from all parts of the command, there could be no question of changing the venue of the concert. When it was certain that ten-tenths visibility existed all the way to the Xanadu airfields, Flight Control lifted the "sock-in" ban. This took off our hands a big backlog of army personnel who had been awaiting transport for days, but it did not affect our four theatricals. Since the General was so confident, Senator Vancourt also decided to wait and go across with them on the following day.

So far as I was concerned, I gave very little thought to the concert. The clear sky came as a godsend for the work that still had to be done in Leromenos. Under the brilliant sun the village looked more possible altogether. Not a vulture to be seen. Kites whirling high in the sky, and lots of smaller birds gaily chirruping in the trees. A big python that had come out into the sun and been killed by the turntable men was slung across a fence like a strip of old carpet. The people were out from their waterlogged huts, aimlessly drifting, their robes bright in damp sunlight. Still rather subdued and listless, they were at least marketing again and making cooking fires. I organized half a dozen gangs for the drains and the ditches and the clearing away of refuse, then went over at noon to Armand's to eat a bowl of his *pilaff*.

Armand told me he had got another girl from one of the villages down the line: while the food was being served she was brought out for my approval. (Approval? For whom?) She was a little more shy, but otherwise indistinguishable from all the others. Perhaps it was no wonder that Fleming never really knew the difference!

While I ate the *pilaff* I enjoyed watching the trains. They were very busy, puffing a lot, competing with whistle blasts, as if they had to make up for lost time.

After I had eaten, Colonel Robarts, the senior medical officer at the base, joined me and I went with him on his rounds, attending to the sick and injured, checking on general health and sanitation. Robarts was a good and efficient doctor, although inclined to nervousness and, on the whole, pretty uncommunicative. So far as his work was concerned, he drew no line between Americans and natives. At the same time, he had a deep-seated suspicion of all that was alien: everything that surrounded the hygienic order and discipline of the military base was a potential source of contamination and medical evil. The whole of Assam and India and northern Burma was to him one great, horrifying, overcrowded lazaret. Leromenos must have filled him with absolute repugnance, and it reflects greatly to his moral courage and strength of character that he carried on his voluntary work there with as much diligence and regularity as he gave to the Army base hospital on the outskirts of Ram-

[115]

part. Whenever I was with him I was always reminded of that terse, dismissive picture of an Indian town given in one of the early Baedekers: "The water is undrinkable, and adders abound!" But I could never quite screw up my courage to the point of quoting it to him.

From a series of almost monosyllabic comments, and curt, squeezed-out sentences, I gathered that he was worried about the possibility of a typhus epidemic, and I interpreted for him while he discussed with the *serang* of the railroad work gangs his plan for general TAB inoculations. (I did not mention to him that I had received a report on suspected cholera from one of the up-river villages. There seemed no point in alarming him unnecessarily. I had already sent one of my own men to make preliminary inquiries, and I could always go up myself within a day or two.)

The new roof was on the rice store, and Quigley's crew was actively stocking it again. The Negro engineers had vanished. Above us the sky throbbed to an intense activity of aircraft, and often the dark shadow of a plane making its approach would come rippling and leaping across the trees and vault the mud-rutted street. I hoped that Benjamin had got his photo planes away.

So the day passed.

When I returned to my office there was a message from Benjamin on the spike asking me to call over at Search-and-Rescue. By this time it was after six, but I took the jeep and drove myself across.

There were only Benjamin and Sergeant Garstein in the cluttered little shed. They looked up excitedly as I opened the door. Spread across the desk was a rough paste-up of aerial photographs. Taken from a not very high altitude and showing in foreshortened unreality a scarred land of cliffs and ravines with little vegetation. Some of the photographs that formed the paste-up had been printed lighter than others, so one saw it as a checkerboard design in tones of grey with an over-all pattern in darker chiaroscuro that would have made an attractive print for textiles. Fronds and veins and stems of things. More like a careful botanical drawing than anything related to ravines and rocks. Or to human lives, for that matter. A section of one of the lower squares had been carefully circled with red crayon.

Benjamin passed me the optical magnifier in its black, truncated stand. He didn't say anything. There was no need to. We had looked at these things before.

Among the dark tones within the red circle there was a pale, blurred fuzz fading away to the left. It could have been—probably was—a drift of smoke, and as it began at a thin and much whiter point towards the right, where the tones anyway were darkest, I nodded and said, "It certainly looks like a signal of some sort. And it's hardly likely to be tribal in origin. There's no habitation in that area that I know of, and the terrain would be too tough for nomads. And nothing much to burn." I handed back the magnifier. "You'll have a shot at it, anyway?"

"Hell, yes!" Benjamin said emphatically. "Well, it's the first break we've had." He pulled at the lobe of his ear. "Not as far north as I expected," he said. "Inside Shingáli, but only just."

"Who's to say? In that area nobody really knows which part is Shingáli and which is us. Anyway, it's six of one and half a dozen of the other. What did the pilot see?"

"Nothing. Well, he was satisfied about the smoke, but he didn't see any activity. He went down pretty low and made three circles. That very dark patch there is what looked to him like a thicket of bamboo and dense scrub. He was too low on gas to stick around for long."

"Scrub perhaps. Not bamboo. Not at that height. Well, what do you want from me?"

[117]

"The usual." His dark little pinched face broke into a rueful grin. "And a *soupçon* of sympathy. Would you believe it, Jacob, it's got to the stage now that when I ask for dropping-planes they look at me as if they suspect I want 'em for political pamphlets! I tell you this is the damnedest, screwiest, frustratingest, disappointingest job in the whole U.S. Army! Believe me, they didn't teach us a goddam thing at Harvard! Next war, brother, I'm for public relations!"

I gave him the information he wanted—spelling out the native names for Sergeant Garstein—and when we were finished we brewed up the usual jug of coffee.

"Time passes," I said. "Aren't you going to the big concert?"

He shook his head slowly, and smiled a little. "Are you?" he asked.

"I suppose so. Everyone is supposed to be there. Frisky regards this as a command performance. Listen, why *don't* you come with me? It will relax you . . . get your mind off all this for an hour or two." I had a real wish for him to come. I would have enjoyed his company.

"Sure, everyone will be there," he said reflectively. "That Jane Carson is quite a drawing card. They'll walk over broken bottles to see her."

"Oh, there are other acts. Frisk swears he has a big hit on his hands. There's a cowboy chap I'm anxious to see. He came in yesterday and—"

"Don't kid yourself, Jacob. Jane Carson is the hit. She's the one they'll be going to see."

"Perhaps she's worth seeing."

"Oh she *is*, sure. I've seen her. I saw her in a couple of movies, and I saw her in the flesh once, in summer stock it was, in *The Little Foxes*. She's good, you know. She's all right. She's worth seeing, sure. But the point is, Jacob, it's a six-hour flight to that place there." His quick finger jabbed

towards the photographic checkerboard on the desk—
"Gentlemen of the jury, I would now ask you carefully to
consider Exhibit A. And at the cost of gross personal
humiliation I've got two dropping-planes fixed to take off
at midnight. So! I guess I'll eschew the fleshpots and take
a walk over to the freight bay and help them get those
political pamphlets aboard. Time, tide, and the 69th Parachute Squadron wait for no man." He grinned at me. "Maybe
Jane Carson would," he said, "but that's another thing."

"Please yourself." I shrugged. "In which case do you
think Sergeant Garstein could run the jeep back to Fleming's
pool some time? Then I can walk across to the hangar."

"Why, sure," said the sergeant. "I gotta go across anyway
for the emergency medical stuff, and to pick up the G clearance."

So, what with one thing and another, it was ten minutes to
eight before I made my appearance at Hangar A-2. The
opening had been set for nineteen-hundred hours, fifty minutes earlier, but it was quite clear that nothing had started
yet. Nothing even looked like starting!

I had half a mind to walk back across the dark airfield
to help Captain Benjamin bundle up his political pamphlets.

12

THAT enormous place! I had forgotten how big it really was, and it seemed half as large again without the aircraft in it. More or less of the same pattern as the standard army Quonset hut, but enlarged to proportions where it could, and quite frequently did, accommodate around twenty of our largest transport aircraft, the eighty-sixes, and still leave enough room for maintenance and repair work to be done.

Now it was packed with close to two thousand restive men in khaki. Impatient, disgruntled, sweltering in a humid confinement. Even standing well back from the wide, open end of the hangar—and I did not have the least wish to approach any closer—I could feel the air gusting out like the blast from a furnace. Even outside there was little relief, for the night air was breathless and sticky: I could feel nothing but sympathy for those poor devils in the hangar . . . every man bound by the rigid after-sundown anti-malaria order of ankle-length pants, socks, sleeves rolled down and buttoned at the wrists . . . every man in the close-ranked seats rubbing against his neighbour . . .

The mosquitoes were already in full cry, and in each of the four aisles that separated the seating blocks a squad of

GI's methodically paraded up and down misting the already heavy air with DDT "bombs." The operation appeared pretty ineffectual, with that great curving space of stifling air above, and the men seemed aware of it. At the rear of the crowd, near where I was standing, and away from the senior officers, the embarrassed disinfecting squads were taking a lot of badinage from the troops.

The makeshift stage, however, was most impressive. Including the enclosed areas to right and left, which I assumed to be the dressing rooms, the improvisation extended the full width of the hangar. It was astonishing how much had been accomplished in such a short time. Heaven only knew what materials had been pressed into service—timber, wallboard, lengths of the tube-metal scaffolding which was used on aircraft overhaul, shielded runway lights, even a real curtain in shimmering vertical bands of red, white, and blue which had been fashioned from our coloured nylon dropping-parachutes. Somebody with a considerable talent for the *trompe l'oeil* had simulated a very clever proscenium front, with a representation of Doric columns in fluted marble at the wings, and, in the centre of the arch, as if carved in relief, were flights of winged cupids holding aloft the various insignia of the units in the command. Was it by accident or intent—or merely my imagination?—that the faces of all the chubby little cupids were portraits of General Frisk?

Yet for all the ingenuity and effort and thought that had gone into these preparations, the plain fact was that the show was late. *Very* late. The curtain, however cleverly improvised, was still drawn across. (Twitching mysteriously every now and then, as if somebody was peeping.) And the temper of the audience—confined, hot, uncomfortable, impatient—was growing worse with every passing minute.

The mood did not seem to be confined to the enlisted

men. I could see Lieutenant Allison way down front, and even from that distance it was very clear that he was angry, too. He looked pale and agitated, and he seemed to be waving his arms at somebody. A few minutes later he came stumping down the central aisle, his face set, almost jostling aside the men with the DDT bombs. When he came out of the hangar and caught sight of me his expression changed. It was not that he brightened, really. His face remained sombre, but his eyes seemed to quicken with a kind of hopeful desperation. His greeting, nonetheless, was brusque and accusatory.

"For pete's sake, what are you standing out *here* for?" he demanded to know. "Your place is fixed down front there with the senior staff officers! What the hell do you expect to see from way back here?"

"Well, there doesn't seem all that much *to* see," I said mildly.

He flushed and said, "Didn't you get my memo about the seating?"

"I did. I'd prefer to stay here, though. I'm half expecting to be called away. Benjamin's getting some planes off, and he'll probably want me." It came off my tongue glibly enough: I hadn't the least intention of being trapped in that sweatbox! "What's the delay?" I asked curiously. "I got here late. I expected to have missed half the show."

"You haven't missed a goddamned thing!" he snapped irritably. He hesitated, frowning at me through his glasses, then beckoned me to one side, away from a group of GI's, rebelliously cooling off outside the hangar, and regarding the two of us with curious attention. "It's that damned Jane Carson!" he told me in a lowered voice. "She hasn't turned up! She's missing! Jacob, you *must* have seen her!" he said in desperation. "Where is she? For Christ's sake, where *is* she?"

"I haven't the foggiest idea. *I* haven't seen her."

"Well, she can't just . . . just vanish!"

"No, I don't suppose so. But why appeal to me? I haven't even set eyes on the woman since the night before last." If this sort of thing continued I would almost begin to think she *was* "my" Jane Carson. "Have you sent across to her quarters?" I asked.

"Are you crazy?" He glowered at me. "Of course we've sent across to her quarters! A goddam sergeant's been posted there for the last hour!" My rather stupid suggestion had obviously made him more flustered than ever. "Oh, for God's sake go down and find your proper place, Jacob," he said impatiently. "You're somewhere near Quigley and Fleming. It's on your goddam paper anyway. I've got things to do."

I don't quite know what prompted me, but I said, "It's just a thought, but Major Peabody might know where she is."

He looked at me blankly for a moment, then turned on his heel and went at a trot towards his jeep. The whine of the gears as he backed out sounded like a new expression of his anger.

His anger, though, was nothing to what was beginning to manifest itself inside the hangar! By now they were really furious. They had begun to clap in ironic rhythm, to stamp their feet against the cement floor: there were angry, sarcastic interchanges between two groups across the aisle from each other: a sudden wild scuffle in which one of the men with DDT was sent sprawling. There were men standing and shouting and waving their fists . . . dark patches of sweat on their clinging shirts—at the back, across the shoulders, beneath the armpits . . . a slapping at insects that was almost as regular, almost as rhythmical, almost as ironic as the sardonic clapping of their hands.

The agitation had spread now to the front rows. I could not discern Frisk's rotund little figure, but I saw two of his staff officers hurrying in behind the stage, their lips compressed. The curtain twitched, then billowed violently as if somebody had lurched against it; there was a roar of disapproval from the crowd; the stamping of the feet rolled like thunder. In the rear rows quite a number of the men were beginning to leave their seats and jostle their way out. There were now clotted groups of noisy rebels crowding the hangar opening. In one of the aisles a pallid-complexioned p.f.c. with a fanatical voice was shouting for a mass walkout as a gesture of disgust . . .

I found myself wondering how Senator Vancourt would be reacting. And I wondered—I wondered very much—about Jane Carson. . . .

Considering the wildness of the scene, the show began so unexpectedly that I could only suppose the curtain had slid back as a result of a direct military command, conveyed from the General by the two staff officers who had gone backstage.

There was a sharp roll of drums, a single, high-pitched, throbbing chord on a clarinet, and the curtains parted—I remember praying that they would not catch on anything: they opened smoothly and professionally—and there against a painted backcloth of crazily tilted skyscrapers was a seven-piece Negro band, all in neat regulation khakis, all smiling, and already into full stride with a "hot" arrangement of *Darktown Strutters' Ball.*

It was a good band. Without any break at all it moved into an easily digested salad of popular jazz, the blues, old nostalgic favourites. The rebels began to squeeze back to their seats. The pale-faced p.f.c., not yet over his frenzy, was pushed into his. Within a few minutes the Orpheus miracle had been reaccomplished. The men were jigging in their

[124]

chairs, laughing at the drummer's clowning, applauding the virtuosity of the huge Negro with the clarinet. (It gave me a curious kick of pleasure to recognize him as the Memphis sergeant who had been in charge of the gang working on the railroad washaway.) They deserved the ovation they were given. And in the reverberations of the applause Vince Readaway walked on from the wings.

He looked very smart and very theatrical in a well-cut tuxedo of burgundy corded velvet, with a matching cummerbund around his waist, and a pencil-thin tie. He carried a hand microphone with a trailing cord. As he moved without haste to the centre of the stage he made a droll business of slapping at mosquitoes and pulling rueful faces. It got a good laugh from everybody, although there was scarcely a man in the hangar who was not slapping at his own mosquitoes. Sympathetic magic. Like music, one of the Orphic mysteries. We underrate our sorceries.

I cannot remember now what he spoke about. Certainly he made no apology nor gave any explanation for the long delay. I have no recollection of anything striking in his patter or memorable in his jokes. With an all-male audience there was nothing very subtle in his act: scatology, the sexual message, random notes from the Readaway blue period. Yet he succeeded in putting his personality across. With his teasing gibes and the red jacket and his extravagant handsomeness and that loud, professional air of self-assurance, logically he should have been detested by those crowded, regimented, sweltering men in their routine khakis, fixed to their disciplined, routine purposes. He was, I felt, a deliberate affront to them, a denial of their validity. I remember thinking that one could not see *him* as real if Captain Benjamin was *also* real. Or Peabody or Sergeant Pendlebury, or even Hathaway, with all his affectations and conceits. The fact remains that his audience warmed to him. The Negro band had largely retrieved an ugly situation: it was Readaway who consolidated the gain. Disliking the man as I did, I was forced grudgingly to admit that Frisk's earlier observation had been valid enough. Readaway was a trouper.

The act that followed was Jack Consadine. I have long since lost track of Jack, but I still vividly remember that performance of his. I suppose, had I given the matter a moment's serious thought, I should have realized that those hard-headed men in Washington would scarcely have arranged priorities and transport all the way to Xanadu for some second- or third-rater: yet the personality of the man himself almost obliged one to expect something rather gauche and amateurish. And I am sure that when he slouched on to that stage most of the audience felt the same, for there was a ripple of uncertain laughter, a shuffling of feet, a stir of comment.

The stage had been dimmed to a single light. Jack Consadine seated himself on a hard wooden chair. He stared down at his guitar as if he was not quite certain what the object was. After the splendid opulence of Readaway he looked an absurdly shabby figure, with that ludicrous pearl-grey hat pushed back on his head and his spidery legs in those frayed, faded blue jeans so awkwardly spread. He did not look at the audience, and it must have been the better part of a minute that he sat there in silence staring hopelessly down at the instrument. When he began to play it was done so quietly, and with such a nervous air of searching from some forgotten trick of fingering, that an appreciable interval passed before one realized how good he was.

He never once looked out beyond the stage: he seemed to be playing for his own joy and sadness, not for any audience. It was just Jack Consadine and his guitar. He played to it. He sang to it. Sometimes he would lower his

[126]

thin, melancholy face almost to the strings across which his fingers seemed to float in some caressive private communion, and when he did this that remote, shy smile would flicker across his face.

There was nothing very special in his repertoire. He sang a couple of cowboy songs—for *The Streets of Laredo* he hunched himself over the guitar with his head bent low, so that nobody saw his face, nor the tears that were on his cheeks—and a group of haunting little folk melodies, and a sad song about a southern chain gang . . . and a spell of the purest enchantment spread throughout that vast and sweltering hangar. When his act was done, and with a quick, diffident bow he had vanished into the wings, the applause was like a thunderclap.

But it was his wife Judy who skipped out to take the encore. She was wearing something tight and spangled, and she looked roundly, rosily, undeniably female. There was much delighted whistling from that woman-hungry audience. She sang a couple of songs into the microphone with a husky competence but no special distinction. It did not matter in the least. The uninhibited gestures of her plump little body were valid to the words, and the words recalled the almost forgotten litany of a stifled suffering. There was no movement of her generous figure that did not carry deep significance . . . here was Lilith, Eve, the Mother Goddess, the figure of erotic magic and fertility, the enduring thread of an everlasting pattern . . . here, curved and living and moving, and with these men reaching towards some dreamlike coalescence of spirits that were lonely and hungry, was a woman of one's own kind. Judy Consadine, artificial blonde curls tossing, her fixed smile set beneath the mascara, her exuberant body playing to every muscular cliché of the provocative rite, was perhaps for the first time in her life playing the role of all women to all men. . . .

The sad thing was that after her the program moved to a complete anti-climax. The supposedly comic juggling act by the fat cook from the base transport pool was embarrassingly unfunny and lamentably in need of further rehearsal. Even worse was to follow. A pianoforte solo by an earnest young lieutenant from Ordnance Supply—two of Chopin's etudes and Debussy's *Reflets dans l'eau!*—elicited only very lukewarm applause, and even that was discounted by the scattered catcalls which accompanied the clapping. The situation, one saw very clearly, was again slipping out of control.

Readaway made a gallant enough attempt to retrieve it, but I think that by this time he, too, was afflicted by the general tension and the growing restlessness of his audience. Perhaps he tried too hard; at any rate his jokes fell flat, his personality entirely failed to come across, and he withdrew without suavity. The reappearance of the Negro band introduced the last element of desperation. One knew, finally, that crisis could no longer be forestalled.

The plain fact, of course, was that they wanted Jane Carson. It was as simple as that. They had come to see Jane Carson. Little Judy Consadine had whetted their appetites, but Judy Consadine was not Jane Carson.

By the time the curtain slid across the last brassy Dixieland echoes, the men had begun, raggedly at first and then in unison, to shout her name.

I craned my neck to see how Frisk and the Senator were taking it, but there was too much movement around me. The whole place was in an uproar again. I am sure there was nothing else that Readaway *could* have done, but the duplication of acts, his own reappearance and the repetition of the Negro band, must have confirmed in the men's minds the suspicion that something had gone wrong.

Yet for the second time—and as suddenly and as unexpectedly as before, but more dramatically—order was restored.

The curtains peeled aside. This time no roll of drums nor scream of clarinet. Dead silence. A confluence of spotlighting in the very centre of the stage. And Jane Carson standing there, effulgent against the darkened backdrop, quite magnificent in her beauty. She was wearing the sort of gown which was, I suppose, standard for an appearance of this sort. Dull greenish silk which the spotlights shot with gold and purple. A long skirt tightly sheathing thighs, hips, stomach, waist. Bare shoulders above a low-cut, strapless bodice. With a thin black ribbon she had caught back her tawny, lovely hair in a kind of wilful disarrangement. Her arms were bare. She wore no jewellery.

From those hundreds of massed, staring men, came a long, low exhalation of breath, like a great, drawn-out sigh. Nobody applauded.

There is a world of other experience to which I am a stranger, and "show business" is a part of it, but I have to suppose that the "personal appearance" of a woman like Jane Carson should, logically, involve no more than the term connotes. She should not, surely, be supposed to act, nor have talent for acrobatics or juggling or conjuring tricks. She need not tell risqué stories nor play the violin. To possess any attributes beyond the physical attribute of being herself, in full flesh and blood, would surely smack of a redundancy. The cult idol, logic would insist, has merely to reveal herself, as in ancient times a goddess was expected at intervals to reveal herself. For she is there, fundamentally, to personify the truth of a myth—in Jane Carson's case the myth of feminine allure, of what at that time was always referred to as "glamour," of that rich sexual Eleusis whose local votive shrine was the bamboo board above the pilots' bar.

[129]

Indeed, in this she was immediately and strikingly successful. She fulfilled her purpose in those first few seconds, merely by standing there in all her womanly loveliness, and the great concourse of men in that vast, utilitarian structure were for those few moments hushed, reverent, almost, it seemed, overcome by awe—worshippers to a man at the oldest shrine of all. Had no more been demanded of her than that—and what else, really, was there to ask of her?—the disastrous fiasco that followed perhaps could have been avoided.

Because I knew from the first moment of her appearance—knew it with an odd instinctive certainty—that disaster was somehow inherent in her very presence there. What fixed this intuition I never knew. I simply sensed that there was something wrong. Wrong about *her*. Something tense, stiff, something nervous, something withheld. It was some cramping thing inside her, at any rate, that erected this barrier between the woman and her worshippers. To the hushed audience she projected nothing of her personality, nothing of that warmth and charm which she had displayed so readily in the pilots' mess. She gave nothing whatever. It was not even that she was cold. She was simply negative.

Well, she sang a song. One of those old, nostalgic numbers that seem to go on being popular forever. Was it *Night and Day*? Or *Stardust*? I no longer remember. She did not use the microphone, and her voice was pleasant enough. Twice in the course of her song she hesitated, and frowned slightly, and her hand would move in a half-brushing, half-slapping gesture, as if the mosquitoes were annoying her. When she did it the second time the feeling came to me of a sort of sick sympathy for her. Of sympathy—and yet of something sad and forlorn. Of foreboding, in a way. . . .

She drew applause that was vigorous enough, but it was certainly not the ovation that Jack Consadine had won, and there was a discernible note of uncertainty in it. The realization came to me suddenly that she was on trial. That she herself knew she was on trial. And that persisting instinct for her told me that she would not meet the trial. I was so sure of this, so profoundly certain, that I began to move inside the hangar as she began to sing again. I had hoped desperately that she wouldn't—that the bumptious Readaway would appear again in his red coat, scattering his wisecracks like cheap fireworks—that Jack Consadine would charm them once more with his alchemies of simplicity—even that the fat cook would sacrifice himself to derision for her sake. Nobody emerged to save her.

The great hangar was hushed again, so deeply held to a waiting silence that you could hear the droning ping of the insects all around.

Her encore was another song of the same genre—*Deep Purple:* this one I remember, for to this day I cannot hear it without experiencing a little prick of pain. But now she left nobody in doubt that the insects were irritating her. (And how was anyone to know that the mosquitoes were merely the visible scapegoat for some deeper torment?) She slapped several times at her wrist and forearm, at her naked shoulder, and once she moved a finger against her cheek as if to rub something away. A few moments later she broke off singing altogether and bit her lip and cast a desperately imploring glance towards the wings. There was no laughter from the audience. With Readaway it had been a funny little trick, meriting the response it received. There was no laughter for her. A goddess is not permitted fallibility.

There is no point in drawing out the sad, sorry business any further. *Deep Purple* was never finished. Quite suddenly—so suddenly that after one single sustained gasp there was a soundless pause in which a dropped pin might have been heard—she turned on her heel and ran off into the wings.

Then pandemonium began. At first it was mystified and questioning, not quite critical—and things were happening down front which riveted attention. I caught a glimpse of her by one of the improvised dressing rooms. Readaway was there, too, and Allison. She had a silk wrap around her shoulders. An arm was flung up, wildly gesticulating.

Most of the men were standing now, and shouting. I could see her hurrying up the second aisle, the black ribbon gone and her golden hair tossing. I began to push my way towards her, but was blocked by a group of soldiers jostling around an overturned chair. She was still ten feet away from me when I saw the big sergeant rise from his seat and deliberately move in front of her. I knew him slightly. His name was Jorgensen and he was a flight sergeant with the 69th Parachute Squadron. He had done a fair amount of dropping for Benjamin's unit. Of Danish extraction and slow-spoken and built like a tree. I had always found him pleasant.

He planted himself firmly across the aisle, his hands loosely on his hips, so that she had to stop or collide with him. She stopped. Very abruptly. Her green eyes stared at him angrily. He said nothing.

"Please, do you mind?" she said tensely. "I'd like to get past."

"Say, how much do you weigh, Miss Carson?" he asked, the words slow-spaced, deep in tone, pleasantly inflected.

She flushed. "Let me pass, please," she said impatiently.

"Why, sure. Just as soon as you tell me how much you weigh. It's something we gotta know, Miss Carson."

For one horrible moment I thought she was going to slap him across the face. Her fingers had stiffened, her arm had already begun to move. I prayed that she wouldn't. I felt a deep pity for her. I seemed to share her humiliation, her isolation among all those faces and voices that surrounded her—yet I also felt a deadening disappointment in her. I prayed that she would not make it any worse than it already was.

She lowered her arm, and for a moment bit at her lip.

"One hundred and eighteen pounds," she said frigidly. "If it's anything to you. Now please let me pass!"

"Hundred and eighteen pounds, eh?" He pursed his lips and stared her up and down appraisingly. "Why," he said agreeably, "that's around three cases of beer we could fly over there to Xanadu. The boys sure get thirsty for beer over there." He moved to one side, and with a slight, stiff, mocking bow said, "It's all yours, Miss Carson. There's the door. Good night."

As she hurried past her eyes seemed to meet mine, but there was only a wild, tortured anger in them, and no recognition.

The hangar by this time had become a bedlam. I caught a glimpse of Frisk's face, suffused with spleen, his white hair tossing. Senator Vancourt was in the corner of the hangar, pacing backwards and forwards with his hands linked behind his back, his heavy sculptural head bent in thought. Poor Allison floundered on the outskirts of confusion, his stricken face withered by the General's wrath. Readaway, his thin bow tie tilted awry like an airplane propeller, was bawling orders from the stage apron. The men were standing, many of them on their chairs, yelling back at him; others were expressing their disgust—and perhaps seeking physical relief—by pushing out of the hangar, jostling me this way and that.

I suppose, in fact, that all this occurred within the space of a minute or two, because most of the men were still in their places when the lights dimmed and the hush fell, and

[133]

there was Jack Consadine sitting on the hard chair in the middle of the stage, smiling down at his guitar as if nothing had happened. Perhaps to him nothing *had* happened! It was, at any rate, the way he played and sang. I left soon afterwards. By this time most of the men had gone back to their seats. Jack Consadine was playing—

> For it's dark as the dungeon
> And damp as the dew,
> The dangers are double, the pleasures are few,
> Where the rain never falls
> And the sun never shines:
> O, it's dark as the dungeon
> Way down in the mines . . .

A plane was just coming in on the far runway, its landing light spreading a zinc-white fan across the tarmac, its red and green wingtip lights winking on and off. Lozenges of other lights, gimcrack jewellery simulating the ruby and the emerald, topaz and diamond, planet-still or flashing, scattered on the black velvet of space, weaving the arabesques of their ordered orbits. Which was the real and which the artificial in this messy jumble sale of existence?

I made my way across to the far side of the airfield, crossing the wide runway between one plane's take-off and another's landing. The deafening, throbbing, urging-onward thunder of the first, and the straining tunnelled *swooooosh* of air as it rushed past with the tail already lifting . . . and the other plane making its landing behind the basilisk beam of its nose light, almost in silence, the lowered flaps and landing wheels singing their low, moaning threnody, the motors soft and coughing, muted as a failing breath, and then the soft, pained squeak of the tires hitting the concrete, and then the rolling past in a slow rush of air that was like a long sigh of relief. A signal lamp winked from the

[134]

control tower. Nervous jabs and darts of white light, spelling something out. Another plane, glinting red and green, was low over the trees that shielded Rampart, circling on its approach. I trotted across the runway.

About a hundred yards up from the Search-and-Rescue hut there was a parked line of three-ton trucks. I pulled open the cabin door of one of them and climbed into the driving seat to watch the planes touching down or taking off along the carnival-lit avenue of the flare path. Behind the black shapes of the trucks the red marker lights on the perimeter fence glowered like the eyes of beasts.

As I sat there, moving the thick, cord-bound wheel in my fingers, fidgeting with the gear shift, staring through the windshield glass, I was at first afflicted by the deepest sense of melancholy. Staleness, fatigue, heat, disappointment. A feeling of loss, too, in a way—a loss that was deeply personal yet infinitely remote. Like Olga, I thought. The idea startled me. Because how could it be anything to do with Olga when it was Jane Carson who was in my mind? A sense of having been failed, at any rate. That for certain. . . .

I tried to leave it at that—no more than a hint, a whisper of connections between a past, a present, and perhaps a future—but thoughts kept intruding, sly thoughts forcing self-examination. Was she in truth, if unwittingly, becoming *my* Jane Carson? Firmly I tried to put the idea away from me: the last thing I wanted to do, the last thing I *could* do, was to have any involvement whatever with a woman like Jane Carson. The very thought of it was ridiculous, destructive, unthinkable! And yet in some queer, inexplicable way I knew I *was* involved with her. It had been evident at that moment when she had appeared on stage and in an almost psychic moment of premonition I had suffered her own torment—even stronger the involvement later when, powerless to intervene, there had been nothing left for me

[135]

to do but to share her humiliation. A sick despair began to weigh on my spirits as I stared through the grimy windshield of the truck.

The night was still clear enough, although the stars had grown misty, and the sad sickle of a rising moon looked like a paring of crumbly yellow cheese. I remember the concert breaking up in the big hangar across the airfield. I could see the black shapes of figures streaming away, endlessly flicking against the repeated studding of the lights, and the headlight beams of trucks and jeeps and staff cars swinging their bright little abstracts against the darkness. It seemed some time before the last lights in Hangar A-2 were extinguished. The clock on the dashboard of the truck marked eleven thirty. I checked it with my watch, and it was ten minutes slow. On the runway the planes were still coming in or leaving.

Time must have passed, because then I remember that the remaining lights had grown moist and blurry, diffused into foggy radiations and darting crystals. A plane came in to land and its nose light was a dazzling smear that had no shape. I realized that the windshield was a blur of water, and drops like glycerine were gathering at the tip of the wiper and dribbling down the glass. It was raining again. Getting heavier. A grey, vertical mist was forming on the far side of the air strip. Once more I glanced at my watch. Two minutes past midnight. Just about the time Captain Benjamin had been expecting to get his planes away.

13

I MADE my escape from the problem deliberately.

First thing in the morning I requisitioned a fifteen-hundredweight half-track from the transport pool, with a native driver, and while I was waiting for him to have the spare petrol cans filled and some winching chains put in I wrote out a careful, confidential memorandum for General Frisk— to keep him informed of my movements, at least, if not of my reasons. When my corporal had taken it off I felt better. I had no intention of getting entangled with Jane Carson, or with Jane Carson's difficulties. There were any number of her compatriots around, I reflected with a queer little stab of bitterness; she could keep *that* within the colours, too!

Since it was Sunday, I realized that I had yet another commitment, so I walked through the rain to Fleming's quarters. I found him in his khaki underdrawers, shaving.

"I have some business away from the base," I told him. "It's just possible I shan't be back tomorrow night. So if you plan on going to Armand's it will have to be solo."

"That's okay," he said. "I'd figured to pass it up, anyway. I guess I've kind of gone off that. Well, it's a pretty crummy way of doing business, when you get to thinking about it. Where are you heading for?"

"Well . . . I'd rather this didn't get talked about, Garnett. But the fact is a signal came in last night. I've been half expecting it. From one of the villages up-river. It seems they have cholera."

"This goddam country has everything!" he said, squeezing at a blackhead.

"It's not absolutely certain. But probable. Best I go up and see for myself."

"In this effing rain! Christ! Am I sick of this lousy climate!" He pursed his lips disgustedly. "That trail will be something."

"I'm taking one of the light half-tracks. And they've given me Alimú. He's about the best of the native drivers. And he knows this particular village. I'd be grateful if you kept this to yourself, though. If Frisk hears he'll go into an absolute flap. Medical parades. Shots for everyone. Off-limits signs planted all over the place. The native labour locked out, and everybody bitching about it."

Fleming grinned. "But you have to tell the bastard something, don't you? Or do you just go A.W.O.L.?"

"I told him it was political." I smiled. "Delicate situation developing. Troublesome headman rumoured to be turning seditious. Just a hint of Moscow gold."

He chuckled contentedly. "Old Frisky's stuff, eh! Jake, I love you! So have a good picnic."

Neither of us mentioned the concert of the night before.

The road petered out at the edge of the midden which marked the sordid last environs of the village proper, less than a mile north of the railhead. From that point there was only a muddy trail cut between clay banks which fenced the

[138]

jungle off on either side. Less a trail, really, than the gouged-out course of a river torrent.

For the first few hundred yards the persistent vegetation of civilization continued to survive here and there among the strangling vines and the high-rooted jungle trees—scraggy little patches of barley and wild rice, rogue tea bushes, stunted mangoes and nut trees, and stands of banana holding their own more staunchly with the rain hammering drumbeats from the thick bent leaves.

I was very glad I had requisitioned the half-track, for no jeep would have made it after the first half mile. The clumsy vehicle was slow, noisy, wet, excruciatingly uncomfortable, and it stank of petrol fumes and hot oil, but the slapping, rattling caterpillar tread did grip the mud and the slime and the ridges, and no obstacle interrupted our clanking, lurching, slithering progress to the northward.

Alimú, a slight, strong-wristed young man with a skin of honey, had never got over that first childlike love of machines which all but the most stupid of Assamese seem to develop when they are given the chance. As he wrestled with the stiff and difficult controls, one sensed very clearly the fierce joy he derived from his task. A kind of sweating, grimacing ecstasy which not only embraced that element of conflict which racially would always form the core of his being, but sang to him of *mastery*—of the slave as master—of his private conquest of the elemental. To me, observing the rapture of his labour, he was potent and poetic proof of a primitive aptitude able to harness and enslave the white man's elaborate magics. I found myself reflecting on Frisk's pompous insincerities, *"the ultimate pageant of world brotherhood."* But should the native come to possess our machines and still retain this gift of zealous ecstasy, what, I wondered, would Frisk have to say then?

Although Alimú spoke very good English, we both fell

[139]

instinctively into the local tribal dialect even before the mean rooftops of Leromenos had been sucked away behind us in the grey desolation of the rain. A few minutes later we saw a leopard slinking across on the road ahead, and this time it was my heart that leapt to the sting of a pure rapture. Alimú's too, I expect.

The clouds, ragged-edged blendings of two tones of a dismal yellowish-grey, were so low that the tops of the taller trees were hidden in a muddy-looking fog, and as the trail narrowed and the jungle arched overhead it became so dark that Alimú turned on the headlights. We got only a kind of reflection back off the driving slant of rain, which accentuated the wet gloom beyond. He switched the lights off again and we slid and clattered forward through the soaking, cheerless half light. On either side, only a few paces in from the outer trees and the undergrowth, the jungle was a wall of impenetrable darkness—not a night darkness, but a sort of greenish-black, like old velour— pricked here and there by the eerie, cave-coloured, phos- phorescent glow of fungi in the soil and on the tree boles. The weird ghost light illuminated nothing but the rank, soggy growths themselves. I flashed a torch sideways and at once they changed to drab, knobbly parasites glistening in the wet. The jungle floor, under its black sheath of fallen leaves, shone like polished ebony. No living thing moved in the rain, although one could hear the grunting of the toads, and one knew that the leeches were there, maggot-like on every leaf.

A strange, lonely journey, but exhilarating in its way. And a change, certainly, from Zone Q-4!

We had lurched out of Leromenos soon after eight o'clock and the village which was our goal was roughly twenty-three miles away, but it was five in the afternoon before we got there. The rain was still heavy and a squally wind had risen. Our approach was effectively heralded by the din of the half-track, so that quite a few of the villagers were out along the trail awaiting our coming. They seemed intensely curious about the vehicle, but responded rather apathetically to my greetings.

The village was wet and huddled and running with water and crouched despondently beneath a ridge of black, storm-tossed trees. The usual thing. Four or five hundred huts and houses squeezed inside a roughly circular stockade of spiky palisades, and a spindly temple just inside the main gate, its eaves tangling with the stockade's slats and bedraggled bantam hens roosting among both. A few low knolls outside the settled area, terraced to the deep chocolate line of the ridges and sparsely planted. A series of water levels for the irrigation, collapsed now under the rain and forming a series of unlovely, muddy puddles stretching all the way down to a slatey, brackish arm of the river, hedged by plumed rushes which tossed dementedly in the wind. Lean-flanked, very hairy pigs nuzzling everywhere. Little bright-plumaged bantam cocks strutting. Some buffaloes in a distant field, wallowing in the mud.

They rang the bell for us above the gate, but it was cracked and gave out a suitably mournful sound.

The village headman, wearing a tweed jacket and a trilby hat for the occasion, was waiting inside the gate to welcome us. I had a twinge of guilt for the story I had conveyed to General Frisk. I had known Sitokó for years—how grey and grizzled and shrivelled he had become since last I had seen him—and I knew that he didn't have a kopek of Moscow gold in his pocket nor an ounce of sedition in his make-up.

Sitokó, in fact, had always seemed to me so exactly the epitome of melancholy failure, of the person so incapable of any profitable opportunism, that I had come, jokingly, to look on him as the eternal incarnation of the father of his race. According to the legend of these people they were once one of the only three races that inhabited the world. There came a day when the headmen of all three peoples were summoned by God and told to bring baskets with them. Our man—let us call him Sitokó—forgot to take his basket. His forgetfulness was unfortunate, for God was dispensing all the things of plenty—rivers, lakes, arable fields, orchards, benevolent seasons, hardy work animals, and industrious women. Sitokó returned empty-handed to his poor country. Many ages later God again summoned the three headmen. Sitokó took with him the largest basket he could find. The other and wiser two—aware of their defections and expecting punishment—went empty-handed and in humility. This time God was giving out evil spirits, and there was nothing to carry them away in but Sitokó's big basket. So he returned to his sorrowing land with nothing but the evil spirits of all the world, and ever since that day they have never ceased to plague his country. So the story goes. Sitokó the headman, in his sagging grey tweed jacket and rain-sodden trilby hat, standing miserably by the patched wooden gate, seemed to vouch for its validity.

We were escorted to his shabby little guest house while several of his women, chased, cornered, and finally despatched half a dozen of the strutting little bantams for our supper, and after the ceremonial washing and drying of hands Alimú was able to beg his leave to withdraw to the hospitality offered in the house of a cousin.

The headman and I found a reasonably dry patch on the leaking verandah, and a servant was sent to fetch my agent, Jidal, from the house of illness at the far side of the village. While we waited we chewed on flat, tasteless little cakes of ground meal, not unlike Tibetan *tsampa,* and dipped our fingers in a paste of cinnamon, and talked of cholera.

How does one *talk* of cholera? As one talks of death, I suppose. In that country, at any rate. It was a fact of being in the same sense that death, in terminating being, was the ultimate fact of being; for while cholera never needed necessarily to be the *final* fact there was always something about its manifestation that demonstrated death's inevitability. There were seasons without cholera, of course. There were even seasons with cholera when the disease would take much less toll than everyday malaria. But there was also the sure knowledge that seasons would come when the plague would scythe through villages and valleys like a rider galloping on the back of death and spurring him along.

Sitting on that leaking verandah with a shrunken little native chieftain, staring out into the gloomy rain pall of a tropic dusk, one felt terrifyingly detached from those factors of certainty which marked the boundaries of Zone Q-4 with a sharper definition than the steel tubing and diamond mesh of the fencing. Nothing seemed quite as permanent, quite as reliable, as one had thought. Like arriving in the Fireball and going on in a plane that had no name. And cholera, the real cholera, could journey those twenty-three miles between the village and Zone Q-4 with greater expedition than we had made it in the half-track. Our magics are profound, except that we are pitiably vulnerable to the secret world of the virus, and we still do not know what an aspirin does to the body's metabolism. Perhaps my thought processes work most strangely on verandahs, talking to natives.

Sitokó had called a woman to light lanterns by the time the servant returned with Jidal. Jidal was half native and half Scottish, the saturnine by-blow of a mining engineer's stay far from the soot and grime of Glasgow—a mistaken reference beached forever on the bleak shore of unwantedness. Loyal, though, and competent enough. No medical training whatever, but a familiar cognizance of the raw physiognomy of disease. Jidal was useful.

He told me there were three cases which he had investigated, all of them confined to one small sector of the village—an old man, an old woman, and a girl of twelve. Living in two huts fairly close to each other. The two females he still felt doubtful about, he explained with a show of diffidence, but the old man seemed definitely to be a case of cholera.

"He is still alive?" I asked.

"Oh yes. He cannot last much longer." Jidal sucked at his lip. I wondered how long it was since he had had a cholera inoculation himself.

"Who was the first to fall ill? The man? The woman? Or the child?"

"This one," he said. "The old man."

"When?"

"Three days ago."

I raised my eyebrows at that. "But how old is this man?"

Jidal looked perplexed and shrugged. "Who can say, Mister Strickland? A very old man." He tilted his head towards Sitokó and quoted the sick man's name. "How many years?"

The headman reflected for a moment as if he were mentally counting on his fingers, then said, "He is older than me. Seventy perhaps."

"Then it isn't cholera," I said. "He'd have been dead by now. I'll go and look at him, Jidal. You'll show me the way."

"Ah, but the rice is prepared," said Sitokó, "and the birds will be ready." He clapped his hands briskly. Two old women appeared from nowhere. He gave them some instructions in an undertone and sent them away.

In Sitokó's world the imminence of death would always wait for the formalities of hospitality. One was an event of the everyday, like excretion or ploughing, the other a rare

[144]

rite to be performed with studied ceremony. I glanced at Jidal, and the Eurasian made a half smile and nodded. There was nothing we could do about it.

We ate seated on the cane-matted floor, which was damp and smelt of formic acid. Highly seasoned rice in a big wooden platter to be scooped up communally with shallow bone spoons. The bantam cockerels—no bigger now than quails—still steaming on metal spits, to be picked and gnawed at in the fingers. A sticky, sweetish liquor made from fermented rice, served hot in tiny cups. Bananas and nuts. And afterwards the formal talk.

"Your wife stays now in the city to the south?" Sitokó inquired politely. "Or in the hills?"

My wife! Olga! For a moment the formal little courtesy shocked me. And then, of course, I recalled that the last time I had visited Sitokó had been many years before, and Olga had been with me then. What had we been doing? I tried to remember. Back there somewhere there were safe memories, too.

"In the hills," I said. The answer was truthful enough. She stayed now in the hills—she would stay always in the hills. . . . "How clever of you, Sitokó, to remember her so long," I said, while I tried to think about it. Carefully. Just to let the panic pass.

"But I remember her," he said simply, and looked towards his wife, an immensely stout woman with straight grey hair and faded, compassionate eyes. She nodded quickly and smiled, and took an obvious pleasure in drawing on her own reminiscences. As she talked, softly with pauses of thought and then in little excited rushes of remembrance, I realized that the span of years had been even longer than I had imagined. Olga had been drawing then and painting. Because of course it was the year she had been helping me— the year that had been supposed to readjust it all. She had

[145]

worked quite hard at the water colours and drawings which were to have been the plates and figures for the book. Well, it had never been published. Never even finished. And where were the plates and drawings now? Jidal listened, nibbling at a chicken bone. Sitokó sipped his sickly liquor and nodded drowsy endorsement of his wife's report. I could feel the tension of my nerves relaxing. On the cane wall the gekkos scratched. The rain drummed and dribbled, and tiny pearls collected along the ragged edging of the eaves and fell one by one into the puddles on the verandah. Eventually the spate of the old woman's memoirs slackened, and Sitokó, sensing the flagging of his entertainment, muttered something to her behind his hand. She nodded and withdrew. I could hear her bare feet splashing away through the mud and water towards the headman's house.

A flash of lightning for a moment lit the tossing trees on the hill behind the village, and from far away a dog howled. One expected it somehow to herald a whole sequence of other sounds, but the cry petered out and there was only a silence held below the watery monotone of the rain.

The woman came back with her shawl soaked, and carrying in her hands a small flat something wrapped around with muslin. She beamed at me as she began to take the wrappings off, and Sitokó chuckled to himself, and Jidal bent over to select another chicken bone.

They were handed across to me reverently—the faded snapshot and the little water colour sketch—and I held them in my two hands with the care they would have expected. I was quite in control now. The discipline was working. My fingers were absolutely steady. I could identify the subject of the painting without remembering anything of her having done it—a crisp, washy rendering of the headman's house, accurate in drawing and pleasant in colour. (I had a sudden absurd recollection of Olga's passionate adoration of the nudes of Russell Flint, and of her insistence on keeping up her subscription to *The Studio*.) Her signature was there, in that bold, bad, suddenly remembered script of hers. *Olga Strickland*. Startling to see it again, scratchy on the grain of the Whatman's paper, fixed imperishably in its fourteen brushed-in symbols. Uneasily evocative, troubling in the meaning that had become meaningless—the lost duality of a name. The faded snapshot evoked nothing at all. A shadowy image in lifeless tones of grey. A fixed, inhuman smile and clothes long since out of fashion and close-cropped hair fuzzing into out-of-focus trees and a sky chemically white from overexposure. An albino figure set against the blurred pallor of a faded world. And behind her the ultimate absurdity of a tennis net, sagging down, and frayed where the net cord joined the mesh. Impossible to imagine that once this anonymous, bleached, two-dimensional cutout had been a woman of flesh and blood and passions. Had been beautiful and faithless. Had loved and betrayed, had lived and died. *Olga Strickland!*

I murmured some politeness and handed them back, and the old woman wrapped them away carefully in the muslin. She would carry them back through the rain to the headman's house. For some reason they would go on being treasured. Strange! And I had never kept a photograph of Olga; I had no single memento of her pursuits torn from a Whatman's block. It was only here that Olga Strickland was preserved, in a squalid little native village in a stockade by a hill. *Very* strange!

Jidal and I took our leave soon after, and with two dancing lanterns we went through the rain and the dripping warren of the huts to the house of the old man. He was already dead. I examined him and questioned the two old women who were there, dry-eyed old women with accepting faces, beating with their palm fronds to fan the evil spirits away. They had nothing useful to say, so we trudged across to the other hut, where the child and her mother lay. There were many relatives in attendance, but Jidal cleared the place of all but the most practical-looking woman among them. She submitted with common sense to my interrogation. There were the symptoms of cholera all right—sudden extreme fever, violent diarrhoea and vomiting, convulsive stomach cramps, lapses into a sweaty coma—but in answer to my point-blank question the woman shook her head. No, she did not think it was cholera. River fever, she said. (It was their name for a dozen maladies, typhoid and amoebic dysentery among them.) Yes, the old man and the woman and the child had all drawn their water from the same drinking tank. But so had fifty other people of the neighbourhood. No, there were no other cases of a similar illness—not of *this* illness. Had melons been eaten? Peaches? No melons had been ripened in the gardens, and none eaten. At my reference to peaches she smiled in a puzzled sort of way and made no comment. The old man, she explained, had been an invalid for years, and toothless, and had lived on meal mash and weak rice gruel. Sometimes he ate soft meat, the chitterlings of a young pig, a piece of chicken or baby kid, but his daughter had always chewed the meat up first in her own mouth and only given it to her father when he could swallow the gobbet whole.

I made a careful examination of both patients—the woman was writhing in pain, the little girl lay rigid, in a sweat as cold as death—and I gave them shots and a medicine and told the woman that we would come again in daylight. I said to Jidal that I did not think it was cholera.

I spent a restless night in the headman's guest house. The

bed was only thin rugs spread across a frame of planks. The mosquito net stank of mildew, and it was full of holes, the larger ones hastily cobbled with strips of dried grass so that it hung in the most extraordinary lumpy, peaky shape. I spent most of the night slapping at the insects trapped within the ridiculous contrivance. The wind howled all night long, buffeting the thatch and blowing in a smell of rank mud and decayed fish from the distant arm of the river. The room was stifling. Each gust of wind seemed to make it hotter. After a time some of the thatch must have been blown away because I could hear a loose bamboo banging on the roof and the rain began to come in and puddles spread across the floor. The water dripped between the planks with the infuriating insistence of a leaking tap. I was in a bad frame of mind, for while I loathed the discomfort of my surroundings I had no real wish to exchange them for the oblivion of sleep, because Olga was still lurking in the background of my thoughts and I was afraid I might dream of her. Still, I must have dropped off or dozed, for there was one moment when I found myself sitting bolt upright in a sudden start of alarm: after a bewildered moment I realized that the "something wrong" which had shocked me was simply the fact that I could not hear the sound of aircraft circling overhead! Perhaps, after all, there was much to be said for the comfort and conveniences of Zone Q-4!

In the morning I went back across the village with Jidal.

The cadaver of the old man had already been laced into the high chair, seated, with his dead hands palms downward on his knees, and a framed photograph of himself as a much younger man tied to the back of the chair with vine tendrils. The mourners were eating cold *pilaff* from a black cauldron. They all seemed pretty cheerful. After the cremation, the chairs and the framed photograph and the old man's clothes would be brought back to the house—the photograph, like the snapshot of Olga, would be wrapped in muslin and preserved as a memento. In the meantime a small, crop-headed boy stood beside the corpse, holding up a black umbrella to protect these valuables from the rain. From time to time one of the women would leave the *pilaff* to take her turn with a palm frond at beating away the evil spirits.

We went to the other house. The woman was still in considerable pain, and they showed me a canister of vomit that was black with bile, but at least she was no worse than she had been the night before. The little girl's condition had greatly improved. "Summer" cholera, perhaps, but certainly not the vicious, lethal "Asiatic" type which Jidal and I had feared. Still, I went with Jidal to the suspect tank to collect samples of the water for analysis back at the base. The tank was edged with a grey-green scum and looked foul enough, but there were a dozen women there drawing water for the day. I took water samples from four other tanks nearby. A leper was sitting by one, alone in the rain. I wondered what Colonel Robarts would have thought about it all. . . .

There was nothing much more I could do. I left Jidal with a kit of drugs and the necessary instructions for attending to the sick woman and the child, and then I found Alimú and we made our formal farewells and started up the half-track.

I must admit that when we clattered through the stockade gate, heading south, I was just as pleased as when we had lurched away from Leromenos, heading north. Home, they say, is where the heart is. And the grass is always greener on the other side of the fence.

14

THERE was a big crowd that night in the pilots' bar, and it surprised me to see *who* was there. My visit to Sitokó's village, coming immediately after the concert on Saturday night, had erased a continuity, so that while I expected to see Readaway there I had not expected to see Jane Carson. But she was there all right, seemingly quite at ease, at a table with some young pilots. Her back was turned to me. A few tables away from her group were Senator Vancourt and Allison, by themselves, talking together quietly. Up in the far corner, tucked against the loose cushions with his knees up, his Stetson hat still on his head, the guitar propped against the wall beside him, a can of beer on the table before him, and a look of melancholic concentration on his face, was Jack Consadine. He was drawing on a sketchbook, larger than the one he had taken from his jeans to show me, and a half circle of pilots stood nearby, totally absorbed, watching. (On the bamboo pin-up board a little pen-and-ink drawing of one of the eighty-sixes in flight had been added to the memorabilia in my absence.) Judy sat near him, drinking something from a long glass.

Vince Readaway was down the room, gyrating carefully,

wriggling his buttocks and slapping at his thighs in drunken parody of some native dance. The few pilots watching him, standing back with their drinks in their hands, seemed rather uncomfortable. No sign of Peabody, of Hathaway, of Strawlings, but Bellini was at the bar, waving a glass around. And just beyond his group, drinking by himself, was Lieutenant Colonel Garnett Fleming! What the devil, I wondered, was he doing there? For over a year on every Monday night at this very hour he had been clearing his throat gruffly, preparatory to going into the shadowy room behind the rattan screen, holding in his fist the small pigskin zip bag with his hair brush and comb and things . . . I moved through the crowd and joined him.

"Hi, Jake!" He was obviously pleased I had come. "Get the hell out of here if you're contagious."

"I'm not. It wasn't cholera."

"Christ! A trip like that for nothing!"

"Nothing's ever for nothing. It was interesting," I said, thinking of the leopard that had crossed the trail, and Olga's water colour. I picked up my drink and looked around the room. "Quite a night," I said. "What is it? . . . some special at-home for transient VIP's?"

"The hell! They're here because Frisky doesn't want 'em there," he said with a touch of cheerful vindictiveness.

"You mean—"

"I mean he just doesn't care to have 'em about any longer."

"Because of what happened at the concert?"

"Well, I guess that's about where it begins. But I suppose there are other angles. Anyway, the old man's got a liver like a used loofah. He'd like to see 'em all to hell and gone out of the place. So we're socked in again. And will you listen to that rain!" He grinned and rattled the ice cubes around in his glass. Above us was the faint sad droning of aircraft in the wet night.

"And the Senator?" I asked. "Is he—"

"That's Allison's chore. Frisky keeps him attached to the Senator like a goddam limpet. Feeding him the P.R. crap. Statistical proof of high morale and top command efficiency. Beyond the call of duty. Jesus, Jake, I used to *know* politics. I figure this guy Vancourt knows politics, too." He glanced towards the quiet table where the Senator and Allison were sitting. "But that moron Frisk plays politics like my Aunt Agatha plays horses or the Stock Market!" Again the ice cubes tinkled.

Jane Carson had turned in her chair to say something to somebody and her eyes met mine and she waved her hand and smiled. There was an interested, faintly quizzical look in her expression. She seemed perfectly composed.

I turned again to Fleming. "You'd better fill me in on some things," I said. "The concert, for instance. What was the reaction?"

"Well . . ." He hesitated and pulled his lip. "Well, I guess it gave everyone something to talk about," he said guardedly.

"Jane Carson, I mean. What did they feel about her?"

He considered this for a moment, staring into his whiskey glass. "Opinions varied," he said.

"They certainly don't seem to hold it against her."

"Oh, some do, I guess. Most of the guys blame Frisky for having insisted on the crazy business in the first place. In that goddam hothouse! And all those bugs! Like asking a stripper to take off her bra and pants in the Hall of Tropical Entymology! The hell with it, Jake, the show was a balls-up long before *she* took a powder. That bastard at the piano playing chopsticks! Boy!" He shook his head in slow disgust.

"And Readaway?" I asked.

"That jerk! Ah, they hate his guts anyway." He made a

vague contemptuous gesture towards the dancing figure at the end of the bar. "Tell you what," he said. "The guy who really comes out of it is old Cowboy Jack up there in the corner. And that Betty Boop wife of his. They're the sweethearts of Zone Q-4. Funny how sometimes the billing doesn't count."

Jack Consadine had put aside the sketchbook and taken up his guitar, and he was smiling down at it as he began to finger the strings. With his first chords there was a good deal of shuffling around as the men began to move over that way. Readaway kept twirling and wriggling his backside and snapping his fingers, but nobody was paying any attention to him. He hitched his belt and went across to the bar and pounded his fist for service, but there was an appreciable delay before the corporal went along to him.

"Well, for Christ's sake, she had the guts to come here and brave it out, didn't she?" Fleming said suddenly and edgily. "Hand her that. And she hadn't been here five goddam minutes, and they were all down on the floor again. So what the hell!" There seemed to be an undertone of bitterness in his words . . . well, perhaps not bitterness exactly, but certainly something different from his usual caustic bluntness. Perhaps he was missing the prophylactic consolation of his lemon-skinned girls. A confirmed smoker who drops the habit is always edgy and irritable for a long time. Possibly one needs an alternative drug to soften the shock of renunciation.

In the general redistribution Jane Carson left her party and came towards us. I had expected that she would; it was why I had wanted to question Fleming.

But her approach surprised me, for she said, "Hullo, Garnett," and put her hand on his for a second. A sentence stirred at the bottom of my mind, like some unpleasant creature moving in the mud. *She shacked up with that slob Fleming, over at billeting, all right.* "And hullo, Mr. Strick-

[154]

land," she added, with the award of a dazzling smile. "We haven't seen you about."

"I've been away from the base. Yesterday and today. I only got back an hour ago."

"I asked about you yesterday. Nobody seemed to know."

"He went up-river," said Fleming. "He keeps a dame there in one of the villages. When he makes these trips nobody ever *does* know."

I asked her what she would have to drink, but she shook her head, and a little frown puckered her brows. "I won't have anything," she said. "I've not been drinking. I . . . I've had a headache all day. It's so crowded in here tonight, and stuffy, and hot. It *is* hotter tonight, isn't it?" She was talking directly to me, as if Fleming was not there at all.

"It's hot, yes. I don't think it's any hotter, really. Depends a good deal on the way you feel."

"You wouldn't want to take me for a walk somewhere, I suppose?" Again it was a question directly put to me.

"*Walk?*"

"Honestly, I must get some air."

"But . . ." I shook my head in bewilderment. "Walk *where?*" I asked.

Fleming was studiedly not interested. He looked as if he was reading labels on the bar bottles.

"I don't have any idea." A strange little smile touched the corner of her mouth. "I thought you'd know."

"But it's raining cats and dogs! And there's half a gale blowing, and—"

"I know. I like walking in the rain. I told you." Her smile broadened. "I have a perfectly good hat, and a perfectly good coat. And a huge pair of boots that Major Peabody found for me. So what's the difference? And rain like this can't mean anything to an old hand like you."

"You make it sound almost like an ultimatum," I suggested dryly. "But the point is I have Fleming here and—"

"Oh, brother! count me out of *this* setup! I even call a jeep to take me back to quarters. You two go have fun at the aquacades. I guess I'll sit around here a while and keep dry." Was there a grating edge to his sarcasm, almost a sneer?

A thought occurred to me, and I said, "Look, stay here a minute or two with Fleming. Let me make a telephone call."

"Don't ask for a Yellow cab," said Fleming. "They won't come this far out." No doubt now about the sneer.

I had to go into the staff office for the telephone, and the call had to be routed through the headquarters central switchboard, so it took a few minutes before the sergeant said, "Flight Control? Hold it," and passed over the handset.

"Sure, take her over, if that's what she wants," the duty officer said, without much interest, when I had explained the matter to him. "Rogers is there. I'll call him and say you're coming. What is it, Strickland? Slumming visit, or just seeing how the other half lives? Guess you'd better explain to her *we* don't give floor shows except on Saturdays."

When I returned she was standing by the door. She had already put on her big gumboots and her raincoat and she was holding the grey sou'wester in her hand.

"You *are* eager to get out in it, aren't you?" I said with an affected levity which did not quite conceal my uneasiness. "Where's Fleming?"

"He went back. Just a minute ago. He said he had some business at his office he had to attend to."

"Everything's gone sudden all of a sudden, hasn't it?" I said. I wrapped on my oilskin and said, "Let's go." I had the queerest feeling that the eyes of all those men were on me.

Outside the wind and the rain slashed at us, and she said, "Where are we going, anyway?"

[156]

"Not far. Just around the airfield here. I don't see much point in just walking. Not in this. So I thought you might like to see how some of it works. That was why I made that phone call. I had to get permission to take you into the control tower."

A harder squall buffeted us, and we had to put our heads down into it, and she took my arm. The squall lasted only a few moments, but her hand stayed in mine. I could make out a dim light blurring in the rain, and I said, "Ah, yes. Let's go over here first."

Only one of the windows of the shack was lighted and I rubbed at the water on the glass and looked through. Captain Benjamin was alone at his desk, his pointed chin resting on his fists, a big book opened in front of him on top of a pile of maps and folders.

I opened the door in a rush of wind and rain, and as we stumbled inside there was a scattering of papers and a lifting flurry of maps. I slammed the door behind us and said, "Sorry for the entrance. I brought you a visitor."

He had risen from behind his desk and he looked very small and neat against the sprawling map contours on the wall behind. His fingers stroked tiredly along the tops of his eyebrows, and then he smiled and carefully closed the big, black-bound book he had been reading. *Applications of Criminal Jurisprudence in the State of New York. Vol II.*

"Hullo, Miss Carson." His voice was warm as he gave her his hand. "This is quite an honour. Hi, Jacob. I hadn't expected callers on a night like this."

"We're not interrupting you in something?" she said anxiously. "I hope—"

A tired, wry smile touched his full, mobile mouth, and he glanced at the big volume on the desk. "That? My Do-It-Yourself kit. Profit from your spare-time hobbies. I'm trying to better myself—studying for the bar. Please do sit down, Miss Carson."

"This is what you were asking me about the other day," I said. "This is Search-and-Rescue." My gesture embraced the cluttered, shabby little office. "And Captain Benjamin *has* studied for the bar. He is, in fact, a very successful New York lawyer."

"Was," Benjamin corrected. "Very much *was*." He smiled ruefully, and changed the subject. "I am sorry I missed your concert, Miss Carson," he said. "I just couldn't get away." I realized from the way he spoke that he had not even heard about the fiasco. "I saw you a few years back," he went on. "*The Little Foxes.* You were very good."

"It's a wonderful play. But thank you, all the same."

"Say, how about I fix some coffee?" he suggested eagerly. "I'm sorry there's nothing else I can offer you to drink, but—"

"We can only stay a few minutes," I put in quickly. "I've arranged to take Miss Carson up to control tower. They'll be waiting. But perhaps if you could explain to her a little bit about what goes on here . . ."

"Sure, if she wants." He gave me a faint smile. "Except that you could explain it a hundred times better."

Anyway, he took her around and showed her the maps and explained something of the activities of the unit, and after about five minutes I suggested that we should move on. When we left he was standing behind his desk again, his fingertips lightly resting on the cover of the big black book.

I paused before opening the door and said, "I forgot. What happened with those two dropping-planes?"

"They never took off. The weather closed in on us. It hasn't cleared since."

"And now?"

"Nothing now. Nothing at all."

As far as I can remember it was the same duty crew in the control tower that had been there on the bad night when Pendlebury had taken me across. Well, Captain Rogers was the duty officer, and Pendlebury was there, and the same radio operator and a couple of other GI's I recognized. The earnest-looking tech sergeant, also, who had been busy with the long-handled squeegee. It was stuck away in a corner this time. The curved glass was rain-smeared and spattered on the outside, but it was not misting up at all inside. In fact, the weather was less violent than it had been that other night, and on the lee side they had half a dozen of the angled windows open to let the air in. It was cooler and more pleasant than it had been in the bar.

They were all very cordial to her, although Rogers, after a quick smile and a hand shake, went back to the lighted black ramp of his control board. It was Pendlebury who made the explanations—how competently and succinctly he presented the complex technicalities to her in understandable terms—while the tech sergeant attended to something brewing on the primus in the corner. While she was occupied I went over to Rogers.

"How does it look tonight?" I asked him.

He glanced up from the microphone and grinned. "Just fine. No problems. Bringing 'em in and sending 'em out."

I glanced over at the flight board. Hathaway's name was chalked up in the pilots' column. His flight was marked as S.F. 862. "S.F." was the designation for "special freight," and it was the only S.F. listing on the blackboard. He had not taken off yet, because the other columns were blank.

"I see Hathaway's rostered," I said. "I was looking for him in the bar this evening."

"He's next for take-off," said Rogers. "He's up there at taxi bay now. Special freighter. Candy bars, I guess. Or gelignite, maybe. You can never tell with these S.F. listings."

I went across to Jane Carson. She had a thick mug of coffee in her hand, black and steaming. I pointed to the flight board. "There's a friend of mine going to take off in a minute or two," I said. "Peter Hathaway. He's rather anxious to meet you, by the way."

"Peter Hathaway? But I *did* meet him. I was with him last night."

"Oh. Well . . ." I managed to shrug it off. Even to smile at her. "I don't have to bother about it then, do I?"

"Stand by S.F. 862," Captain Rogers called into the microphone. "Stand by 862. Taxi to west end Runway C."

"S.F. 862 to control. Roger! Taxiing to west end Runway C." Out of the fabric disc in the bakelite board Hathaway's voice emerged, thin, metallic, strained through space and the magic of this sounding-box suspended in the wet wild night, and yet still carrying that edge of affectation to establish identification with Hathaway's personality.

A long distance away, through the wet-stippled glass and the slant of rain the jewels of his wingtip lights glittered, and the dazzling halation of his nose light moved slowly along to the left and stopped. The lights swung a brief bright jerking beam that scattered stars across the curved glass.

"Tower to 862. Control check."

A pause, then, "Control check completed. All Sir Garney-oh! Am I clear for take-off?"

"Tower to 862. You are clear for take-off, 862. You are clear on a due east course to six thousand feet. Your ceiling here is three thousand. Roll her, 862."

The wingtip lights flicked on and off three times, then began to move towards the right, sliding through the rain, slowly at first, then faster, the zinc-white beam of the nose light expanding and contracting through the wet screen like something explosive. The plane went across us at an

[160]

angle of forty-five degrees, faster and faster, rushing past our immediate line of vision in a sudden brilliant dazzle of light.

"S.F. 862 to control tower." I observed the sudden stiffening of Rogers' fingers on the control key even before I sensed the new inflection in the metallic voice. "Anxious moment. I have too much torque on my rear end. I am not coming up well." A fractional pause, then: "I shall take off anyway because I have no more runway."

The lights vanished suddenly, obliterated by the black wetness of the night. We heard nothing, save the hiss and splash of the rain and the sighing of the wind outside—nothing of the plane going away, nor of the explosion. It seemed to come up so slowly at first, like an incandescent violet bubble, swelling in the darkness outside, a chemical stain thrown upon a colourless slide. Billowing larger. Vomiting up against the sky. Bursting before our eyes in a searing, blinding flash of brilliant orange and sulphur yellow. The control tower shuddered as if a giant were shaking its foundations. The flashing fiery envelope collapsed into distant tongues of blue flame.

"It wasn't candy bars," Rogers said, as if he were talking to himself, and his finger moved to the button. The sound of the siren seemed to come from far, far away, wailing a sobbing keynote to the storm. The hooter of the crash truck was a more strident sound, closer, stabbing at the night with clamorous insistence. The red warning light on its cabin top blinked up at us as it turned and raced away. I caught a glimpse of it as it sped down the rain-shining runway, and it looked absurdly like a clockwork toy.

As I took her away, I could hear Captain Rogers speaking into the microphone. "Tower to Inward 332. Can you hear me, 332? You will continue to circle at three thousand feet pending altered approach pattern. There is a burning aircraft at the eastern end of Runway C. We are giving you flare path on Runway A. Please continue to circle. Confirm with tower, 332."

We had nothing to say to each other as we walked back through the rain. No comment about it. No conjectures. We did not look behind to where the searchlight beam of the crash truck flicked and darted against the low black shapes of trees. Something was burning, but the flames were slow and yellow beneath a lavender canopy of smoke. Again she took my arm and put her hand in mine. The dim light was still burning in the window of the Search-and-Rescue shack. *Applications of Criminal Jurisprudence* . . .

"Where are you taking me now?" she asked finally in a low voice.

"Back to the bar. We've had our walk."

"Why there? I . . . I don't think I very much want—" She broke off abruptly. "Yes, all right," she said. "The bar, if you like. I guess that would be best."

I decided to say nothing to Bellini. At first I thought I would, but I saw that he was pretty high, and I knew that Hathaway had been his special friend. I left her with Allison and the Senator and said good night, and as I walked home through the rain a plane came in and hissed its landing along the central runway. Inward 332. At the eastern end of Runway C everything was pitch black. S.F. 862. All a matter of numbers in a filing system, chalk marks on a blackboard, punch holes in a dark, wet night.

15

HATHAWAY's death triggered off a lot of things. The reason
for it I never heard resolved—an error in loading? a defect
in maintenance? a moment of human aberration?—but the
accident seemed to usher in a period of the darkest mis-
fortune for the men flying out of Kansas. Three other planes
were lost that same night, and from that Monday until the
following Saturday the losses and casualties mounted to a
total of twenty-six aircraft and a hundred and sixteen men.
I seem to remember that it remained the worst week listed
in the records of Operation Xanadu.

To me the immediately shocking thing was the loss within
a few days of both Favell and Hathaway in what were,
after all, normal, undramatic airfield accidents. Normal!
Undramatic! My God, what words we are obliged to use
to strike a fine line of distinction! Yet one had been a carelessly misjudged landing, the other a faulty take-off. Nothing here of those hidden rock crags soaring into the sky,
the mauling of the hurricane, the loneliness of high, lost
places far away from anywhere. And these two had been
among the most experienced of all our pilots: men long since
matriculated to an elite group of the infallible. *Ah, Favell*

and Hathaway could fly a ship through thick clam chowder.
The accolade of one of them. Yet Favell and Hathaway, only
a few days after Peabody had offered the testimony, were
both dead—dead, bodiless charrings in two burnt-out patches
of scrub at opposite ends of Runway C. Names crossed off a
list. Images fading. Who could remember now the peculiar
trick of speech that gave affectation to Hathaway's comments? Or the bearlike steps of Favell's "Svenska Jazzenska"?
Algebraic factors now in a military equation. Concerned
with the ratio of expendability. Jottings in a Senator's notebook. Ashes in a jungle clearing. . . .

The weather continued to be bad, but because of reverses
in the combat areas the logistical pressures grew even more
severe. By Tuesday evening the growth of tension among
the pilots—the veterans, too, not just the rookies—had become an almost tangible force; it was almost as if they could
smell the approach of selective disaster without knowing
any of the rules of selection. Still, had it not been for the
bombastic stupidity of Vince Readaway I doubt if anything
would have happened: they were under stress, certainly, but
they were very far from demoralized.

They were, I imagine, beginning to grow a little uneasy
at the continued presence among them of so many outsiders.
This was natural enough, I suppose; under added strain or
an increase in hazard such a group of men would tend to
draw more tightly together into an almost esoteric community sharing—and being unable to share with others outside
the community—both an expert lore and the experience of a
mutual danger. At the same time I, being an outsider, could
feel a certain sympathy for the visitors. They were not weath-
erbound in Zone Q-4 by their own choice. By Frisk's error
in insisting on his concert, perhaps, but not willfully. That
area was never marked with asterisks in the guide books as
an ideal place for a stopover vacation, especially during the

monsoon! They had not deliberately sought the hospitality of the pilots' mess; it had been offered to them. It seemed to me to be hardly logical to resent them now simply on the grounds that it had not stopped raining. A situation which could not be remedied should, I felt, at least be tolerated.

The trouble was that it was not at all easy to tolerate Vince Readaway.

He had been disliked from the very beginning. Among other men prejudices will always spring easily against the Vince Readaways of this world, but in this case there were other factors of distaste. The latent serviceman-civilian animosity—the active and the non-active, the doers and the don't-doers. Then, his oppressive handsomeness. His clothes. His success. The stupendous amounts of money he earned simply for being handsome and able to cope with certain simple charades. And, above all, his own unfortunate personality.

He had not—I am sure he *could* not—set himself out to please. To impress, yes, but that is a quite different thing, especially as he could never be even faintly impressed himself. From the very moment he had appeared in Zone Q-4 he had been condescending, self-opinionated, ill-mannered, insulting. He was an exhibitionist and a narcissist. He needled the young pilots in the bar at every provocation, and often when there was no provocation, and they were the ones, presumably, who would be stuck with his bar bills. The end of the bar near the bamboo board he had virtually "occupied," but then the general impression he gave was not at all that he was a guest but that he was there by some special Hollywood Act of Annexation! Even before this particular Tuesday evening it had occurred to me that there would have to be a limit to what his hosts could stand. But the way it happened was very different from what I expected.

When I got to the mess around eight o'clock that evening, Readaway was the only one of the outsiders who was there. The place was not too crowded. Peabody was back and so was young Strawlings—still with that morose, haunted expression on his face, although, as I learnt later, he had graduated the day before out of the crew-killing gasoline tankers into one of the general freight squadrons. Steve Bellini was there, too, but he was alone at a table away from all the others. The table was stacked with empty beer bottles, and he was crouched over them with a morose, withdrawn expression on his ugly face. I was surprised to see Captain Benjamin in the mess, sitting at a table with Tommy Updike, who was the ranking officer of the 69th Parachute Squadron. Next to them, at a table alone, was another unusual visitor—Colonel Dorenfurst, a spare, grey, secretive man who was the commanding officer of the security guard at Rampart—and something never specified which was very much more than that. And since he almost never visited Kansas there was something distinctly intriguing in the picture of him sitting there by himself, sipping some liqueur. He greeted me with a slight nod and a chill, mechanical smile. I moved past his table to where Benjamin was sitting.

Readaway at this time was lounging at "his" end of the bar, clutching a highball, his black hair falling in a thick lock across his forehead, his eyes heavy with alcohol and boredom. Just behind him Bellini brooded over his beer.

Peabody, his back against the bar, was talking to a group of pilots. "You can't follow a pattern of weather," he was saying. "Something happens east or south of us, it doesn't follow that's the way it's going to happen where we are."

Shop talk. Interesting enough. To us, at any rate, because one way or another we were all involved in it. (No doubt to Readaway it was boring, but there were racks of magazines in the corner.) Listening, it was a few minutes before

I was able to tie the ends together. Peabody had just come back from a special courier flight to the zone which neighboured us on the south, some three hundred miles away. It was designated as Zone Q-1. It was also a complex of airfields, but with an important difference: where we were "logistical," Q-1 was "operational." It was directly involved in the combat area, and from time to time suffered enemy air attack, often violently. Even geographically and climatically it was almost another world from ours because it was far off the main spur of the great alps, although it did suffer both from the build-up and the backlash of our weather. It was to this zone that Peabody was referring when he said:

"Well, okay—look at it this way. Night before last we had it easy as a piece of pie. But *they* didn't. They got all the weather we missed out on. Two of their ships iced up and spun in. One had forty-six guys aboard and the other had thirty-eight. Add eight for crews and that's ninety-two. And not one goddam survivor."

"That's a lot of horse-shit," said Readaway thickly.

There was a moment of stunned silence as we all turned and looked at him. He was leaning across the counter, his drink in his hand, a cool supercilious smile twisting his mouth. He straightened up and looked at Peabody.

"Sorry." Peabody stared back at him. "You were saying?"

"I was saying, my friend, that's a lot of horse-shit you're feeding us," Readaway said distinctly.

I could feel the tension mounting around us, filling the whole room, as Peabody said, "What makes you think that, Mr. Readaway?" His voice was very quiet, without anger.

"They don't fly passenger ships in the rain, that's why, Buster. That's why. They're not allowed. There's a law against it."

"But I wasn't referring to passenger ships." Not a change

[167]

of inflection in Peabody's voice. Nor of expression on his brown, lean face. "I was referring to two ships that were bringing back wounded. These happened to be some Marines, Mr. Readaway, who'd gotten themselves hurt. Maybe they'd gotten themselves so badly hurt that whoever was in charge of the situation thought they couldn't wait about too long. Maybe they had to be shipped out in a hurry, rain or not. So they flew 'em into a mountain and now they're all dead, so it doesn't matter anyway. They could have waited for the rain to stop, I guess. The point is, Mr. Readaway, that they weren't passengers. They weren't *passengers,* Mr. Readaway, in the sense that one of these days, when the rain stops, you'll be able to be a passenger again."

"Ah, what the hell!" Readaway flung his hand in an impatient gesture that dismissed the explanation as if it had never been given. I realized suddenly how drunk he was. "All you bastards make me sick! Christ! You guys don't talk about anything but rain and weather and the ten best reasons for not having to get off your asses and go out and fly an airplane. No—the hell with that . . . stay in this goddam bar where it's nice and cosy. Just call for the wine card. Brother, we have everything—but *everything* in this joint! Why go out in the rain?"

He drained the rest of his drink at a gulp—a somewhat obvious gesture of defiance—pushed the empty glass across the counter, and slapped his hand down heavily. The corporal, watching intently from further along the bar, made no move whatever. The rest of us were so dumbfounded that we could only stare at him in amazed silence. He was drunk enough to see this as a weakness on our part, because he looked insolently from one face to the other, his smile broadening. At Peabody, Strawlings, Updike, at Leason and Buehle and O'Caffrey—three of the other freight pilots—at

[168]

Benjamin and me. With a slow gesture he pushed his lock of hair back, and hooked his thumbs in his belt, and said:

"Okay—so these other guys hit the deck and get killed. That's too bad. Sure, it's too bad. Do you think I don't feel that too? But those guys were *in* it, for God's sake! Weren't they? They were out there. They were doing something. They weren't just a bunch of corn-fed jerks sitting around in cane chairs waiting for the silver lining. Listen, my friends"—he must have felt that he had got away with it, for he was all bumptious arrogance now—"there's supposed to be a *war* on, isn't there? Or have I got it wrong? Maybe—"

"Why, you loused-up sonofabitch!" It was Captain Updike who made the move, thrusting towards him, swinging. And it was Captain Benjamin who grabbed at his arm and said:

"Hold it, Tommy. Let him alone. He's so plastered he doesn't know what he's saying."

"The hell he doesn't!" O'Caffrey growled. "He wants to make something of—"

"Lay off," said Peabody firmly. "Benjamin's right. I suggest, Readaway," he said coldly, "it might be a good thing all round if you took a little air. It's kind of hotting up in here."

Readaway seemed about to say something, then looked around and blinked uncertainly at the ring of hostile faces. He was drunk, yes, but not drunk enough to be unaware of the danger to himself that now existed in the situation he had deliberately provoked. I realized, watching him, that he-man Vince, the hero of the mesa, was something of a coward at heart.

I knew that the situation was past retrieving when I saw Bellini moving from his table. His face was working. And he was drunker than Readaway.

He said nothing as he took the actor by the shoulder and twisted him around as if he were a child, and his big scarred fist bunched up the shoulder of Readaway's shantung shirt as he dragged him close. Readaway was head and shoulders taller than Bellini, but the Canadian had the shoulders of a bull, and nobody but Bellini knew the roots that went deep down from the awful flowering of his rage. With one hand he held Readaway in front of him—he had to look up into the flushed, startled, scared face above the twisted collar of the shantung shirt—and he shook him slowly backward and forward while he talked to him. His voice was low and hoarse and thick with anger and contempt.

"Listen to me, you pig's ass," he began threateningly. "You want to fly in the rain, I'll goddam fly you in the rain. By Jesus, bud, I'll take *you* flying in the rain! I'll get a special check-out flight tomorrow just to take you flying in the rain. Sure, I'll fly you through rocks, Jasper, and I'll fly you through fire and ice and wind, and I'll fly you through blue lights that'll burn your ass out! You wanner come with me, big boy? I'll fly you through the bones and guts and bowels of a whole bunch of corn-fed jerks who've been sitting round in cane chairs waiting for the silver lining. I'll goddam fly you, Billy the Kid, through burning gasoline and trees charred to cinder stumps and rocks plastered all over with little bits of what's left of bums like us. And then when I've gotten sick of flying you around, wise guy, I'll toss you out where the icicles are hanging like the piece of shit you are. But before we do that, Mister Big Mouth, there's just one thing I'd kinda like to do right now, and—"

The others had been waiting for it too, and they jumped on him as his fist bunched and began to swing, and together Bellini and Peabody and O'Caffrey fell to the floor, violently entangled, as Readaway staggered back, pale and coughing, and slumped against the bar.

[170]

Benjamin grabbed his arm and shook him upright. "Beat it," he said curtly.

"Bastards got no goddam sense of humour," Readaway blustered, shaking his head wildly. "They think—"

"Beat it, I said," Benjamin repeated in a tight, flat voice. "Skip the explanations. Just get the hell out of here. When everyone's cooled off maybe you can tell us about it."

Readaway opened his mouth as if he intended to go on with his defence, but the New York criminal defence lawyer wasn't interested in hearing about it, and neither was I, and together we steered him to the door and got his raincoat and put him out into the wet night.

By the time we had done this the uproar at the other end of the bar had subsided, and Bellini, rocking a little, was propped up against the bar and Peabody was talking to him in a low, earnest voice. A few minutes later the Canadian went back to the table where he had been sitting, and for a long time he stared down at his hands, and then with a sudden furious gesture he swept all the empty beer bottles into a crashing litter on the floor. Nothing was said. Heads turned, and turned back again. The corporal took his broom and pan and the pail from behind the bar and whistled as he cleared up the wreckage. And then, on his own account, he took a fresh bottle of beer and a clean glass across to Bellini's table, and went back to the bar, still whistling.

The night was far from over yet, though.

The others came in about twenty minutes later, Jane Carson and Jack and Judy, and Peabody went across to greet them.

The secretive Colonel Dorenfurst had vanished—"gone" was too mere a word for such an Indian Rope Trick disappearance!—and even his little liqueur glass had vanished with him.

"What happened to Dorenfurst?" I said to Benjamin. "Did he slip through a trap door?"

Benjamin grinned. "The FBI has a special selection board to pick those guys," he said. "They have to pass a test to prove they're made from invisible ink and not flesh-and-blood. If you ever catch one you hold him over a hot flame and see."

We were talking of other things by the time Steve Bellini got up from his table and began to move down the bar towards us. He walked unsteadily, planting each foot well apart at each step, carefully guiding himself along with a safe hand on the edge of the bar counter. His hand gripped each of our shoulders in turn as he detoured around us. He was grunting softly to himself. I had a momentary thought of detaining him, but Peabody was down there, so I let him go past.

"Hi, Beauty," he said to Judy Consadine, and gave her a clumsy bear hug of an embrace that almost toppled both of them to the floor. She laughed and pushed him into a chair quite firmly, but with evident affection, and I heard Peabody say good-naturedly, "Take it easy, Steve. You behave yourself." Bellini blinked round at them all, made a kind of wavering salute to Jane Carson, and slumped deeply into his chair.

"He's okay," said Benjamin. "What were you saying?"

Nothing happened for ten minutes or so. Strawlings had left us to brood in solitude further along the bar. Jack Consadine was drawing airplanes. The corporal was pulling the cork on a fresh bottle of Campari when Benjamin touched me on the arm and said very quietly, "Jacob, suppose we go down there for a bit and sit in on it."

His legal training, I imagine. That experience of the

[172]

nuances of a courtroom's atmosphere. The ability to smell the subtle elements of a juryman's hostility, a witness's duplicity, a judge's prejudices, an opposing counsel's craftiness. At any rate, he had sensed the trouble at the central table before I had even the faintest suspicion that anything was amiss, although in an almost subconscious way a tiny part of my attention had remained with the group from the moment Bellini had gone there.

Benjamin's move was astute enough and quick enough—almost everything Benjamin did was astute and almost everything was quick—for us to get within an ace of saving the situation. The very physical fact of our intrusion—the moving of chairs, the introduction of Benjamin to Judy, his recognition of Jane Carson, Peabody's obviously rather deliberate little explanation of the work of Search-and-Rescue —was enough to establish new tangents for everybody.

For a time Bellini sat quietly, his thick body slumped in the cane chair, his legs sprawled, his arms loosely hanging. Below the widow's peak dart of his hair his forehead was beaded with sweat, and his flat, pockmarked, ugly pug's face was moist and blotched. He was looking directly across at Jane Carson, but his eyes were quite blank, and from time to time he would close them and seem to sleep.

He was like this when suddenly he opened his eyes, blinked a moment, and said, "Hathaway's dead." Again his eyes had nothing in them, except a brown fluid, like treacle spreading.

"That's right," said Peabody quietly. "That's the way it is, Steve."

"Pete Hathaway got burnt out," said Bellini in a low, dull voice.

"Sure, that's too bad," Peabody said soothingly.

"Who was talking to you?" Bellini's voice grated.

"Take it easy, Steve." The guarded watchfulness in Pea-

[173]

body's eyes made me realize that this had been going on before we joined the group.

"I said who was talking to you?" Bellini repeated, with a thicker truculence. His eyes were just as blank as they had been before.

"Now then, Steve," said Judy Consadine in a gently placatory tone, and she reached across and put her hand on his arm. "Major Peabody is just saying that we all do understand how you feel about it, and he—"

"My remarks were not addressed to Major Peabody. They were addressed to Miss Jane Carson." He spoke with the stiff, stilted enunciation of drunkenness, and every sibilant was so slurred that he had to work his jaw to make the sound that followed. With elaborate care he moved Judy's hand off his arm. "You see, Miss Carson and I were . . . were particular friends of Pete Hathaway. That's so, Miss Carson, eh?" There was something terrible about the question coming from beneath those blank, brown, misty eyes.

"Well, I didn't know him the way you knew him, Captain Bellini," she said, and her voice was soft and compassionate. "But I'd met him. And I liked him very much. We were all sorry—"

"He talked t'me about you . . . sure, just before he went off on that flight. *Flight?* One hell of a flight, ugh? He sort of had you—"

"Oh, Steve," Judy put in imploringly, "you must try to stop thinking about it. Stop brooding. You—"

"Shut up, Beauty. I wanna talk t' Miss Carson."

"Yes, but later, Steve," Benjamin suggested quietly. "You're upset now. Some other time. This isn't the time for it, nor the place."

"Sure it's the time. Sure it's the place. Where else d'you talk about a guy that got himself burnt out? You don't think I'm entitled to get the record straight for a buddy of mine

[174]

who got himself burnt out? Okay. Don't listen. You don't have to listen . . . Nobody was talking to you anyway. I made it clear I was talking to Miss Carson, didn't I? So suppose we just do that, Jane . . . suppose we just talk it out together, eh? Just you and me. The poor dead bastard's very special friends. No flowers. No cards. No tears. Jus' talk between friends."

"Steve! I want you to stop this!" Peabody's voice was firmer.

But Jane Carson lifted her hand and said, "Let him talk it out. Please, it's best. Let him say what he wants to say. Can't you see this is something he has to do . . . something he *needs* to do. You just go on, Captain Bellini. You talk it out with me."

"Sure, that's what I said. What I'm trying to point out is that he . . . he sort of had you on his mind in a big way, Miss Carson. He talked to me. We were buddies, see. He talked to me. He was pretty excited about the night before . . . and sure, why not? . . . and then he got his bowels in a tangle because he was the one who drew that number for the S.F. run. I reckon he wanted to stay on here and have another night of it, but that's the way it goes, eh? Now what we got to do, Miss Carson, is we got to try and work out why he went in like that . . . and I can't figure it any other way than that . . ."

"Than what?" she asked him gently.

"Than what I said. Having *you* on his mind. Pete Hathaway just couldn't have nosed a ship in like that unless his mind was kinda twisted up with other things. Well, that's the way I figure it."

"That just isn't true, Steve." It was my turn to try to interpolate reason. "I heard his take-off through the control speaker. He was—"

"Sure, sure, sure." He waved impatiently. "Except you

[175]

couldn't fly an airplane from here to that goddam bar. So what the hell! How would you *know*? Listen, I'm not bitching anybody, brother, I'm just trying to put the record straight for a guy who burnt out." He leaned forward, his head lowered a little, his eyes glowering around. They were still swimmy but no longer blank; there seemed to be little red flares burning behind the moistness, and there were beads of sweat caught all along his heavy eyebrows. His jaws were working and twitching as if he was grinding his teeth. "For God's sake," he snarled, "I don't give a good goddam if some dame with hot pants gives the treatment to this slob or that slob around the base, but I feel kinda sore when it screws up a guy like Pete Hathaway. It seems to me—"

"It seems to me," Peabody said, rising, "you've said what you had to say. And a bit more. So—"

"Oh, for pete's sake! why do you all *sit there* and let this drunken bum spew out his dirty insults!" It was Strawlings, white as a sheet, his face a grimace of torment, his voice edging on the hysterical. He rushed towards us, his big awkward hands and arms reaching out as if he would tear Bellini apart. "Why do you let him go on with this vile, lying, wicked—"

He stumbled into a chair and staggered as Bellini rose to meet him, sending his own chair over with a clatter. The Canadian flung a wild, round-arm swing that missed Strawlings by a yard. The impetus took him clean off balance and he fell across the table with a crash that sent glasses and ash trays flying. Strawlings leapt upon him. Judy Consadine screamed. Benjamin and I grappled with Strawlings, and although he struggled like a maniac we were able to drag him off. Bellini rose slowly and turned and bunched his fists, and Peabody took one slow step forward and caught him on the jaw with a hard straight right that sent him over backwards like a falling tree. The corporal came from behind the bar with his broom and ash tray and pail.

Peabody helped drag Bellini to the wash room and took him home afterwards. I don't know who took Jane Carson to her quarters. The Consadines, I expect. Benjamin and I went back to the pilots' quarters with Strawlings. The kid was in too much of a state to say anything, and we didn't ask questions or make comments. He was pretty much a mess when we left him on his bed.

"Quite a night, one way and another!" I said when we were coming back.

Benjamin nodded. "You know, it's a funny thing, Jacob," he said, "but I only get around to that bar about once every three months, and damn it, if something doesn't happen every time. Whenever I go it's Bingo Night. Last time I was there was when that crazy psycho from Texas brought his .45 along and began shooting bottles off the racks."

"Nobody was psycho tonight," I said. "Just drunk. Bellini and Readaway, I mean."

"Oh, everybody's psycho, I guess. This way or that way."

"Usually it's under control."

"Sure. Usually." He was thoughtful for a few moments, then: "That's the thing I learnt around the courts back home," he said. "Control is one thing and behaviour is another, and there's a reason for everything. The thing is to look for the reason because you can't contend with the demonstration unless you know what's behind it. Yet the hardest thing in the world sometimes is to find that reason. I guess it gets buried right away in a lot of other clutter, and most of us have more clutter than anything else."

"I think the reasons for what happened tonight are clear enough."

"Some of them, yes. Sure, some of them stick out like sore thumbs. Readaway's been sitting around here in the

[177]

rain a whole week now, and he's bored and you can't blame him. Well, he'd be an irritant anywhere, but he just comes out worse here, where he doesn't fit in with anything. Then this poor young bastard Strawlings is just a straight case of injured innocence . . . Adam suddenly confronted by Original Sin. He's crazy about Jane Carson, and he gets screwed up into a knot of real old-fashioned green-eyed jealousy if any other man pays the least attention to her. Poor bastard! At that age, with that type, there has to be a *la belle dame sans merci.* He's just dead unlucky, drawing one like her. Bellini isn't quite so clear cut, I think. Sure, he's on the edge of his nerves, and he was plenty high, but to look at him you wouldn't really think he's the sort of man who could know grief like that and show it. Real grief, I mean. The way it comes out it looks maudlin and melodramatic and oversentimental, but I'm pretty sure that isn't the way it is."

"Peabody had to hit him."

"Peabody had to hit him, sure. Peabody's got his own raw edge of nerves, too."

For a few moments we splashed on through the rain in thoughtful silence.

Then, "You haven't said anything about Jane Carson," I said.

He laughed softly. "Was I supposed to run through the whole cast list?" he asked.

"She's involved."

"Jane Carson's a woman," he said. "A special sort of woman. The sort of woman who has a way of sliding out of the law books, the standard references. You can't look up precedents on the Jane Carsons because they establish their own precedents as they go along. They're tricky, because they're not bound by the rules. And maybe they don't have so much of the clutter. They have something else that keeps the reasons buried." He put his hand lightly on the shoulder

[178]

of my oilskin. "Well, this is the parting of the ways, Jacob. See you tomorrow."

"Where are you going?"

"I'll go across to the shack for an hour or so. I go there most nights. It's a quiet place to read up on things."

16

THE following morning I set out deliberately to try to explore Jane Carson's world. I decided that I would reverse the situation and ask *her* to go walking with me. In the rain.

I thought about it a lot while I was having breakfast: of what Benjamin had said and the way he had stalled, of the implications behind Bellini's outburst and young Strawlings' loss of control, and I told myself that I wanted her to understand exactly *why* the tensions had exploded the way they had.

When I had finished my coffee and checked at my office I walked across to the billetings section. I had not expected Fleming to be there so early, but he was behind his desk, sorting through yellow filing cards.

"Could you give me the number of Miss Carson's room?" I said, and he looked across at me sharply.

"What the hell do you want that for?" he asked.

"Just want to ask her about something. Why?" I smiled. "Is she off-limits?"

"Sixty-one," he said. "Block J." His eyes never left my face. A curious, speculating expression in them.

"Sixty-one. Block J." I repeated the words, listening for the echo of the chord they struck. "But isn't Readaway—"

"He's sixty-two. Right next door. Neighbours." He gave me a wink of complicity. "It's okay, Jake, you don't have to worry. There's no connecting door. I guess it wouldn't matter if there was. They'd be over all that by now."

"Over all what?"

"All that. For pete's sake, man, he was her husband once."

"He was *what?*"

"Hell, what's so odd about that? They're from Hollywood, aren't they? The way they intermarry there it's a wonder all the issue isn't cretinous. After they made *Birth of a Nation* they moved the Ozarks west. Readaway was her *first* husband," he explained with an elaborate show of patience. "She's had others since. She hasn't got one now. Check?"

"I see." I nodded.

"I gather he didn't amount to much. A marriage of convenience, maybe. It only lasted a few months, and anyway that was years back. A case of the first shall be least, if you like to put it that way. Still, I guess our boy Vince was the first to plant the flag. Legally, I mean." He grinned unpleasantly.

I nodded, and thanked him, and went out into the rain.

It was a morning different from those we had had. The rain was light and soft in its descent. More than a drizzle, but less than what we had grown accustomed to. The air was paler and lit by some mysterious pearly radiance—an emanation from some light source that seemed more remote than the sun. There was no line of definition or any change of tone to form a sky. The silvery, wet haze at ground level and the misty damp globe above—how far above? . . . at arm's length or a thousand feet away?—were parts of the same thing. Walking across to Block J was like moving

[181]

through the centre of a damp and shining bubble. It was already hot, and intensely humid.

The door of sixty-two was open. I could see the rumpled bed and the hooked-back folds of the mosquito curtain, but the room was empty. I had never thought of Readaway as the early bird.

I passed along to sixty-one and knocked softly. There was almost no interval of waiting before she opened the door. Her hair was swept up high, carelessly, and caught with a black ribbon. She was wearing a plain yellow dressing gown, man style, with patch pockets. Her feet were bare.

"Hullo." She seemed surprised. "You're an early caller."

"Good morning. I came over to see if you'd like to take a walk with me."

"In the rain?"

"Of course. I shouldn't have dreamt of suggesting it on a nice day."

She laughed softly. "Can you give me ten minutes? I have to dress. And I haven't had breakfast."

"We can get coffee and something to eat on the way, at the airfield. How does that sound?"

"Fine. Where are we going?"

"Just walking. Well, there are a couple of things I could attend to in the village. If you'd like to come with me?"

"I'd love it."

"Splendid. I shall call back for you in ten minutes or so."

"Why? You can come in here and wait." Again that soft laugh. "It really is quite proper. I practically have an apartment. Well, they've given me a screen. Do come in."

It was like all the other transient quarters, except for the feminine things around and the jars on the table and the four-leaf bamboo screen that divided off one corner of the room. Her bed had not been slept in or she had already made it up herself. The room was scrupulously neat. She motioned me to a chair and went behind the screen. I had the faint, pleasant woman-smell in my nostrils; more an emanation than a fragrance . . . how long was it since I had been in a woman's room?

"You must be getting pretty sick of all this by now," I said. "Stuck in a place like this. Living out of a suitcase. Having to slog a hundred yards through the rain to get a cup of coffee."

"Oh, I don't mind it," said the voice from behind the screen. "I'm really enjoying it. Well . . . enjoying most of it. It's strange to me, and rather exciting."

When she came from behind the screen she was wearing a simple oatmeal-coloured dress of cotton, quite plain, with a shirt front. She always wore the simplest clothes. I never saw Jane Carson with a bow or a flounce or any of the other curlicues that women seem to love. I don't remember that she ever wore jewellery. She went across to the mirror to brush her hair, then left it loose while she put on her raincoat and sou'wester and the big gumboots Peabody had found for her. Evidently she used no make-up.

"I'm ready when you are," she said, smiling at me.

"Let's go."

"Do we have to go to the airfield? Isn't there some place in the village where we can get coffee or something?"

"There is, yes." I hesitated. "I'm afraid it's the local brothel, though. There's no other place."

"Why, it sounds wonderful. It's every woman's desire, isn't it, to be able to go to one of those places, just to see?"

"Oh, you won't *see* anything. We're out of business hours. You'll only see Armand. Still, he does make good coffee. He has some private black market arrangement with the PX."

We approached the village through a mad clamour of frogs. The curious atmosphere of the morning seemed to

[183]

have driven them into some frenzy of vocal activity—mating, or merely barometric pressure?—and passing some of the swampier patches we could barely hear ourselves talk for the demented croakings and whistlings and gobblings of their grotesque batrachian chorus. It was a hidden madness. We did not see a single frog. At the last fields before the untidy sprawl of the village huts we ran into the butterflies.

This I had seen before many times. It was a manifestation of every monsoon, yet I never found an entirely satisfactory explanation for it. The butterflies would come from somewhere in swarms of hundreds of thousands—of millions, perhaps, for who could count the components of that pale, shimmering veil of movement trembling across the rain-soaked fields? They would dance down from the misty trees in vast clouds of vibrating colour. Small butterflies, most of them, of a lemon-yellow colour, but there was never any total concentration of a single species for among the fluttering lemon mass one would see black butterflies and red, violet and viridian and blue, white ones and orange ones; big creatures six or eight inches across and dwarfs scarcely bigger than gadflies; graceful swallowtails and stubby-winged varieties of drabber hue that looked more like moths —all involved and fluttering in this phenomenal rite of light and air and moisture. A dance of death, really, because they would go down one by one, all of them eventually, I suppose, borne under the weight of the rain; going down in a desperate palpitating resistance, then quivering for a moment or two in the brown puddles or the sodden grass, and finally quite still, as gay and lifeless as blown petals.

I shall always see the chromatic shimmer of myriad butterflies when I think of Jane Carson, because she stopped at the irrigation channel that gave boundary to the first field, and after a speechless, almost breathless pause she jumped the narrow barrier and walked in among the whirling, flying specks of colour. I followed her.

"But . . . but this is so beautiful . . . so wonderful!" she whispered. "Heavens! I've never seen anything like it before! Does . . . do they often come like this?"

"No, not often. About once every year. It's sad in a way. They're dying all around you."

"In a way that makes it more beautiful, don't you think?"

I had to pause before I could answer her, because her own loveliness was enough to make one catch one's breath. She was standing ankle-deep in the soaking, vivid emerald of the young grass, stooped over a little, and the field stretched away behind her as a glossy green background to the sweep of her tawny hair underneath the wet grey hat. Her eyes were greener than the grass, her lips as red as the butterfly which seemed to dance upon her shoulder. And behind her, shimmering in the air like a pointillist mirage of colour, the drifting clouds of living vapour danced and fell.

"I think they're going away." I could think of nothing else to say.

And they were. What strange natural magic called them? What made them all, as if a signal had been given, turn at once in their countless, confused variety, and begin to fly away towards the distant perimeter of the field? The vast cloud receded, rising and falling, dancing onward, fading into something hardly less nebulous than the grey mistiness of the day, then turning in unison to make a brief, bright kaleidoscope in the air as if a rainbow had splintered into a million fragments. Quite suddenly they vaulted the dark line of hedge that marked the far limits of the field and vanished. All around us the dead were scattered, in the long grass, across the spikes of new grain, on the clods and hummocks of shiny clay, drifting this way and that in the uncertain eddies of the water channel, as if the dying flowers of a whole autumn had been shaken to the ground.

For what seemed a long time she stood quite still, staring away towards the far, stained outline of the hedge, and when finally she turned to me—so slowly she turned—I saw that her eyes were glittering and wet. "Thank you," she said, almost inaudibly.

"For what?"

"For that," she said simply. She bent over and picked up the body of a small orange butterfly and held it in her hand, then dropped it gently into the water channel and watched it drift slowly away.

"Good heavens, I didn't arrange *that*. It happens. But it's not predictable. It can't be arranged. Nobody can tell *when* they'll come, any more than they can say where they come from, or where they're trying to get to. It just . . . well, happens. You were jolly lucky to see it."

"Yes." She smiled a little. "I wondered if that was why you asked me to come walking."

"No."

"To hear the frogs then?" The smile at her lips grew more pronounced, twisting her mouth in that odd, attractive tilt of amusement.

"No."

"I guess it had better be the direct question then. Why did you want me to come?"

"I just wanted to talk to you."

"About what?"

"About last night," I said deliberately.

"Last night?" The smile faded.

"Yes. About Steve Bellini, rather. I don't want you to . . . well, to get him wrong."

"I don't think I got him wrong," she said guardedly, her eyes watching me.

[186]

"I thought I'd try to explain him, that's all." There was suddenly something strangely private and appropriate in my talking to her in this field among the dead butterflies with the soft rain falling into the soaking grass. So soft the rain that it caressed the red-brown water in the channels into an almost breathing movement without pricking the surface, and the wings of the fallen butterflies stayed stiff and glossy, not bedraggled at all. In this peasant's field we seemed more isolated than ever within the damp and shining bubble of the day. In every quarter the world ended at a given point just beyond our reach. Certainly we could not prick the skin of the bubble, but neither could anything reach us from beyond the skin. To one side of us the sordid purlieus of Leromenos were not visible, did not exist, could give no substance to the fact of coffee being prepared in a ramshackle bordello owned by a degenerate half-caste. To the other side, the calculated efficiency of Kansas and Rampart, the mess lines and the fatigue parties, the metallic agitations of the base, were less real than the dead carcass of a lemon-yellow butterfly stuck by the rain to the floppy brim of Jane Carson's sou'wester. Outside did not exist. The melee in the bar the night before had no more continuing reality than the mist of butterflies that had danced in the rain and vanished across the distant hedge. For the discussion I felt to be necessary, I told myself, the circumstances were safe.

"What I wanted to say," I began slowly, "is that Bellini's own position should be appreciated. He was pretty drunk, of course. And then he had been rather badly affected by Hathaway's death—they were the only two Commonwealth men in the group, you see—and the accident had cut him up considerably. Not only that, there was a rather nasty incident just before you came to the bar. It was Readaway who was responsible, but Bellini got involved in it, and I expect that after that he was in the mood to make trouble. I do want you to understand all this. He's a good chap, actually, and—"

"Jacob." Her voice was very soft, but her use of my Christian name, for the first time, brought my explanation to an abrupt halt. "Jacob, are you trying to defend him or defend me?"

I made no reply.

"You are very innocent in some ways, aren't you?"

"*Innocent?*"

"Yes." For the moment she had nothing more to say. She just looked at me, with that odd, twisted little smile at her mouth, as if she were summing me up, speculating on my possibilities. She remained where she had turned away after following the dissolving flight of the butterflies across the hedge. We were still six yards apart from each other. The grass around her feet and all the ground between us was littered with the dead scraps of colour, like torn fragments of carnival paper. The rain hissed softly down upon the two of us. Even as I looked at her the dead yellow butterfly was washed from the brim of her hat, and it fluttered to the ground like an autumn leaf.

"I don't know," she said, and shook her head a little. "Maybe that's not what I mean at all. It's hard to find the right word. You are strange, I know that. Every person I talk to thinks you're strange. Don't get me wrong. They like you. But they all think there's something . . . well, something *odd* about you. Not just your being English, being different from them . . . I don't mean that. More intriguing than that. Maybe innocent isn't what I mean . . . maybe it's something else . . ."

"We were discussing Bellini," I said.

"*You* were discussing Bellini. I was discussing you."

"We weren't supposed to be."

"Well, we are," she said firmly, and came across the strip of wet ground that divided us. A fixed resolution seemed to move her towards me. Her face was set and determined, almost proud. Certainly—this was a thought that came later, for I was not at that moment aware of her intention— it was not at all the face of the confessor, for there was nothing of penitence in it, nor of guilt. Not even the face of the sinner appealing for sympathy or understanding. Just the face of Jane Carson with the rain on it, and her red-gold hair incandescent against the diminished enclosure of that damp dun day.

"But we'll talk about Captain Bellini first," she said surprisingly, "if that's what you want."

"Good. That *is* what I came to talk about."

"Did you object to what he had to say?"

"I didn't necessarily object to it. I wanted to explain it, that's all."

"Why? Why should you? He was justified in saying what he said. I invited him to say it, didn't I?" She paused then and looked at me carefully. "I knew what he was going to say."

"And you wanted him to?"

"I knew he *had* to. One way or another it had to come out of him. Peter Hathaway meant too much to him for him to keep it bottled up inside himself."

"You realize what he was implying?"

"I may be lots of things, Jacob," she said evenly, "but being a hypocrite isn't one of them. Oh, he'd gotten it twisted up. And he was drunk. But he wasn't telling lies. I don't happen to agree with his conclusion, that's all."

I left the question unstated.

"I did go to bed with Peter Hathaway the night before he was killed," she said. "But it doesn't follow that that makes me responsible for his death."

"You'd never even *met* Hathaway until the night before his death."

"That's right," she said, and her green eyes looked at me calmly. Her voice was set to a lower key and was not quite so resolute. "You see, Jacob, I'd honestly rather you heard it from me than get it bit by bit, the way you'd hear it from the others. I've been around. I know the way men talk. And I'm not blaming them either, do you understand? If they've got reason to think I act like a tramp I guess they're entitled to treat me like a tramp . . . to talk about me as if I were a tramp. That's the way it goes. A woman will always get out of it what she puts into it. At least that much. Maybe a whole lot more. And that's all right. You can't do a black thing at night and expect it to turn white in the daylight."

I looked down uneasily at the damp, dead butterflies strewn across the earth, at the muddy pools and the scribbled water channels trickling down the clods, thin and silvery like the trails of snails. There was a frog, a deep jade-green frog, squatting on the ridge of the irrigation dike, its swollen throat palpitating like a heartbeat. It made no sound, and after a while its back legs flexed and flicked and it was gone with a plop into the muddy water.

I made myself look up and meet her eyes.

"You had heard the stories anyway, hadn't you?" she asked quietly.

"I heard some gossip. I didn't give it all that much attention. With a crowd of chaps who've been away from wives and sweethearts for God knows how long, these are the stories one always hears. You said you know how men talk . . ." I broke off with a shrug, but I could see by her face that the lameness of my explanation seemed to offend her somehow; I realized, quite suddenly, that she was not asking to be excused or defended; her desire, rather, was to have it all exposed, and examined. So I said, "They talked

[190]

about you and . . . and Fleming." I spoke very carefully, hating myself for saying it and yet knowing it was essential that I should engage myself in some impossibly subtle exorcism which she felt to be necessary.

"Yes," she said, without a trace of emotion.

"And Strawlings?" I put it to her as a question. Best to clean it all out. Get it over and done with. Certainly the situation, however deeply one felt for her, was too untenable to be maintained for very long. I had a sudden recollection of Benjamin's comment the night before: there was no precedent for Jane Carson; she established her own precedents as she went along. Yet what woman's secret sense had told her to choose *me* for this bizarre moment of self-revelation? What freakish intuition had informed her that I was safe?

"Yes," she said again, but in a lower voice.

"Peabody?" I pursued the examination dully. The cold pungency of a courtroom examination. Or the calling of a roll?

"No!" The sudden vehemence of the denial startled me. She looked across at me quickly, her mouth firmly compressed. "No!" she repeated it flatly. "Not Major Peabody." She hesitated a little, then lifted her head higher, not really defiantly, but something like that. "I wanted to," she said steadily, so steadily that I could not help feeling that she was deliberately driving herself towards some mysterious goal of verbal expiation or absolution. Or perhaps it was no more than a determination to prove that hard core of honesty around which her strange, twisted, troubled character was built. "I wanted him to," she said. "But he wouldn't." Once again she paused. "I went to him twice. That was why I was late for that damned concert," she said with an inflection of bitterness. "I went to his room. I knew he had to go away and fly at ten, and I knew he was very upset about

[191]

that friend of his who was killed, and . . . and I tried to make him do it. But he wouldn't. I stayed with him until he had to take his gear and go. That was why I was late. That was why I ran out on it."

She stood there quite stiffly, looking at me, waiting. What reaction was expected of me? What was I supposed to say? "Why do you tell me, Jane?" I said. Whatever else had happened, we had clearly moved to the informality of Christian names. "Why do you feel that I have to know?"

"I . . . I'm not sure, Jacob." For the first time she seemed uncertain of her objective. "I think I *have* to talk to you. But I don't know why. It . . . it comes from inside, but I can't explain it . . ."

"I'm not standing in judgment on you," I said.

"I know you're not. Maybe that's why . . . why I have to tell you . . ."

"Well . . . as long as that's understood." I managed a smile. "Look, suppose we move on now and see about that coffee," I suggested. I mistrusted this new tangent. I had no intention of probing further. She had had her confessional, for what it had been worth to her. I had put my case for Bellini. There was nothing more to be said, nothing more that could be said without putting us on very false ground with each other. "I think it really is time we had that coffee," I said.

"Yes," she agreed, and without another word she followed me across the irrigation channel to the road. Within five minutes the brown squalor of Leromenos formed its squat, shapeless ugliness out of the soft grey mist, and we walked all the way to Armand's place in silence.

He made good coffee and brought hot wholemeal cakes and wild honey for her to eat, and inquired, rather quizzically, for Fleming's health. I told him Fleming had been very busy with an unexpected influx of important people.

Armand smiled and went away, and after a time the lemon-skinned girls came from inside one by one and sat by the rattan screen to look at Jane Carson. Finally all twelve of them were there, silently staring. I tried to pick out the newcomer among them, but I could not identify her. An odd thought came to me. Was my role with Jane Carson the same, really, as my role with Fleming? Someone to talk to after the necessity of the act . . . return to the haven? Life very seldom neglected to seize an opportunity for irony.

While we were there the sky became much darker and the mistiness cleared away, and we could hear the growl and mutter of distant thunder from behind the black wall of trees. The rain grew heavier, and the verandah began to leak, and Armand sent all the little girls scuttling inside.

On the way back to the base we passed the field again, but all the butterflies had disappeared, their bright bodies washed away by the downpour or obliterated by the mud.

17

THE RUMBLE of distant thunder we had heard in Leromenos, so deceptively like the sound of the flatcars coming up the railroad from the south, and the quickening of the rain into what was a torrent by the middle of the day, were not so much ominous of what was to happen that day as symptomatic of what had already begun to occur. For the deterioration of our weather came several hours after the great electrical storms hit the alpine areas.

By the time I got back to the base much had already happened. My corporal met me in some agitation, with a fistful of messages. All but one were terse and urgent. Three were more or less duplicate requests from Benjamin to come at once to his office. Two were from Flight Control, one asking me to go without delay to control tower, the other—timed twenty minutes later—repeating the request and suggesting that I bring Benjamin with me. The corporal said that Benjamin was already there. There was a terse memorandum on one of General Frisk's pink forms ordering me to attend him in his office at 1500 hours. The remaining message, rather surprisingly, was a handwritten note from Senator Vancourt. Could he drop by some time at my quarters for a friendly chat? There was nothing pressing about it, just when I had an hour or so to spare. I folded his note with Frisk's pink form and stuffed them in my shirt pocket.

I drove the jeep fast around the airfield, skittering and side-slipping in the soft mud although the chains were clattering on the wheels, but in the control tower Benjamin greeted me with undisguised impatience.

"Holy mackerel! we've been looking all over. Where the hell have you been?"

"Walking. I went in to the village."

"You sure picked a fine time."

"What's the trouble?"

"Plenty! Five ships have spun in. In a bunch, almost. All outwards. And all on our side of the range."

"Crews?"

"We don't know. They all baled out. All five were in contact with Captain Peachey." So Captain Peachey was duty officer, and not Rogers. I hadn't even looked across at the control board. Now I saw that Pendlebury was not on duty either. "We've got fairly good plots," Benjamin said, "and now we want to put together the general S.R. picture. We've checked most of it, I think, but I guess you can fill in a detail or two. Let's get down to it with Garstein now."

It did not take very long. Not one of the five planes had got within a hundred miles of the main summits, and all had crashed in a fairly concentrated area that was reasonably accessible either by helicopter or from one of our outlying Search-and-Rescue depots. (We never found the crew nor any trace of one plane, but within the course of the next week fifteen of the sixteen men in the other four aircraft were brought in by helicopter, all alive and not very much the worse for their experiences.)

Each plane had reported violent gales, tremendous turbulence, and the most alarming electrical disturbances. In

[195]

the case of two planes no clue at all was offered as to the cause of disaster, only the desperately curt announcement that the crews were jumping. In the case of two of the others the airframes had been virtually wrenched apart by the violent up-draughts and down-draughts. The signal from the remaining plane was merely: "Losing height steadily. Can't pole-vault this one. We'll try it on foot."

By about two o'clock we had done all that could be done, and I drove back to the Search-and-Rescue hut with Benjamin and Sergeant Garstein. Benjamin brewed up some of his thick, black, almost undrinkable coffee while the sergeant splashed off to get rolls and cheese from the airfield canteen.

"Well, it's not as bad as it might have been," I said, as we chewed on the rolls and stared down at the maps spread all around us.

"A million bucks' worth of U.S. property junked in the air, and twenty human lives in jeopardy . . . bad enough," said Benjamin. He took every plane loss as a personal challenge to his ingenuity and his sense of duty.

"Well of course it's bad enough. But it *is* an accessible area. The chances this time are a good deal better than even money. And you don't often get odds as good as that in this gamble."

He nodded slowly, cupping his fingers around the thick mug. "You don't count up your day's winnings after the first race," he said, staring into the steam off the coffee. "The gamble hasn't started yet. I take it you haven't been in contact with the G side today."

I shook my head.

"Because they're the ones who are holding the bookie's bag. They're calling the odds. Not us. It seems, Jacob"—he looked up and smiled his thin tired smile at me—"we're involved in a military situation. Over there we've had what the communiqués call a 'temporary reverse.' It's all part of that business Peabody was talking about, where those Marines got kicked around. So what we've got to do is deliver—and deliver but fast—a lot of high priority stuff like bombs, ammunition, mortars, and medical supplies. So they posted the order at nine this morning. Simple enough. 'Freight schedules in all groups will be maintained strictly at F.E. standard from 1000 hours until further orders.' You know what that means?"

"Yes, I know." F.E. was the designation of "Flight Emergency" and the F.E. standard simply meant that no freight schedules were permitted to spread beyond the three-minute interval between planes taking off for the designated emergency area. Regardless of weather conditions. Presumably, regardless of losses also, although this was not specified. The Law of Expendability, at any rate. Logical enough, thinking of those poor devils of Marines. Logical enough anyway. We might lose some men and some material, but we were not a combat area; our job was only to deliver what was needed. Our losses would be slight compared with the losses already sustained in the area of "temporary reverse"; negligible compared with what we might be able to prevent. Yes, logical enough. Yet how sad that the logic of war could not hear the thin sound of a voice coming through the crackle of static to say, "Can't pole-vault this one. We'll try it on foot." (It was his plane we never found.)

I drove the jeep straight across to Frisk's office, and got there a minute or two before three. I knew as soon as I was admitted that he was in a bad mood. You could tell that, anyway, by Allison's face. Frisk came straight to the point.

"Strickland," he said brusquely, "those natives of yours at Rampart." They were always "my" natives when something was wrong. "I want a sharper check kept on them.

We're getting complaints. Snooping. Rubbernecking around. I don't like that. Neither does Colonel Dorenfurst."

"Yes, sir. But what *are* the complaints exactly?"

"I've just told you, man. Snooping. Meddling in things that don't concern them."

"I don't see how they can be. There are five work parties detailed to Rampart. They're under picked overseers. They work with a security guard. They're checked at the gates going in and coming out. They're trucked straight back to their own compounds. Frankly, sir, I don't see how there is any way for them to . . . to snoop."

"Well, you check, Strickland. They're slippery as eels, these goddam niggers. You've got to watch 'em all the time. I don't want these complaints to continue, that's all. Make a check on your overseers, too. Wouldn't trust any of 'em."

"Yes, sir." He frowned up at me and lowered his fine white head. I waited a moment. "There's nothing else?" I said.

"That's all." He tapped irritably at his blotter with the miniature *kukri*. "Unless you know when this damnable lousy weather is going to let up on us," he said sourly.

"No, sir, I don't know that."

"I'm damned sick of it!" he said fiercely, and glared at me as if I were to blame.

"Yes, I think we all are, General."

"Are we? Hmmm. All right. That's all, Strickland. Allison, let's get on with these orders."

Since it would still be more than two hours before the Rampart gangs finished their day's work, I turned the jeep and drove across to the guarded airfield. It was the first time I had ever gone there without Frisk in attendance. I told the sentry at the gate that I wanted to see Colonel Dorenfurst, and I was instructed to wait in the jeep until he phoned through. After about five minutes two of the white-helmeted guards—one with a Tommy gun and the other with a .45—came across from the administrative block, and escorted me back there, one on either side, not talking. I felt like a prisoner on his way to Alcatraz.

Colonel Dorenfurst was in his neat, bare office, sorting through folders in a tall, olive-green, steel filing cabinet. He welcomed me with a faint smile and a gesture towards the hard chair beside his desk, frowned for a moment over the folders, then closed the cabinet and locked it. He turned then and leaned his spare figure against the cabinet, linked his fingers together, and said, "Now, Mr. Strickland. What can I do for you this afternoon?"

"I've just been with General Frisk," I explained. "He says there are some reasons for complaint against the native work gangs here at Rampart."

"Yes?" It was a prompt to continue, not an affirmative. His grey, metallic eyes examined me carefully.

"I'd like your permission to check with the gang over-seers," I said. "I know them all. I consider them reliable men."

"What precisely are these complaints, Mr. Strickland?" he asked, with a subdued interest.

"The General's word for it is 'snooping.' Rubbernecking around. He said you had objected."

"Did he?" He unclasped his fingers and passed one hand slowly over his neat grey hair, and a faint smile seemed to flick at his lips. I thought he had nothing more to say. My eyes moved around the bare, sterile room. Very secretive, like the man. Locked cabinets, screens across the windows, papers hidden in taped folders. No triangular name block on the desk. Not a single photograph. Not even an ash tray to point towards a human weakness. I thought of the tiny liqueur glass on the table in the pilots' mess. That would be the limit of Colonel Dorenfurst's excesses. "Did he make a specific statement," he said at last, "to the effect that I had complained about the conduct of the native workmen?"

"Well, that was the sense of it. He said he didn't like it and neither did you."

"Yes." His neat narrow fingers continued to smooth his neat grey hair. "In fact, Mr. Strickland, I think there *is* evidence of a security weakness . . . there *has* been some unfortunate curiosity concerning the Rampart activities. I must say I had not suspected the native work parties. They are under the strictest supervision, as you well know. However, I am sure General Frisk's concern is sound. It would be wise to make a thorough check of both workmen and overseers. Let us by all means be on the safe side. But I should prefer you to do this, Mr. Strickland, when the gangs are returned to their compound this evening. It would be very complicated to interrupt their work at the moment."

"Whatever you say, Colonel. I'm perfectly confident the suspicions will prove to be quite unfounded."

"Of course, Mr. Strickland." His slight, chilly smile was a dismissal, but as I rose and began to move towards the door he said, "Most interesting yesterday evening, over there."

"Yes," I said, "it was quite a night."

"Do they always go on like that? I mean, is it always so out of control?"

"I should say last night was rather exceptional. There's been a good deal of flying strain these last few days. And the liquor was circulating rather solidly."

"I thought that actor man was aggravating, too."

"He was pretty unbearable. I imagine he's suffering from *non*-flying strain. And this weather doesn't help one's neuroses."

"I must go there again some time," said Colonel Dorenfurst. "An interesting place. Well, so long for now, Mr. Strickland. Thank you for your co-operation."

The two guards were waiting outside the door to see me safely to my jeep.

I spent over an hour that evening at the workers' compound, and I questioned every overseer and practically every man who worked at Rampart. The General's charges, I was absolutely sure, were arrant nonsense. I went back to my office and wrote brief reports both for him and for Colonel Dorenfurst. By the time I had sent them to Message Centre it was too late to arrange any appointment with Senator Vancourt. Tomorrow, I told myself, was also a day.

At eight o'clock, when I walked over to the pilots' bar, I had no idea what was in store for me.

The Senator was already there, and his surprising companion at the centre table was Colonel Dorenfurst. Against the background of younger faces in the bar they were an interesting-looking pair, grey, sculptural, in some way stony figures—the lapidary Roman and the chiselled Etruscan. When the corporal had mixed my drink I went across to join them.

"I did get your note," I said to the Senator, "but I've been in a bit of a flap most of the afternoon and—"

"Don't worry, Mr. Strickland. Any time at all. It's not all that pressing. Tomorrow morning, maybe?" He smiled pleasantly.

"Yes. Or we could talk here if you like."

"Tomorrow would be better. At your quarters, if that would be no inconvenience?"

"None at all. Shall we say ten o'clock?" He nodded. I turned to Colonel Dorenfurst. "On that matter we discussed this afternoon," I said, "I have made a thorough check, and I'm confident there's no foundation at all for suspecting the natives. I've made out a report to you."

"That's fine. You will send it over? I like to have these things in writing."

"It went to Message Centre half an hour ago."

He nodded with that chilly dismissiveness I had come to expect of him, and allowed his attention to move to his more general surroundings.

I was momentarily surprised to see that Readaway was in his customary position at the far end of the bar, lounging in nonchalance as if nothing had happened the night before; indeed he looked perfectly capable of continuing from the exact point where he had been interrupted by Bellini. But Bellini was not there, nor any of the other pilots who had been involved in the incident.

The atmosphere of the place was noticeably more tense and nervous. Few of the pilots seemed inclined to stay at the bar for any length of time. They came and went, and on the rain-damp, mud-clotted square of flooring near the main door there was a constant, fluctuating movement. Men taking off waterproofs. Or putting them on. Brief, over-loud greetings. Curt farewells. A tighter ring to the little jabs of laughter.

Jane Carson had not yet put in an appearance. The extraordinary interlude of the morning continued to tease my mind. For the first time I found myself disturbed by her absence. With a vague sense of uneasiness, I wondered where she was; for the first time, I realized, I was deliberately *wanting* her to come. The thought, once admitted, gave me an uncomfortable twinge of guilt. Was *I* getting like young Strawlings and the others? So I turned again to Colonel Dorenfurst, and said:

"What brings you back here so promptly, Colonel? Are you expecting more frolics?"

"I never expect anything, Mr. Strickland. Therefore I am seldom disappointed."

"That was a philosophy I rather clung to myself for a

time," I said equably. "Then I decided it would have to end up in pure solipsism, so I let it go."

Dorenfurst glanced at me sharply, then looked away. The Senator, a slight smile twitching at his mouth, said, "How do you define pure solipsism, Mr. Strickland?"

"Oh, the fixed belief that nothing really exists outside the cognition of oneself. With the rider, of course, that nothing is valid that is outside one's own experience." I glanced in the direction of Readaway, and said, "I think you have a pretty good example of the dedicated solipsist over there at the bar." I was aware of the Colonel's steel-grey eyes fixed upon me. It might be rather enjoyable, I thought, to try to chisel some mark in this hard Etruscan surface.

"Perhaps you discarded the doctrine because you were disappointed in spite of yourself," Senator Vancourt suggested.

"Oh, but one *must be*. Inevitably. I'm pretty sure that even Colonel Dorenfurst must be occasionally." I looked at him, but he had detached himself from the discussion and was inattentive.

"And what was your particular critical disappointment, Mr. Strickland?" the Senator asked.

"My wife," I said. "So I eliminated her. And went off on a new tack of my own."

"Non-solipsist?" he said, with a soft laugh.

"Absolutely."

He nodded good-humouredly, and changed the subject. "I understand you have been checking on a cholera scare," he said.

"Yes," I admitted, and looked at him with interest. How on earth would he have found out about that? From the laboratory, perhaps, where the water had been analyzed? From Fleming? "It turned out not to be cholera," I said. "I had the reports in this evening. It was suspected in a village some distance up-river. Even had it been cholera I doubt if it would have come this far."

"But your responsibility then is not confined to this base? You have to think of the natives also?"

"Naturally. They *are* part of the base. Everything around us is part of the base, if it comes to that. The whole country. The people in it. The jungles and mountains. The weather. We're just a little bit of it fenced off, like Colonel Dorenfurst's airfield over there. But it's what is *outside* that really counts."

We talked generalities for a while, but Dorenfurst remained withdrawn and the Senator seemed to have something on his mind which he was not prepared to discuss—I could not have known at the time that the former was there to watch Readaway and the latter was waiting to watch Jane Carson!—so I left them. Heaven alone knows what impulse it was that took me across to where Readaway was standing, but I regretted it the moment he greeted me with a brassy, "Hi, Strickland, what's new, old cock?", with the "old cock" delivered in bad stage Cockney, presumably as a witticism on my nationality. He had nothing more to say for a while, and I was about to take myself off when he nudged me and said, "Say, you were here last night. You heard what I said. You saw what happened. Well, goddam it, you just listen to this bunch of jerks along here right now, and tell me if I wasn't right." He spoke in a low voice that was bitter and contemptuous. And resentful. Very resentful.

His "bunch of jerks" were five second lieutenants standing next to us beside the bar. Their faces were familiar, but I knew none of them by name. All of them flew gasoline tankers, so none of them could have been long in the command.

"You just listen to these bastards a minute or two," Readaway whispered thickly. I listened.

[204]

The one who was talking was a blue-eyed youngster with curly hair and a boyish face with a golden, downy look, as if he hadn't had to learn to shave properly yet. It seemed he had flown through the fierce electrical storm that had cost us the five planes during the morning. Apparently his had been quite a crossing, for while all the outside of the aircraft was alight with St. Elmo's fire, an electric "fireball" the size of a basketball had manifested itself *inside the fuselage,* and for a minute and a half this spluttering sphere of cold blue flame, with the bucking of the ship in the turbulence, had rolled back and forth along the metal catwalk gallery built above the central belly tanks into which the high-octane gasoline was loaded. As the fireball had rolled up and down they had watched it in horrified fascination, expecting the plane, which was stinking with the fumes of gasoline, to be blown to Kingdom Come at any instant. When nothing happened, and this ball of electric phenomena continued to roll around, the crew chief sergeant went in and clambered down the gallery—how gingerly one can imagine him stepping past that fearsome sphere of ice-blue incandescence!—and opened the emergency escape door which air crews use when they have to jump. On the next upward kick of the plane the pilot made a slight left-hand bank, the fireball rolled down to the tail and out the door.

"Jesus! The crap these slobs feed each other!" Readaway said scornfully. "I get sore just listening to 'em."

"It isn't compulsory to listen," I said. "And, as it happens, it isn't crap."

"You been around these bastards too long."

I turned away from him deliberately, and spoke to the group of pilots. "That was quite a trip," I said. "You were pretty lucky, lieutenant."

The downy boy flushed and nodded.

"What time was this?" I asked.

"Nine thirty this morning," he said shyly. "Maybe a little after."

"Yes, roughly the same time that those five other planes went down?" This was strictly for Readaway's benefit.

"That's right, sir. Around that time. They were all ahead of me. Three of them were from our outfit." Again he coloured. He blushed very easily. "I suppose you wouldn't have had any reports on them, sir?"

"We know they all baled out in time," I said. "And I think they're located."

"That's swell. That sure is."

"The country isn't too bad in that part. They can get 'copters in. So I imagine they'll be all right."

"That's good news, sir. That sure is good news." He smiled nervously, but his neck was brick-red again as he turned back to his companions.

Readaway stared at me for a moment, then, "So you want to play this game too," he said in a low, gritty voice.

"What game?" I tried to be patient with him, but he was becoming very tiresome.

"All this crap about who's to be today's big hero. Who can invent the biggest goddam lies. Brother, am I getting—"

"Readaway, you're the stupidest and most offensive bloody man I have ever met!" I snapped, suddenly very angry indeed. "You made a complete damned idiot of yourself last night, and now you want to do it all over again! You think—"

"If you want to make something of it, bud . . ." he began with a show of truculence, but I cut him short.

"Shut up!" I said curtly. "Shut up and listen to me. What I want to make of it is perfectly simple. I want to make you realize what a confounded, idiotic, fatuous, self-opinionated lout you are!" I knew that I was shouting at him, and I did not care. At that moment I hated Readaway more than I had hated anyone in my life.

[206]

There was a sudden hush in the big room, heads were turned, figures arrested, the group of young pilots had moved in closer, watching us with wide eyes. But mostly I was aware of the effect my outburst had on Readaway. He was leaning so heavily on the bar that he seemed to have sagged. His mouth had fallen open slackly and there was a dribble of saliva pendulous on his lip. His eyes were cloudy and uncertain. His head with the lock of black hair fallen across his forehead swayed stupidly. I reached across and took him by the shoulder and dragged him erect, and I had a surge of wild hope that he would aim a punch at me so that I could drive my own fist into his handsome, horrible face. But he hung there limply in my grip with his head swinging and I knew that he was afraid.

"I wish to Christ that Bellini had gone ahead with it last night and knocked some flipping sense into your swollen bloody head!" I said furiously. "Why don't you do as he suggested? Go flying, Readaway! Go flying with him and see for yourself what it's *really* like! Make up your own hero stories!" I shook him violently, but his only response was a kind of weak, protesting gesture of his hand, and the muscles around his mouth jerked in a tight spasm as if he was about to vomit. "Readaway, these chaps have been telling you the truth," I went on, and although anger kept my voice harsh I managed to give it a little more restraint. "Five planes *did* smash up in the air this morning. These fellows are doing a job that you're not prepared to do and wouldn't even be capable of doing. And they don't do it on celluloid, Readaway, they do it for real! So I'd suggest you keep your bloody mouth shut until somebody really asks for *your* opinion! Which will keep it shut for quite some time, I imagine. I'd also like to suggest that you finish up your drink and get the devil out of here, but since I don't have that privilege I shall have to do the next best thing. Because

[207]

as far as I'm concerned you drink by yourself from now on!"
I released him with a shove that must have been more violent than I had realized, for he reeled back against one of the bar stools and sent it over with a crash, and almost fell himself.

As I left the mess I was very conscious of the stillness, of eyes looking, of heads turning to follow me. Senator Vancourt. Colonel Dorenfurst. The pilots. The mess sergeant transfixed in the door of his office. Jane Carson had just come in. The shoulders of her raincoat were running with water and her grey sou'wester was in her hand, and she opened her mouth as if she wanted to say something to me, but I brushed past her with a brief nod and took my slicker and went out into the rainy night. I had no doubt at all as to where I wanted to go. I turned around the corner of the pilots' quarters and headed across the airfield to the Search-and-Rescue shack.

The effect of my outburst was very curious, although I was not to realize this until some time later.

My anger with Readaway had been an uncontrollable flaring up of a deep personal dislike of the man, and an unwillingness, if you like, to go on suffering a fool gladly; but in the pilots' mess it was given a much deeper interpretation. It began, as it were, an open declaration of hostilities against him.

My own unique position in the mess—a foreigner and a civilian, yet an "outsider" who had a role and a stake in their affairs and who had long since been accepted as one of them—in the eyes of the pilots gave a quite special emphasis to the situation. I had passed a judgment which, to them, was final, impartial, and unimpeachable. To them I did not represent the sudden, frenetic denunciation of a Bellini driven out of control by alcohol and personal anguish.

Nor was I, as they all were, subjected to the strains and tensions and buried fears which might so easily give distortion to their own judgments and prejudices. Since I was not one of them I could judge impartially, and I had judged against Vince Readaway, for whom they already had sufficient reason for dislike. It was enough.

I suppose, too, that they were influenced by the very visible evidence of Readaway's cowardice. It had been very clear during my attack on him that, like most bullies, he lacked any real guts. There must have been some special satisfaction to them in seeing this godlike dummy revealed as nothing more than a charades hero with six-shooters cut from cardboard.

They began what was later referred to as "The Treatment." Whether there was a calculated deliberation in the method, or whether it simply developed of itself, I cannot really say; all I know is that by the time the pattern of attack had crystallized they had developed a system of psychological warfare that was horribly effective.

I suppose they could have expelled him from the mess, but not only did they allow him to stay there, they encouraged him to do so. They went back to drinking with him. They competed with each other to pay for his bar chits. And they talked to him. They talked to him, and they talked among themselves when he was with them, about flying. Each flight was examined now in every detail of its hazard—perhaps hazards were invented when the drama was insufficient. Deliberately and cold-bloodedly they described flights made through ice and blizzards, through the fearful madness of electric storms, and they told of hair-raising escapes among unmapped peaks and cloud-hidden rocks. In devastating detail they recalled accidents where planes had had their wings wrenched off in air pockets, or had somersaulted down precipices, or had disintegrated in flame. They spoke of the cannonshot clatter of ice flung back from propellers against the fuselage, the eerie terror of St. Elmo's fire. They talked of men reduced to gibbering idiocy by stark fear in that black high sky, of others lost and raving in the desolation of Tibet, or the victims of jungle head-hunters. With a technical dispassion they described the ratio of their losses, the obsolescence and the vulnerability of their machines, the shortcomings of their equipment, and the hazards of their landing fields. And in vivid, searing pictures they envisaged that moment of pure panic when a man must make that jump into the whirling black chaos of an alpine night, not knowing whether he is to freeze to death or perish from lack of oxygen or find a more lingering fate in the unknown wilderness below—whether his parachute will open or fire will burn him or his neck will break on the hidden rocks or only the slow agony of starvation be his fate.

And through it all, like a measured ticking metronome stroking at the cadences of inevitability, they kept making him see that time ahead when he, Vince Readaway, would have to attend that shabby briefing room on the edge of the airfield to learn the contents of a jungle pack, the method of jumping, the way of pulling a ripcord—the flimsy armour against the forces of hazard.

It was the full treatment—a war of nerves that was cruel, deliberate, and merciless. Within forty-eight hours Vince Readaway had forgotten that airliners flew out of Dallas or Salt Lake City without waiting for the rain to stop.

All this I found out later. That night I sat with Captain Benjamin in the Search-and-Rescue shack, and we talked about constitutional law and Oliver Wendell Holmes and about Mozart and botany, and the door of the shack was open to the warm rain and we watched the lights of the freight planes coming in and going off.

[210]

18

I HAD been seeing Senator Vancourt as a heavy head and shoulders above a table, and I had forgotten how short and slight he was until he came to my room.

Except for brief, distant glimpses of him as an upright figure—stepping briskly through the rain towards the mess hut, pacing up and down during the concert fiasco—I had usually come across him in a group around a table. Now, standing beside me in the high, cane-walled room, dwarfed by my own excessive tallness, he seemed out of proportion or in some vague way deformed. Like one of those old-fashioned cartoon figures in which the head is always drawn much larger than the body. One half expected him to speak in the form of lettering drawn in a balloon swelling from his mouth. Caricature of a political figure. William Jennings Bryan attacking Darwinism or shouting for Prohibition. Or something out of a Max Beerbohm album.

I offered him the cane armchair, and at once his proportions fell into place again. As if the slide had been changed in a magic lantern, a different personality instantly appeared; one was sharply conscious of the strength in the craggy, heavy-lipped face, the forceful lines incised around the mouth and nose, the alert intelligence in his piercingly blue eyes.

"This is your permanent home, Mr. Strickland?" he asked, after a careful examination of his surroundings. "Or do you regard it as something temporary?"

"Well, nowadays everything is temporary, I suppose. But this is the only home I have, if you like to call it that."

"You keep it very impersonal."

"I try to be very impersonal. It suits my outlook." I knew what he was driving at. Apart from the few books on the shelf beside the bed—and even the books were neutral, meaningless entertainments, there to while away a leisure hour or so, giving no reference to interests or to character—the room was quite bare of any evidence of a particular occupancy. The standard furniture. A closet in which I hung my clothes. A tin trunk in which I stowed the overflow of papers from my office. Not much else. No photographs. No pictures on the wall. No letters or newspapers left around. No postcards surviving from a Christmas or a birthday or the journey of a friend. Nothing of the past nor of memory. The functional reduction. The last thin shell around Jacob Strickland reduced to what was necessary to keep out the wind and the rain.

He nodded and folded his small hands neatly across his little paunch and said, "I figure you're a busy man, Mr. Strickland, so I'll come directly to the point of my visit."

I inclined my head and went across and sat on the bed, facing him.

"I assume in a place like this one gets to know what's going on," he said gravely, "so I guess you would know that one of the purposes of my visit is to investigate questions of general morale. Not only in the advanced combat areas, but in all areas where our boys are stationed."

"I had heard something to that effect."

"Please understand, Mr. Strickland, that you are not obliged to make any comment whatever. I realize you are bound by certain undertakings of loyalty to the outfit in which you are working. On the other hand, you are not now a member of the fighting services, nor are you a compatriot of mine. This puts you in a rather special position in Zone Q-4. For these reasons I must tell you that I've paid rather particular attention to you since I came here." He glanced at me sharply. I nodded and waited.

"The brief talks we've had together I've enjoyed a lot. I'd like you to know that I appreciate your appraisals and attitudes in general, and I think I'm in sympathy with your views. Aside from that, you've won respect here. And I'm not unaware of the fact that the angle of native affairs and native labour here is one of the least troublesome aspects of work at this base. Which, as you know, Mr. Strickland, is not always the case in a foreign country."

"You're very kind," I said, thinking of General Frisk and his "goddam niggers."

The Senator's heavy mouth twisted almost into a smile. "And just man to man," he said, "I also happened to like the way you handled that loud-mouthed bastard in the mess last night. But that's beside the point. What I'm getting at, Mr. Strickland, is this—you can be valuable to me because you're *objective*. And that's what I'm looking for. Objective comment. Objective criticism. You know the setup here as intimately as anyone can know it. But in a way you don't belong to it. You can see it from outside as well as from inside. You don't have that close involvement that the others have. You don't have an axe to grind, if you want to put it that way. That's why I'd like to talk to you. Within these four walls. Just to get your views."

"Well, go ahead," I said. "I don't really know whether I can help, but—"

"I guess we'll find that out, won't we? The question then is general morale. Around this place right now there are some pretty disturbing aspects, wouldn't you say?"

"Are there?" I said guardedly. "There have been losses and casualties, but—"

"Not that," he interrupted. "Not the flying side. We've already discussed that. I was thinking of the more general picture."

"General Frisk runs a good base," I said. "It's efficient and it gets things done. It works, and it works without too much fuss."

"Go on, Mr. Strickland," he said patiently. "You talk to me."

He closed his eyes and sat quite still with his hands clasped across his stomach while I talked. I gave him a brief, rather laudatory picture of the development of the area from a crude jungle clearing beside an antiquated rail-head to the complex network of Kansas and its environs—capable now of maintaining its F.E. schedule even under the worst possible conditions. (Frisk had been in command since the inception of the base and I gave him, justifiably enough, even though personally I disliked the man, full credit for the achievement. Frisk ran his command fussily, pompously, and with a good deal of unnecessary authority-by-paper—"bumph" was the word we used to give it—but he ran it with purpose and energy and it had always functioned efficiently.) I had been talking for about five minutes before I realized that this wasn't what the Senator wanted to hear at all.

"That concert," he said, "was not altogether what you would call a success." He spoke rather absently, as if he had not been listening to me. His eyes remained closed.

"The idea was all right," I said. "If it had come off the way it was planned the men would have enjoyed it enor-

[214]

mously. Even as it was, it got by." I thought of Jack Consadine and his guitar.

"I doubt if it was all that good for morale." The bright blue eyes were looking at me now. Watchfully, as if he was expecting me to admit an error.

"The conditions were all against it. It was a choice between the rain outside and the heat inside. The boys made a pretty good stab at it." I thought of Captain Allison and the improvised stage.

"But it didn't rain."

"They weren't to know that, were they?"

"Let's get to the point, Mr. Strickland. That woman loused it up, didn't she?"

"What woman?"

"Jane Carson. That wasn't much of a deal, when you come to think of it."

"She had a lot to contend with."

"Maybe she did, Mr. Strickland. That's hardly the point, though, is it? She'll have a darned sight more to contend with when she gets to Xanadu. Still more when she goes to the forward areas. That's what she's sent out for. We can't build an air-conditioned Carnegie Hall and truck it out ahead of her." He paused and stroked at his chin. "When you were in the British Army did you have entertainment shows for the troops?"

"Of course. But usually in base areas. They were very popular . . . and good for morale."

"Sure. Did you ever come across a woman like Jane Carson in one of those units?"

"I've never come across a woman like Jane Carson anywhere before," I said quite truthfully.

"Well, that's it. Let's come to the point, Mr. Strickland."

"We seem to be taking quite some time getting to that point," I suggested dryly.

[215]

"All right. Are you aware that after that performance one of the enlisted men made a direct attack on her? Told her she wasn't worth the payload space on an aircraft flying to Xanadu. Told her they were going to fly over a crate of liquor instead!"

"I am aware of the incident, yes. It was not expressed quite so bluntly as that."

"That was the substance of it, wasn't it?"

"Well, yes."

"Do you consider that an incident like that is conducive to good morale, Mr. Strickland?"

"Frankly, I don't think it has anything to do with morale."

"You don't? Maybe we'd better define morale."

"To me, that was simply a matter of pique," I said. "The natural indignation of a man who'd been kept waiting too long in a hotbox with a plague of mosquitoes. I happen to know the enlisted man in question. He's attached to the Parachute Squadron, and I do a lot of work with them. He's a very efficient flight sergeant. He's human, too. That night he got angry, and he said his little piece, and I can't say that I blame him. But since then he has done his job just as efficiently as before. Just as willingly. Just as ungrudgingly. What I am trying to point out, Senator Vancourt, is that his morale has not been affected in the least by Miss Carson's perhaps natural reluctance to finish her encore. I simply don't believe that that has anything whatever to do with morale. Morale, to me, is another thing altogether."

Suddenly, I was intensely irked by his attitude. I wanted to talk to him of the implications of the F.E. standard; of poor Hathaway's last cool words, *I shall take off anyway because I have no more runway;* of the gang of singing Negroes working on the railroad washaway; of Quigley's GI's putting to rights the derelict village rice store; of Pendlebury's exhausted eyes; of little Captain Benjamin poring

[216]

over his maps in a rain-lashed shack; of a baby-faced second lieutenant making his left-hand bank to flick the fireball out. There was plenty of bloody good morale around Zone Q-4 if anyone wanted to take the trouble to look for it! And, in any case, why should I have to waste my time trying to connotate a word to examine which a whole Senate sub-committee had been appointed? They were perfectly capable of examining it without *my* help; of defining it, analyzing it, setting up new orders around it, wrapping it up in reams of printed paper, and, so far as I was concerned, shoving it up their bums when they were finished with it! I had become impatient with the senatorial investigation!

He must have sensed my petulance, because his thick lips formed a lopsided, tolerant smile, and he cleared his throat in the way a politician does, and said, "Yes, yes, Mr. Strickland. But let me explain a little further. You see, this entertainment unit to which Miss Carson has been appointed is very much in the nature of an experiment. We have not before sent civilian entertainers into our advanced combat areas. So the problem of the effect of this sort of entertainment group does become one of very special importance. Is it to be a good thing or a bad thing? Here, with the monsoon, and the obvious strains and pressures that are operating, we find among the men a certain degree of nervous tension, a temper easily touched on the raw. At Xanadu that uncertain element of stress will be even more evident. In the forward combat areas, very much more so— particularly with the added responsibility involved in the presence there of unarmed civilians. You do see what I am driving at?"

"I see all that, of course. If you are so concerned about it, though, why were they sent at all?"

"For the good of morale. If it *is* to be for the good of morale. That is what we have to find out. The experiment,

[217]

Mr. Strickland. An experiment, I regret to say, already placed in jeopardy by Miss Carson's behaviour. I'm sorry she had to be one of those selected for this first trial."

"But why?"

"Because I think she is highly unsuitable. Disruptive, shall we say?"

"Really? You approve, however, of Mr. Readaway?"

"As a person, Mr. Strickland, he's not even a good skunk. The sonofabitch stinks! I do not, on the other hand, find him disruptive."

I looked at him in blank astonishment. "Senator Vancourt," I said slowly, "I'm coming to the conclusion that you and I are completely at odds on the connotation of various words. So may I make myself quite clear, and say that I think Readaway is just about the most disruptive bloody bastard I've met in many a long day."

He chuckled. "I think our connotations are the same," he said. "We differ only in our interpretations. I do not at all approve of Readaway's personality or behaviour." He chuckled again. "Last night, had I been twenty years younger and a foot taller, with a little more heft on me, I would have very much enjoyed punching him in the nose. But that's not the point. He can't affect the morale of those boys he keeps trying to needle. He can only make them stiffer and tougher, out of sheer goddamned cussedness. After you'd gone last night you would have seen that in the mess. Those kids can handle our friend Readaway. You bet they can!"

"But Miss Carson is something different?"

"Miss Carson is something entirely different." Again the somewhat artificial, political clearing of the throat. "We are speaking, of course, in the strictest confidence. Within these four walls, Mr. Strickland." He paused and frowned. A heavy, Roman, stony frown. The bright blue eyes were all

[218]

wrong. They should have been stone-coloured too, and sightless, as they were in the sculptured busts in museums. "I don't think I really have to tell you," he went on, his voice heavily keyed to his expression, "what she's been doing since she's been here, do I? The dogs bark it now. There's a whole bunch of GI wisecracks about her. Rather bitter cracks, most of them, since the enlisted men aren't getting any. I had coffee over at the Signal Corps mess yesterday, and they were having a joke about getting up a kind of lottery pool to pick the name of the next officer who sleeps with her." He stared across at me grimly. "She's been laid by a different guy every night since she's been here," he said.

"Well, what of it?" I spoke lightly enough, but the very directness of his words disconcerted me. Hurt me, almost. I remember a momentary sensation of chill, as if a cold draught of air had stirred in the humid room. I suspect now, although it did not occur to me then, that this was the precise moment when the thing began to turn in on me. It was not merely that I had seemed to become involved, unwittingly, as her unofficial sponsor and guardian: I had become involved with the woman in a deeper and far more frightening sense. And I was incapable of involvement. This was the moment when I should have rejected her. Instead, I continued to defend her. "Mightn't that be a jolly good thing for morale?" I asked, still with the forced tone of levity.

"Are you serious?"

"Perfectly serious. For heaven's sake, look at history. Napoleon carted women along with the *Grande Armée* because he found the practice good for the morale of his soldiers. Camp followers, tarts, the officers' mistresses, even wives, were the normally accepted thing until we got puritanical about it. Blame the Duke of Wellington for a good deal of that. Nelson was another thing. You wouldn't suggest that his morale as a sailor suffered because he was immorally involved with Emma Hamilton, would you? Nowadays, of course, we look at these things differently. Now we have bromides. And blue light outfits. And prophylactic stations in the selected brothel areas. We also still have syphilis and the clap. What the hell are we getting all moral about Jane Carson for?"

He tilted his head back and unclasped his fingers. He seemed startled. I was rather startled myself. I had not meant to display such vehemence, but a muddled picture, a montage really, had flashed across my mind. Concerned with Garnett Fleming. Fleming squaring his thick shoulders as he came out on to Armand's verandah, his system satisfied by a little dark-eyed girl with lemon skin who didn't even have a name . . . Fleming standing uncomfortably in the doorway of his quarters with that ridiculous short towel around his loins . . . The more I thought of it the more muddling it became, because I had no idea at all what Jane Carson's habits had to do with a Senate subcommittee investigating questions of general morale and command relationships. Unless—and possibly this was the crux of the matter—we were again out of harmony on the use of words. I thought I had better point this out, so I said, "We are discussing morale, Senator, not morals."

"In this case I believe the subjects are related," he said firmly.

"I'm sorry. I simply cannot agree with you. There is nothing in any manual of the military sciences to suggest that occasional immorality makes for bad soldiering. Rather to the contrary, I should imagine."

"This isn't *occasional* immorality. This is chronic!"

"For God's sake, Senator, what are we standing in judgment *on?*" I protested, losing patience with him. "What *is*

[220]

this? *The Scarlet Letter,* or a Salem witch trial? Look, it's not my prerogative to brand Jane Carson as a . . . a floosy! I doubt very much if it's yours, either. All I can say to you is that I do not consider her disruptive to the morale of this command. Personally, perhaps she *is* disruptive—the haves and the have-nots—but that's a perfectly normal aspect of the battle of the sexes here or anywhere else. At one time I was involved in it myself, and I've no doubt you have been, too. But surely the only valid question is whether she is disruptive in the over-all military sense. You are not seriously suggesting to me that these officers she is supposed to have been sleeping with are now unfit to perform their military duties efficiently! And if they are," I added dryly, "you must at least concede to her that she has spread her damage lightly . . . and over the widest possible field."

For a long time he looked at me, his neat fingers stroking slowly at his square, strong chin. "Mr. Strickland," he said at last, "I guess we are a little at cross purposes. In all fairness to you, maybe I'd better make myself a bit clearer on exactly how I come into this. I have noticed that you and Jane Carson seem to enjoy a rather particular kind of friendship. She talks to you, goes walking with you. She—"

"I assure you I've not had the pleasure of sleeping with her, if that's what you mean."

"That was not what I meant at all, Mr. Strickland. I am trying to keep this quite objective. But I happen to know she does have a kind of special respect for you. To be quite candid, I have discussed you with her. It seems she has some . . . well, I can only say some particular feeling of *trust* in you. Something like that. I'm not sure if that's the word. But, to be quite frank, I came here because I rather hoped you could talk to her and—"

"*Talk to her!*" I stared at him in complete amazement.

He nodded. "Yes, I figured that maybe—"

"Talk to her about *what?* You mean I'm supposed to tell her to be a good little girl? Hang your clothes on the gooseberry bush, but don't go near the water! Mustn't speak to strange men! Oh, come now, Senator Vancourt!"

"May I please continue, Mr. Strickland?" he said very quietly. "You see, I'd be mighty happy if this experiment worked. I might as well tell you that primarily this entertainment group is here because of me. It was my suggestion originally to the War Department. It wasn't all that easy to get approval through some of those Pentagon departments. I wouldn't like the project to fail now, on its first trial. I'm not denying there's a selfish angle, but that's wrapped up in Senate politics, and I guess you wouldn't be interested in that. What I am saying, Mr. Strickland, is that for this to lay an egg on us—and while I'm here on the spot, supervising so to speak, looking after my own baby—would give a damned big laugh to a lot of people back in Washington, and wouldn't be much of a help either to me personally or to the political causes I happen to care about. You appreciate that I am being entirely honest with you?"

"Yes," I said, but I could not refrain from adding, "You do have an axe to grind then?"

"I do, Mr. Strickland. But don't forget that sharp axes clear wildernesses, and there's still a mighty lot of clearing to be done in my country." He made the noises in his throat. Rather self-consciously. "Let me get one or two other angles straight," he said. "General Frisk, as you probably know, was very sore about the lousing up of his concert. And, since he's no man's fool, he will have heard all these stories that are going the rounds. He told me yesterday he was most distressed about the situation." The Senator studied me carefully. "General Frisk," he said quietly, "is very well aware of the intricacies of Senate-Pentagon politics, and he knows exactly who among the top military brass in Washington were opposed to my proposals. A career soldier could legitimately regard some of these figures as powerfully influential."

"More axes to grind?" I murmured.

"Exactly. The General has, in effect, issued an ultimatum. He has threatened that if the personnel of the group are not removed soon to Xanadu he will ask for its recall to the United States, and give his reasons for doing so. He is, after all, the commanding general in this area."

"And hasn't drawn a lucky ticket in the lottery," I suggested tartly. "How would he explain why the unit did not proceed to Xanadu when the crossing was perfectly clear for the personnel to go?"

Vancourt smiled. "I am quite certain, Mr. Strickland, that General Frisk is an old hand at explanations like that. I understand," he added dryly, "that his meteorological officers, not he, were in error, and have been reprimanded in an official memo." A slight, rather wistful smile gathered on his heavy face.

"We used to call it 'passing the buck.'"

"Sure. It's a popular pastime in politics, too."

"My point is, Senator, that I don't see why we should pass one to Jane Carson, too."

"I think you have made yourself clear, Mr. Strickland. I respect your stand, and I admire your loyalty to her."

"This has nothing whatever to do with loyalty. Nor with this particular woman, if it comes to that. Senator Vancourt . . ." I hesitated, because I sensed that the subject was already wound up, then decided to go on. "Once a long time ago I pointed the accusatory finger at a woman who was weak and . . . well, morally irresponsible, if you like. I am not prepared to do it again. It didn't work then. It wouldn't work now. And one way or another it doesn't

[223]

affect the organizational morale of this command by so much as that." I snapped my fingers.

"Well, thank you, Mr. Strickland," he said briskly. "I must confess I always do enjoy talking to you." He stared at me fixedly for a long moment, and for the first time I noticed how shaggy his eyebrows were. Then he sighed, rose from the chair, and even though he squared his shoulders he instantly became slight and diminutive again. He shook my hand firmly and walked slowly towards the door, but there he paused again and turned to me with a wide grin on his face.

"Listen to me, my boy," he said, "if this project does fail—and it looks to me as if there's a darned good chance it might—I guess I could fix it with Washington to organize a division or two of harlots and concubines. Why, we could package 'em up just fine!"

He was still chuckling to himself as he splashed off briskly through the rain.

I had a sudden considerable liking for the little man as I watched him walk away.

19

THE discussion with Vancourt, however inconclusive it had been, teased and tormented me for the rest of the day. I accepted without any question the basic truth of the charges against Jane Carson. Not *every* night, as they claimed. Peabody had rejected her. She had told me that. But fundamentally the picture of her immorality, or amorality, was clear enough. What I found disturbing was this involvement of myself in a situation which, by every rational standard, did not concern me in the least degree.

Why should Senator Vancourt have sought *me* out? What was *I* supposed to do about it? The more I thought about it, or tried not to think about it, the more ridiculous the situation became. The woman, after all, was only a transient personality in the fixed life of Zone Q-4. When the rainclouds lifted she would vanish from it as completely as the butterflies had vanished from the sodden field near the village. Where, I found myself unconsciously adding the rider, she had looked so beautiful. My preservation of the image gave a new, uneasy tangent to my reflections—I remembered, with a sudden twinge of misgiving, my concern when she had been absent from the mess the night before, my impatience for her to appear . . . To hell with her! A day. Two days. Three days. She would be gone. One way or the other—off to Xanadu or back to the States. I was damned if they were going to force on me any deeper personal involvement with her problems. I could not allow myself to be involved: already, almost insidiously, there had been a deeply disturbing invasion of my privacy, that essential protective privacy I had been at such pains to preserve over all these years. I was determined that it would go no further.

The problem, however, was not to be so simply discarded. Before even this first day was over my involvement with Jane Carson, whether I wanted it or not, was to be far, far deeper than I would ever have dreamed to be possible.

It began, one realizes now, that very morning. After the Senator had left me I drove across to Search-and-Rescue. Tommy Updike was there with Benjamin and the sergeant. They had plenty on their hands, and I fulfilled no particular function by being there. I stayed anyway. Long association enabled me to fit in harmoniously enough. I listened idly to their talk. It never occurred to me that there were things I could have done in Leromenos. Quite a number of things, including a few minor duties which I had neglected to do when I had taken her to Armand's for coffee. I could have made another check on the Rampart work parties. It had been in my mind to contact Colonel Robarts to find out if he was still worried about typhus. I just sat in the swivel chair at Sergeant Garstein's desk and listened. (It was not until afterwards that I realized how subtly I was invalidating my own argument to the Senator: I may not have slept with Jane Carson, but she was already affecting my morale; I was not performing my duties as efficiently as I should have been!)

The F.E. schedules were still being maintained, evidently at the cost of considerable strain. There had been no further losses, but seven pilots had been "grounded" by Colonel Robarts, and two others by the medical officer at Xanadu, as psychologically unfit for active flying duty. Benjamin was pessimistically sure the worst was yet to come. He was right. The rot began to set in that afternoon.

Since young Strawlings was involved in that rot it seems queer and disturbing that they should have been discussing him that morning. I think one has often seen this happen, but in hindsight there is always something a little alarming about it. As if a secret force has shaken the fixity of one's natural beliefs. My own experience hardly fits me to believe in personal fates that are preordained. Yet occasionally it seems that there is a dark, fluid stream that runs silently beneath our experiences and our contacts, and sometimes we hear the whisper of its movement: we feel the faint, stroking touch of a current that has already passed along. We become, unconsciously, part of a future moment.

It was Updike who began it. They had finished their technical discussion and the four of us were sitting over the inevitable mugs of coffee, smoking our cigarettes, drifting into the verbal therapy of airfield gossip.

"Somebody ought to take that poor bastard Strawlings aside and have a talk with him," said Updike. "I saw him in the briefing room this morning. Then we had coffee before he took off." He pulled a mouth and shook his head slowly. "Brother, he sure is a case!" he said.

"What sort of case?" Benjamin wanted to know. He was invariably way behind on any sort of gossip.

"Well, Christ! You took him back to his quarters the other night. You were there in that business with Bellini. You ought to know."

"Oh that," said Benjamin disinterestedly. "Well, that's all over."

"The hell it's all over! Are you crazy? It's not all over for

[227]

that poor sonofabitch. He's got that dame in his crop like a turkey with a tennis ball. He can't think of anything but Jane Carson. He goops around all day like a martyred saint, and then hangs around in the shadows half the night watching her room. She goes to the mess, he never takes his eyes off her. He's rostered to fly and you'd think he'd rated a twenty-year stretch in Fort Leavenworth. Man! Is *his* morale low!"

I looked across at him sharply, but it was Benjamin who said, "He's just a kid. He's a romantic. He'll grow out of it."

"He wouldn't have grown into it if he'd had any goddamned sense," Updike said with a grin. "Not with this baby! She doesn't want romantic kid stuff. She wants variety. All fifty-seven that Heinz puts out and a whole lot more! And he just can't *see* it. He thinks just because he laid her the first night she was here he gets some right of total possession."

Jane Carson again, I thought wearily. The *second* night, I wanted to say. I had a dull desire for technical truth. At least let us keep the records straight. Was that my function in the setup? Evidently I was the only person capable of separating the reality from the legend. A bloody odd thing that. Apparently I had been about the last to suspect the woman, and the one man, by the Senator's and even by tacit definition, without an axe to grind, but I was the only one who had the documentation reasonably correct. Strawlings was the second night . . . Fleming the third . . . then it was Peabody, but Peabody hadn't . . .

I didn't say anything. I just made an excuse and left them talking.

And I suppose it was in the pattern of things that since I had been thinking of Fred Peabody I should have run into him, over at the central administration block, coming away from the white building where the Star-Spangled Banner

[228]

hung still and soggy in the rain above the dripping thatch.

"Summoned to see the gallant General," he explained, with a crooked grin. "Let's go and have a drink."

"I've some gin in my room, if you'd like to go there," I suggested, because my quarters were barely twenty yards away, but he shook his head.

"I've had your gin before, Jacob. No ice, and tepid water. Let's go to the mess."

The place was empty. We took our drinks to a table and Peabody lit a cigarette and said, "What's got into Frisky's hair?"

"Why?"

"He called me over to see if we could get a special authorization to fly that entertainment bunch across to Xanadu. For *me* to fly them, specifically."

"Now? During the sock-in?"

"That's right. Now."

So the battle was on. Senate *versus* Pentagon. Issue had been joined. Over the body—the beautiful body—of Jane Carson. . . .

"What did you say?" I asked him.

"I said sure I'd fly 'em." He shrugged. "But I said he'd have to get the S.A. clearance from Flight Control. So he had Allison call 'em up. They gave him the flat no. They told him the sock-in order was fixed by Washington, that weather conditions right now were plain lousy, and that the met stations on both sides of the range predicted even further deterioration. There wasn't anything Frisky could say. I left him chewing on his lip."

"I know why he wants to get them away," I said deliberately. "It's because of Jane Carson."

"What has she got to do with it?"

"She's disruptive," I said. "She made a fiasco of Frisk's concert. And she's playing fast and loose with too many officers on the station. Undermining morale. That's the charge."

"What sort of bull is this?"

"That's the charge," I repeated.

He gave me a long, careful look, and then for quite some time he was very thoughtful, staring at his drink. "That's the way it is, eh?" he said at last, glancing up.

I nodded, then filled him in briefly on the salient points of my talk with Vancourt. When I had finished he lapsed again into a thoughtful silence, from which he finally looked up to say:

"I wish I'd known this when I was talking to the General. I could have straightened him out on one or two angles."

"Such as?"

"Well, his concert, for one thing. I loused that up. It wasn't anything to do with her. I was with her over in my room. I kept her there." He glanced at me quickly, as if he expected me to make some comment, but I just watched him and waited. "I didn't lay her, if that's what you're thinking," he said quietly. "We talked, that's all. Just talk," he said reflectively. He had the same expression on his strong, dark face as on the night he had first met her, when he had sat with me afterwards at the bar staring up at her photograph.

"I wasn't suggesting anything," I said.

"I know you weren't," he said quickly. "I was just anxious to get the picture straight. I guess it isn't easy in a place like this. Not with a woman like her."

"No," I said. Did *anybody* have the picture straight? Frisk and Vancourt, even Tommy Updike, all thought she affected morale, but none of them had the picture straight. Did Fred Peabody have it straight? I remembered what he had said before she had even got to Assam. *There are tramps and tramps. She takes it farther than most. . . .*

It was almost as if he had read my thoughts, because he

said, "I guess they all think she's just a cheap little two-bit tramp, and . . . well, she certainly doesn't try to pull any of this cloistered nun stuff. She *is* messed up, sure. But, do you know, Jacob, she isn't really what you think at all. I mean she's not just a goddam nympho. I'll swear to that! It's not what Steve got so het-up about. She's not just a dame with hot pants chasing around after any guy who'll throw her on her back. She's not even a tramp . . . not in the way we think of it . . . not in that cheap, dirty way. There's something else about her that's honest, and good, and true in a way. Hell, I don't know. I don't have the words, I guess." He glanced at me awkwardly. "She's a woman, anyway," he said firmly. "She's a real woman, by Christ!"

"Perhaps that's precisely what Frisk is worried about," I suggested.

"How come?"

"Women don't really fit into a place like this. You have to consider how men's minds work, as well as women's."

He thought about this for a few moments, then, "That may be," he said, "but I guess we ought to try to understand something about her before we start lashing her to the stake. I know a bit about her. We've talked about a lot of things." His fingers kept rubbing at the table as he talked. "She's scared, and kind of lost, and I guess she's looking for something. Maybe it's not even a man she's looking for . . . it might be that she only wants someone to point out a direction." The lean brown fingers went on rubbing, rubbing, rubbing. "You see, Jacob," he said, "we get all hot under the collar just because this sonofabitch Readaway doesn't understand—or doesn't take the trouble to *try* to understand—this environment of ours or the work we do or the way we behave or the problems we've got to contend with. But don't you think we're just as guilty as he is when we make our snap judgments about *her?* We don't even try to find out what's behind it, or what *she's* had to contend with, or what makes her act the way she does. It's simpler for us to snigger behind our hands and write her off as an easy lay. The way Readaway writes us off as a bunch of corn-fed jerks. It just seems to me that it isn't only Readaway who's making hasty, superficial judgments."

"I haven't been passing judgment on her," I said.

"No, I wouldn't have expected you to." He looked at me curiously. "There's something alike about you and her. It's funny. She sees that, too. She talks about you quite a lot. She said a queer thing to me the other night: she told me she had the feeling there was something buried away inside you that was very like something she had buried away inside herself."

"What did she mean by that?" I asked, feeling the touch of panic at this new, sly intrusion into privacy.

"I don't know. I guess you'd have to ask her." He gave me that slow, easy smile of his. "I got to get along," he said. "There's a noon briefing."

We went to the bar to sign our chits, and I said, "Perhaps we can talk more about this tonight."

"Maybe. Don't hold a seat for me. We're all flying freighters now."

At the door he put his hand on my shoulder. "Say, listen, Jacob, if you want to talk more about it why don't you go talk to her? She's a good dame. She's worth working on. And I figure you're just about the one guy here she'd listen to."

20

It was Jerry Buehle who provided us with the only reasonably clear picture of young Strawlings' death.

Until Buehle checked in after his own inward flight, in an empty eighty-six from Xanadu, Strawlings was just one of four names listed on the control tower blackboard against blank spaces in the final column. It was Pendlebury who took the message from the flight room, and he called it across to Benjamin, who told him to tell Buehle to come right over.

Dusk had just settled over the big airfield and the lights in the slow rain had a smouldering glitter, but there was still a strip of dirty yellow sky above the trees that sheltered Rampart. Sometimes against the strip of yellow you would see the black shape of a plane circling in low to make its landing—a chip of no significance save the fact of its movement.

Buehle came in his flying kit, wet with rain, and his oxygen mask was still slung around his neck, and under his arm he carried his clip board, trailing the straps which held it around his thigh when he was flying. His heavy, stolid,

Germanic-looking face was unshaven and his eyes were unpleasantly bloodshot. He looked very tired.

Benjamin called him over to the cluttered table where he and Sergeant Garstein and I were sitting. Buehle put his clip board down on the spread of maps. There was nothing written on the blotched, rain-cockled pad.

"Hullo, Jerry," said Benjamin. "Nice to see you. Pull up a chair there." Buehle sat down and rubbed his eyes, and looked carefully round the room. "Okay, let's have it," said Benjamin. "You don't mind if I ask the questions?"

"Shoot," said Buehle, stifling a yawn.

"What was your flight number out of Xanadu?"

"Fifty-four."

"Time of take-off?"

"Eleven forty-six hours."

I looked up at the blackboard. His name was there, with all the entries completed, two lines above Strawlings' name. Strawlings' take-off time was chalked in at 1153 hours, and there was nothing chalked in against the next column.

"Tell me about the conditions," said Benjamin.

"They were pretty good. Pretty good at first. Better than this side. Tail wind. A whole lot of visibility. We could see way down past Old Baldy. We had fourteen thousand feet of ceiling for more than an hour out."

"You took off just before Strawlings?"

"That's right. He was two flights behind me. When I was at the end of the runway, gunning up the motors, I saw him coming up the taxi strip. Jennings was in the bay behind me, waiting. Jennings got through okay."

"Yes, Jennings got through okay."

"I saw Strawlings wave to me as I started rolling."

"Well, you take it from there. One thing first, though. Did you fly a compass course?"

"Sure." He gave the compass bearing and said, "There was

a big arch in the overcast, and I took her that way, over towards that big lump they call The Hammer. There was a lot of it clear, right up to the shoulder of the main spur."

The Hammer! The peak I had set out to climb years before.

"Good, this is just what we want," said Benjamin. "That gives compass bearing from Xanadu, and a geographical point to check drift, if any. You see, Jerry, Strawlings wasn't in radio contact at any time. We didn't get any signal."

"You wouldn't have got any signal," said Buehle quietly. "He wouldn't have had any time for that."

"You tell it your way."

"Well, I was taking it kind of easy. Cruising along. Looking at the scenery. We haven't had much scenery the last week or so. Anyway, I'd been on extra roster, and I wasn't exactly caught up with that dynamic feeling, if you follow what I mean. Well, taking it easy. As I said, cruising along." He rubbed at his reddened eyes again. The lines around his mouth and nostrils looked quite black, as if charcoal had been rubbed into them. "I was taking her along cosy just underneath the overcast when I saw another eighty-six over on my right, coming up pretty fast and drawing in on me. After a bit he came right up close and I could read the number on the tail. It was Strawlings. He sure was pushing her along fast, but he eased her back a bit, and we flew along together for another ten minutes or so. Say, thanks!" he said gratefully, as Pendlebury handed him a mug of hot coffee. "I sure can use this!"

"There's a slug of bourbon in it bigger than your fist!" Pendlebury said with a grin.

Buehle took two big gulps at it and pulled a face and set the mug down on the clip board. "I guess that can cool off a bit," he said.

"You still had The Hammer in sight at this point?" said Benjamin.

"Sure. Right over the nose. About thirty miles ahead. That was why I decided it was time I started to get up. Besides, there was nothing in front but great black thunderheads all the way along, with a lot of that nasty firecracker lightning running through it. Like an electric bulb flicking on and off inside a burlap bag. So I pulled on the stick, and as I began to climb I saw that Strawlings' ship was starting on down."

"*Down!* You mean—"

"Oh, *he* was doing it. He was flying her down. The ship was handling just fine, the way it looked to me. He just wanted to get under, that's all. I flipped my wings two or three times to try to tell him to come up where there weren't any goddam rocks. I guess he didn't see me. Anyway, then I was in the thick stuff, and I lost him. I figure he must have thought he could fly it through *under* the overcast. Boy! How crazy can you get!"

"And that was the last you saw of him?"

"No, it wasn't. This is the screwy part of it. I guess it must have been around ten minutes later. I had plenty of altitude, but it was thick as chowder. And then—you know how it is—suddenly the clouds rifted. One hell of a rift! . . . Like a great shaft tunnelled down all the way to the ground. Well, sure, it's pretty high ground around those parts, but still . . . It was Andy, the crew chief, who saw him. He kept tapping me on the shoulder and pointing down, so I banked her a bit, and there was Strawlings, way down. Jesus! . . . *Way* down!" He took up the mug of coffee and blew into it, but it had cooled off and he drank it all, and twisted up his face and said, "That really did have a lacing of bourbon, man!"

"Go on," said Benjamin quietly.

"It's hard to say," Buehle went on thoughtfully, "but I guess by this time he would have been moving around the west face of The Hammer. Well, that's the way *I* figure it.

Everything looks kind of different at ninety degrees, especially when you're seeing it down a rift like that. He was flying along a sort of deep gulch, pretty wide, but he was weaving this way and that as if he was looking for an out. I guess it wasn't wide enough for that. He seemed to be flying the ship all right. He'd just picked the bastard of a place to try it in, that's all."

"What happened then?"

"I didn't see. But I could see ahead of him and there wasn't anything there but just clouds. The dirtiest, thickest overcast you've ever seen. Black as sin and piled up to thunderheads or all mixed up in the general shit, and those lights flicking on and off behind the burlap. Just then the rift closed in and I didn't see any more." He blinked at Benjamin and began to rub his knuckles into his eyes.

"But why the hell would he *want* to get down as low as that?" said Benjamin impatiently.

"I guess he figured the holes went through all the way to the other side. They didn't, that's all. Maybe he thought this was the short cut, the quick way home. So it is, when the clouds aren't full of rocks."

"And that was all you saw, Jerry?"

"That was all. Afterwards, when I calculated we were over, I took my ship down again, but above the secondary range it was still thick, so I went on a ways and then tried down again. This time we didn't get clear of the overcast until four thousand feet, and even then it was patchy. I circled around a couple of times waiting to see if he came out, but he didn't come. That's all. I came on back here. He hadn't checked in."

"He still hasn't checked in," said Sergeant Garstein.

"You see, Jacob, it's what I said the other day," Benjamin said in a low, tight voice. "These bastards always know best! They won't fix a course and go through with it. They think

[237]

they can get home faster by sliding underneath it—and there's *no* underneath it!" His fingers rapped nervously on the desk, then he looked up at us from his pinched, sallow face, and stroked his knuckles across his eyebrows. "Well, thanks a lot, Jerry," he said. "That's all we need from you. I guess you'll want to hit the sack right now."

"Brother!" said Buehle, with a slow, tired smile. "I guess that bourbon has made me kind of sleepy."

"Sergeant Garstein will take you over in the jeep. You've helped us a lot, Jerry. At least we've got a bearing and a position. We can send out a recce plane to look around."

"For what?" said Buehle, rising stiffly. "What do you expect to find?"

Captain Benjamin shrugged, and said nothing.

"I'll take a ride part of the way with Buehle," I said, and the three of us went away together.

All that Buehle said in the jeep was, "Crazy young bastard, that Strawlings," but he didn't seem to be speaking to the sergeant or to me.

I left them at the pilots' block and walked back.

21

THE death of Strawlings had moved me profoundly. I knew he was dead. I knew that Jerry Buehle and Benjamin and Sergeant Garstein all knew he was dead, too. A recce plane, of course, would still be sent out, if the weather permitted. To find what? It was the question Buehle had asked, the obvious question, and there was no answer that needed the formal framework of words. The answer framed itself in the imagination far too readily. That twisting, narrowing gorge, with no room in it for an "out." That wall of terrible opacity hanging there in front of him like the arras of death. The frantic, desperate guesswork, the trying to remember, the half-recalled images of valleys and peaks . . . the swishing change in cadence of the engines' song as the ship plunged into a rushing blackness with the pearls of moisture skittering an insane dance upon the plexiglass . . . the howling blackness of eternity and oblivion and death. . . . Well, he would have seen nothing, and it would have happened quickly. Instantly. One single, flaring flash of extinction. Smothered at once in chaotic darkness. . . .

There had been some strange, fixed pattern to young Strawlings which I could see now in a kind of poetic clarity.

I could see him standing among the feathered cornstalks on his father's farm in Indiana . . . the broad mouth, the big rural hands, the simple innocence in his undisturbed grey eyes. I remembered with a painful vividness that evening in the bar when he had tried in vain to express in words the magic he had felt flying the twisted gorges on that clear blue day, coming back from Xanadu. And then later, the baffled pain of metamorphosis . . . that slow staining of innocence in eyes that had grown hungry, resentful, tormented . . . the agony that was there and the bewilderment, the rage and the hope. Shadows cast across naïveté, like a portent of destruction—and the darkened image of a final moment of tragic poetry, searing it all away in obliterating flame. "Crazy young bastard, that Strawlings!" Jerry Buehle's words. What epitaphs they gave! But whom the gods loved they first made mad. Perhaps. . . .

Were they *all* mad?—Favell, Hathaway, Strawlings, all the others? I was afflicted suddenly by an oppressive sense of the superstitious: events passed, events happening, events yet to come, were all bracketed together within set boundaries that were dark and ominous. One could almost see a kind of twisted validity in all the absurd little taboos and fetishes of the base, in the mascots carried for luck and the queer little formal rituals of behaviour.

It was out of these morbid and melancholy reflections that I came to realize, as I walked back through the rain, that I would have to talk to Jane Carson. I would have to tell her. Through the dark imagery of Strawlings' death I was committed to involvement with her.

I went to Block J, but there was no light burning in No. 61. The door was locked. There was no response to my knock. I moved along under the verandah light to look at my watch. Seven minutes to nine. Nine hours, to the very minute, since Strawlings had set off from Xanadu to come back to Zone Q-4. Yet not until midnight would Pendlebury take his damp sponge and wipe his name off the blackboard so that a new roster could be chalked in. Until then, in a queer way, Strawlings still existed.

At this hour, I decided, it was most likely that she would be at the pilots' mess. I was reluctant to talk to her there, in the setting of all those faces, but there was no choice. If it came to that, when did we really have choice? I walked very slowly across to the bar through the lash of the wind and the rain.

It was easier than I had expected. There were not so many people in the mess, and most of them were concentrated around Readaway. Giving him "the treatment." Even Jack Consadine had abandoned his usual corner. His sketchbook neglected. His guitar propped against the chair in which usually he sat. His long, lugubrious face was fixed in an expression of rapt wonder as he stood there with a can of beer in his hand listening to the pilots' stories. Jane Carson and Judy Consadine were sitting together at a table.

"Could I have a word or two with you later, Jane?" I said when I went across to them. "Somewhere. Just the two of us." I smiled my apology at Judy. "Not necessarily now. Just when you have a few spare minutes."

"Of course." She gave me a quick, quizzical look, then smiled and said, "But won't you have a drink with us first?"

"Thank you." I went across to the bar and got my negroni and brought it back.

Judy said, "Say, I guess I'll *have* to go up with Jack. Will you just *look* at him, for land's sake! Mouth hanging open like the town idiot! And that hat! If that boy could only *see* himself!" She sniffed, and began to rise.

"Please don't go," I said quickly. I had an illogical wish for her safe third presence. But she rose with her friendly smile, and left the two of us together.

[241]

"What did you want to talk to me about?" Jane's green eyes were very direct.

"About Strawlings," I said.

"Yes?"

"He crashed. I've just come across from the control tower. There are four planes missing. One of them was Strawlings'."

She lowered her eyes. I saw that her hands were trembling a little. "Missing?" she said. "You mean he might still come in?"

"No." I shook my head. "He won't come in. Another plane saw him. He was down very low. He hit the mountains. Around the middle of the day."

"I see." It was no more than a whisper.

"I thought I had better tell you," I said. "I wanted to tell you."

"Yes." She looked up at me. Again there was that direct, controlled look in her eyes. "Do we have to talk about it here?" she said, her voice almost calm. "Can't we go somewhere else?"

"If you like. We can go to my room. Or to yours."

"Let's go somewhere, anyway," she said.

We went to her room. The same bottles. The same screen across the corner. The same unruffled bed. The same tidiness. Nothing changed. She was even wearing the same oatmeal-coloured dress.

"I can't give you a drink," she said. "I don't keep anything here."

"That's perfectly all right, I don't really care for anything." The words sounded stilted and formal, but I suddenly felt awkward, restricted, uneasy. Now that I was here I did not know what more there was to be said. Yet at the same time I had a deep-seated awareness of being committed to something which, while yet unspecified, would prove to be of vital importance to both of us. In the lamenta-

[242]

ble poetry of Strawlings' death was lodged some hidden symbol which the two of us would have to expose. Something which had been put aside and evaded in a field scattered with dead butterflies would now have to be taken up again and examined.

She seated herself on the edge of the bed and smoothed her skirt carefully across her knees.

"Will they blame me for this, too?" she asked rather harshly.

"Why should they?"

"Do you blame me?"

"I'm not standing in judgment. I've told you that."

Her expression clouded a little, as though she were mystified. Her obliquely tipped eyes, beneath the fringe of soft shining hair, eyes so deeply green and so moistly glittering, were like those hidden secret pools one comes across in a lonely forest clearing. Yet not a tear formed to mark its wandering course across the pale, sharp-contoured loveliness of her cheek. And as I looked back at her in the long silence her brimming eyes grew dry again and no tear fell.

"Will you tell me about it?" she said at last. Her voice, under control also, carried little trace of emotion.

"He crashed. He's dead. That's all. I felt you would want to know." I was less in control than she was; I could detect the flicker of panic in my own voice.

"But what will they say? Go on. You can tell me."

"They don't even know about it. Aside from a few chaps, that is. Officially he won't be posted as missing until the midnight roster change."

She gave a short, angry little laugh. Not a laugh at all, really. "And then? Then they'll say Jane Carson destroyed him. The Jinx. The Vampire Woman. The Succubus. Poor baby," she said. "Poor boy," and looked down at her fingers

[243]

still smoothing at her skirt. "It's what they said about the other Peter, isn't it?"

I made a short, impatient sigh. "You're just harking back to that Bellini business. I thought we'd thrashed that one out. Look, if you really want to know, I have heard one comment. Only one. Somebody said he was a stupid young bastard."

"He was young," she said. "Dreadfully young. But he wasn't stupid."

I said very carefully, "He was obsessed about you. He tried to get back here too quickly. He crashed."

"And he's dead." She said it on a falling note that was inexpressibly poignant, and I suddenly heard the director's voice saying *Can we just take that one again, honey? You gotta feel it the way this poor dumb kid gets killed because he was crazy for you. Get the pathos into it, honey. Right? Lights! Camera!* And because this was so cruelly unfair to her I dodged back behind neutrality, which, heavens knows, was a good deal safer for me, too.

"The real tragedy of very young people in love," I said, "is that they always have to *make* it so bloody tragic. And you were—I didn't say this, somebody else did—you were his *la belle dame sans merci.* There has to be a *la belle dame* for the Strawlings of this world."

"I didn't see myself in the role," she said, and looked at me straight and clear. "Honestly, Jacob."

"That's all right." I still managed to preserve neutrality in spite of those eyes. "The facts are sad but very simple. He tried to fly under the weather. He had been warned about it—warned about it long before you ever came here. All right, he may have wanted to get back here in a hurry because of you. On the other hand he may simply have been deceived by the look of the weather over the Xanadu strip. This was his first monsoon, remember, and in Indiana they

[244]

don't have monsoons. We come back, you see, to the question of experience."

"Yes." Her eyes were downcast now, the heavy ivory uptilt of the lids, the silk fringes of the lashes. As if she were veiled. "All things are a question of experience," she said. She seemed to think about this for a while, and just as I was beginning to relax a little—it was going to be all right, after all—she looked up quickly and turned the full barrage on me, the dazzling green barrage. "But I have the feeling, Jacob, that in fact you *do* think me responsible," she said. "I feel this very strongly. Well, otherwise there's no reason why you should repeat to me the *la belle dame sans merci* bit, or point out so carefully that the poor kid was obsessed and hurrying to get back to me. There is a kind of an accusation, isn't there? And there wouldn't be unless you think I really am responsible."

Panic flared again, stronger now. "Good God, Jane, do you *want* to be responsible?"

She leaned forward suddenly, with one hand stretched out and cupped in an almost childlike little gesture of appeal. "Look, it's my pain, Jacob," she said. "Don't make it any worse. I so desperately need someone to help me. Help me, Jacob. Please help me."

I could feel a pulse in my throat beating, beating. A yellow gekko no longer than a lapel pin was flicking on the wall behind her head, where a loop of the mosquito netting rubbed against the cane. The throbbing nerve in my throat seemed to make my voice thick. "How can I help you?" I said.

"Just tell me what they are saying. Then I will know."

"Some of the pilots seem to think," I began tonelessly, and felt the thickening-up again, and paused, and began again. "Some of the pilots seem to think that Strawlings' morale was shot to hell because of his infatuation for you. Or his jealousy. Whatever it was." Her only reaction was an almost imperceptible nod. "Senator Vancourt," I continued, "considers you disruptive to morale generally." Again that faint, almost convulsive little nod. "And General Frisk, I gather, is more than half inclined to ship you all off back to the United States."

The ghost of a smile, half-angry, half-mocking, lifted the corners of her mouth. "In disgrace? Because of me?"

"That's only Frisk. And as far as he's concerned, you'd really be a pawn in some intricate game of military politics he's probably working on. Hardly a social problem. Or a moral one. But he's a past master at passing the buck. Which means you could become the scapegoat, of course. I think he'd see to it that it would certainly *look* as if you personally had blotted the copy book. The gallant General is inclined to find very special uses for civilians."

"Wheels within wheels," she said. "But you still haven't told me what *you* think."

"I had not quite finished. Captain Benjamin says nothing about you that isn't nice. Fred Peabody thinks you are a very fine woman."

"But you, Jacob? What about you, Jacob Strickland?" She whispered it, half-smiling, and my heart seemed like a great black bat hanging in my chest, a great black bat that stirred. The panic welled up like a nausea.

"I have told you that I am not your judge," I repeated. "I defended you to the Senator. I defended you to Bellini. If it were necessary I would defend you to General Frisk."

"Which doesn't alter the fact that you think I am a tramp, don't you?"

"No!" I exploded. "For Christ's sake, no!"

"You *do* think I'm a tramp, Jacob, but yet you'll still defend me. It's funny, that. Fred Peabody would defend me,

[246]

too, but he doesn't think I'm a tramp. And Captain Benjamin doesn't really know me at all, does he?"

I had to ask it. Thickly and shamefully. But I had to ask it. "You weren't in love with young Strawlings, though, were you? You couldn't have been. Not you."

"No. No, I wasn't in love with him, Jacob."

"Hathaway?"

"No."

"Fleming? No . . . of course not."

"Of course not," she repeated. "I'll tell you something, Jacob Strickland." Her voice was as bleak as a cry on the wind. "I have never been in love. I've never been in love in all my life."

"Look," she said. "Women need to love. Not only to *be* loved, but to love. Did you know that? Every woman needs to love. There isn't one, I swear, who hasn't dreamed of a Lancelot or a Tristan or an Abelard. No. Not dreamed. Believed in. Not even that. Who hasn't absolutely taken for granted the existence of, somewhere in the world, at some point waiting in the future, a point of fate as inevitable as the seasons . . . or death. Her own Lancelot or Tristan or Abelard—some man who will be so noble and kind and good and wise and brave that she will be able simply and naturally and totally to do what her instinct tells her is good and beautiful and true. To love one man with all her body and all her heart. To cleave to him. To be one flesh. Don't laugh, Jacob."

"I wasn't laughing," I said. I wasn't, either. If my hands were over my face it was only because I could not have borne her to see the expression that must have been on it. "But I wonder," I said, "how many of your Lancelots or Tristans or Abelards keep those future appointments punctually."

"Some, I think. It happens. For the lucky few. Maybe it happens for people like Fred Peabody and his wife." She made a funny little gesture. Almost rubbing her knuckles into her eyes. "But most women are in such a hurry to get on with loving that they mistake the spurious for the real. Or just settle for something. That's easy enough. They suffer later. Some women become impatient and take what's about and make the best of it. Or deliberately throw Lancelot's mantle over some shabby little fifth-rate Gawain and lie to themselves and to him for the rest of their lives. I guess they're the worst of all. But what I'm getting at, you see, is that the need is very real."

"The need might be real. The Lancelots aren't. They're only made of mist."

"Are they? I've been wrong then?"

"Wrong?"

"Believing it. Believing that somewhere in the world there was someone for Jane Carson. Someone reckless enough and brave enough to accept the most that I could give."

The most that she could give. An involuntary tremor shuddered through me. For a hideous second I hated young dead Strawlings.

"Because you see, Jacob, I have believed that," she said. Her face was grave, yet oddly alight in a way, with the eagerness of telling, I suppose—something of the same sort of vibrant intensity that had characterized her confessions on the day in the field of butterflies. "I *have* believed it. All the way through to here. All the sordid, dirty, cheap, nasty way to here, Jacob. Through all the jackal-men and the panther-men and the wolf-men who demanded their toll for every single step of the way."

"But you paid it, didn't you?"

She looked at me directly. There was a tiny puzzled pleat between her brows. "But of course," she said. "I'm not dishonest. I'm not a hypocrite. I pay the price for what I want if I want it enough. I wanted to get to the top. I knew I was good enough to be there."

"And what happened to poor old bloody Lancelot?" I said, with a bitter sarcasm.

"Don't," she said. "Oh, don't, Jacob." Perhaps her lips trembled then, but her chin was high and there was no change of expression in her eyes. "I am not particularly interested in conventional moralities. They hardly apply in my world, and they're usually hypocritical anyway. But all right. Technically, I was not innocent. But don't you see I *was* innocent, Jacob? There is the innocence of the believer who goes on believing in spite of all evidence and proof to the contrary."

"Oh Christ!" I said, and I could not keep the tone of disgust out of it. "*Readaway?*"

"You can call it a mistake if you want to be charitable. Although I'm not asking you to be charitable. A mistake. Or overeagerness. Overgenerosity, if you like. But a mistake anyway. There are thousands of women who would have made the same mistake. There are thousands who would now. You should see his fan mail." She pulled a wry smile. "I soon got over that," she said.

"And went on believing?"

"Yes. And went on believing. At least for quite a while. Through other mistakes. Through straw-men and baby-men and girl-men and little-boy-men. A slow sapping of confidence, perhaps, but that's all. Because I was good at my job. I *am* good at my job. And there has always been the excitement and the adulation that go with it. It was quite a long time before I began to feel . . . to feel deprived."

I took a long, deep breath. "*Do* you feel deprived?" I asked.

"Oh yes," she said. "And so do you. Don't you, Jacob?"

[249]

She said it so gently, almost sweetly, and she leaned towards me with her eyes grown soft and deep and a faint questioning smile on her mouth.

"No!" The denial came out almost as a cry, as if jerked out involuntarily by a sudden sharp stab of pain. "Oh no!" I said harshly. "You don't involve *me* in this!"

"Yes," she said. "I must. Because we are alike, dear Jacob. We are both displaced persons longing for a home. We can save each other. Maybe neither one of us can do it alone, but perhaps together we can save each other."

Sounds from outside, intruding. The whine of a truck's gears. Rain falling. Inside the room a fly buzzed, caught in a ragged trap of torn cane, pinged the irritation of its release, flickered away in a soundless, senseless activity. A draught ballooned the mosquito net above her head. The water dripping from the ragged eaves seemed to be falling like leaden pellets into the bottomless emptiness of my being.

"I have to involve you, Jacob." Her voice came to me across the void. "All the time I've known you . . . that isn't very long, is it? yet it seems so long . . . I've had this feeling about you. It's why I had to talk to you that morning in the rain. Why I wanted to talk to you after that awful concert party . . ."

"I wasn't even here," I muttered. "I had to go away."

"I didn't know that then. I saw you in the hangar that night among all those howling men. *Howling!* My God! And then the next day and night you didn't come near me, and I could still see your face among all those other faces, and I thought you despised me. And that night," she said, "I met Peter Hathaway."

I thought of the flames snuffing out Peter Hathaway's life in a violet bubble of light exploding into a wet black sky.

"Why weren't *you* here, Jacob?" she said.

"I had to go away," I repeated stonily.

"You were the only one who might have understood . . . the only one I really wanted to understand. If you were prepared to understand, that is. After you had come back, and I'd talked to you . . . after Peter Hathaway's plane blew up, even then I remember thinking that you might have gone away just as an excuse, just so you wouldn't *have* to be involved."

She paused then, but I said nothing.

"Maybe that's the way it was," she went on. "Because, you see, Jacob, I think I know now what it is that is . . . well, odd about you. You live behind a barricade, a sort of outer wall you've built up. You only want to involve yourself in things that exist *outside* you. I guess that's why you're so good at the base here. You can give everything to the outside things. Your natives, that village by the railroad, the railroad itself, the brothel man, the place you went to up the river, the pilots in the bar over there, that nice little man in that shack on the airfield, those people in the control tower. All these things and all these people that aren't *you* at all."

"That is my job, after all," I said.

"Yes, but they're like a great crowd pouring out of a subway between you and the steps leading to somewhere. Or between you and somebody you're supposed to meet and aren't too sure you want to meet. So you don't have to look at the clock to see whether it's time for you to go. Because with all this crowd in front of you, you can't see the clock anyway, and you can't see the steps, and you don't know whether the somebody has come or not, or whether they've decided not to, and you don't have any idea whether it's time for you to go or not. Why, you don't even have to look, when there are so many things in the way that there's no point in looking. Isn't that it, Jacob?"

I said nothing.

"But *why?*" she said suddenly. "What is it? Where are

[251]

you?" The questions were like fingers reaching out, feeling for me, exploring. "Is it that this is why we're alike?" she said. "That we're both . . . both *blocked,* in some way . . . that we've got something corrosive inside us that we can't seem to remove. Is it that?" Her words petered out in the soft, humid air. From the sodden thatch little leaden lumps dropped into the emptiness. "Who are you, Jacob, to forgive *me?*" she said suddenly.

"I am . . ." I began, intending to tell her about the emptiness. "I am . . ." Again I stopped. And then at last I raised my eyes to hers and said, "When I first came here, Jane, more than ten years ago, I was married."

"Yes. You told me that."

"Did I? How odd. I hadn't remembered. Her name," I said, making the words ride above a dark, sluggish stirring where my heart should have been, "was Olga. Names don't really matter, except that they establish a sort of reality. If I think of her as Olga she remains a kind of visible personality. Rememberable, at any rate. If I think of her as my wife—my *late* wife," I amended carefully, "she has no more human reality than your jar of cologne over there."

"But she's dead now," she said, puzzled.

"She is dead, yes. She has been dead for more than five years. I killed her," I said.

Even then she only looked at me with a kind of patient, puzzled interest, as if she had not quite comprehended the sense of my words and was waiting for me to explain a little more.

"I *killed* her," I repeated, and the sluggish thing inside me became the hideous black bat, and the thing lurched and was still. Quite still. "I killed my wife in the hills over there beyond the river. Do you understand?"

She made a faint inquiring breath of sound, and put one

[252]

hand up as if to ward something off. "But why? . . . *why* . . . ?"

"Why?" I began to laugh. Well, it had the sound of laughter, but there were tears in it. The clichés of laughter. I laughed until tears poured down my face. I could hardly speak for laughing. "I killed my wife because . . . because . . . she was . . . just like you."

I suppose it still came out articulate enough, although each separate word seemed incomplete, and not true and yet not false either, with my own laughter sobbing through it, and the sense of it all seemed to choke and die in my throat, like a river emptying its waters into the dry sands of the desert, and only the echo of the words kept beating and beating in my brain.

22

I HAVE no clear memory of taking her back to the bar, of how we conducted ourselves, or even whether I sat with her when we got there. Looking back on it now, it seems likely that I must have involved myself quite deliberately with Readaway simply as a way of not having to be with her. Evasive action again, yes, but I could plead in my own defence that the hour spent in her room had left me in a wretched state emotionally, and I was utterly incapable of going any further.

The background to the events that were to take place, however, remains vividly in my mind. The war of nerves against Vince Readaway had greatly intensified, but it had moved to a subtly different level where the younger pilots were, I think, unconsciously the victims of their own state of nerves.

The apparent improvement in the weather out of Xanadu —that brighter lifting of the overcast which had encouraged Jerry Buehle to look at the scenery and had sent young Strawlings to his death—had been grimly misleading. Over the whole length of the alps storms of brutal violence had begun to develop by the middle of the afternoon, and al-

[254]

though the score of missing aircraft had already increased to seven there had been no relaxation of the F.E. standard, nor was there any evidence that there would be. (What had happened was that the military situation in the combat areas had deteriorated so alarmingly that even the outlying stations of Zone Q-1 had come under direct enemy attack. The fact that the dangerous situation was retrieved three days later by a brilliant and courageous counteroffensive was in a very large measure due to the materials flown in from Zone Q-4, and to the human sacrifices it cost us in doing it.)

God knows what the pilots had been pumping into Readaway, but the change in the man was almost shocking. He was, admittedly, very drunk—probably alcohol was the only defence he had against the unremitting assault upon his nerves—but while drink had made him bleary-eyed, incoherent, dishevelled, something more than whiskey had fashioned that mask of terror that lay dumb behind the twitching nerves and muscles of his face.

Perhaps because of my own shattered state and the emotional sickness that cramped my stomach, I had an odd, sudden sympathy for the poor bloody drunk. The story that Jane Carson had told me had filled in gaps in the portrait. Much as I abhorred the man, I could see now the pathetic, worthless emptiness of his personality. She had known emptiness and I had known emptiness, but never the awful, spiritless vacuum of this self-obsessed dummy of a man. And the death fear to him would be a deeper terror than she or I could ever know. To our sort of tormented, self-tortured people the death wish is invariably a pipe dream for occasions. But to Vince Readaway, the self-idolator, the very thought of extinction must have been too much to be borne—the total obliteration of an ego that was all he lived for and all he believed in.

A sallow-faced, sandy-haired young lieutenant, whose

name I did not know, was working on Readaway. He was describing, in careful detail and with sadistic relish, the fate of the crew of a gasoline tanker which had been forced to make a bellylanding at Xanadu because of a faulty undercarriage.

"They skidded her in okay," he was saying. "Sure, they put the ship down okay." He was leaning forward tensely and talking directly into the numb, stricken mask of Readaway's face. "Then two guys jumped out and started to run for it. Only just then the gas tanks exploded, and these two poor bastards got caught in the jet of high-octane, and we just had to stand there and watch while they ran on and on, all caught alight and burning. I figure they must have run ten, fifteen yards like that before—"

"Sorry to break this up," I said politely, "but I had promised to take Mr. Readaway back to his quarters."

Readaway stared at me stupidly, and in the sudden hush that fell I realized that he was not the only one who had been drinking too much. I saw in the faces of the pilots a kind of set antagonism which, fixed for so long upon their victim, reacted against my interruption with a strange slowness, like a sequence from one of those old slow-motion movies. And behind the hard, baiting faces, there was the absurd, improbable figure of Jack Consadine, seated crosslegged in his blue jeans and Stetson hat on the top of one of the tables, his hands clasped beneath his long chin, his face fixed in an expression of the purest enchantment. For all the world like that old academic painting of the boy Raleigh—or was it Drake?—listening to the tales of the Elizabethan mariners on Plymouth Hoe which used to hang on the walls of every schoolroom I ever knew as a boy. Obviously in Jack's trancelike state of bliss—tales of flyin' an' flyin' machines such as he had never heard before . . . Man!—he was quite oblivious to the mood of his narrators and to the condition of the person to whom the stories were directed. How infinitely wide is the range of human perception . . . the tales of paradise for Jack Consadine, the terrors of hell for Readaway.

"Let's go, Readaway," I said crisply. "I'll help you get your coat."

He blinked at me for a few uncomprehending seconds, then, "Why, if it isn't our goddam limey frien' Mister Nosey Parker Strickland," he said thickly. "Jus' lemme alone, willya! Who the hell was talkin' to you, Buster?"

"Nobody was talking to me. I just came to see you to your quarters."

"Lay off him, Strickland," the sandy-haired lieutenant said aggressively. "He's okay. He's doing fine." His mouth formed an unpleasant grin. "We're explaining to him the way we do our flying out in these parts."

"Yes, well you can continue the explanation some other time, can't you? Come on, Readaway, let's get cracking."

He was suddenly quite docile, and he allowed me to take his elbow and lead him away. After his token show of aggression and the formal insult I suppose he was relieved to have the avenue of escape organized for him. Going past the lower tables Jane Carson's eyes met mine, but I looked away deliberately, making a pretence of guiding Readaway's stumbling feet around the high stools at the end of the bar.

Outside, splashing through the slow dark sibilance of the rain, he was quiet for a time and allowed me without protest to steer him on an unsteady course towards the billeting blocks. He was in pretty bad shape, and I had to put my arm around him to prevent him stumbling headlong into the puddles and the ditches. His breath came stertorously, so that after we had covered about seventy-five yards I led

[257]

him to the shelter of a tree and propped him up against the damp, crusty trunk so that he might rest a while.

I lit two cigarettes and put one in his mouth, but after one puff at it he began to snigger and it fell from his lips into the mud. "Brother!" he said with a snort of triumph, "did I tell those goddam craphounds back there just where they got off! Boy, did I give it to 'em!"

"Good for you," I said dryly.

"Say, why is it that every bastard who flies an airplane thinks he's God?" he asked thickly, swaying a little even against the thick trunk of the tree.

"Is that what they think?"

"Sure 'swhat they think. Goddam little tin gods, playin' with their toys!" His drunken laugh honked out again. "They can't see they're through here. Jus' a bit longer, brother, an' they're through. Maybe they'll ship 'em back home then to fly kites. They're through. I told 'em. Boy, did *I* give it to 'em!"

"Why do you think they're through?" I asked, to humour him.

"You don't *know!*" He weaved forward and grabbed unsteadily at my shoulder. He thrust his face to within a few inches of mine. I could smell his hot, whiskey-sodden breath. He laughed suddenly and I moved my head aside distastefully as a shower of spit fell on my cheek. "Well ain't *that* something! Mister Nosey Parker Smartypants Strickland doesn't even *know!*" he crowed delightedly. "You're not kiddin' me, Strickland?" he said owlishly. "You're not tryin' to take me, are you, Buster?"

I reached out and pushed him firmly back against the tree. "For Christ's sake, pull yourself together, man," I said, "and let's be on our way."

"Oh no," he said solemnly. "Oh no. We're not goin' any place, Buster. We got things t' talk about. So you don't know

[258]

about this deal at this other airfield over there. Boy, that's a laugh! I figured you were Mister Wise Guy . . . I thought you were supposed t' know every goddam thing about this joint."

"What other airfield are you talking about?" I asked him quietly.

"Hell, that one over there," he said. "Forgotten the name . . . why should . . . I dunno . . ." His words blurred together.

I shook him firmly by the shoulders.

"Rampart," I said carefully. "What do *you* know about what's going on over there? Listen to what I'm saying, Readaway! Answer me!"

"Ah, the hell with it!" He pushed my hand away, and he lowered his head and swayed it slowly from side to side, like a bull preparing to charge. But then he straightened up again stiffly, and said, "When I'm in a place I like to get around. I like to get to know what's goin' on. I don't care for goddam mysteries. So I wanna find out what's the deal around a place, I find out. That's the way I operate, Strickland. *Any* place."

"And what did you find out about Rampart, Readaway? Tell me what you found out about that."

He looked at me blankly. I grabbed his shoulders again and shook him hard. "Tell me!" I said sharply.

"Okay, okay. Suppose you lay off pushin' me aroun', Jackson. I don't go for that stuff. But okay, I'll tell you anyway. They're makin' a big new bomber base out there, Buster, that's what they're doin'. They're tryin' to keep it all hush-hush, but I'm the sort of baby who finds these things out, see. They're makin' a big new hush-hush bomber base for those big new Superforts, Buster, an' they're goin' to bomb the shit outa the Nips all the way from here. So we'll have *real* guys here, flyin' *real* airplanes, doing a *real* job for a goddam change!" He gave an emphasis to each repetition of the adjective by jabbing a wavering finger at my chest. "An' when they come here, Buster, they can make baggage porters of all these other useless bastards, these fair-weather falcons, or ship 'em back home to write crap stories for the pulps! Boy, I can see their goddam faces when some *real* flyers come here! I can hear the bastards telling their stories!" He began to laugh again, but it choked in his throat and turned into a violent paroxysm of coughing and retching. I thought he was going to vomit, and I moved aside. But the fit passed. He groaned in self-pity. "Gotta get m'self t'bed," he gasped. "Boy, do I feel low! Those goddam sonsabitches laced that Scotch with something."

"Readaway, did you talk to those pilots in the bar about this?" I asked him.

"Chrissakes, waddayou think? Sure I told 'em. Why not? Why the hell not, Buster? Bastards might as well know how they rate for size." He swayed suddenly and lurched forward. I caught him and propped him up again, but his knees were sagging. He was mumbling incoherently and dribbling spittle from his mouth. I pulled his arm across my shoulder and levered him up to take his weight.

When I got him to his room I took his boots off and his coat and rolled him on his bed. His hair and one side of his face were caked with yellow mud where he had fallen. His jaw had dropped and his mouth was open and his skin had sagged into ugly folds and pouches, and his black hair was plastered across his forehead. He didn't look at all like the hero of the mesa or the idol of Hollywood. I pulled the mosquito curtain around him. He was snoring when I left him, and grinding his teeth.

Outside the door of his room I hesitated for a moment. I knew that Jane Carson would think I had made an excuse of it again. I had left her and gone off with somebody else

[260]

. . . absorbed myself in some other problem so that I might avoid further involvement.

I had a desperate wish for postponement, but I did go across to the bar. In a way I was relieved that she was no longer there.

It was after eleven and now some hours since I had checked on the flight situation, and I knew that I should call Benjamin or go over to the control tower. But even if the casualties had increased, or continued to increase through the night, there was nothing much we could do about it until daylight. I killed a few more minutes by asking for my drink chits and signing them, and then I went back to J Block and knocked on the door of Room 61. There was no answer.

I got out the jeep then and drove across to Rampart.

Approach to the gates of Rampart at night was quite a different matter from what it was in the hours of daylight. At least fifty yards before I had reached the fence I was sharply challenged by a white-helmeted guard who came from the shadows of the trees with a Tommy gun levelled.

"Okay," he said curtly, walking around to the rear of the jeep. "Get out. Walk up there in front of the headlights. Now, turn round. Okay, what's your business out here?"

"I'm Strickland," I said, blinking into the dazzle of the headlights. "Civilian liaison officer. I wish to see Colonel Dorenfurst."

"Isn't it kinda late for calls?" said the voice out of the dazzle.

"I am perfectly aware of that," I said irritably. "It happens to be urgent."

"Okay. Let's go to the guard post. Just turn around and walk straight ahead. I'll keep you company. We'll leave your jeep just where it is."

The sentries at the gate were hardly more accommodating. It took several minutes of argument to persuade the sergeant in charge to telephone his C.O. There was another long delay before he came out to me and grudgingly said, "Stick around. They're sending an escort." It was at least fifteen minutes before the inevitable pair of custodians arrived. White webbing and "S" helmets. One with a Tommy gun and one with a .45. I knew the drill now and moved smartly between them; we about-turned and set off at a brisk march. I changed step to break the rhythm, but they immediately shuffled into step with me again and we went towards the low administrative block like a well-drilled squad. None of us said anything.

I suppose the delay had been necessary to give the Colonel time to dress, because he was waiting for me in his bare, clinical office, wearing his uniform, badges, and campaign ribbons, and as spruce and fresh-looking as if he were about to take a morning parade.

"Please sit down, Mr. Strickland," he said, without any preamble. "Eleven thirty-five. A late call."

"I'm sorry." I took the hard chair facing him across the tidy desk. "I felt it to be necessary."

"Naturally. I would not expect you to come at this hour merely from sociable motives. So let's have it, Mr. Strickland." He folded his thin hands across the blotter.

"It's to do with this business of snooping here at your field. You suspected that my natives might have been the culprits."

"I don't believe I ever suggested that, Mr. Strickland," he corrected me mildly. "But please go on."

"I've an idea I know who your snooper is."

"Readaway?"

I looked at him sharply. "You knew already then?"

"Suspected, shall we say. He's been poking around outside from time to time. Tell me your story, Mr. Strickland."

"But then . . . that was why you went across to the pilots' mess. You were watching him?"

"Not watching, exactly. Listening. Men who are as inquisitive as Readaway are usually loquacious."

"It seems he was loquacious tonight. And also very tight."

"I would suggest that the condition is hardly unusual with Readaway."

"Quite. Tonight, I gather, he was explaining to a group of pilots the object of the activities here at Rampart."

"You say you 'gather,' Mr. Strickland. You did not actually hear these—er—these explanations?"

"I didn't hear him talking to the pilots. He told me about it when I was taking him back to his quarters."

"What *did* he tell you, Mr. Strickland?"

"That Rampart is being built up as a secret bomber base from which we intend to fly Superfortresses against the Japs."

"I see."

"Is that right?" I asked. "Is that what is going on?"

He smiled slightly. "The truth, Mr. Strickland, continues to be a classified matter whether Readaway is telling it or not. Shall we leave it at that? From the security point of view, the unfortunate thing is the *fact* of his inquisitiveness and loquacity, not necessarily the content of it." He held up his hands and examined his fingernails. "Mr. Readaway," he said, "has acted very foolishly. He has involved himself in a breach of security."

"Well, he was probably so drunk that nobody paid the least attention to what he was saying. You will understand that my concern is less to act as informer on him than to protect the integrity of the natives in my charge."

"Of course. I entirely understand. Since you are a Britisher, Mr. Strickland, you will doubtless remember the poster which your country issued early in the war, with the slogan Careless Talk Costs Lives. Careless talk such as Readaway's, whether delivered drunkenly or soberly, could cost lives here, too, you know. Do you realize that with this push the enemy has made around Zone Q-1, he is practically in a position to launch very heavy offensive air attack against *this* base?"

"I hadn't realized that," I admitted.

"Let us indulge ourselves in hypotheses, Mr. Strickland. Supposing that with great secrecy and at enormous cost the United States Army Air Force did establish here in Zone Q-4 an advance airfield from which big, ultralong-range Superbombers—aircraft still on the highly classified list— could make massive offensive air strikes at enemy targets as far distant as Singapore, Hanoi, Canton, Hong Kong, even the Japanese home islands. And supposing these plans were revealed prematurely to the enemy. In the first place, the priceless element of surprise is lost. In the second place, the enemy cannot be subjected to demoralizing mystification as to where the attacks are coming from. And, finally, he will surely make the most prodigious efforts to attack and neutralize the potential source of danger." He returned his hands, folded, to the blotter. "Well, so much for idle theories," he said. "Now, to get back to Readaway. I do not think he has been actually *inside* the area proper. Perhaps some of your natives have talked to him?" The metallic eyes watched me steadily.

"In what? Esperanto? Or do you think Readaway has been attending Berlitz classes on the local dialects? Quite apart from the fact that not one of the natives would know a Superfortress from a yam!"

Colonel Dorenfurst lowered his head and laughed very softly. I had never heard him laugh before. It was not altogether an appealing demonstration. "Then obviously someone else must have talked to him," he said. "It's possible. We

have our own security guard here, certain technicians, sometimes G.I. work parties are detailed to us by General Frisk.
One of these men may have been susceptible to the status
and personal magnetism of Mr. Readaway. There are some
Americans, Mr. Strickland, who worship the figures of Hollywood in exactly the same way as ignorant savages worship
their little wooden idols. They think they are both omniscient
and omnipotent. To be able to talk to one of these godlike
figures *in person,* Mr. Strickland, to feed information to such
a deity, might give great satisfaction to a person stupid
enough to cling to such forms of adoration." Again he spread
his hands and studied his fingernails with great care. "General Frisk, on the other hand, seems firmly convinced that it
is your natives who are responsible for the leakage," he said
smoothly.

"General Frisk is a bloody fool!" I said angrily. "He knows
nothing at all about them!"

"Where ignorance is bliss, Mr. Strickland, 'tis folly to be
wise. And let us take the political angle. From General
Frisk's standpoint—in the event, shall we say, of War Department hearing that a major and dangerous breach of
military security has occurred in Zone Q-4—it would be much
more comforting to pin down the source of leakage to a group
of natives working under the control of a foreign civilian
officer than to loyal American servicemen under the direct
command of a Major General of the United States Army.
Here we have, I think," he added slyly, "a clear-cut issue of
general morale and command relationships."

"And Readaway?" I said coldly.

"Ah, this is also an interesting situation. If the major cul-
prit in the matter happens to be a very famous American
cult idol, then presumably General Frisk must also take into
account the possibility that there might also be important
officers in the Pentagon, or even in the Administration, who

[265]

are also susceptible to the power, the magic, and the influence of our national cult figures." He glanced up from his fingers and smiled at me. "I have reason to believe, Mr. Strickland," he added blandly, "that our commanding General is becoming very uneasy at the continued stay here, not only of Mr. Readaway, but of Miss Carson also."

"He is taking consistent action everywhere to pass the buck, if that's what you mean," I said bitterly.

"But he has his own position to protect, Mr. Strickland. He did not ask these people to come here. If they are upsetting his operations, or threatening the morale of his command, he is perfectly entitled to various forms of action. To self-protection, in a way. Surely you would not deny him that right, Mr. Strickland?"

"I am hardly in the position to do so, am I?"

"Nor, I hope, would you deny me my right to take whatever course of action I deem best to safeguard *my* particular responsibilities in the command," he went on.

"I don't deny you your right. I just think it would be bloody unfair if innocent people were victimized simply because—"

"My dear Mr. Strickland, who suffers *personally* in these issues is not really the important thing, is it? The vital question is that the task must continue and the objective be achieved. In war, personal sacrifice is as much a strategic material as steel or gasoline or aluminum." He rubbed at his fingers and said, "So far as you are concerned, Mr. Strickland, I would say don't worry. I shall make it quite clear to General Frisk tomorrow morning that you and your natives are completely exonerated from suspicion as far as I am concerned. I shall also take up with him the subject of Readaway. But I am not at all able to predict what course of action, evasive or otherwise, the General will want to take

[266]

from that stage. Well, thank you for coming, Mr. Strickland." The dismissive twitch of a smile was at his lips. "I think it's time we all got some sleep."

He rose, shook hands cordially, opened the door for me, and passed me on to the two waiting guards.

23

When I had put the jeep away I walked across to my office and unlocked the door and went in. There was a typed message asking me to contact Peabody, but on it my corporal had written, "Checked this but the Major is on special courier ferry to Q-1 with G staff personnel." I telephoned Benjamin. He sounded sleepy and he had nothing particular to report. He told me that there had been no improvement in conditions over the main range, but losses for the midnight-to-midnight span still remained at seven. It surprised me vaguely to realize that it was already past midnight. Strawlings' name would have been wiped off the blackboard. . . .

"If you could drop around about seven I could use some filling in," Benjamin suggested dispiritedly.

I felt despondent enough myself as I walked slowly across to my own quarters. There was a plane sobbing somewhere overhead, and another roaring its motors at the end of the runway, and a nervous jab of lights rippling above the trees. Although the rain was still slanting down cheerlessly I thought I saw the glitter of one star over in the west, but a second glance revealed it as the wingtip light of a plane moaning in to its touchdown. The realization of my mistake added to my sense of discouragement.

Suddenly I was fed to the teeth with the whole bloody business! The noise of aircraft engines in the night, never ceasing . . . the rain that eternally pissed down . . . the mazy disorder of unending involvements. Intrigue, gossip, question-and-answer, buck-passing, duplicity . . . a futile and perpetual striving towards some orderly pattern of things in a world where everything was a muddy flux of intolerance and misrepresentation, of ambitions twisted by spurious values, of obeisance to the safe stereotype at whatever the cost!

Why in the name of God did a man like Benjamin keep on trying? In the long run, what the hell did it really matter? Planes fell from the skies. Well, that was another aspect of the law of gravitation, nothing more. Planes smacked into mountains. The law of diminishing returns. Men with tight lips tested parachute harness and took the blind leap into howling space. Some were lost. Some were found. There would be a law of averages about that, an equation of expendability. Sometimes it cost months of work and only the War Department knew how many tens of thousands of dollars to bring in a man so that he might exist in a madhouse or spend the rest of his living days stretched out on a hospital bed, drawing a full pension and reading fictional adventures in a mirror. The law of logic. Where, in all that, for God's sake, was the orderly pattern of things? Was this the ultimate fruit of the logical, dedicated, sacrificing, legal mind of a man like Benjamin? Yet Benjamin *believed* in what he was doing! He would always believe in what he was doing. Christ, it was only a few days since I had believed in it myself! And now?

Now other images intruded. New problems were superimposed. The phony, brassy obbligato of film music drowned out the plaintive droning of aircraft in the sky. Huge, warm, swollen, beautiful faces on a screen, as animated as if they really lived, obscured all the true-living, true-dying things. Now we had other more important things to think about than men meeting death alone in the high dark nights. Strawlings, perishing on some alien wall of rock that did not even have a name—a life that had hardly begun charred away in that dreadful smell of burning . . . of smouldering rubber and hot, buckling metal. Why consider Strawlings now? The sponge has wiped him all away. Now we have other images to obsess us, and possess us. We must give our attention now to the myth hero, twenty times life size, whiskey-stinking and mud-plastered and retching in the rain. To the myth goddess, with the dying butterflies aswarm in her tawny hair, and only her libido to consider. Bow to the keener intellect of Colonel Dorenfurst. Knuckle the forelock before the ruthless efficiency of General Dalton Frisk. Symbols of security and morale. The precious repositories of organization, know-how, and true patriotism. What are idols for if not to be worshipped? To the devil with people. . . .

Bitterness and despondency were my companions on that slow walk back through the rain. My irritation was ridiculously intensified when I saw that I had left my light burning. I pushed petulantly at the door.

She was there, sitting on my bed, in her hands a magazine she had taken from the shelf.

She smiled with a kind of tense timidity. "Your door was open," she said, not too confidently. "You didn't lock it."

"I never lock it." I tried hard to keep my voice steady. "I've never felt there'd be anything here that anybody would want."

"There is now."

"What?" I asked, moving towards the chair, still trying to grapple with the shock of seeing her there.

[270]

"You," she said quietly.

Panic clutched at me. I had a sudden desperate longing to possess the metallic rigidity of Colonel Dorenfurst, the chilly smile, the steely eyes, the established composure of the man. Talking to me across the desk he had stroked the palm of one thin hand with the forefinger of the other, and the gesture had produced a slow, dry, scraping sound that had somehow been intimidating. I sat down carefully and began to drum my fingers against my knee, then realized that it only betrayed the panic. I clasped my knee tightly, but the skin showed white on the knuckles of my hand. I lowered my arm, but even then there were loose straws sticking up from the dry grass mat and I began to pluck at them. The room smelt of mildew, and the grass straws were soft and unpleasant, damp to the touch.

I rose jerkily from the chair. "I can offer you a gin and lime," I said, getting a grip on myself. It was essential that I stall off any resumption of the earlier conversation. I was not going through *that* again! "Or gin and tonic. Although it won't be very cold. I'm afraid I've no ice."

"I didn't come for a drink" she said.

"Do you mind if I have one then?" My heart was pounding, but I was not to be panicked. I went to the cupboard and took out the gin bottle and the lime juice. I used the jigger meticulously, poured the drink with a connoisseur's care. My hand, I saw with relief, was absolutely steady.

"There isn't much time, Jacob," she said in a flat, quiet voice. "They *are* sending us back."

I turned to face her, my fingers tight around the long, tepid-feeling glass. "Who said so?" I asked.

"Judy. Someone told her this evening . . . the sergeant from Garnett's office, I think it was."

"For God's sake! How the devil would Fleming's sergeant know?" I sounded more snappish than I had intended, I

think because she had called him Garnett and not Colonel
Fleming.

"But *you* thought they would do this," she said. "You told
me earlier." She glanced away and I saw that she was biting
on her lip. "It will break their hearts if they don't go," she
said. "Jack and Judy, I mean. It . . . it means *everything* to
them. They don't look on this as . . . well, just a stunt, or
an adventure, or as some kick for their own egos. It's something almost . . . almost religious with them. They're like
pilgrims going some place. And . . . and I think it would
break my heart, too, Jacob, if it was all ruined for them
because of me."

"Oh for heaven's sake, Jane! Some cock-and-bull story
circulated by an NCO sitting behind a typewriter in an
office!" The drink tasted awful, like swallowing a throatful
of the wet warm heavy gasping air. But there was safe
ground between us now. Something else had intervened
between us and the ghastliness of our earlier discussion. We
had taken a new tack. I could go back to my chair. "If one
were to listen to all the stories and rumours that float around
a place like this!" I sat down and stretched my legs out. I
even managed to sound briskly impatient. Who was I de-
ceiving?

"Tell me the truth," she said. "You've already told me
that General Frisk had this in mind. Were you only breaking it to me gently?"

"It isn't my business to know these things, Jane. It isn't
my department." I could feel the sense of relief solidifying.
"General Frisk likes us to stick to our own departments," I
said. "It prevents confusion higher up. Or lower down, if
you like. What I told you was simply part of the usual pro-
cess here of transmitting facts, lies, rumours, speculations,
hints, and wishful-thinkings. The *modus operandi*. Standard
Operational Procedure. In this case it seems that Frisky

dropped a hint to Vancourt. The Senator passed it on to me. I relayed it to you. That's all I know." I felt at ease now, in command of both myself and the situation. The other matter had been put aside; she had come back only to check on a disturbing rumour. "Look, Jane, why not forget it, and have a drink? The gin is remarkably potent this evening." Like you, I said to myself, out of my new confidence. Like your mouth and your hair and the pain lodged in your eyes and your lovely throat straining so unhappily. It was a mistake even to think it. Women are telepathic to the slightest brain pulse of the amatory.

Rather to my surprise she responded.

"Yes, fix me a drink, please," she said evenly, but without any change of tone she went on to say, "I can't help thinking that you're dodging again, Jacob. And I wish you wouldn't. I wish you would let yourself be involved just for once. For me, Jacob. Couldn't you be?"

Even then I managed. I got to the cupboard and worked the cap off the gin bottle and measured out her drink and put the cap back very neatly and took the drink across to her. It worked. In that tiny, smelly cane box of a room even the small pattern of progression of chair to cupboard, cupboard to water jar, water jar to bed, gave me an illusion of freedom. I might even have walked out the door, I thought, and gone away.

"If you want to know," I said, "I doubt the sergeant's story very much. And shall I tell you why? Because I happen to know for a fact that the General wanted to send you all over to Xanadu today. He called Fred Peabody in. He wanted Peabody to fly you across. So there you are."

"Is this true, Jacob?" She seemed startled. "Then why . . . ? Oh, I get it." Her eyes clouded. "And Fred wouldn't?" she said.

I felt a sudden ache of sadness for her. She was so entangled in this mesh of guilt and trouble that every state-ment and every fact were suspect. In all probability, I re-alized, she thought that Peabody had refused to fly her as some sort of tacit endorsement of Flight Sergeant Jorgen-sen's contention that she was not worth pay load space that might better be allotted to a freight of liquor.

"It wasn't what you think, Jane," I said gently. "Fred was quite prepared to take you over. Flight Control refused the clearance. That's all. And a jolly good thing too," I added firmly.

She looked across at me questioningly.

I said, "Just another of Frisk's little chicaneries. He wanted to pass the buck, that's all. And he didn't get away with it, which is just as well. The weather was absolutely bloody then and it might even be a damned sight bloodier now. Do you realize we've lost seven aircraft already? And that was—"

I broke off. "What on earth's the matter?" I asked, even as I saw my own blundering insensitivity. For a chisel of terror had jabbed between her brows. Real terror. Unmistakable. And a tortured something else, which may have been only a reminder that Strawlings would have been one of the seven.

"I'd forgotten," I said awkwardly. "You're scared of fly-ing, aren't you? You told me before."

She made a quick little nod. "I always have been," she said. "Almost pathologically. Still . . ." She shrugged.

My very first meeting with her, I realized, had arisen directly out of her reaction to this fear. I could only guess at the degree to which it had been intensified by her en-forced stay at the base and her apprehension at the thought of having to continue on that more perilous flight across to Xanadu. To what degree had she identified herself with the pattern of danger to which the rest of us, in a sense, had become more or less immunized? Or been affected by the

[274]

cold-blooded "treatment" directed at Readaway in the pilots' mess? And, even more than all this, how could I even begin to appreciate the depth of her *personal* involvement in those ever-recurring crises of tragedy and suspense that marked the monsoon flying days? Strawlings? Favell? Hathaway? The violet fire bursting in the night? (She was there, too, in a Senator's notebook, a table of logistics, among the voices in the static, lodged in the unwritten annals of a noncombat zone in a time of war.)

"Look here, I am sorry," I said. "I . . . I didn't mean to upset you."

"It's all right," she said quietly. "I do get a bit scared thinking about it. Sometimes I do. But I don't think I'll be frightened when . . . when it happens." She was silent and thoughtful for some little time, and then, "Jacob," she said, curled up damply on my damp, drab bed, "if you could tell me something about it I think . . . I think it might make it easier."

"Something about what?"

"About over there. Xanadu. You have been there yourself."

"Oh yes. Many times." A sudden curious peace seemed to be established between us. It was false, I see now, no more than a temporary lulling of our separate fears. Yet it was there, existing between us. She looked relaxed, and a kind of subdued, almost childlike curiosity had moved the panic and the trouble from her eyes. She was seeking comfort from me, I realized, and reassurance. I filled her glass again and mixed another drink for myself—that was a mistake—and felt the quality of mercy dropping as the gentle rain from heaven—it was drumming down outside—and I thought that Jacob Strickland was God.

And "God" said, unsatisfactorily but with truth and from the gentlest motives: "China is a state of mind. Xanadu is a point in logistics. Or a problem of organization. There *used* to be a country there once, I think. Sometimes I almost remember it. Or possibly I only *seem* to remember it. It's all so long ago, you see. It isn't anything with immediacy or reality any longer. A mood? A feeling? Put it this way—to me it's come to be like something which one knows actually exists, but which lies beyond and quite outside the stretch of one's imagination. Like the far face of the moon, for instance . . ."

"Oh, but *I* know what's on the far face of the moon," she said, surprisingly. She had kicked off her shoes earlier, and she was sitting on the narrow bed with the mosquito netting looped above her and her legs tucked beneath her, and her glass was held, gripped almost, in both curled hands. (So that any trembling of her fingers would not have been apparent? I suppose an experienced actress would have known many little tricks like that.) Outside the rain went on drumming and drumming, and the warm wind blowing in made the mosquito curtain seem to breathe in uneasy forced breaths, like an asthmatic. The pale, musty-smelling, almost transparent material made shapes above her head—a dancer's *tutu*, a Turk's trousers, a carnival balloon, grotesque faces, puffing out their cheeks, pouting, swollen into hilarity, then all the images sagging into sad, damp drapes, with old rust stains in the folds. I could hear the lizards scratching along the walls, scuttle and pause, scuttle and pause, and the faint stabbing whine of insects, and even the distant impatient uproar of the planes.

The memorized detail is still as clear as that. Clear, and yet out-of-true somehow, in the way the twisted distortion of a dream is often imprinted with all the precise and colourless clarity of a steel engraving: perhaps it is that one only sees now in visual terms the falsity of that strange calmness that seemed to join and surround the two of us. For we were both afraid—of different things, but both afraid—because I also remember thinking that there was another sound among the motif of sounds, and it was her heart pounding in terror. Muffled, dark, alive. Or had that been *my* heart?

"Shall I tell you about the far face of the moon?" she asked. Her face, tilted a little to one side, seemed very young.

"Tell me." I nodded, humouring her.

"Well then . . . The far face of the moon is something else," she said gravely. "Anyway, I guess this is what they used to believe hundreds and hundreds of years ago. They used to think that on the other side of the moon there was nothing but huge storerooms and lockers and cupboards and closets and chests. Things like that. Things for . . . for putting things in." She raised her glass and put an imaginary something into it by way of illustration.

"What kind of things?"

"All the things of everybody's life that had never been completed," she said, with a sort of reflective earnestness. "Stored away there forever. Unfinished business . . ."

"Go on." I smiled a little, to prompt her.

"Well, things like promises that have been broken," she said thoughtfully. "Vows unfulfilled. All the appointments one never got around to keeping. Unfinished books. Dreams that have never been realized. Wishes never gratified. Failed ambitions. Broken trysts. Suicides planned and never carried out. Murders too, I guess. Unconsummated loves." She paused there and looked at me across the rim of her glass. That green, soft, marvellously brilliant look of her eyes! "Things like that." She ended the explanation with an almost careless, dismissive little gesture. "Unfinished business," she said, and looked down into her empty glass and laughed very softly before she held it out to me to be refilled.

I had the sensation of having to wade to reach it. As if the air had clotted around me. Like walking through warm treacle. I cannot pretend to explain now how extraordinary it seemed that Jane Carson should be sitting on my bed holding out a glass for me to fill, how dreamlike and yet utterly familiar this fusing together of time sequences that were not even related: as if the soggy cane walls that kept the wind and the rain off Jacob Strickland had been built only to contain *this*, had been mute and impersonal for two whole years just to chamber this misty, swirling, chaotic moment in time.

A loop of the mosquito curtain brushed my head as I bent for the glass and I had to duck beneath it.

"Unconsummated loves," she said. "Things like that." And kissed me full on the mouth. And reached for me and pulled me down against the firm, rich, desperate suppliance of her body. And as the panic boiled up to engulf me I heard the empty glass hitting the grass mat and rolling.

24

It was because she was still crying that I began to tell her. She was sitting up quite straight, her hands held loosely on her bare knees, palms upward in a kind of unconscious supplication, and although her head was high it was no longer proud. Nor, distorted as it was by a sort of ferocious anguish, was her face really familiar to me any longer. She was still racked by loose jerking abandoned sobs—how dry her eyes earlier in the evening! And I remember thinking that when Olga had cried—and she had cried very often—the tears had always become dark and muddy from her make-up, and there would be unsightly smears of mascara down her face which she would have to wash away.

A space—a void, rather, immense and empty—seemed to lie between the two of us, although I was so close to her that I could feel the warmth of her spent body, smell the sweet tingling female smell of her in my nostrils, and with hardly a movement of my hand my fingers could have touched her shining hair. This did not matter. It was not physical space that divided us now. Physical links, or divisions, had been abrogated in that earlier frenzy of desperate despair and frustration and humiliation, in the writhing struggle which had driven our naked, sweating, impacted bodies to the ultimate distance of pain and failure, to my own deadening realization that the void was there forever and that the nightmare of five years ago was still the nightmare of now. It was not that I had to *tell* her, because it was all too bitterly evident: more that one had to somehow make an explanation as a substitute for peace.

The planes were droning in out of blackness, seeking the bright sanctuary of our base, and the yellow lizards were busy on the walls, and a sticky fly pivoted drunkenly on the rim of the glass that had fallen to the floor. I remember the burnish of the lamplight streaking the loose dishevelled fall of her hair, the play of shadow curving from her armpit to her straining breast and the nipple was angrily dark and still erect and hard with some obstinate, still unstifled sexual desire, the sharp bone of her tear-glistening cheek bright as a knife before my eyes, the glaze of sweat across her flank and belly, even the clean wet gleam of her flesh reminding me of when the raindrops had moved on the face below the grey sou'wester on the night I had first met her. (I tried to picture the small table in her room where the jars and lotions were kept. I could not recall whether I had seen there a little flat oblong case and the tiny black brush for mascara. Eau-de-Cologne, shampoo, a vial of perfume. Nothing else. Olga's dressing table had always looked like a pharmacy. It made no difference, though. . . .)

"She was over there with me, of course," I said, forcing a level tone. "Over there in Xanadu. I shall have to tell you about it now. I hadn't intended to, but now I must. We can at least add it to the anthology." I tried to keep the bitterness from my voice. "Tales from the Far Face of the Moon. Complete and unabridged." The gall was there, an acrid coating on the words.

It will not be forgiven you, I told myself. Neither that,

nor this, nor anything. But I told her anyway. We had come so far there was nothing else to do.

I talked at first with my back turned to her, standing by the frayed cane drop of the window, staring out at the sliding shimmer of the rain, and the flick and dazzle of the lights, blue-white across the parking compound and road to the landing field, and a sort of dirty yellow where doors and windows were open in the billeting blocks. There were only a very few of the yellow lights burning. It was quite late. I thought of all the hundreds of transient human bodies, sweat-wet and restless in the humid darkness beneath the dank drape of mosquito netting.

When I turned to face her she still crouched on the bed in the same position, but she must have moved while I was not looking at her, for she had pulled the bed sheet around her body, tight against her nakedness, rather like a sarong.

"Her name was Renneck. Olga Renneck," I said, striving for a factual, almost dossier-like accuracy so that emotion might be held below the surface of narration: and for a time, indeed, the story did come out easily and without particular pain. . . .

I had first met Olga at a dull residency party in one of the southern seaports, to which I had gone to recuperate from malaria contracted during a longish exploration in the swampy delta tracts of the Arakan. I was then not long down from Cambridge. She was the niece of a prosperous but alcoholic planter and was on her first trip out from England. She was a quite pretty girl, and vivacious, with something to be rubbed off from Swiss finishing schools, but intelligent enough to let new experiences work upon her. She had an immense romantic excitement about this exotic tropical world she had come to. Nowadays she would have worn tight pants and striped sailor's shirts and her hair in a ponytail, and she would have read Henry Miller and liked Scarlatti. That sort of girl. She was twenty-two when I met her.

I was both impressionable enough and lonely enough to find an extraordinary stimulation in her company. I remember her as a kind of gay, effervescent, intensely *living* sort of person who provided the most exhilarating contrast to all the dreadful dried-up women of the residency officials, the desiccated partners in Christian Endeavour of those dull but dedicated missionaries whom I would meet from time to time on my scientific wanderings, to all the gabbling shrews and harpies who lived around the tennis courts and yacht clubs, and the beaky, mean-faced, high-complexioned naval wives. She was—or at least regarded herself—as "advanced." She liked to make statements such as, "The real problem for our kind is to accept without prejudice the fact that while we are monogamous by conditioning we are polyerotic by inclination." We were, in those early days, always classified as "our kind." Perhaps in testimony of her advanced social consciousness, she permitted me to make love to her on the first night I met her, rather uncomfortably in the cramped cabin of a friend's two-berth cruising yacht.

We were married a year later, when I returned sick with a recurrence of the malaria and desolate for my own sort of companionship.

During that year she had stayed on in the seaport. The gay, loose mixture of the formal and the informal suited her temperament. She had enjoyed the social protocols, the occasional emotional dramas, the frivolous escapades of the young naval officers, the flux of faces and personalities occasioned by the changing dispositions of the R.N. flotillas and the visits of cruising yachts, and by the intermittently wild carousals of miners and traders and planters and airline men from the hinterland. She had made amusing liaisons

[282]

among the men and satisfactory enemies among the women.

Yet I suppose there must have been some element of boredom or satiation attached to it, because she accepted my proposal of marriage eagerly, and with it the new, exciting prospect of joining me in what she considered, I am sure, my intrepid adventures in the back-country. At this time, with a grant from the University of Basle, I had already begun work on an extensive botanical survey of the areas flanking the eastern spurs of the Himalayas and the basins of the great rivers—the areas later to be known as Zone Q-4 and Xanadu. . . .

Jane had remained perfectly still during my careful explanation of these preliminaries, and although the sobbing had ceased an occasional little freshet of tears would impart a wet glitter to her eyes. But she was quite still and absolutely silent. The directness of her gaze and the rigidity of her posture gave the impression that she was listening intently to every word I uttered, but I still had an uneasy feeling that half her concentration was barricaded off from me. That "blocking" she had referred to? Well, I reflected savagely, we were coming to *that!*

"So," I went on doggedly, "we were married and she came up here with me. For a time it worked. She found it exciting for a while, and she played along with the discomforts. But then . . . No, it wasn't her. I don't think it was her. It was me. Because after a time she began to get on my nerves. Her talk, her gaiety, her enthusiasms mostly. Her almost delirious desire to *share.* Because, of course, one can't possibly share all things, one can only share some things . . . and where science and scholarship are concerned one can't really share at all. At any rate, after a few months I found I just couldn't stand her. It's possible that where my work was concerned I had already grown habituated to a serious solitude. The sexual act, frequently repeated—and she wanted it frequently repeated—did not make up for the loss of that essential intellectual privacy. Or so I told myself. Well, the excuse came when she went down with a pretty bad attack of fever: when she was over the worst of it I sent her back to the seaport, to stay a while with her uncle.

"And now we come to the illogical angle," I went on. "Are all human relationships largely illogical? I suppose by their very nature they must be. At any rate, the fact remains that once I had sent her away I began to miss her terribly. When I tried to analyze it I told myself that it was not for her companionship or her talk—which still irritated me when I thought about it—nor even that irritation itself can be a valuable palliative for tedium, so I came to the conclusion that I missed her simply for the sexual comfort she provided."

Did I imagine it, or did Jane compress her mouth at that, as though I had touched a bruise? Her eyes never left my face.

"I'd better give you the rest in précis form," I said. "It went on more or less like that for several years. I would send her away and want to have her back again. For quite long periods she would be in the seaport, then I would summon her and she would rejoin me. Then after a while, and perhaps not unnaturally, she began to be a little less responsive to my demands. Weeks would pass after she'd received my telegram before she would even make a reservation on the plane. Even so, it was a long time before I began to realize what was going on. In these small, isolated communities, in foreign countries, gossip always runs on swift feet, but I was a long way off the couriers' beats. Olga by this time had begun to develop a reputation which could hardly have remained a secret, even from me, although I know the cuckolded husband is always the last person to find out. One realizes now, of course, that she had hardly had much of a

[284]

chance to be other than she was, but it was difficult to see this then."

I went across and poured myself another drink, because I had almost come to the point where my thoughts would have to be very carefully assembled. Her eyes, I noticed, did not follow me. They remained fixed on the chair where I had been sitting, just as intently as when I thought she had been looking at me.

"Well, from this point," I resumed, "things became pretty strained. And violent, too. I mean, it wasn't just that I rather went on like the classic jealous husband . . . I mean violent in various other ways. Quarrels, accusations, recriminations—all that, yes—but also the violence of sexual excess between us. Almost as if I had to prove something to her and to myself as well. Rather horrible, really. Perhaps she had something of the same feeling . . . it's difficult to say now. Anyway, the point I'm coming to concerns only me, and this was obviously something quite different from whatever agitated her." I paused carefully, marshalling my thoughts into correct order, trying to present it as cold-bloodedly as I could, but the bitterness welled up in me again, chokingly, and I said, "This fiasco we've just enjoyed—or endured—well, it has to be explained, I suppose. In fairness to you." I stared down at the floor as I spoke, afraid to meet her eyes. "It . . . it isn't the easiest thing in the world to get off one's chest, you know, but I'll have a shot at it anyway." I waited, looking down. There was no sound from her.

"I'll try and keep it on medical grounds," I said carefully. "You may know, or possibly you don't, that men who stay on for long periods in tropical climates without relief stand a pretty certain risk of suffering changes in metabolism. Sometimes these changes can be profound. One effect is a form—er—a form of sexual debilitation. I don't mean just a lowering of vitality, a physical lassitude, which is normal enough . . . I'm talking of an actual pathological condition. It derives from a number of things, or so the experts say—the attrition of a constantly bad climate, recurrent fevers of various sorts, more especially the constant prophylactic doses of drugs like atabrine and quinine . . ."

I heard my voice as from a great distance, coming across that immense and empty gulf. It sounded precise, detached, unaffected by emotion. Scientific, almost. I was gratified that those years of self-discipline and control were working automatically for me now. Yet I could not have looked at her just then for a million dollars. I could hear both her breathing and the thudding of my own heart. And I could hear the rain still beating and beating down.

"Of course this doesn't happen with everybody," I heard myself saying. "I suppose there has to be something there in the individual's basic metabolism to begin with. I had been warned about it, in fact. By a doctor who worked for years up here among the natives. Degenhardt. Kurt Degenhardt. He was a lapsed Lutheran. A funny little man with a squint and a rabbitty face, who went around in a soiled white suit with hypodermic syringes stuck in his coat pocket like fountain pens. He died a few years back of bubonic plague, and I was the only person around to bury him. Well, as I say, he'd warned me about this business. Very solemnly. And I had laughed at him. I was still only in my twenties, remember, and besides he had some pretty eccentric ideas about medicine, anyway. Poor old Degenhardt. He lived for years and years with a little Kachin girl, and Martin Luther would never have approved of his absolute enjoyment of her. What I'm getting at is that I'm pretty sure Degenhardt would have considered impotence a fate much more tragic than death by plague."

She made such a funny sound then. Not a grunt, exactly, but a sound almost as ugly. Of rejection? Of disbelief? God knows! I think I could have lifted my head and looked at her then, except that I was staring across the intervening years to that clearing of sunlit stubble at the edge of the jungle. Staring at it from far away, in a sense, for I still had to get up to that part. And the really hard bit came before.

I took a long, tight breath and some dissociated area of my mind shaped the vision of a little circle of sunlight—bright, hard, hot, screaming with insects and hidden birds. And then began:

". . . on this particular night I tried to, but I couldn't. Just like us, Jane. I lay there under the mosquito net with her body naked against mine. Sweating. Suddenly fearful. Thinking of what Degenhardt had told me. She made me try again. She had all the ways of making you try again. And still I couldn't. God! It was an insane nightmare that had nothing to do with sleep. It was horrible and I was sickening for a bout of fever, and it's . . . it's like delirium now because it seemed to go on all through the night. And it wasn't until just before dawn that the awful realization came to me—Jesus! how awful it was!—that she was teasing me, goading me, torturing me, laughing at me. I thought that my rage with her then would turn the trick. That sheer brutal sadism would give me the power to ravish her. And still I couldn't . . ."

And then the clearing came rushing up at me suddenly, before I expected it, and it filled my whole vision, and I was there, dizzy, sweating. The dry smell of the grass stalks. The dry snapping of twigs. The dry yellow dust blowing. . . .

"We went out to shoot pheasants next morning. The fever was coming on now. Sweats and shivers. Blind pain in my head. So dizzy I couldn't see properly . . . everything sort of fuzzy and out of focus. I am not pleading this as an excuse, mind you. I . . . I just want you to understand it as it happened. Well, because I couldn't see properly I missed two birds I tried for. Both dead easy. And I missed by yards. She was just a little ahead of me in the break of the trees, about ten paces away, when I tried another shot at a rising bird. I missed again, and she turned and stood there laughing at me. And suddenly I couldn't see anything of the trees behind or the dry stubble." (I could smell it though. I could still smell it even then, as I talked to her.) "I could only see her the night before, and the folds of the mosquito net around us, and her naked in the bed, laughing at me. I . . . I don't know what happened then. I remember breaking the gun and shoving two cartridges in. I remember her calling something about birds, calling to me through her laughter. I must have shot her down while she was still laughing. Both barrels . . . one after the other, I suppose . . ."

And she had lain down in the grass stubble and drawn up her knees convulsively and turned her head and become quite still, just like Jane Carson on my bed. So now I had shot them both.

"I was able to carry her back (Jane Carson with her dead face and her hair falling and falling with the stubble chips caught in it instead of butterflies!) and to explain to the houseboy that there had been an accident. He helped me dig a hole in the ground and we buried her, and then I collapsed. The boy nursed me through the fever, but I was in bed seven days and I was still pretty groggy when I got up. Then we had to make a ten days' journey overland to get to the post where Degenhardt was working. He filled out the formal report of her death in a shooting accident, and signed the certificate. He didn't question it. Then I asked him to examine me."

In the long silence the outside sounds invaded the room. The mosquito curtain bulged and contracted in the warm wind.

"So that's why I couldn't," I said. "That's why I can't."

She neither moved nor made a sound, not even when I rose and moved across to her and sat on the bed and touched her hair. And I knew, in a way that was a terror of fresh illumination, that I had stumbled at last into that desert of vast eternity from which there would never be return. Not for me. I lay beside her on the bed and pushed my face against her hair and wept.

25

ABSOLUTE exhaustion must have made me sleep, but the invisible time switch of the mind wakened me at six, and I knew that Captain Benjamin would be expecting me in the little shack on the airfield. I lifted my legs over the side of the bed and sat there, staring down at the clothes strewn across the floor. Her clothes and mine.

She was sleeping. The sleep of exhaustion, too: blank white eyelids, pale sealed mouth, the delicate blue veins at her throat and between her breasts, and those supple muscular hands curled into fists—sleep had taken her in the midst of struggle. I had to close my eyes against the pain of the memory, the sickness of recollection. I winced again at the stabbing images that still formed behind the flowing red darkness of my tightly closed eyes. She had tried again. Twice more she had tried. Once with a tender, soothing solicitude; once in an abandoned, passionate, sobbing frenzy of proof and longing, and then she had cried herself to sleep, and for a long time I had lain beside her, staring up at the thatch and thinking that one could almost feel one's own soul shrinking and withering into nothing.

The mosquito curtain was still looped up high above us,

where I had flung it because it had kept brushing against my head. There were insect bites on my forearm and wrists, and one tiny pink swelling on her thigh.

The bitter gall was no longer only across words and tainting thoughts now; it was a foul taste in my mouth, a corrosive acid burning behind my eyes, concentrated into a leaden weight that dragged insufferably at my failed and useless body.

After a time I was able to get up off the bed, and I picked up her clothes and folded them carefully and put them across the back of a chair. I ransacked the drawers of the cupboard until I found a clean muslin sheet and with it I covered her nakedness—that body of hers!—and lowered the mosquito curtain around the bed. An enshrinement rather than a protection; the mosquitoes had vanished with the coming of daylight. When I had done this I washed and dressed; and then I found a spare key and hung it on the inside doorknob. When I went out I locked the door with my own key in case one of the dormitory boys should come to clean up the room and find her there.

There seemed to be nothing much more that I could do.

At the airfield canteen I stopped the jeep to drink black coffee laced with a double brandy, but it was still before seven by the time I got to the Search-and-Rescue shack.

Benjamin was already there. Alone.

He greeted me, and said, "Did Fred Peabody find you?" I shook my head. "He called here," Benjamin said. "Wants you to contact him. I told him I'd let you know."

"Thanks. I'll get in touch with him. I thought he was flying courier?"

"So he was. He checked back in earlyish last night."

"I'll see him later. What have you got on your plate?"

His face clouded. "Nine," he said. "And four, I guess, are hopeless." A gravity as old as human history moved in

[291]

his Jewish eyes. Strawlings, I knew, would be one of that four. "The other five are promising," he said.

"Well, shall we get started now?"

"I stayed up all night," he said. "To tell you the truth, I think we're in pretty good shape. I'm just waiting around now for Updike. So it's okay by me if you want to go find Peabody." He gave me a long look, and said, "What's got into you, anyway?"

"Me? What do you mean?"

"I don't know. You look as if you've just found the turd in the punch bowl. You also look kind of tuckered out, man. You know what's wrong with you, don't you?"

"What?"

"You're trying to bite off more than you can chew. You're spreading your resources over too wide a field. You can't go on playing Figaro to every goddam outfit in the setup, Jacob. Why the hell don't you take it easy?"

"Listen to once-a-fortnight talking!" I retorted, trying to make it come out lightly. Inwardly I accepted the unintentional irony of his comment.

Figaro Strickland! Spreading his resources over the problems of Readaway, Jane Carson, Dorenfurst, Senator Vancourt, and Major General Dalton Frisk! How long was it since I had been to the village? What was happening there? Sanitation? The rebuilding of the huts? Food supplies? The threat of epidemic disease? Distribution of the emergency rice ration? I hadn't even sent the official confirmation of Jidal's final report up-river to Sitokó's village. There had been half a dozen times when I should have called Benjamin and hadn't. Last night I had known that seven planes were missing and I hadn't even gone back to the control tower. Now the score was nine. . . .

"Look," I said, "if you're absolutely sure you don't need me for the moment . . ."

[292]

"We'll be okay. Shouldn't be any problems."

"Then I'll push off, I think."

"Roger."

"I really should go in to the village."

"Do that. I'll let you know what the deal is later, after Tommy calls."

As I went away I was very conscious of his warm, shrewd eyes watching me.

While I was driving back to the administrative block, driving very slowly, the real truth of it all began to come to me, and I wanted to think about it first, so I detoured back across to the airfield canteen and ordered another mug of coffee. With another lacing of brandy.

A frayed cane chair in a scabby Quonset hut, staring out on the rain sheeting across an Assam airfield, with the monsoon heat prickling at one's skin: a dreary fulcrum this upon which to test the balance of one's destiny! It began, I remember, with images, for I found myself wondering whether she had awakened yet, and dressed herself, and found the key where I had left it, and gone back to her own room; and I had to close my eyes against the picture of her that took possession of my mind. Then I realized again that the closing of one's eyes did not expunge that sort of image, and this flash of logical examination at once changed the image into something else. Now it became that awful desolation, trackless and empty and without configuration, which I had seen stretching ahead of me during the night. I seemed to see this untrodden territory of despair more calmly now, with the eye, as it were, of inevitability. However unpromising the adventure—however terrifying the thought of going alone into that unwelcoming void—it was quite clear to me that the journey would have to be undertaken. Because there was no longer any other way to go. It had become as simple as that. I had come to the end of all the beaten trails; no further alternative was offered; there was no other journey to make. Every journey, one had to suppose, in the long run was only a movement to catch up with oneself, although the random byways and the evasiveness of the detours often made it all very deceptive.

Once I had this settled in my mind I walked across to the bar counter and got myself another brandy, this time without the coffee. I thought of it as a kind of stirrup cup, and I took it very carefully across to the table beside the old cane chair. For quite a long time I stared into the glass, as if the oily-looking topaz skin of the liquid would shimmer and break and form some other image. But one doesn't find the translucent orb of the clairvoyant in Martell's Three Star, so I took up the glass and drank the liquor down.

It had the effect, not of warming me, but of freezing into an icy core of awakened cognition the truth of what had happened. *The structure had collapsed!* Again, as simple as that! Everything fallen into a messy ruin, like the miserable little huts of Leromenos battered into rubbish by the monsoon rain.

Worse, my interest in the shape of the pattern had totally vanished. I knew with absolute certainty that I would not build the structure up again. That, in fact, *I could not*. I had forgotten the shape of it already. I had even forgotten how much careful planning and work had gone into its construction . . . how intricate the detail, how skilful the attention to joints and strains and stresses.

So there it was. All those years which so sedulously I had built around myself, as if I had been making a stockade in the jungle to keep the wild beasts out, had fallen into a sorry heap of muck and debris, like the mud-soaked wreckage near Armand's brothel. And I did not care, I told myself.

[294]

For what the devil did I care now, what did I *really* care, about Benjamin's pored-over maps, or his neat paste-ups of badly printed photographs? Or crayon marks on a grid scale? Or Pendlebury's tired eyes roving in a half-lit room? Or the disease fear and the hunger fear written on the pock-marked face of some skinny naked native? What did I care about the serious entries in a Senator's notebook or the calculated duplicities of a West Point General? Vultures in the trees, Negroes singing, the shadow of a plane skipping a mud-rutted road, flames in the black night, rocks in the sky, noises of despair screaming in the neutral static—what were these things to *me?*

My only concern now was myself, and the journey that must be made.

In a way—there was no point in denying this or trying to evade it—she had been responsible. If she had not come to Assam . . . or if the monsoon had not forced her into this long stopover . . .

Rationally, one could hardly make her responsible for the monsoon, but I have an obsessive desire to finish the story honestly, and it was at this point that an evil distortion began gradually to twist my thoughts. Were there extenuating circumstances? The events of the previous night had torn my nerves to shreds, and I had the feeling, physically, that my body had been beaten with metal rods. I had already drunk three double brandies on an empty stomach. I was in a suicidal mood of depression and futility. And I still had the uncomfortable, guilty sensation of Benjamin's eyes staring at my retreating back.

It was very possible, I told myself carefully, that with Jane Carson I had strayed too far into the territory of mercy. That I had invested her with my own wistful, romanticized interpretation of her moral frailty. But supposing she was really no more than a woman obsessed by sex—a case, not

[295]

for the romantic lover, but for the psychiatrist; a clear example of the wilful nymphomaniac, threading men to her casual tally like shell beads on a belt of wampum? Now perhaps poor, deluded Jacob Strickland was only another bead, a broken bead, hung there with the others to mark a wanton's progress . . . hung there among *all* the others—Strawlings and Hathaway and Fleming and only she would know how many more running all the way back to the nauseating Readaway!

It was very odd that after I had made my terrible confession to her—offered it, really, so that *her* self-respect might be maintained—she had not once even mentioned the crime I had committed. The murder of my own wife! Not even by inference had she given *that* the least attention. Oh no! Her interest had been entirely concerned with the other thing. My completeness as a man. Hers had been an organic problem, not a moral one. My usefulness as an instrument to satisfy her sexual appetites. God! She had even had to try to prove it for herself!

I stared at the empty brandy glass, my thoughts dizzily dissipated in a sudden wave of nausea. The hot taste of the cognac seemed to well up from my stomach and atomize in my throat, acrid and choking. I felt weak and faint. I didn't know whether I wanted to put my head down or go outside and be sick around the corner.

I pushed the glass away and folded my arms across the table and put my head down. And in that red running darkness behind my eyelids the images stalked me . . . stalked me in the blind red darkness through the full circle of vision, as if I had an insect's eyes. Everywhere the image of Jane Carson, the thousand differing images of Jane Carson, in front of me, on either side, behind me, above me. The multiple-lensed retina of my own shame and cowardice flicking the images back at me. Sharply focussed. Insistent.

My soul the ground glass. Warped and stained, but still the frosted frame on which the image of her face advanced against the receding shimmer of the butterflies in the soft rain, and her grave green eyes asked for truth, and her soft voice pleaded for one man's charity and understanding. Was this nymphomania? My tears in her hair and her tears on my face in that moment when we were completely merciful to each other. And surely it had been her mercy that had forced that last wild abandoned wish for proof? *Surely?* She had called me her love . . . her own love. . . .

"Mr. Strickland, suh? You feeling all right, suh?"

A soft hand fell gently on my shoulder. I looked up dazedly to see the negro GI from the canteen standing beside me, teeth set in a white smile below troubled eyes. "You been curled up here with your head down, suh, best part of an hour or more. You care for aspirin, Mr. Strickland? Or maybe I fix you another brandy?"

I controlled a shiver and shook my head. "Thank you, Harry. Nothing more. I'll push along now."

"Sure there's nothing wrong, suh? Nothing I can do?"

"No, no. I'm fine. Tired, that's all. Thanks very much, Harry."

My jeep passed Peabody's, coming out to the airfield, on the way in to the administration block. He waved, and we both stopped, and he reversed and pulled in beside me.

"Where have you been?" he called. "I've been looking all over. Didn't you get my messages?"

"Yes." I nodded and climbed out from behind the wheel and went around to him. "I intended to contact you."

"I was looking for you last night," he said.

Again I nodded. Another defection! He had been back from his courier flight early; I could have tried to contact him after I had got the corporal's message. "I got your message," I said, "but my chap had indicated that you were flying some personnel down to Q-1."

"I got back around nine thirty. I wanted you to come along with me to talk to Senator Vancourt. The way it worked out it was okay, anyway." He looked at me carefully. "Say, you got ten minutes or so? I've got to go over to my room. Could you come on over behind me, and I'll tell you about it."

I nodded and went back and turned my jeep and followed him down to the pilots' block.

Peabody's quarters consisted of two rooms divided by a half partition, and were an incredible clutter of books, magazines, newspapers, bottles, flying gear, service equipment, a pennant with Nebraska printed on it, and countless photographs of children, dogs, horses, airmen, family groups, some elderly women and one pretty young one, and airplanes. Thumbtacked to the dividing partition were two things which had been added since my last visit—one of Jack Consadine's drawings of an eighty-six taking off from the Kansas runway, and an eight-by-six glossy photograph of Jane Carson with something written on it across the corner.

He caught my eye and grinned. "Guess you'd never have thought I'd go in for pin-ups," he said. "But she *is* the only actress I've ever got to know, and the flesh, after all, is weak."

He tossed his cap on a table littered with opened letters, V-mail forms, and airmail envelopes, straddled a chair, and came straight to the point.

"It's about her," he said, with a jerk of his head in the direction of the Jane Carson photograph. "I got to thinking over what you told me about your talk with Vancourt, and coming back from Q-1 last night I began to figure something out. I realized I'd have to get the Senator in on it, though, and that was when I thought it might be good policy if you came along with me."

"You had to get him in on what?" I asked.

"Well, I had a quiet check with Allison, and it seems old Frisky wasn't kidding about his intentions. Either Jane Carson got off to Xanadu in the next roster period, or Jane Carson got shipped back home with a flea in her ear."

"So?"

"So the way I figured it, flying back here from the south, I thought we'd better get Miss Carson off to Xanadu."

"How?"

"Well, this is where the Senator had to play along. You see, I knew I could work it with Captain Ryeland at Flight Control to make a special request signal to Air Transport Command in Washington, but there would have to be a reason for the request, and that's where Vancourt had to come into it. He came over here to my room last night, and we talked an hour or so, and then we went across to Ryeland, who's an old buddy of mine, and Vancourt even helped draw up the signal. This is what we sent, if you're interested." He took a folded slip of paper from his shirt pocket and handed it across to me. "It was coded, of course, but this is the broken-down transcript in clear."

I unfolded the slip of paper slowly, and read:

BASE HQ KANSAS Q-4 TO OPERATIONS OFFICER GHQ ATC:

URGENTLY REQUEST ON BEHALF SENATOR CARTER VAN-COURT SPECIAL PERSONNEL FLIGHT AUTHORITY FOR VAN-COURT AND ENTERTAINMENT UNIT FOUR PERSONS TO XANADU STOP VANCOURT DISTURBED BY REPORTS OF ENEMY PRESSURE AGAINST OUR POSITIONS Q-1 AND ELSEWHERE FEELS STRONGLY THAT ENERGETIC ATTEMPTS BE MADE TO UPHOLD MORALE STOP HE INSISTS THAT THIS WAS WHOLE PURPOSE FOR WHICH ENTERTAINMENT UNIT WAS ESTAB-LISHED AND URGES SPEEDIEST POSSIBLE TRANSPORTATION TO FORWARD AREAS STOP SOCK-IN CONTINUING BUT CONDI-

"You're taking a hell of a risk, aren't you?" I said, looking across at him. "Who said conditions are improving?"

"Well, hell, Jacob"—he spread his hands and grinned at me—"they've got to improve *some* time, don't they?"

"So if this comes off," I said bitterly, "that bastard Frisk gets away with it, after all!"

He studied me curiously. "Jake, what the hell's gotten into you?" he said slowly. "Why do you just have to feel bitchy about the goddam General? Couldn't it make you feel good about *her?* She wanted it, didn't she? She wanted it pretty damned desperately. Couldn't you feel good that it's come off for her?"

I looked at him blankly for a moment. "Come off?" I said. "You mean . . ."

"Sure. Approval for the S.A. clearance came through about two hours ago. I called Frisk and told him, and I'm damned if I know whether he sounded pleased or sore."

I looked at him, and I didn't know what to say.

"I'll be flying them over," he said quietly. "That's why I'm here, to get some gear together. I figured I'd spend a couple of days with 'em on the Xanadu side, while they get themselves settled in."

Again, I had no words. My mouth was dry and my body seemed weighted with lead.

He looked at me with a trace of that easy, slow smile of his just discernible on his lips, and then came across and put a hand on my shoulder.

"You see, Jake," he said quietly, "riding the ship back last night, I had a bit of time to think a whole lot of things out. And I figured that if both of you couldn't be helped it might be a pretty good idea to try to help one of you."

[300]

26

I cannot remember how long it was after I left Peabody's quarters that I realized it was not raining. The clouds were still grey, but no rain was falling. Normally one's first instinctive action on coming out of doors was to look up into the sky to assess the weather—Benjamin, like a tribal ancestor of his, would have had a dove in readiness—but on this morning my grip had loosened on the orthodox.

As I walked over to the jeep park I had a queer sensation of the day having advanced farther than was proper—something of that feeling of strange disorientation, of time having passed unwatched, of things unsuspected having already happened, which one always has in coming out to a daylit street from a matinee performance in a theatre. Now, with my awareness that the rain had stopped, I was also conscious that the day had changed; one had the uneasy feeling that it had grown much larger. There was still no direct sunlight, but the light was brighter and more white than grey. The grooves in the cement had dried out, so that one could see dirt and chaff and used matchsticks embedded along the cracks, and the oil stains on the concrete were clearly defined in black and brown like old hypothetical

maps of undiscovered continents, and in the puddles the
whorls of spilt gasoline had taken on their rainbow tints
again. There was even dust rising behind an eighty-six
gunning up its motors in the first taxi lane.

I had a splitting headache.

I drove back to the administrative block slowly—I had
a distinct feeling of a need for postponement, without knowing precisely what it was I wished to postpone—and while I
was parking the jeep the eighty-six which I had seen kicking up the dust took off overhead in a hollow rush of air.

When I got to my office I thought the corporal gave me a
curious glance from behind his desk.

"Any messages?" I asked.

"Some," he said. He tapped a little stack of papers. "Nothing special. I've dealt with 'em. Miss Carson called over,"
he said. "She wanted to see you."

"When?"

"Oh, it must have been an hour ago, I guess. She wouldn't
leave any message. I suggested it. You want me to run over
and fetch her?"

"No. Skip it. It doesn't matter. If there's really nothing
pressing I think I'll trot along. I should go in to the village.
If anyone's wanting me that's where I'll be."

"Yes, sir."

He was still looking at me curiously as I went out.

I hadn't reached the jeep when I heard Fleming calling
me from the porch in front of his office. He looked almost
gleeful. I went across to him.

"Say, Jake, have I got a laugh for *you!*" he chuckled, and
made a comic feinting punch at me. "Boy, have I got a
laugh! Let's go in where it's quiet."

"Well," I said doubtfully, "I should go along to the village."

"Hell, it can wait. Come on."

[302]

I followed him into his office. He gave me his swivel chair and seated himself on the big desk and swung his leg. He kept rubbing his hands together briskly. The swinging leg and the rubbing hands were equally expressions of the delight that creased his handsome, heavy face.

"It's that buddy of ours, Vince Readaway," he said happily. "Jesus! you wouldn't believe this! The bastard's chickened!" He took a long, satisfied breath, his eyes sparkling as he watched my face. "The bastard's chickened out, Jake! How d'you *like* that?"

"But what do you mean?"

"I mean he's quit. That's all. The remarkable Mr. Readaway, old he-man Vince, our great big bee-yootiful matinee idol, has gone and chickened out. He won't go through with it. He's refused point-blank to fly over there to Xanadu."

"You can't be serious."

"The hell! Not only that—he's asked for passage back in the Fireball. He's decided he'd rather get right along back to the land of the free and the home of the brave."

"But how can he do this? He—"

"He can do it, my friend, because he's a civilian, he's not under direct army orders, it's a free country, and he's got the shit scared out of him!"

"You're sure it's not something to do with security?"

"Sure it's something to do with security. *His* security."

"I don't mean that. I mean military security."

"What the hell has *that* got to do with it? Jake, what are you getting at?"

"Nothing. I heard some idle talk."

"You heard some idle talk." He mimicked my accent good-humouredly. "Security! Boy, that's a laugh! How would that dumb bastard get involved with security? He never knew his ass from his elbow at the best of times." He laughed. "No, Jake, this is a plain case of how chicken can you get. What happened was the whole bunch of them got alerted for stand-by this morning. Their S.A. clearance came through on a special Washington priority this morning, sock-in or no sock-in. Anyway, the way this weather looks to be lifting, maybe there'll be no sock-in. The point is that our boy Vince, as soon as he heard about it, came haring in here like Becky's ghost, white as a sheet, sweating all over, practically wringing his goddam hands, and pleaded to be put on the outward Fireball. Brother, *I put him!* Priority A, and the best seat on the plane. And *bon voyage* to him, the loused-up sonofabitch!"

"He hasn't gone already?"

"He's out at the field now. He leaves"—he looked carefully at the clock on the wall—"in exactly seven minutes. And in three days' time he'll be back there in Hollywood, blazing away with his six-guns!" He slapped his thigh. "Those bastards!" he said contentedly. "God how I love 'em! When I was in combat we had a bunch of correspondents come up to see how we were shaping under fire. The day they arrived we had one of those routine little air strikes on the strip, all of four miles up the road. One stick of bombs. Hershey Bars! From where we were you could hardly hear the explosions. But, would you believe it, one of these guys reports straight off to the PRO, asks for air passage back to the base area. Claims he's suffering a punctured eardrum from bomb blast. Four goddam miles away! Some blast, eh? They sent the jerk back. Another of these cardboard heroes. But, Jake, you should have seen the crap that guy wrote in the papers. Holy Mother of Christ!"

"I really think I'd better push along," I said. "I should go in to the village."

"Sure. I got a million things to do, too. I just wanted you to know this Readaway deal."

I nodded and rose from the chair.

[304]

"Say, listen, Jake," he said, "when you're in the village howsabout you book a table at Armand's? We could take a run in this evening, eh?" He eased himself off the desk and stretched his big strong body, and looked down at his wrist, turning it this way and that. "I could do with a bit of set-ting-up. I'll fix with the sergeant about the ice. We could go in about the usual time. What do you say?"

"Of course. I'll pick you up here." I had a tiny swift rush of gratitude to him. Relief, almost. Thankfulness, I suppose, that some small move had been made to patch up the fallen structure. The sensation was momentary; the recoil from it shameful and sickening. The first patch in the ruin, and such a cheap, sleazy, sordid patch it was! And I had found myself grasping at it, grateful even for this grisly crumb of resurrection!

Outside there was no way of avoiding her. She was stand-ing under the thatched verandah across from where my jeep was parked. As I walked across the compound her eyes followed me unwaveringly. I went past the jeep and across to where she was standing.

"Hullo, Jacob," she said quietly, her gaze still quite steady.

"Hullo."

"I found the key. Thank you for thinking of that." She paused. "You know we're leaving? For Xanadu. We've been alerted."

"Yes, I heard. Peabody told me. It appears to have worked out then, after all."

"We're to take off around noon apparently."

"Well . . ." I forced a smile. "It's good to have something definite after all this waiting around and . . . and suspense. The weather's lifting too, by the look of it. That's a break. You should have a perfectly good crossing."

"Does this mean that the monsoon is over?"

"Oh, the worst of it, I should say. After this it'll just be heat, insects, dermatitis, athlete's foot, and insufferable boredom." Small talk. The safe evasions. But that, clearly, was not what she wanted.

She said quickly, "Jacob, do you think we might talk somewhere else? Would you mind very much? Please."

Block J was just around the corner. We walked to her room in silence.

Her bag was open on the bed, almost completely packed. The little table was now bare, so I could not check about the mascara. In the room's emptiness there was a melancholy look of impermanence—the folded screen, the open suitcase, the few garments interleaved with tissue paper and neatly folded on the bed, a spill of screwed-up paper and some crushed, empty cigarette packs pyramided neatly beside the ash tray, a pair of stockings hanging over the chair-back: already the impersonal sadness of a cheap hotel room had invaded her surroundings.

I decided to re-establish the conversation at a level where both of us could be secure. "This change in the weather rather sneaked up on me," I said. "I'm jolly pleased, though. I mean, it takes a load off your mind, doesn't it? Especially with Peabody flying you over. You've nothing to worry about, you know. It'll be an absolute piece of cake."

"Oh," she said. "That." Her mouth was trembling a little, I thought.

"Don't be frightened about it," I said.

"I'm not frightened. I'm glad we're going. I honestly *am* glad." She spoke with some firmness, either to convince herself, I thought, or to control that little quiver at her lips. "Did you know that Vince isn't coming?" she said.

"I heard. You're getting *all* the good breaks, aren't you?" I said lightly.

She didn't respond to this. She was looking at me quite

[306]

steadily, but in a way remotely. "At least I'll be able to find out for myself, won't I?" she said at last. "What the far face of the moon is really like, I mean. That will be something, won't it, Jacob?"

"Yes," I said awkwardly. "Yes, I suppose that will be something."

She began to speak, hesitated, then said, "Will you come to see me off? Or not?"

"Not, Jane."

"I thought that," she said, and turned quickly and took up the folded oatmeal-coloured dress and put it carefully in the suitcase, and then began to pack the few other things that were laid out on the bed. I watched her in silence. In sick, sad silence. It took only a couple of minutes for her to finish, and then there was nothing more for her to do than close the case, which she did with a kind of crisp, decisive neatness.

"You've forgotten something," I managed to say, and pointed to the stockings.

"No," she said. "I left them out to wear." She picked them up and stared at them and put them down again, and I saw that suddenly her hands had begun to shake violently, and when she lifted her face I realized, for a second, what Jane Carson might look like when she was old. The spasm passed and she straightened slowly and gave a funny little sigh.

"Love," she said, very softly. "My own love." And came to me and put her hands on my shoulders and her face against my breast. Achingly, I held myself rigid. I could feel my own heart beating through her body. She stayed like that for a little while and then she let her hands fall slowly, running her fingers down my sleeves and over my wrists and hands, and then she stepped back.

"We still could save one another, you know," she said very

[307]

softly. I looked at her in silence. "There are other doctors, Jacob," she said carefully. She had half turned away from me and was staring at the stockings. "There are other doctors besides an old German buried away for years in the jungle."

I said nothing.

"Have you talked to the doctor here at the base?"

"Colonel Robarts? No." I had the sensation of a great hammer beating in slow, heavy strokes at the centre of my brain. I think I said something like, "It's hardly the sort of thing that one would—" but she cut me short.

"There have been enormous advances in medicine in these last few years," she insisted. "You just can't accept this and—"

Rage and shame came up like a great red choking clot. "For God's sake!" I shouted at her. "Drop it! It's finished! Christ, woman, don't you have any pity at all?"

And then she was shouting too: "It isn't finished! I won't *let* it be finished! I love you, you fool! And I'm damned if I'll pity you!"

I don't know how long we stood there staring at each other in this baffled fury and rending desperation. I think truly we might have killed each other then. I wrestled for some shred of self-control—my blood seemed to have turned to ice—and when I could trust myself to speak, "Just supposing," I said with great care, "that medical science has advanced so far that this little difficulty of mine presents no great problem. All right. Haven't you still forgotten one other thing?"

"What?" she whispered, and now she was really trembling.

"That I killed my wife. Murdered her."

For an agonizing interval those brilliant green eyes

[308]

stared at me. Shining. Jewel-like. As if tears, like blood, had frozen. "Oh my *God!*" she whispered.

I turned away and began to move towards the door, but her voice, soft and pleading, arrested me before I had reached it.

"Darling, how can you know?" she said, as I stared at the dark rectangle of slatted cane. "It's been haunting you for years, Jacob, but . . . but how do you *know?* Darling, you must listen to me . . . you must let somebody else talk to you about it." She spoke in a voice that was low and tense and terrible. "Oh God! Do listen to me, Jacob, *please!*"

I turned slowly and looked at her. She was crouched on the edge of the bed, arms stretched out towards me, her fists clenched.

"Jacob," she said, "I don't believe you murdered her. I don't. I *won't!*"

"You know nothing about it," I said.

"I know you. And . . . and I know you couldn't have killed her intentionally."

"She is dead," I said. "Degenhardt is dead. The house-boy is dead. *They* might have known. Not you."

"Jacob, it could have been an accident, don't you realize that?" she said with a furious insistence. "All right, it can haunt you for the rest of your life as to whether it was deliberate or chance. It will always be something awful and horrible. But you were sick and half crazy with anger and you were dizzy and you couldn't see properly and you were shooting wildly. What you remember is your rage with . . . with her, and you see everything through that frame. You told me she called out something about birds. How do you know you weren't aiming at the birds and shot her by accident? How do you *know,* Jacob?"

"How do you?" I said, as quietly as I could.

"I don't. I just believe. Jacob . . . darling . . . it isn't

[309]

as bad if you're only haunted by yourself saying, 'Did I murder her?'—not 'I *did* murder her.' It's bad enough, yes . . . it's terrible . . . but that's the only way you can think about it. God, darling, you *have* to think of it this way or it . . . it'll destroy you!"

"Does it matter?" I said. "However you think of it, there's no way of knowing, is there? Not now."

"But if one person believes, don't you think it matters? If *I* believe? Isn't that important?"

"Jane," I said, and moved towards her.

I remember the suitcase falling to the floor, and for a long time we lay together side by side, held in each other's arms, but without any speech or any movement, and it was like a flowing together of both our essences, so that nothing more was needed, or even possible, for whatever span of time was necessary to enclose our silent unity.

There was a peace then, such a peace as I have never known since. Something absolute in its perfection. Perhaps that was where we should have left it, in the balm of its own eternal mystery.

But then she was talking, her face pressed against mine, and her face was hot and wet with tears. "I have to save you, Jacob," she whispered. "I *have* to. I have to save something . . . somebody . . . I can give life as well as death. I *can!* I have to! Oh God, *I have to!*"

Her body came hard against me as she reached back her hand to loosen the zipper of her skirt. Her mouth was open against mine, devouringly. Her lips still trembled. I could feel life moving in me, filling, swelling, hardening, beating the pulsing rhythm of my heart and brain, and my arms locked around her so tightly that it was perhaps this that forced from her mouth that strange little choking gasp that was almost an incoherent prayer as I pressed down upon her.

[310]

27

I WAS almost in sight of the village—at the edge of the field, in fact, where we had seen the butterflies—when I stopped the jeep and backed up against the bank and turned on the rutted road that was already drying into dust. I drove back very fast, skirting the block of administrative buildings and taking the narrow direct road to the airfield.

A yellow tractor was towing one of the eighty-sixes down from the big hangar. By the time I had parked the jeep and walked across, the plane was standing in front of the briefing room on the oil-stained hardtop, with a gasoline truck alongside and a group of men in olive-drab fatigues up on the wing, feeding in the hose. Fred Peabody, in flying kit, was strolling pensively around the undercarriage and nosewheel, kicking his boots at the thick rubber tyres.

He waved as I approached and ducked his head beneath the silver-sheening wing assembly and came across to meet me. "Hi, Jake," he said. "Come to sing *Aloha?*"

"I thought I'd just say good-bye," I said. "You heard about Readaway?"

"Yep." He nodded. "Poor bastard," he said.

"Have the others come yet?"

"Sure. In there." He jerked his thumb towards the briefing room. "Learning all about it. What to do with a parachute pack. How to go out head first. The ripcord and its functions. The emergency pull. Contents of a jungle kit. Medicinal value of oxygen. What to do till the headhunter comes. The ten minute Do-It-Yourself course." He grinned. For Peabody, he sounded very chipper.

They emerged from the shed a few minutes later, a straggling irresolute quartet all bunched together as if there was some security in their civilian solidarity among about twenty servicemen in regulation khakis from one of the airfield maintenance units. It was odd to see the different ways they carried their parachutes.

Senator Vancourt, who had reverted to his GI issue khakis, the webbing belt, and the heavy strap-over combat boots, kept the parachute harnessed on as they had shown him, and the thick pack bumping around his backside gave him a grotesque enlargement in width, so that he looked smaller than ever, like a deformed dwarf. Jane Carson carried hers slung across her shoulder by the webbing strap. Jack Consadine cuddled the pack across his stomach, his fingers drumming on the canvas as if it were his familiar guitar he held against him. Judy moved toward the plane like someone in a trance, carrying the parachute before her in a sort of offering way, like a housewife bringing a big cake from the oven.

I thought I was the only person who had come down to see them off until I observed Allison hovering in the background, frowning. General Frisk, I presumed, would have made his farewells officially—and no doubt thankfully—from his own headquarters.

I knew she had seen me—there had been a sudden quickening of her glance before she had looked away—but I was acutely conscious of Peabody standing beside me, so I

[312]

balked the issue and made a point of offering my hand to the Senator.

"Well, it came off," I said.

"That's right, Mr. Strickland. Or let's put it this way—it's come off to this point. Now I guess it's up to us."

"I'm sure you'll have a good crossing. Rather ironic, that. I mean, your getting a special clearance. The sock-in would have been lifted some time today anyway."

"When you get to my age, my boy, you might find yourself in agreement with me that it's the little ironies that are the punctuation marks of life. Still, this special dispensation did give me a chance to talk to Major Peabody, and I'm that much the wiser on quite a few things." He made his throat-clearing noises. "I'm kind of glad the weather looks good for her sake," he said gruffly, and I thought he intended to add something more, but the GI's began filing towards the boarding ladder, checking their names with the flight sergeant, and we had to move apart. When we came together again we were away from the others on a patch of oil-stained cement, and he was on another tack.

"I guess you'll be happy to know we left General Frisk in a much better humour." His heavy lips twitched. "Well, I've only got to put one foot wrong with that West Point bunch now and, boy, has *he* got me! He can throw the whole book at me! Cowardice, conduct unbecoming, immorality, general disruption of morale, violation of military security, and the iniquitous wastage of the taxpayer's money joy-riding that jerk Readaway all the way out to Assam and all the way home again!" He chuckled. "Once we get over the other side there, Mr. Strickland, why I guess we just *better* be good! Well, it'll keep us on our toes." He wiggled his bottom and reached back to hitch the parachute pack. "Ah, I guess this is it, Mr. Strickland," he said. "That guy's giving me the signal." He held out his hand. "I've certainly enjoyed our little

[313]

talks. Maybe we've helped each other. So long, Mr. Strickland." "Good-bye," I said. "Good luck."

I walked over to Judy Consadine. Her eyes were wet and blinking very fast, and of a misty blue like the first break of the sky through rainclouds. The mascara had run like ink blots. Her face was dazed and ecstatic. "Oh, Jacob, isn't this just wonderful!" she gasped breathlessly. "Isn't it just so . . . so terrific that we're going? I . . . I just can't believe it. That it's really happening. That we are *going!* Why, I guess we've been just dreaming of this moment for . . . for . . . well, I just can't *tell* you how long!"

"Good-bye, Judy," I said. "Good luck, and happy landings. Happy landings always."

"Oh yes," she breathed. "Oh, yes, yes, yes!"

"Man, am I getting experience!" said Jack, dreamily offering his hand to me. "Oh *man,* am I getting experience!" He moved towards the metal ladder like a sleepwalker, clutching the parachute pack to his chest.

I was conscious of the slide and shuffle of feet across the concrete as I turned at last to face her, the soft rasp of canvas, folds of khaki, the glint of metal, the click of boot heels against the aluminium steps of the ladder like coins dropping in a slot, the subdued murmur of fading voices. I was aware of figure after figure vanishing in a shaded oblong above our heads, of the gasoline truck backing away, the grunt of rubber, of two GI's in drab overalls malleting out the wheel chocks. I knew that all the others were aboard the plane. The flight sergeant tapped a pencil against his clip board. There were only the two of us together in the long truncated shadow of the wing. How curious to see the dark edge of a shadow printed against real sunlight!

She searched my face very slowly, very carefully, as if to make quite sure. "So," she said in confirmation. Then she touched my cheek with a fingertip and turned and climbed

[314]

up the sloping metal ladder. The parachute pack bumped awkwardly against her thigh, and a hand reached down for her, and she vanished in the dark shadowy oblong without looking back. The two GI's rolled the ladder away. The door closed. I saw the handle turn and lock. From the high shining nose came the whine of the ignition.

When the GI's had gone away, following the gasoline truck, I waited by myself in the big concrete bay until the eighty-six took off. I stood there watching as it began its slow, cumbersome, gathering roll down the runway—Runway C, with Favell's ashes at one end and Hathaway's at the other—and behind me the grey buildings rattled and shuddered in the gale of the slipstream, and the gritty dust and blown paper whirled around my head until I had to duck away and turn my back.

It went low over the trees beyond the control tower, where a white signal lamp nervously blinked, and the tops of the trees rolled green in the wind-flurry and then were dark and still again. I walked across to the jeep as the plane tilted over to show its shape to me in a slow turning bank above the Rampart fence.

I climbed into the seat of the jeep, and I sat there behind the wheel and I watched it come round again, much higher now, and with the look of a slow, sluggish thing above the skittering rushing race of its shadow on the ground. It headed away towards the east, climbing higher, growing smaller, glinting and darkening in the play of sunlight and cloud shadow, heading towards a bright blue gap of sky above the mountains. The day had lifted, and the peaks of the high alps hung in the clear air like a remembered dream. My eyes began to smart as I tried to follow the plane. It diminished to a speck, then, with a final prick of light that was like a pin driven into my eyes, it vanished altogether. I tried to pick it up again, but there was nothing to be seen.

I turned the ignition switch and pressed the starter.

Now, what did I have to do? There were things to do, yes. But what sort of things? Well, I still had not made my visit to the village. I had Fleming's business to fix up with Armand. I would have to check with Benjamin. And when these things were done? What then?

I let in the clutch carefully, and drove slowly towards the dusty road, trying to think of the answer.

But, of course, there was no answer then. There is no answer even now, for Jane Carson, as all the world very well knew at the time, died exactly ten days after she left Zone Q-4. She was killed when a liaison plane which was flying her to a guerrilla unit operating behind the enemy lines was shot down in the jungle just north of the Red River.

She is out there now somewhere, on the far face of the moon. Unfinished business . . .